⚙ Visit ⚙

www.**DarkandDay**.com

Become a Fan and Like the book on Facebook

http://www.facebook.com/pages/Dark-and-Day-book/102844399757795

See artwork at Deviant Art.com

http://jono-wyer.deviantart.com/favourites/#Dark-and-Day-art

Also by Israel Grey

✿

DARK & DAY (series)

Dark & Day 1

Dark & Day 2: The Withering Mark

Dark & Day 3: The Angels' Masquerade

With more to come!

Praise for Dark & Day

"A well-crafted novel, its universe holding together without the inconsistencies sometimes apparent in the fantasy genre. There are excellent fight scenes and illusion. Some of the themes and literary references present in best representatives of the genre are apparent here: echoes of Genesis, for example, are in the telling of the creation of Jonothan's society at the beginning of the novel. There are also themes of the Cold War in the depiction of two cultures divided, armed against each other, almost too paralyzed with fear to act.."

San Francisco Book Review

"An imaginative feast for younger readers. Grey's message is laudable, expressed the Sage of Ages: 'What is there to gain in heaven if we lose ourselves along the path to it?'"

Kirkus Indie Review

For Ani

Doubt thou the stars are fire

Doubt thou the sun doth move

Doubt truth to be a liar

But never doubt I love you.

By

IsraelGrey

Cover Art by Andrew Hou, Tyler Edlin, Lianna Tia & Israel Grey
Interior Art by Israel Grey, Andrew Hou, Tyler Edlin, Lokman Lam, Lianna Tai

Any sufficiently advanced technology is

indistinguishable from magic.

Arthur C. Clarke

Dark&Day

The Revelations of Wood

9.1 And thus the rule of angels forever changed.

9.2 He that once defended the balance of light and dark, whose fiery chariot carried light across the sky, was most distraught when the old mother's light receded.

9.3 Spite conquered His thoughts and verily the seventh angel over the earth had lost himself to the endless Pit.

9.4 The earth was torn and the Pit of the abyss opened.

9.5 Darkness went up out of the pit, like the smoke from a burning furnace. The sun and the air were darkened because of the mark of the Pit.

9.6 The old mother Sol, looking upon her desperate flock, offered unto them her only sun.

9.7 Oblivion offered only darkness.

9.8 Dark and Day were thusly segregated.

9.9 The fifth angel sounded, and the seventh angel, lost amongst the endless abyss, appeared as a star from the sky which had fallen to the earth. The key to the Pit of the abyss was given to him.

9.10 His deceit was set to reveal truth unto the peoples of Earth, before the lifting of the veil.

9.11 The herald angel of the abyss returned as king, with judgment over fate, between oblivion and life beyond.

9.12 His name was the Abysmal King, Attrayer.

Chapter One

The Wizard Invasion

*U*ntil the sirens blared, Polari was the safest town in the Dark End. The permanent canopy of twinkling twilight was home to simple folk of blackrock miners and muscow herders. The sky gave everything in the sleepy town a tint of blue. Far from the hustle of steamy cities and mech bases, the people living in this quiet valley would have never known much about the Day if it weren't for the propaganda from the capital city, Eies.

Across the Dark End of Earth, posters plastered the sides of brick buildings and wrapped around buzzing lampposts, alarming citizens to the horrors threatening their peaceful way of life. Soldiers with powerful mechanix installed in their bodies looked bravely from the posters to share the same dire warning:

Magic was coming.

Maybe not this wake, and maybe not the next, but at any moment the Day could strike with a barrage of magical spells and an army of dragons, basilisks, and tortogres. All it would take was the slightest excuse: one stray mech patrol, one missing Day diplomat, one tiny spark to start the fire.

"No small spell is safe! Report magic use at once!" one poster would say out loud to passersby. All posters offered directions to the nearest anti-magic bunker.

"Don't be caught under the Day's spell! Know your emergency safety plan!" said another.

Under Twilight, people of all species—human, alien, and the rest—

lived at peace with the notion that the belligerent politics that roused the tempers of the Lords of the Day or the Empress of the Dark End were a distant threat. They walked through the staged anti-magic drills, huddling in bunkers and practicing covering their eyes from incantations as though it was a joke.

Until the sirens blared.

The shrill noise echoed through the grassy valley as the dreaded herald of war arrived without regard to their past indifference. It offered no time to ease into the end of the world, no patience for their dream of neutrality. There was only time to scramble to the closest sheltered nook and hope for the best.

Sheriff Burt Thoone knocked over his coffee as he tore off a dirty apron and locked a burstcannon onto his metallic right arm. The rest of his diner's patrons huddled beneath their yellow tables. Thoone twitched his handlebar mustache with fear and determination.

"It's magic, sheriff," gasped Corbin Dobbs, with sweat streaking down through the blackrock dust on his face. "The Day is coming for us!"

"Let's hope to the stars it's not. Y'all stay down and quiet." Thoone mustered his courage and thundered out the door. "Beth, what do we have?" Thoone mentally whispered to the bionetic communicator installed in his brain. He grimaced as the answer came into his mind.

A bell above the door rang, joining the chorus of blaring horns placed on each corner of Main Street. Polari looked abandoned.

A large wooded park stood at the center of the town with the capital building, bank, and school lined around it. The last of the people still in the streets scrambled out of sight, while Gus, the only junker of a battle bot Polari called its own, stood on a corner looking around like a lost dog. Gus was shaped like a portly bar tender, with a powerful engine in its gut and slumped head on its neckless shoulders. Its rusty humanoid hull was speckled with patriotic stickers like *I got your .50 caliber magic right here* and *Cast a spell on this!* stuck onto the bot's rear end.

Thoone waved his arms at machine.

Gus shrugged. No one had bothered to update the bot with the terrible news.

"Wizard!" yelled Sheriff Thoone over the sirens.

Thoone noticed Gus freeze, just for an instant. The bot had seen war and knew exactly what the warning meant. Spells. Pixie fire. Burnt circuits and melted wires. Its past combat files activated and in an instant the sluggish bot engaged its arsenal of lethal and slightly less lethal weaponry. It stomped across the street as Sheriff Thoone waved it toward the old school ahead of them.

Groandring Elementary had seen better wakes. Its blue paint had been flaking off for years, but it was the popped red balloons and half-hung *Welcome Back* sign that made the wake of failed celebration all the more tragic.

"Beth, tell me this ain't true," Thoone said.

Her charming voice re-entered his mind. "Still no sign of magical discharge, but the wizard was last seen entering the north side of Groandring just before the bell rang. I have the witness and her mother here with me now. Cameras caught a spark of orange behind the school, but the lab can't confirm it was a spell quite yet."

"You tell me the instant they can."

"Our wizard friend must have thought he could sneak through the Twilight without a trace. Didn't count on a town being out here in the middle of nowhere."

Thoone glanced at the battle bot beside him. "He probably didn't count on old Gus either."

Beth switched the comms to include the rusty battle bot. "Sheriff, one ex-soldier and one busted down battle mech isn't gonna count for much if we got more than a rank six wizard in there. No offense, Gus. Is there any chance we can just let this Day Ender move on through and let the Empress' army handle it?"

"Too late for that," said Thoone. "If the wizard was aiming to move on, he'd have done it. This mage is holed up in the school. We can't abide by hostage taking or, stars forbid, blood magic."

"Burn'em wizard!" Beth swore. "What kind of person hides behind children?"

Thoone starred at the windows to catch any sign of movement. "The Day, that's who. Keep your eyes tight on Groandring and you let me know if so much as a blade of grass moves funny. What do we have that can see through invisibility capes?"

"Only Chester has the latest eye installs, and he's out on vacation. I could bring down the goggles, but who knows what type of capes the Day is using these wakes."

"No, Beth. You stay put. Gus and I are going in to test his metal."

Beaten metal doors leading into the halls of Groandring creaked as they opened. Gus shuffled in with the sheriff behind his thick metal hull.

"Listen Gus, I know you were decommissioned from being a combat bot before getting left with us, but there is no margin for mistakes here. These folks ain't built for mage fighting. You and I are Polari's only line of defense. If we fall here, that wizard could enchant the whole town with no one to slow him down. If his wand hand twitches, you twitch faster, you hear me?"

Gus nodded.

"Beth, send me and Gus the witness' sketch. We need to know what we are lookin' for."

"Done."

An image of a wizard in a thick blue coat and furry hood hovered over Gus' arm. The wizard wore a strange mask and carried a bag of wands on wheels.

"Burn'em Day folk can't handle the cold," muttered Thoone. "Why can't they stick to their sunshine?"

The two officers crept down the hallway as lights flickered and poster boards on the walls rattled in the draft around them. The sheriff pointed to the first classroom.

"Gus, get your eyes in there and have a look."

Gus looked back at him sheepishly.

"Go on. Get. You're metal. We can fix you."

Gus peered into the room with his round metal eyes. The bot pulled back from the cracked door and nodded.

"We got confirmation on the invader," Thoone said. "Gus, lock in on to the target. We move in nice and easy, but be ready for trouble."

Thoone peered through a rusted hole in Gus' metal shielding as the door opened.

Students were huddled below their desks. All the magic drills since birth couldn't prepare them for what it felt like to be truly under siege. A box of name tags had spilled around the warped linoleum floor. Children shook with fear and some cried as quietly as they could manage, but from below one desk in the back came a stuttered mechanical breathing.

Curled below his desk, Jonothon Wyer was on the edge of tears. The nine-year-old boy had pulled his furry blue hood over a mop of brown hair and the old breathing mask that hugged his face like a foggy fishbowl. He clung to a long metal machine on wheels that had two wires snaking from a flashing panel to disappear under his shirt. His paralysis was the product of a lifetime of anti-Day propaganda. The fragile boy was frightened to the edge of death as the sirens exclaimed the war of magic against machine had finally arrived.

Thoone stepped cautiously into the room.

"Gus, relay your sight back to the station. Beth, ask the witness . . ." He pointed at Jonothon. "Is that the wizard she saw?"

Across the Line, a young girl's frightened voice replied, "Yes."

Sheriff Thoone lowered his cannon and frowned. "Burning stars." His hand shook and his voice cracked with relief. "Thanks, darlin'. Gus, call it off. Let the mayor know it was a false alarm. It was a mistake about the Wyer boy." Thoone pointed at Jono's mechanical contraption. "Gus, does that look like a wand carrier to you?"

Gus shook its metal head.

"Me neither." Thoone sighed. "Come on out, kids. This was all a big misunderstanding."

After a moment, one student rose and then another until all but Jono had crawled out from beneath their desks. The poor kid's breaths still came in erratic wheezing. He was likely so afraid his heart might burst altogether.

Thoone leaned down and tried to put on the most sympathetic face he could muster after nearly becoming the epicenter for the next world war.

"Tough way to start off your first wake at school, eh Jono?" Thoone tried to smile, but it came out like a sneer. "The good news is we all get to keep on living."

Jono's breath was loud and mechanical as he inhaled and exhaled. The end of the world may have come and went, but he would not be so easily convinced.

Chapter Two

The Boy with the Broken Heart

*J*onothon's nervous breath fogged up an old glass window
and blurred the tiny *Congratulations Graduates* banner that
hung along the wall of the school in the distance. The whole
town looked much farther than it was down the grassy hill from his
home.

It had been two years since he was transformed from the sickly boy
nobody knew into the notorious mistaken wizard. While the sting of
jokes and pretend spell casting had lessened, the situation hadn't
improved much. The damage was done, and there was no undoing it.

Jono had always been scrawny and exceptionally pale; blue veins
crept out of the edge of his face to compliment his cloudy blue eyes. A
mop of brown hair fell over his face and made him look like
shipwreck survivor.

He was not an average kid for his town. He wasn't even a normal kid
for his family. His sister was unstoppably confident and had more
friends than even she knew. His mother was the most beloved
member of the town council, and his father was a rising star at the
environment conditioning plant. But because of his fragile heart and
feeble lungs, Jono wasn't any of those things.

His home rested on a hill outside of town. Whenever he came down
into the valley, he would breathe in the thick EC vapors mixed with
the mining dust that lingered in the air and got into a severe coughing

fit.

He wanted to go back to bed and hide beneath his comforter. He wanted to lose himself in the stories of *The Adventures of Illius* that had been his closest thing to a friend.

A blond head popped up from below the window and his sister, Dahlia, began puffing her cheeks against the warped glass. Her curly hair bounced around her cheerful face.

Jono frowned at her sense of humor, but Dahlia was eternally unfazed. She waved at him to come out and Jono begrudgingly met her outside the front door. Dahlia wore a red sweater with the Groandring's Marauding Muscow mascot on it.

Jono doubted a muscow had ever done anything close to marauding in the entire history of the universe, but he was never asked his opinion on the matter.

A gentle breeze graced the Wyer's rickety porch on that morning in Jeweleye. The stars twinkled brighter in the summer, and the thermal steam pipes made the air warm enough for everyone but Jono to walk around without wearing a heavy coat.

Dahlia wrapped an arm around her younger brother and gazed proudly at the town below them. "Your last wake at school. You made it through."

"I don't have my test back," said Jono.

Dahlia laughed. "Are you joking? You'd crush any kid in the Dark at mathometry and half the adults down there too! And I bet the Empress would kidnap and brainwash anyone in the Day that could code like you do. Your scores will be more than good enough."

"How did you do?"

Dahlia winced. "Fine, I guess. But it's wasn't the same for me."

Jono nodded. It wasn't the same at all. Not for Dahlia or anyone else in Polari. Their lives would barely change, while for him, everything would.

Jono looked down the hill. "I don't know what happens next."

"I do," said Dahlia. "You're going to make it in. That deal's welded. I can tell."

"No one can tell the future."

Dahlia smiled. "I can. Things are going to look very up for you."

"What if I'm not ready?"

"No one's ever ready. You just learn as you go. So?" She nodded to bubbly music that wandered up from a decorated field beside Groandring. "Shall we go?"

Dahlia raced down the hill ahead of him, likely eager to meet her friends at the End of School Fair.

Everyone would be there, whether they wanted to or not. The last wake of school every year was always celebrated with rides, games, and enough muscow burgers to feed an army. To everyone else the test scores were just another exam, the last thing between them and summer break. They would be free to go to high school and go on get jobs in the mine, with the herds, or work remotely for the capital. But for Jonothon, those scores held the key to one of two fates. If he had passed, he would be whisked away to a life in the military where powerful installs would fix everything that was wrong with him and grant him amazing powers to defend the Dark. But if he failed, he would be doomed to a short life gasping for breath through his deteriorating mechanical mask.

Either way, his destiny was already written down in a code of scores—Superior, Good, Average, Tolerable and Unacceptable. All that was left to do was find out what it was.

Jono strapped on his mask and wheeled his heart regulator behind him. The school wasn't a far walk from home, but the dread of arriving for the rambunctious wake made every step heavier than the last. He stopped at entrance to Burt's Beers and Biscuits, and stared at the poster on the diner's door. A friendly soldier saluted a red star and said: *Be all the Machine you can be! Join the Empress' army!* The soldier looked so proud and invincible that Jono doubted he could ever be like him.

Sheriff Burt Thoone waved through the diner's window with a giant smile beneath his graying mustache. He pointed to a bacon-crumble donut on the counter.

The bell above the door rang and Jono found himself at the counter with the last free donut he might ever have shoved half way in his mouth.

"That'll put grease on your gears," Thoone said with a laugh.

Jono smiled, but never knew what to say. Old Burt Thoone didn't mind. He could always talk enough for the both of them.

"Can you believe that I learned to bake those back when I was a cadet? This was at Crossridge, mind you, not Windom, with all the techy geniuses like yourself, Jono. Now that school, stars above, that would be the place to go if I were to enlist again." Thoone would carry on as he washed dishes and ignored the loud snores that came from the wrangle haired Mister Dobbs, sprawled out in a yellow bench after a sleep hours shift in the mine, "There was this time at Crossridge, my squad and I would go out on training missions so close to the Dawn that a crack of orange cut across the horizon like the Earth was cutting through the dirt and sky like a sword on fire. I was with LeAnne Yesler at the time, she's the yeton lady in charge of the steam season each year, you've seen her around town, I'm sure. Well LeAnne came back to Crossridge showing the world how the sun had tanned her white fur. She was so proud, but I don't think an electron microscope could 'a told the difference. Ol' LeAnne would show off her tan like she had baked in the dead desert itself. Those were the wakes. I wouldn't trade my time at the academy for the stars themselves."

Jono looked down at bacon fragments on his plate. He nodded at the sheriff's stories and tried to avoid looking at the clock behind the counter. Thoone noticed and leaned in with a friendly smile.

"You know Jono, out those doors, and just one block over is the start of life so full of adventure you're gonna have stories to tell for a hundred years. Out there you'll make best friends with a new squad each year and be stronger. Out there, you'll be doing the Empress' work keeping magic at bay. Out there, you'll be a hero. You just gotta take the step, that's all. Let the world do the rest."

"I guess I should go." Jono slid off of the chair and the bell above the door rang again. He stopped. "Thanks for the donut, Sheriff Burt."

"Any time, Cadet Wyer," Thoone said as he dried a mug with the towel tied to his apron. "Any time."

Jono found himself on the edge of the block. The school loomed only a block and a half ahead and, as though stepping past Mortimer's Mech Merchandise and onto the new block signaled the breach of the event horizon of a black hole, Jono sighed, embraced his fate, and walked on.

The crowd of noisy students and faculty were every bit as intimidating as Jono had imagined. Red balloons and banners cluttered the air, harshly festive against the drab building. Hordes of classmates gorged themselves on candied flowers and glowing lava sticks. They raced down a huge inflated bowl in puffy suits until an elastic cord strapped to their backs reached a critical point and flung them into the air. It was a poor town's carnival but judged by the wide smiles of the students recently freed from the burden of intellectual pursuits, it was heaven.

As children screamed in joy and teachers barbequed, Gus meandered around the school grounds, ignored by everyone around it. When Jono arrived, Gus waved lazily and Jono waved back.

Jono sat alone along the side of the school, grumbling to himself about having to wait for his test scores. He spotted his sister running wildly about with more friends than he knew of. For Dahlia, friends seemed to multiply at random intervals.

Across the field he could see Aram Holinger hanging upside down as Dahlia climbed after him. "Did you use your tickets for the sling bowl yet?" said Aram as his coat slipped off his shoulders to flop over his face.

Dahlia Wyer shook her head, her blonde curls bobbing side-to-side. "I was waiting for Layla, but she's too busy helping Mister Reynaldo set up the raffle."

"Do you want to go together?" asked Aram. "I bet if we hold hands we can stretch it enough to get higher than the roof."

Dahlia's blue eyes lit up.

Jonothon watched from afar as his sister got suited up for the sling-bowl. He tried to ignore it, but the fun she was having made him feel even more alone. He heard voices approaching and tucked his legs close. Tripping someone would only become that wake's new spell from the world's weakest wizard.

"You wouldn't believe how messed up it was," said an athletic, black-haired boy of no more than fourteen. "The head's still fine for a trophy, though. My da' says it's one burn'em catch for my first hunt."

Four older boys had turned the corner while Dietrich DuLac showed off the hovering images of a dead pungrus. The thick antlers and tusks that lined the beast's head spiked out in all directions while its purple tongue hung limp beneath its rumpled snout. The other boys leered over his shoulders and nodded at the splendor of his skill.

"You shouldn't go hunting that close to Dawn," one of the boys said, scolding Dietrich. "I hear Day Enders like to sneak across the border to kidnap kids."

"Why would they kidnap kids?"

"To use in their potions, you clunker. Children's blood is pure and innocent."

Dietrich laughed. "I'm not afraid of some scrawny witch with a sleeping spell! My da' has a model SX Crunch Hog. I'd love to see a wizard try to stop that mech once it's rolling!" Dietrich mimed a frail wizard waving a stick. "Oh no! My whispy fire spell isn't working on six tons of reinforced steel! Splat!"

Jono thought they would continue straight to the End of School Fair, but Dietrich glanced to his side just in time to catch Jono trying to make himself invisible.

The boys stopped.

Dietrich strolled over to the cement corner, looking down on Jono with exaggerated confusion on his face. He acted as if he wasn't sure that Jono could see him at all. Dietrich leaned over, his head close to Jono's mask, and rapped on its leathery forehead with his knuckles.

"Look who it is!" Dietrich said in mock kindness. "Hey, Mister Wizard, we were just talking about your friends. You might want to take notice that there's a fair going on. Right over there, you see? That's what all that color and noise is." Dietrich breathed on Jono's eye piece and rubbed it clean with his sleeve as the other boys laughed.

Jono knew he should just stay quiet and ignore him, but he hated himself for being afraid. "I know what it is! I can see it just fine."

Dietrich leaned in again, smiled, and gave Jono a forceful slap on the shoulder. "Those are Dark Enders. They won't bite."

"Wyer's scared there's a witch in the weeds," said another boy. "I bet he's wet his self."

"Watch out, Wyer! I'm a wizard here to zap you with my lightning stick!" Dietrich said to a chorus of laughter. "You stay vigilant, mage hunter. We're gonna go over here and have some actual fun."

The boys joined the festivities, leaving Jono to feel even lonelier.

"I'm not scared," Jono mumbled to himself.

It was all he could do to stare at the cracks in the cold ground: loud breath in, loud breath out. His mask's eye pieces fogged up when he tilted his head down, and he didn't bother to wipe them off. He wondered what made people become like Dietrich DuLac. Was he overcompensating for other problems? Was his family mean to him? Was it a natural, genetic tendency?

Jono sighed and leaned more comfortably against the wall.

Thinking was the only thing he could do well. It made him feel better to ponder how the world worked and what made people the way they were. It took the sting out of insults, the terror out of monsters under the bed. If he couldn't be strong or dashing, Jono was determined to be wise.

Jono spotted Dahlia across the field the instant after she broke her grip with Aram's hand and they both went soaring into the air. Their padded bodies looked like blue gazberries as they flew well above the school roof. Their landing and subsequent bounce brought them back above the rim of the bowl. They finally bounced to a rolling stop, bursting with laughter.

A smile cracked the contours of Jonothon's face. That really was a good sling.

In the spirit of opportunity, or because his body was sore from sitting on cement and moping, Jono stood and wheeled his heart reg toward the crowd.

Mister Sniffen, the only mustecrat teacher at Groandring Elementary, was judging a handstand contest where the students balanced upside down in the air with their hands pressed against small floating pads. Sniffen stood only as tall as his students. His plump, furry body and whiskers that accentuated his toothy smile made him everyone's favorite.

Judy Jupiter, the school cook, was handing out muscow burgers under a plain white tent. She wore a concerned smile as Mark Yoshiburi stuffed an entire burger into his mouth and then darted off with his cheeks puffed out like balloons.

"Your ticket, sir," said a voice behind Jono.

Jonothon turned around to find his teacher, Ms. Einhart, holding a yellow ticket in front of him.

"It's for the raffle, Mister Wyer," she stated with a kind nod to a pile of assorted items that looked like presents on a Giftmas morning.

"You may be interested to note that the library has donated a large collection of used books for one of the winners."

"Really?"

A small box sat on the table with corners of books pointing out above the rim. He wondered what adventures could be held within that mysterious box. But every other student had a ticket just like his, and he had never won a raffle before.

"I bet my chances aren't very good," he said, resigned to the loss but starting to guess at what those unfortunate odds might be more precisely. Number of students divided by the number of prizes . . .

"Oh, I don't know," said Ms. Einhart as she laid a hand on his shoulder. "They may be better than you think."

After scribbling his name on the ticket and dropping into a raffle box, Jono filled a plate with a muscow burrito and a scoop of mashed mushrups. Jono watched a teacher juggle fiery sticks as he squeezed a torn piece of burrito under his mask and plopped it into his mouth.

The End of School Fair really wasn't all that bad. The wake was warmer than usual, and no one really bothered him much; they were too busy enjoying the festivities. He let himself become mesmerized by flashes of orange flame as his mind slipped away to imagine the unlikely possibility of winning the box of books.

A scream cut through the boisterous noise and jerked him out of his thoughts. The shrill sound brought everyone's eyes to the blonde girl in the red sweater as she flew out of the sling-bowl with a snapped safety wire flapping behind her. The small figure sailed over the rim and thudded on to the grassy field.

Jonothon was running to his sister before he knew he had even stood up. He was deaf to roars of the crowd's chaos. All Jono saw was her limp, red sweatered body.

He ran ahead of the rest, pushing himself, desperate to get to her—

to save her. His feet beat against dirt and pushed him closer and closer until he froze. For one terrifying instant, his hand moved to his chest at the realization that the cables connecting him to his heart reg had ripped out. The crippling sensation spread through his limbs; his body went limp, his legs twisted; Jono tumbled and crashed face-down in the dirt and grass.

He struggled to look upward through impenetrable green blades. Everything in him fought against the prison of his own body, trying desperately to reach toward that tuft of unmoving blonde curls until everything went black.

Jonothon breathed in loudly.

It had not taken long for the nurse to resuscitate him.

"You really shouldn't push yourself like that. Ever," the nurse insisted. "No matter what happens, Jono, you cannot lose control. You'll just cause more damage to yourself than whoever you're trying to help."

Jono agreed without really listening. On the wall hung a poster with an army medic holding a large syringe. *Science heals! Magic is poison!* He felt for the plugs connected to his chest. He didn't feel healed.

"Dahlia's fine," said the nurse. "Just a broken arm. You're alright to go back to class but be sure to go straight home afterward."

Jono slid off the nurse's chair and pulled his heart reg beside him as he left. His relief for Dahlia did nothing to ease the anger he felt at himself. He felt broken and useless. He was supposed to better than that. He should've been able to protect others, like Illius did in all his stories.

Jono made his way to his classroom, finding it empty as neither the other students nor his teacher had come in from the fair yet. Jono held back tears that stung the corners of his eyes and sat motionless at his desk until the other students finally shuffled into the classroom.

Jonothon told himself he didn't care when Terrance Fungston shook his head at him.

Ms. Einhart shut the door after the last girl scuttled in. The room was full of cheerful chatter disturbed only by Jonothon's deep, mechanical breathing.

Ms. Einhart cleared her throat to quiet the classroom. "I hope you have all had an enjoyable wake. It's always a little sad to say goodbye, but there was something particularly special about this class. I know what you've been waiting for," she said in a light tone. "But you don't have to worry. I was very impressed by the turnout of your scores. Cumulative marks were up nine percent over last year. You should all be very proud of yourselves."

She went down the rows, handing electronic papers to each of the children. As she passed by Jonothon's desk, she slid the page face down. "You got the highest mathometry scores I've ever seen for your grade." she whispered. "Good luck, Jono."

Jono's hand hovered over the paper. He hesitated, thinking about the infinite paths his life could take and how his options were swiftly narrowing down to one. Everything he would or wouldn't do depended on the accomplishment of this one thing. He took a deep breath and turned the page over. On the SGATU scale of Superior, Good, Average, Tolerable, and Unacceptable, Jonothon had received three S's, four G's, and only one A.

Jonothon Wyer's breath was silent as he starred knowingly at the paper in front of him.

He had done it.

Everything would change.

Jonothon collected an assortment of trinkets he had kept in his desk over the years: a colorful pen with scales on it, a scroll with half its viewing pixels blanked out, and a small plastic action figure of the mythological Titan Warrior he'd brought with him on his first wake of school for good luck.

He found an old pamphlet he received at the assembly at the end of each year. It was labeled *Friends Don't Let Friends Dabble in Magic! Report Illegal Spells at Once!* Jono had never seen anyone use magic, but at every assembly the principal warned them how dangerous and addictive it was. "Stay vigilant," Principal Hairgrave would repeat. "Open eyes can save lives."

Jono was the last to leave the classroom and by the time he started on his way, the streets were quiet with all the other children home and safe behind glowing orange windows. Jono buttoned up his thick blue coat and pulled his hood up to guard against the growing chill.

His every step along the familiar cement sidewalk was calculated as he wondered if he would ever look at those particular cracks again. The cement soon gave way to gravel, and the gravel was soon lost amid the grass.

His nervous heart could not stop its pace from quickening at the sight of Dahlia sitting on their rickety porch bench as she waved with her one good arm.

"Check it out," she laughed, lifting up a cast-covered arm that glowed a faint green. "You just have to hold it up to a light for a while."

"You're alright?" said Jono.

"Of course." Dahlia shrugged as though she cheated death twice a wake before breakfast. "D'you get your scores?"

Jono nodded.

Dahlia turned her head with obvious curiosity. "And?"

Jono meekly nodded again and sat next to her on the bench. Dahlia didn't say anything. She put her good arm around his shoulders and they watched dull lights fill up the windows of houses in the valley.

The smell of steaming noodles filled up the house and fogged the windows. Charles Wyer slurped up the noodles being as loud and playful as he could be. Dahlia laughed and mimicked the technique.

Beky Wyer slurped politely and brushed a fallen strand of blonde hair back into her bun. "That is truly fantastic news, Jono. I'm proud of you."

"I knew you could do it all along," said his father. "How do you want to celebrate?"

"We could go to Jupiter Gorge," said Dahlia. "They added a new ride down the canyon."

"We can't forget the shrine," said his mother. "It would be good if you consulted the angels before you leave, Jono. You may not get another chance."

Jono shrugged. "I'm kind of tired already. I may just go to bed and read."

His mother nodded sympathetically. "I like that idea. We don't have to do anything exciting. It's nice to just savor a quiet evening at home."

"Not many of those left," said Dahlia.

Charles kicked her from below the table and glared.

"Ow!" Dahlia rubbed her shin. "Sorry."

After Jono finished dinner he retired to his room on the second floor of the rickety house. His windows looked out at the slanted hillside. Grass rustled in an uneven breeze. The hill and the town and distant mountains all appeared motionless and permanent, as though he were looking at a giant's painting.

Jono didn't know what else to do, so he turned away from the open world and climbed into bed. He pulled the red comforter up to his chest and slid an open book from the end table. Orange candle light flickered over the pages and helped the words dance to life.

He shut out the world and along with it a future coming too quickly. Jono buried his mind onboard the deck of the Integress with Illius at the helm. He could almost feel the bursting sails above him and the gentle rocking of the wooden deck beneath him as the ship sped across liquid seas. He forced his ears to ignore the subtle ticks and tocks of the clock on his wall and instead imagined the *kaw* of seagulls and the crashing of waves.

He lost himself to that world of wonder. He fell asleep with a smile on his face as the weary flame beside him died without a whisper of dissent.

Chapter Three

The Recruit's Reward

Out of the still world came a muffled thump. It beat three times then silenced. After an uncertain pause, it beat thrice more like an eager, nervous heart.

The pounding heart beat again, followed by something creaking and shuffling along wood and linoleum floor. Jonothon woke. He blinked and rubbed his eyes. The thump against the door beat twice more before the cranky lock and creaking hinge silenced it for good.

The front door opened as Charles's tired voice cracked out, "Hello?"

Jonothon peered out of the window as warm steam rolled down the hills like it always did when the summer was still young. He slid out of bed, wrapped the comforter around him, and cracked open his bedroom door just enough to see the three soldiers that stood on the front porch. They looked powerful and imposing. Their metal armor was bulky, with jagged plates colored in dark blue with trims of silver. Their helmets were white in the front with jutting cheeks and hollow eyes that resembled a monstrous skull.

Jono feared and admired them.

"Charles Wyer?" grunted the soldier in the front of the pack.

"Yes, sir."

"The convoy of the Forty Second Brigade of Her Noble Empress' Army has arrived in your . . ." the soldier cleared his throat, "village. We have been informed of the successful application of military academics by one recorded at this residence, a mister Jonothon Amleth Wyer. Is he present?"

Charles was flustered. He was a thin man with a caramel complexion and thick black hair. He was exceptionally good at many things but didn't take well to surprises.

"Yes, of course he's here, but . . ."

Jono's eye caught movement from the door across the corner from his own. Dahlia's blonde curls bobbed out of the darkened room. She looked at the open door below them and then to the one exposed eye of her little brother, her face full of concern.

"Very good," the soldier interrupted. "Have him gather his belongings and we'll take him to the convoy with us. You will receive confirmation of his safe arrival to the city in just under—"

"But it's the middle of sleep," said Charles.

The soldier stopped. He looked like he was just accosted by an absurdity of false logic.

"We were told we he wouldn't be leaving until two wakes from now," said Charles.

The soldier looked at the disheveled man, unfazed. His clenched, exposed jaw beneath the helmet indicated he wasn't going to bend to ridiculous schedules that included a regimented bed time.

Charles pleaded. "Sir, this wake we promised to take him to the angel's shrine before he left. We need time to say goodbye as a family."

The soldier popped his clenched jaw. "Angels? Even out here in the middle of nothing I didn't think I'd come across Dark Ender believing in that Day Ender nonsense," he muttered. He sucked in a deep breath through his nose then exhaled in frustration. "The convoy is scheduled to disembark on Redwake. You can bring him to us at the west gate of town. Be sure to have him there well before o-seven hundred hours. You have to understand, Mister Wyer, that this is a courtesy on our part and not one that we enjoy. Just because your boy can't take the mineral train like any other cadet from this town doesn't mean we owe him special treatment. We will not wait. If your child misses the appointed time, do not be surprised if his application is denied. Our commanders do not look favorably on those who do not fulfill their commitments."

With that, the soldier in front clicked his heels together and the three of them turned from the porch and marched down the hill.

Charles stared after them without moving. The distant sky held the same subtle twinkling pricks of light they always did, only this wake, a canvas of gray clouds crawled from the distant horizon to gobble them up.

The lights in the kitchen were already on when Jonothon woke for the second time. The house seemed brighter, and he suspected that his mother did it on purpose—more light to brighten their moods.

Jono crept down the stairs. A chocolate corn cake with one delicate blue candle waited for him on the dining room table. His parents and Dahlia were already gathered in their pajamas at the wobbly kitchen table.

"Breakfast is served!" said Charles. "Nothing but the best to get the wake started, right? Happy recruitment wake, Jono."

"Happy wake," Dahlia and his mom added.

Jono forced a supportive smile, shut his eyes, and blew out the candle. He was overwhelmed with a tangled mess of emotions that he didn't know what to do with. He was excited about the idea of being fixed and of becoming stronger than he was, maybe even braver than he was. He imagined being a soldier more like Illius, daring and courageous. At the same time he was terrified that he would fail. He was scared to leave his family, and in the pit of his stomach he felt like the city would be too much for him to handle. What if they brought him all the way to the academy and then realized that he was a loser? What if they sent him home? A preemptive wave of shame bubbled in him and he hadn't even failed yet.

In that split second, he pretended to be making a wish but there were a million thoughts and fears running through his mind and he couldn't weigh the various consequences of each wish that popped up. He ended up not wishing at all.

His family clapped and wished him a happy recruitment again as Charles stood up to cut the cake. They had all known, or hoped, or more rightly worried, that this wake would come.

It was at the wise-old-age of seven that Charles sat Jono down on the rocking bench and explained to his son how he was going to live.

In the Dark End of the world, the Empire of Eies had established a program that offered the poor and sickly a chance to overcome the regrettable lot that had been dealt to them—a life destined to end too short. If a child, not unlike Jonothon, survived to the age of eleven and was judged of useful intelligence then he would be taken to Eies, the capital of the Dark End, and undergo the surgeries that would fix all that was wrong with him.

He would finally become whole—a real boy.

The only cost was his freedom. Jono would be forced to join one of the great military academies in the Dark and be trained to serve the rest of his life in the army of the Empress.

"We're lucky enough that convoy is coming through Polari," Jono had overheard his father mention months earlier. "Otherwise, I don' know how we could get him to the city. He couldn't breathe through the dust on the mineral rail, even if we could afford the ticket to get him on."

The four Wyers sat quiet at breakfast, spooning cake into their mouths with awkward smiles on their faces.

In a spark of recognition, Dahlia dropped her fork and dashed away from the table. After a few confused moments, she returned with her hands behind her back.

"We got something for you," she said. "A reward for all your hard work, making it into the academy."

She looked to her parents, who nodded, and then she showed it to him. In her outstretched hand was a tiny copper pocket watch. On its cover were the embossed images of a phoenix and a capricorn, both stared upward to a distant star.

Jonothon carefully took it from her hands and clicked open the cover. At first it was just a simple clock with a time display, but when he ran his fingers over its face, the clock disappeared. The holographic image of Dahlia flickered above the screen. Her tiny hand waved back at him.

"Hi Jono!" the imaged squeaked with a slight electronic version of Dahlia's voice.

The tiny Dahlia stepped aside and the image refocused on the outside of their house, whose lights glowed orange against the blue world.

"Remember this old place?" the electronic Dahlia squeaked. "Welcome back home!"

"We all recorded stuff for it," the real Dahlia explained. "So you remember what we sound like wherever you go."

Jono took the memory watch and looked at his family. "Th-thanks," he stuttered, not knowing what else to do.

Dahlia hugged him, the watch squished between them. Tears burned under his eyes, and his parents knelt and joined in the hug. His mother kissed his forehead and wrapped her arms around him.

"By the burning mother," she whispered, unsuccessfully trying to hold in her tears, "you come back to visit when you can, okay?"

Jono knew he had to be strong. He couldn't cry, beg to stay, or try to hide. He couldn't live with the thought of leaving his parents with any regret when he knew they made the right choice, as hard as it was.

Jono swallowed his last piece of cake and emptied a glass of muscow milk. He didn't know what to do next, so he sat still in his chair, soaking in the feeling of the only home he ever knew, silently saying goodbye.

The Narrow Path

*T*he Shrine of the Seraphim was a few kilems outside Polari along a rocky dirt road that wound into a thick forest where towering trees and wild mushrups grew untamed.

Most people in the Dark didn't approve of anything to do with angels or other superstitions, but being so far away from the capital, people in Polari looked the other way without incident. The Twilight had a reputation for independent thinking. The land was rough and living was simple, so if you found the right person to do the job, it didn't matter if they believed in ancient stories or not.

As far as Jonothon could deduce, consulting the angels was almost always a formality. It was more like trying to find peace with a decision you've already made and just needed the extra ounce of confidence to go through with it.

The last time they had gone to the shrine, it was after months of 'passionate' (meaning: loud) 'arguments' (meaning: repeating the same, seemingly sound reasoning again and again) made by the two children of the Wyer family about how beneficial it would be if they were to get a werepuppy. After deliberation on parental side of the debate, his mother took them to consult the angels. Unfortunately, but to no surprise to Jonothon, the whispers of the angels informed his mother of a polite but definitive, no.

After an hour of rattling, the Wyer's rusted yellow truck stopped in front of a vine-covered cottage half-eaten by the thicket of trees. The road ended here. Beside the flower infested home, there was a path that led deeper into the forest. Blocking the entrance sat a sturdy yellow gate.

The cottage's red door cracked open, and an auburn-haired head in a pointy red hat poked out. The figure looked around before he recognized them and came out. The short, skinny caretaker in a red coat trotted over with a wide and genuine smile. His clothes were baggy and flopped about as he hurried over.

Alexsayter Aquinas was a tumnkin. He had mostly human features, but his body and face were trimmed with fur. His ears were large and pointed outward. Short, curled horns grew out of his thick, curled hair. It was a rare thing to see a tumnkin north of the Dawn.

"Welcome, welcome!" Aquinas cheered as the family unloaded from the truck.

Aquinas met them in a line and shook all their hands vigorously.

"This is a fortuitous wake indeed," said Aquinas. "Such a decision to be made! Come. I shouldn't keep you waiting from your calling. The woods have been a flutter with whispers for some time now. Although for good or ill, I cannot make out amongst the shadows and noise."

Aquinas paused and for a moment his face flashed with a nervous look. "Unless, you'd rather stop inside for a tick and a tock? I certainly don't want to push you along the path. There's no rush, nor worry. I've made fresh tea and there are biscuits and cookies."

"I think we should probably head out, Mister Aquinas," said Charles.

"Quite right," said Aquinas with an uplifting smile. "I have tea ready in thermoses on Celeste for the trek."

The Wyer family followed Aquinas around the back of his house to where the vines grew rampant over an old wooden stable. Under the wood planks and vine covered canopy stood a large yellow bird about the size of a duskhorse. It had four clawed legs, a long neck, and a thick tail with scales on its underbelly. The riding bird had thick wings on both sides, but Jonothon was quite sure such a heavy beast was unable to fly.

Aquinas walked up to the bird, stroked its bushy feathers, and tightened a series of leather satchels beside its saddle. Celeste cooed as the tumnkin attached another large pouch to her side. Her eyes sparkled in the dim light.

"Alright, come along, Jonothon," said Aquinas. "She's ready to go."

Aquinas held out his hand. Jono walked over to him, his heart regulator bumping along behind him. As the tumnkin stepped forward he took the small machine and lifted it into the new pouch, ever careful not to disturb the delicate green and yellow wires that connected it to Jono's heart. Aquinas was only a head taller than Jono, despite being full grown and quite probably older than Jono's parents, although he didn't look it.

"Just hold my shoulder," said Aquinas, "and put a foot on my knee."

Jono hesitated.

"Wark." Celeste titled her head impatiently. The curve of her beak hinted at a smile.

Jono smiled back. He leapt and slid onto the saddle.

"Well done. Everyone else ready?" said Aquinas a smile, taking pleasure in the small success. "Off we go!"

The path through the forest was narrow and the lush green depths that surrounded them were littered with pale glowing mushrups. His family hiked ahead of them as Jono, Celeste and Aquinas followed.

The forest crackled and squeaked with life. A flock of flarks fluttered among the branches, flying in a helix pattern. An embermander stopped mid-step up the trunk of a tree. In a puff of steam, its molten skin cooled and a dark black crust formed over its body; camouflaging it amongst the tree bark.

The journey through the forest would take them most of the early wake.

Aquinas held Celeste's reins as they walked. "In ages past, there used to be thousands of shrines across the Dark rings, but now, you're lucky to have one of the few active ones so close."

"What happened to them?" Jono asked.

"The Empress happened," Aquinas sighed. "Oh, she didn't send anyone out to tear them down or anything so blatant, of course. Her machinations are of a much more subtle nature. She let them drain and wither. Many remote shrines fell into decay and were followed by the independent towns all across the Dark. The weaker they became, the stronger she has become. More and more people were forced to move deeper into the Dark End—closer to her iron grasp. Tragic really. It stands to no reason to leave warm lands for the cold."

This was not the first time Jono had heard bad things about the Empress. Every wake closer to his enrollment in the army, his doubts grew, but he continued to ignore them.

"These wakes most people on the Dark End have to travel for many wakes on end to consult an attended shrine," said Aquinas. "I guess it just makes all those that remain ever the more precious. She can't take them all, not while the Fellowship can still cross the globe."

"Do you know of anyone who has gone into an academy?" asked Jono.

"I have known a few, sent from Polari like you, and others under different circumstances." Aquinas shook his head. "I apologize. I have no place to weigh your spirit down with thoughts of mine, Jonothon. Yours is a tenuous predicament."

"I don't know anyone. I don't even know what to expect."

"It will be many years before you could ever earn the freedom to return home, even for a visit. Most of the recruits I've known never do. Perhaps they find it easier to simply cut off the life they once knew. Perhaps something they experience, or something they become under her command, makes it hard to face this humble way of life again. There was a young man who returned a few years after I first crossed the Dawn to Polari. There was a great celebration, but the joy was short lived. It was nothing he expressly did, but there was a difference in him, and the town knew it. There was something important in his spirit that was lost."

"Do you think I'll be like that?" asked Jono.

Aquinas smiled. "Whatever course you tread, I have faith that your heart will guide you well."

The honest bit of confidence put Jono at ease and gave him a swell of pride. "Do you think it was the Empress that changed him? I heard at school once that she has a webmind and can control her army with a thought."

"It is true that she can command machines by thinking. Some say she is a machine, herself. Only following her programing as it deteriorates into madness. I cannot know if it was her that changed him, or if it was the life she forced him through."

"Have you ever seen her?"

Aquinas bowed his head. "No. But I have seen what she is capable of. I've seen my share of deserted homes and abandoned cultures. I've seen the fields at Eve's Dale."

"Where is that? I've never heard of it."

Aquinas looked up at him, and then looked back at the ground. He didn't answer.

The path had led them so deep that the light from the cottage was now lost in the canvas of trees, shrubberies, and vines. As they continued on the winding trail, Aquinas kept furrowing his brow and muttering to himself. "The problem," Aquinas finally blurted, "is not with her rule, as such. No, she would boast a noble, free, and powerful kingdom, but therein, you see, she would claim such ends are her virtues to own. That she is in all things benevolent and good! But if you were to scratch below the surface, if you were to see that truth she hides to all below the blackness, you would be stricken to know such horrors were laid bare in order to build her narcissistic enterprise. Jono, there are dark deeds that haunt the halls of that city—the city that burns against the black night.

"It is your position," Aquinas whispered gravely, "that tells the tale of her true character. The least of all of us, is you—the weary, the down trodden. And from you, and others so desperately in need, she takes her deepest tax. Her harpy's sting cuts into the weakest of her brood and usurps their potential for her conniving machinations! Such ambitions that she keeps . . . there is no good in it, Jonothon. Of taking a life in exchange for what are trinkets and trash to her, but would mean life for you? Were I possessed of such aid I would give them to you free, unconditional. But to grant life only to demand the same in payment? What monstrousness is that? It surely takes a steel, dead heart to tick within the bosom of the Empress of Eies—black as her night, black as her mechs and the oil they bleed. Mark me, Jono, it is a sign along a path best not trodden."

The weight of his words brought up all the doubt and fear Jonothon had pushed back. He didn't want to go, but to stay would be a death sentence, condemned to be nothing more that the frail boy he was now. Jono thought of Illius and Sheriff Thoone. He ached to be brave and kind like them. They were always surrounded with friends, and even kings and mayors consulted them for their wisdom. The price for that future didn't seem so high, and still he was afraid to pay it.

Twisting through a thick nest of trees, the small caravan finally came upon their destination.

The shrine was a short white-brick building with a metal tiled roof that peaked high in the middle and curved low at its base. Around it were stone temples and rock sculptures that barely poked out from the dense underbrush. A fence ran along the building on either side so that you could get to the area beyond only by going through the shrine.

It was meant to be a place of seclusion, mediation, and prayers to the seraphim that watched over the world. And occasionally, a place of answers.

Celeste walked up to the shrine, and then Aquinas helped Jono dismount. His parents and Dahlia arrived with encouraging yet rehearsed smiles.

"Here is the attunement broth," said Aquinas as he handed a bottle to Charles. "It is potent enough for the gate to recognize it, but I have diluted it a great deal due to being drunk by one so young and small. I'll leave Celeste with you. Take all the time that you need."

The tumnkin tied Celeste's reins to the branch of a sapling.

"Celeste can guide you home when you are ready. If you need to speak with me, just push that button on the Thinker's belly." He pointed to a statue of a chubby gnome that sat cross-legged.

"Jonothon," Aquinas said as he rested a hand on his shoulder. "Follow the path and listen to the whispers along your way. They come through the calm, through the core of your true self. Don't try to force them or change them. Just listen. Let truth be truth and care not for all other concerns."

Aquinas patted Jono on the shoulder, waved goodbye, and then disappeared down the path back to the cottage.

The shrine's doors creaked as Charles pushed them open. Six wood pillars held up the roof. The only light came from steady candles with thick, perfumed smoke. Decorative markings and symbols were carved into the wood. Six statues lined the walls, guardians of different virtues and environments of the world, they represented the angels themselves, that heavenly protection over the sphere, but one was missing.

The seventh angel, Ariam, the brave and wise, was the shrine's patron and her statue lay at the end of the narrow path.

The four Wyers removed their shoes on the wooden floor and set them in slots by the wall. The air was clear enough that Jono did not need his breather mask, and he set it beside his shoes. Incense burned from lanterns on each of the building's support beams, their scented smoke wafted upward in lazy curls and out of harm's way.

Together they stepped onto an elevated green floor and knelt on purple mats. Everyone except Jonothon bent over. They whispered prayers for his safety and for the wisdom to make the right decisions. They would have been laughed at by most people in the Dark, but more than a few of their fellow Polarins had made their way to the shrine more than once. They held their heads in their hands; his mother thumbed the beads of her necklace and asked those that watch over the Earth to pay special attention to one undistinguished boy.

Jono leaned toward his father. "Do I have to go?"

"Jono, what else can you do?" Charles whispered back. "We can't ignore your condition and hope things will get better. I'm your steward and that is a duty that can never be shirked. This has been our last chance. This is my last gift to you. There are few certainties in this world, Jonothon, and when opportunities arise, I want you to seize them. Take it wherever it leads you. I want you to find friends there, and joy and laughter. Let yourself be whole. There is no greater honor you could do me than to take the opportunities I have steered your way and make the very most of it."

"I'll try," Jono said with complete honesty.

"You will do great, Jono. I know it. Here. Take a sip of this."

Charles poured the amber broth into a small ceremonial bowl and handed it to his son. "And when you go through that door wait a moment to let it scan you. You'll feel kind of funny at first, but that should subside."

Jono took the bowl and lifted it to his face. It smelled bitter and unwelcome, but it would be a terrible slight to come so far and not drink it. The strange brew tickled as it went down. It felt warm going down his throat even though the drink was cool.

"It will help you hear their whispers and see any signs the angels may send," said his mother. "They are subtle, so be watchful. Go ahead whenever you're ready."

After a moment of absorbing the tingly new experience from the broth, Jono cautiously walked past the gray stone statues that seemed to peer down at him with unflinching, judgmental eyes. He felt small and fragile compared to the complete commitment of their stone bodies. With every step, his gaze turned nearer to the ground.

On the far end of the shrine, there was another area for shoes beside two ornate wood doors. He reached the end and looked through the shelves for a new pair of shoes, but they all seemed insurmountably larger than his own feet. He looked back at his family, but their heads were all down, as they were supposed to be.

Jono put on the smallest shoes he could find. The doors to the path were solid and heavy. Jono pushed, but they didn't budge. He tried again, and the most movement came from the rattling of the metal knockers. He was about to turn around in frustration when he realized the latch was still down. He lifted the latch and the doors opened gently onto a long, narrow path that cut through the lush woods.

Chapter Five

Whispers in the Woods

*J*ono stepped onto the narrow dirt trail and felt a tingling in his head. He walked on, feeling light, like he glided across the ground. The path itself was smoothed; no large rocks or roots obstructed the way. The dirt seemed to have been combed. Along the straight path ran a silver hand bar.

Jono tried to breathe slowly and listen for the whispers, but the forest was vibrantly alive with twinkling pixie flies and glowing mushrups that grew fat on the ground or thin on the trunks of trees. The Terralunis light illuminated the forest, the massive city that covered the whole moon shone brightly down at them.

Jonothon shut his eyes, took hold of the silver bar, and walked the seraphim's path.

At first he could only hear the chirps and rustles of the forest. Time lost its meaning; his body felt connected to all the sounds around him. There were near infinite layers of sound, close and far, loud and soft— differences to every rustle of leaves, to every chirp or scrapping claw against bark.

The instant he heard it, Jono almost lost his grip on the bar and fell.

It was a breath of a voice nestled between the rustles of two trees. He looked around but saw no one in the shadows. The further he went along the path, the more it seemed as though he could hear them. They spoke through the trees and throbbing light of the pixie flies. More and more voices joined the chorus all around him, but their words were hushed and hurried and he couldn't understand what they said. He strained to hear, but their words were always beyond him.

Near the edge of the path stood the hull of a massive metal mech. It was ancient and rusted through. Holes riddled its frame and tore upward like petals on a flower. A thick tree had grown up through the mech in the decades since it found its rest in the forest. Mushrups and ferns sprouted over the forgotten remains of a battle no one remembered.

Jono starred at the skeleton of the mech and wondered how many pilots it took to control. How many pilots died when the monstrous machine crashed to the forest floor? How many mages did it take to bring it down? What spell could tear through solid metal?

He let his mind wonder at the sight of the empty tomb. The whispers lurked in the shadows, yet he began to grasp the tone of their words.

It was a deep and chilling dread.

Between the gnarled shadows of metal and plants whispered a terrible secret in a language he couldn't understand. Above tree limbs, they rustled a warning dripping with fear. A howl bellowed far through the trees. A distant branch snapped. There was a growling overhead and then it surrounded him all at once. Jono's head pulsed with the harsh whispers on the wind. The growling grew louder and louder until it roared over and through him like the earth itself was moaning. Large black shapes darted across the sky, and the woods bowed to their terrible majesty then shivered back as the creatures disappeared.

The shadows around him grew larger and larger. They crept onto the path, stalking him. It was this that the whispers were warning of. They were coming for him.

Jono grabbed his heart reg and charged madly through the underbrush. He smashed through branches and ferns, running as fast as he could anywhere away from them. Jono forgot all about the path as he passed the point where the forest began to crawl up the mountain side.

His body ached and pleaded with him, and eventually he stopped to look around as he gasped for air. He was lost in thick blades of grass and plump mushrups. Jono panted and leaned against the top of a huge mushrup. It puffed glowing particles into the air. Its trunk was sturdy but still swayed under his weight. He couldn't see the stars through the thick canopy.

The nearby underbrush rustled and jerked Jono's attention to the ground. Fern fronds swayed. Something gurgled, growled, and then charged forward.

Jono froze.

The creature burst from the foliage. Jono screamed and fell back on the ground before he could see it. His heart raced, but his regulator was still plugged in. The fear of impending death made his muscles clench hard as stone.

Just as he was about to die of fright, a white wrangle-furred frog hopped gingerly onto his knee.

"Reelloo," ribbitted the woolly frog.

Jono released his held breath and laughed.

His life wasn't over just yet. He laid his head back in

relief and began to slide backward down a brush covered, muddy ravine. He crashed through underbrush, gripped tight onto his reg, and with his free hand he grasped for something to stop himself. Spatters of mud and a whirlwind of scratching leaves flashed around him. He covered his face and tried to reach out but could do nothing until his back slammed into a dirt covered boulder.

"Great," Jono moaned.

He whipped chunks of mud from his face only to notice his whole body was thoroughly covered in gooey soil.

The canopy above him appeared to melt into the brush that covered a sheer rock wall beside him. The mud was part of a large indent against the rock where the forest and mountain met.

A trail of underbrush rustled in his direction before the woolly frog hopped into the open and squatted beside him.

"Rello. Rello."

"Hello," Jono replied.

Jono gathered himself up and then knelt over the small creature to pet its thick and now muddy fur.

"I'm glad you're not going to eat me."

"Reat me?" replied the woolly frog.

Jono looked around. In the rock wall, there was a cave with thick-leafed plants wrapped around its entrance. Jono pushed the leaves aside and poked his head in. The cave was wide, but no more than ten feet deep—a perfect place for a pungrus or mire bear to hibernate after a hearty feast.

The woolly frog hopped boldly inside and looked around. Its feet crackled against the ground, which was odd because as far as Jonothon was aware, stone or mud did not crackle when walked upon.

He crawled inside the cave and brushed the less muddy dirt aside. Below it was strange and gray and not natural at all. He dug at it some more. He tried to grip it and pull it up, but the flat plastic matter spread out wide and was pinned down by layers of dirt and plants.

There was a hole in the gray plastic moss growing along its rim.

Jono glanced back at the woolly frog that stared curiously up at him.

"I don't suppose you know what this is, do you?"

The woolly frog just sat there with its black eyes, reflecting Jono's face back at him without offering the courtesy of a reply.

The hole was an inch larger than his fist, so Jono followed the only logical course of action and stuck his hand into the black unknown. He hadn't thought his hand might have been chomped off by a violent creature hiding below, but by the time that idea popped into his brain he was already committed, elbow deep. It was fortunate for him no such monster lived in the pit, or at least it wasn't home at the time.

His fingers dug into the dirt.

All he felt was more dirt and mud, but then his fingers touched something cold and hard. It could have been a rock but the shape of it convinced the haphazard explorer that it was something else, something metal.

Jonothon pulled a mysterious metal object from the hole and held it up to the dim light. It was circular, like a medallion, with a red spherical jewel in the middle on both sides. Jono took the odd relic out of the cave to get a better look at it.

The woolly frog followed him with continued interest.

Mushrup light glistened off its rough and jagged silver edge. Along that round edge were strange writings, eroded and illegible.

Jono pushed the center gem in, and the relic popped out of his hand. It flopped through the thick ground leaves and then plunked into the muddy ground.

The woolly frog hopped back. It looked up at Jono, back at the greenery where the object lay, and then it darted in the opposite direction, disappearing into the forest.

The metal circle lay on the ground with its front side open around the blinking red gem lighting up Jonothon's concerned face. The inside of the medallion was empty. He picked it up again, pushed the center gem to close it and put it in his jacket pocket.

The forest was quiet.

"I need to get back," Jono whispered aloud.

Jonothon followed the cliff face back the direction he had come. He hoped to once again find his way to the cave. His body felt less tingly after all the running and excitement, but his head still swam from the broth.

The whispers had left the woods altogether, and Jono took comfort that at least the shadows didn't seem so alive and menacing.

The rocky mountainside curved back to the path. The narrow dirt road now had rocks sticking up from it.

Jono climbed the stairs at the end of the path. He brushed the purple curtain aside and entered the cave of the seventh seraphim.

Inside was indeed the statue of Ariam the wise. The arms of the once burning Mother wrapped around her from behind. There was a crack down the center of both statues. Any jewels that decorated them were now chipped off and littered the floor. The heads of both great angels were shattered at the ends of their barren necks.

The cave held no answers at all.

When Jonothon returned to the shrine he was met with smiles and hugs. They were surprised at how muddy he was, but didn't ask a single question about his journey.

Jono was just happy to be done with it.

As the Wyers trudged back through the woods, Jono spotted the foliage ahead moving. It shuffled violently before a red hat poked through the green leaves.

"You won't believe it!" Aquinas burst out, panting. "She . . ." The tumnkin struggled to control his breathe.

"Aquinas!" said Beky. "Are you alright?"

"She . . ." Aquinas wheezed. ". . . is coming."

"Who?" asked Jono parent's in unison. But Aquinas's wide, fearful eyes told them. It was her.

"Are you sure?" asked Charles.

"Yes," Aquinas said.

"You can't be serious, Mister Aquinas," said Beky. "There's certainly no reason for it at all!"

"At least none that we know," Aquinas replied. "For whatever the cause, the Empress herself, mistress of all the Dark End, will be here on the morrow! This is a telling omen to be sure."

Jono's family looked at each other, confused and unbelieving. Aquinas's gaze fixed on the young boy as well as the red and silver mechanical relic that poked out of his jacket pocket.

"By the stars, Jonothon!" Aquinas gasped. "What did the whispers tell you?"

Chapter Six

The Friendly Sergeant Tombs

'Home', they say, is a feeling.

It's a sense of the familiar, a place that is a part of you where everything is set in the right place. Or even if it's not right, it's yours, and that's enough.

In his final hours at home, Jonothon felt that sense of rightness slip away. He didn't want it to change, but the wind doesn't stop blowing just because you stand in it.

Jonothon sat on his bed and pushed the red jewel on the old relic: in and out, in and out.

There was no going back.

The army would take him away to a whole other world, leaving his life and his family behind.

In some ways it was everything he had wished for. He would travel the world. But it felt like a lie.

The fact that the Empress herself was coming to Polari was truly remarkable, but it seemed to have left Aquinas far more shaken than anyone else.

Aquinas had asked to see the relic Jonothon had found. His furry hand shook when he touched it.

"Do you know what it is?" Jono had asked.

Aquinas shook his head, but his breathing grew more rampant as he looked it over. "I have seen drawings, quite similar to this, but that was a lifetime ago . . . . I'm sorry, but I have to leave."

Aquinas dashed through the underbrush and was gone.

When the Wyers passed the cottage, orange light glowed from every window. They could see Aquinas was inside, walking in a circle, talking to himself as he flipped through books and then tossed them onto the floor.

Jono squirmed in bed. He picked up the book next to him, opened it to a red velvet bookmark, and buried his mind in it.

Illius stared across the desert, beyond the sparkling old city and toward the distant sea. To him, the world beyond the square earthen walls and bustling bazaars, beyond that glistening barrier, all was unknown. His father stood silently behind the thin drapes of their castle balcony, praying his son would change his mind, praying he would stay and one wake be king. Within his kingdom, no one aged. There was never drought and never fear, and nothing could ever change. It was a kingdom of peace and bliss, frozen in time. Illius stared down at the barrier of water from which no traveler could return.

Jonothon's lips mouthed the words as his hero spoke them—the words that had been forever imprinted on his mind.

'What am I, if I feast on food I've been given and rest in beds I have not made?' Illius whispered to himself and to the night of a world under a moving sun. 'Is that all there is to life? To sleep and feed?'

'Some may say such a life makes you lucky,' replied the King.

'It makes of me a beast, no more.'

Illius stared back at his father, who knew the bold words of his heir were true.

'Are we here to let all our capabilities, all our reason, just in us, unused?'

It was long into sleep hours before the weight of his eyelids forced Jonothon to finally shut the book. He knew it would be the last time he would read in his bed, in his home, with his family near to him.

He pulled the covers tight over his shoulder. He dreamed of joining Illius, sailing the liquid seas, fighting monsters, and rescuing maidens. In his dreams, he was never afraid, never weak.

Jonothon dreamed of who he could be. If only he wasn't who he was . . . .

As moments of dread often do, the wake came far too swiftly.

On this particular wake, Jonothon's dread was waiting for him. A strange man sat at the kitchen table, eating a biscuit he had dipped into a steaming cup of coffee. He wore the same soldier's gear, as those who came the wake before, with its light mechanized exo-skeleton and packs of ammo and pixel cannisters, except his seemed dull and worn. The skull-like helmet covered most of his face, but the stubble on his chin stuck freely below it. Strands of long blond hair dangled out the back.

The man was chatty and energetic compared to the sullen face of Jonothon's father. His mother took another batch of biscuits from oven. She glanced up at him with worry in her eyes.

When the soldier noticed Jono coming down the stairs he waved with a hearty smile despite the half chewed biscuit in his mouth. "Oi there, recruit! I was just telling your father, here, what an exciting time it is to be joining through the academy."

Jono cautiously stepped down the final stair and approached the table.

"The Terraloonies are looking weaker than ever, on account of our resistance to the blockade," the soldier continued. "I suspect by the time you graduate, we'll be guarding past the atmosphere again!" He winked through his mask and took another crumbling bite of the biscuit. "The Day pretends while the Dark ascends, eh?"

"Jono, this is Sergeant Tombs," Charles said, failing to hide the trembling in his voice. "It seems the army is eager to have you on your way."

"Quite right," said Tombs. "It's a habit of maintaining efficiencies, but you'll learn all about that. I do have a bit more for you to sign, Mister Wyer."

The soldier dug through his bag, retrieved an electronic scroll, and placed it in front of Jono's father. The words moved up and disappeared from the page as Charles scanned through the document then signed beside the X at the bottom.

"That takes care of all the technicalities," Tombs said. "Time to grab your things, Jono. Oh, and you should grab some breakfast before we go. Long travels ahead. Thanks for the grub, Misses Wyer."

"Do you have to leave now?" asked Beky.

"Time's more fleeting than you know, ma'am. I'll be taking the recruit down to the convoy, and we'll be off to the city in quicktime."

"You're not staying?" asked Charles. "The Empress is coming this wake."

"Oh." The soldier was visibly taken aback by the idea of not leaving immediately. He cleared his throat. "There's that, yes. Of course, we're on separate schedules, you know. The Empress and us dregs, eh? I hear there'll be a bit of a parade in her honor. Rightly so, rightly so. I'll take Jono down to the convoy myself. I don't want you to have to miss out on all that."

"No, we're happy to take him," Beky insisted.

Tombs paused for a moment, his smile frozen on his face. "As you like it." Tombs snatched Jonothon's hand and shook it. "Let me be the first congratulate you, Cadet Wyer. Welcome to the side of the good guys."

Beneath a tear in the soldier's armor, Jono noticed the lower half of a tattoo: a circle with jagged cracks. It was a symbol he'd seen before but only on gravestones. It was the symbol of the dead sun, Sol.

Tombs clapped his hands together. "Shall we be off?"

Jono lugged his heavy suitcase down the stairs that threatened to snap under its weight. The soldier waited on their porch as the family filed out the door.

"Have all your things, do you?" Tombs smiled at Jono. "Wouldn't want to leave anything precious behind."

Jono nodded. The memory watch was firmly attached to his shirt, but it was the strange, dented relic in his pocket that he felt for.

"I've got it all," Jono answered.

"Good lad," said the sergeant with a hard slap on Jono's back.

Chapter Seven

An Empress in Polari

Main Street was a jungle of activity.

Despite short notice for such a grand occasion, Polari had the streets decorated with patriotic flags celebrating the Dark End and the capital city. The symbol of Eies, a red circle gear with it central spire touching a star, hung down from banners on nearly every building. Giftmas decorations were repurposed to give the otherwise drab street lamps and building walls a garland of green, red and silver.

Dahlia succumbed to a giddy smirk at the crowd of excited pride around them. Despite the revelry that took hold of the town, Jono couldn't share his sister's emotions. He was resolved to move forward through the crowd and on to his destiny, but that didn't mean he could muster a smile along the way.

They turned off of Main Street, but the crowd was so thick that they had to maneuver around people at every step.

At the end of the western road stood a metal gate and on the other end rows of bulky military vehicles. They were shaped like fierce robotic beasts with metallic faces and gnarled claws that could rip you in two without any effort.

The Wyers approached the edge of the convoy and waited. They looked around, but Sergeant Tombs was nowhere to be found.

"Where did he go?" asked Dahlia.

Charles shook his head. "I don't know."

Another soldier stepped forward. It was the one from the wake before.

"You're late."

"Only barely," said Beky, "and with all this commotion for the arrival of the—"

"Yes. Fine. Is this the recruit?" The soldier nodded toward at Jono.

"Yes, sir." replied Charles. "This is Jonothon."

"We'll be disembarking shortly. Reno!" The soldier waved at a new soldier jogging up to them. "Collect his effects and put him over in the third B.O.A.R."

His mother turned Jono around pulled him close to her.

"Promise to be safe, alright?"

Jono nodded. "I will."

"Be safe. And make lots of friends." she said, her eyes tearing up.

Jono nodded and, in a moment, his family was led away. He waved, not knowing when or if he would see them again. Metal doors shut as a solider locked Jonothon in the belly of a troop carrier.

The early wake waned, and still the convoy didn't move.

Jono waited with patience at first, but as time passed it seemed less and less likely that they were actually going anywhere. He threw down the third book he tried to start reading back into his suitcase and shut the lid. He looked out a view slot on the side of the interior wall. Every time he looked, fewer soldiers seemed to be hanging around the convoy.

There was a loud clank as the door handle twisted. Jono spun around, unsure if he was already doing something wrong. He we met by the smiling Sergeant Tombs.

"Hey there, boyo."

"Hi," replied Jonothon in an unsure tone.

"It turns out the convoy's not leaving for some time after all. They said it's on account of restocking issues, but I wager they're all sticking around for a glimpse of the Empress themselves. I'm probably not supposed to be letting you out of your cage, but, stars, these chances don't come around often, do they?" Tombs grinned below his skull shaped mask. "Come on. I'll sneak you out into the crowd and we'll get a glimpse of our fearless leader."

"Don't you think we'll get in trouble?"

"Not a lash!" The sergeant laughed. "Most of the troops have already shuffled off. There's no one around to reprimand us for the same crime they're all committing."

Jono looked around. It was true, the convoy was nearly abandoned.

Together, they hid behind the gigantic tire of one of the carrier tanks while another soldier wandered past. Jono and Tombs ducked and darted through the west gate, snaked down back alleys, and made it to the throngs of people where colorful balloons and streamers pulsed along the Polari Main Street.

On a nearby street corner, a man had set up as a one person band. His two human arms played drums and a keyboard, while his four mechanical arms played a guitar and a self-blowing trumpet.

They pushed through the crowd to a dessert cart covered in chocolate rasbunches and vanilla twisps. Tombs bought each of them a twisp.

"Let's go around the back of this building and cut around to that space over there," he said, pointing to a gap in the sea of people at the rising steps of the Polari Trust Bank. "We'd get a better view."

Just as Tombs was sliding between a rather large man and a brick wall, something familiar caught the corner of Jonothon's eye. He stopped to poke his head through the jungle of arms, legs, and bodies to spot Sheriff Thoone across the road.

"Wait!" Jono shouted over the music to Tombs. "I want to say goodbye to someone."

He clenched his heart reg close to his chest with both hands and lunged forward, spilling drinks and thumping elbows as he went.

"Jono, come back!" yelled Tombs. The soldier squeezed from behind the large man, but Jono was already lost in the crowd.

Jono shoved his way through the mess of elbows and legs until he finally broke through to the open street. As he reached the middle of the road, he froze.

On the far end of Polari, past the north gate, a black spire emerged through the mist—a carriage growing out of a cloud. Around the carriage floated smaller vessels. Jono squinted. The flying objects looked like people, only with black-metal wings and robotic bodies. The carriage came down the weathered street, hovering above old buildings—towering and intimidating.

Alongside the carriage marched the Empress's mechguards. Their bodies were fused with bionetic mechanical arms and legs. The mechs took the shapes of monsters: towering tyrannosaurus, snake-bats, gorillacs, and wolvyerns. The wave of marching black metal spread over the town like a fog of charcoal.

The Empress was here.

Along the peaks of the black carriage, sparkling light ignited. Cannons boomed, and the foggy sky erupted in dazzling waves of red, white, and green. Fireworks formed creatures that swam through the clouds before crumbling into glittering rain.

The crowd had been silent until that point, but at the sight of the brilliant fireworks, Polari's citizens exploded into a roar of cheers.

Jono ducked into the crowd.

He pushed through a row of children that jumped and clapped at a firework butterfly. He couldn't see the sheriff anymore. He looked back across the street and realized he'd lost Sergeant Tombs as well. Jono realized that the other soldiers may leave before the parade ends, and he might not make it back in time.

The ground vibrated as the mechguard stepped closer and the carriage of the Empress grew nearer.

Hordes of people pushed past Jono. He was knocked forward and back and then slammed against a brick wall. Jono pulled himself close to the wall. He was blocked off from the road. He had to get back to the convoy. He should have never come to the parade.

Jono spotted an opening in the crowd and darted forward. He turned a corner just as a burly man stepped in his way. They crashed into each other. The man stepped back, but Jono bounced off and rolled to the cement. A foot collided with Jonothon's stomach and another crashed down an inch from his face.

"I'm sorry. I'm sorry," insisted Jono, although he was the one that had taken the brunt of the abuse.

Jono's hand touched his heart plugs, and he was relieved to find them intact. Then he saw the relic had slipped from his pocket. It slid along the cracked sidewalk. Jonothon reached for it, but a careless foot kicked it into the crowd. The relic smacked against the base of a lamp post, its red gem hit squarely, and the relic popped open.

That exact second, the parade of mech-guards stopped.

Jono crawled through the forest of legs, snatched the relic, and then closed it. No one had noticed anything had changed. The crowds still cheered as sparks of fireworks rained down on them.

Jono peered up at the dark metal guards only a few blocks away. A creeping fear infected his blood. The deep breaths he took through his mask grew faster as the noise of the crowd became slower and muted. The people themselves were slowing down, their motions drained until they weren't moving at all. Arms remained up in the air, excited expressions carved on people's faces.

The vibrant cheers and bursts of fireworks melted into echoes until an eerie silence possessed the world. The last twinkling colors descended quietly from the heavens as Jono stood in the crowd of statues.

The carriage jolted, and the mechguards charged forward—not marching, but in full speed down the road.

Jono held his breath in shock. He was the only one not frozen. What was going on? Should he pretend to be still like the others? Should he run and hide?

In a roar of engines, a group of flying mechguards soared overhead. They zoomed up the road together in a line then spread out. Their heads turned left to right, their eyes scanning the crowd in search of something.

Jono tried to step into crowd. He hoped to hide between legs and frozen bodies to blend in. Each centimeter he moved was calculated with the utmost caution. He made his way to the front of the line of frozen people and leaned fearfully forward to get a view of the street. The mechguards had left the main road and had fanned out amongst the crowd. The front of the carriage was still as two round metal guards stood watch at either end. The center of the carriage's chassis melted into black stairs.

Jono stayed as still as he could, his gaze fixated on the black stair case.

Chapter Eight

Attrayer's Key

At first there was nothing but shadow.

Then came movement beneath the dark, and a red figure stepped from the oily carriage door. Even under the blue-tinted sky, this red didn't bend into purple; it refused to shift from its regal crimson.

Red was the color of her gown.

It was thick and soft with a plush fur collar. Its wide and low neckline revealed ivory skin glistening against the dull town. The carriage's oily liquid door clung to her long black locks as she moved from shadow onto the Polari street. Upon her head rested a black crown and from it a veil, ornate in its beauty and terror, covered her eyes.

The first thought that formed in Jonothon's mind was the Empress was astonishingly young! An adult woman, no question, but her youth was stark against the black metal army. Her every motion was full of grace.

Jono forgot he was pretending to be frozen, but his body remained still—mesmerized by the sight of her. His heart rate slowed and his breaths were their natural loud and grating noise; he caught his breath when he heard it. Surely they would hear him, but there was no way for him to hold his breath for long. He had to escape!

The sound of metal scrapping against cement came closer. Jono peeked as a spidery mechguard charged, its skinny mech legs stepping loudly inbetween the frozen crowd. There was no time to think. Jono was about to turn and run when a man darted into the street.

"Jono!" called Sergeant Tombs. The soldier's eyes were wide when he spotted him. His mouth was covered by a clear mask. "We have to go! Now!"

The spider-mech jolted backward and darted at Tombs. Jono ran in the opposite direction through the alley. He turned down the first corner, hoping to lose anyone chasing him.

He kept running down barren streets until he came to the edge of an open road. Before he could move, something came from behind, covered his mouth, and yanked him backward. One moment he was standing on the sidewalk and the next all was dark.

Jono tripped and tumbled backward. His hands went to his heart reg. The plugs were intact. He blinked against the darkness, trying to get his eyes to adjust faster. The room stored large crates and a menagerie of odd items stacked on top of each other. Jono heard scuffling before the tip of a wand flashed a bright light on beside the face of his captor.

"Aquinas!" he gasped.

The tumnkin pulled Jono away from the wall.

"Quickly! Move back," said Aquinas. "I have to lock down this wall. This room's illusions will keep us safe for a moment, but it would be death to expect that to stop her for long."

"Everyone is frozen. They won't move," stammered Jono. "It's like . . . like they're dead."

"It is Orpheus drought," said Aquinas. "It is a pausing agent. The Empress has used it before. Trust me, Jonothon, they will be alright. She wouldn't harm them. There's nothing in it for her."

"What's going on, Mister Aquinas? Why did she do it? Why is she even here?"

"You haven't realized it yet, have you?"

Jono's head was swimming. He didn't know what Aquinas was talking about.

"I have been preparing for her to strike for ever since I came to the Dark," said Aquinas. "I expected her minions to finally break the spirit of this town, but never did I imagine it would be under events such as this, when her vile heart is manifest."

"I don't understand," said Jonothon.

A roar of engines came from directly above them. "There's   no escape, is there?" said Jono. "They have eyes that see through walls and ears that hear our heart beats. They'll find us!"

"We are not alone, Mister Wyer. Help will find us. Until then, we must count on the speed of the seraphim. Follow me."

Aquinas pulled a short wooden staff from his cloak. The top was covered in jagged crystals. He waved the staff in front of a painting in the corner of the room.

"Aperio," Aquinas commanded. The painting promptly melted into stairs leading to a tunnel.

Jonothon gasped in horror. "That was magic? You know magic!"

"The Empress is nearly upon us. There is not a moment to squander in doubt," said Aquinas.

"But . . ." he was supposed to be a soldier. He was supposed to protect the Dark from magic. "You're a wizard."

"Jonothon, I know you've been told many horrible things about magic and the Day, but please consider. Did magic do this to your home? Did magic leave you sick to barter for your life?"

"Are you going to enchant me?" Jono asked.

Aquinas leaned back, appalled. "I would never. You've known me your whole life. Jono, if you could set aside the lies that the Dark End has told you about magic, you would know in your true heart that I could never mean you harm."

"At school, they said magic is addictive," said Jono. "You shouldn't cast spells."

"All power is addictive. I only use it now to save you from her."

"Why now? All I wanted was to go to the academy and be normal. Why is she here?"

"Everything changed, because of you," Aquinas whispered. "If you come with me you will be saving both Ends from a fate most terrible. All these serendipitous events are not without cause. Think on it, Jono. Right after your walk along the path of angels, the Empress comes to Polari! Right after you bring that relic out into the light? It can only be because she knows! Somehow she has discovered it, saw it with her eyes that spy in every corner of the Dark. And now her cold hand is stretching out to take its power for herself. She is afraid. This, Jono, is the thing she fears the most. This is the hour to end her rule or the end of us all. Hold to faith, Jono. The light will not be swallowed by shadow. It can't end like this. She will not have the key."

"The what?" Jono asked.

"The key, Jonothon!" Aquinas grabbed him by the shoulders. "That very relic you discovered on your consul with the angels. It is none other than Attrayer's Key! The key of destruction! The power of the sun itself may fall into her hands. The light of my home would be extinguished. The Day doesn't deserve its fate to be in her clutches. It is up to you to prevent the night from covering the entire world. Jono, I can't make you believe me or to not be afraid of magic. You have the chance to be the hero that saves us all. The choice is yours."

Jono heard metal footsteps outside get louder.

Aquinas leaned toward him. "Tell me you trust that metal monster out there that froze your home in an instant and we'll surrender now. But if you doubt her oily heart then come with me. Save the world from her madness."

Jonothon looked down the tunnel and then back at the screech of metal. In that instant, the fate of the world weighed down on his frail, trembling shoulder. For so long, he had always felt so afraid of life, but now that salvation fell to him, he wasn't afraid. He knew exactly what he would choose. Even sickly and alone, he would never turn his back on a world in need.

"Okay." Jono summoned all the courage he thought he didn't have. "Let's go."

Aquinas' smile was wide and trembling. "You've chosen wisely. Quick! It is a gift from the angels that Polari was built on black rock mines. There are tunnels entwined with tunnels littering the whole valley."

Together, Jono and Aquinas ran through a hallway, racing deeper and deeper until the walls turned from cement to stone and dirt. The mining tunnels beneath the town were long emptied of any useful blackrock, but the barren mines were secured for the occasional school field trip. Jono had always had his parents sign a waiver, and now he pressed his mask against his face to keep the fine dust from his lungs.

A thunderous explosion crashed from above, sending both of them falling down opposite directions in the tunnel. Dull blue light cut through swirling billows of dust. Jono coughed through his air mask and pulled it close to his head.

Through the cloud of dirt, a behemoth metal arm rose from the hole it had just created. On the street above, a gorillac mech stuck its head down the hole.

"Run!" yelled Aquinas.

Jonothon lifted himself up just as the mechanical head jutted into the tunnel. The metal gorillac's mouth opened as if to crush him in its teeth.

"Cover your eyes!" Aquinas yelled as he pulled a turquoise egg from his cloak and flung it at the mechguard.

The shell collided with the monstrous face and burst to pieces. A thousand butterflies swarmed out of the shattered shell in a cloud of fluttering lightning that shocked the metal beast. The mech pulled out from the hole and reared back as though the machine was in pain.

"Now! Go!"

Jono and Aquinas charged down the depths of the dimly lit tunnels. The route twisted and turned. They passed through cell doors, one after the other, until Jonothon was certain they were completely lost.

It seemed they had run for an eternity.

All of Jono's muscles ached from carrying his heart reg and holding his mask tight against his face. As they ran, he panted and fell further behind.

After the last heavy metal door shut and locked, Aquinas finally let them come to a stop.

Jonothon crumbled to the ground, his chest heaving with effort.

Aquinas struggled to catch his breath as well, but at least he still stood upright. He took out a staff from his cloak and lifted it up in the dusty air. The crystal at the top lit up and projected a map above them. Aquinas touched the air to move the map around. When he found what he was looking for, he tapped the base of the staff to the ground, and the light went out.

"Was that all magic too?" Jono gasped.

"A spark egg. Magic of a sort." Aquinas replied. "It's the only thing that works against those metal brutes. We must be prepared, however we can. The fragile peace of this world is at stake. Catch your breath. We'll be alright here for the moment. It's a sterile chamber the miners use. The depth and the extra lining should shield us from whatever those creature use to see and hear through matter."

Aquinas waited for Jono to catch his breath. One he did, Jono took out the small metal relic from his pocket to examine it. He ran his thumb along the edge but made a careful point to avoid the red gem in the center. He worried the mechs could sense its power.

Aquinas glared at the relic, his beady eyes full of worry.

"So who is he?" asked Jono. "Attrayer?"

"The Biblios says he was once the seraph that guarded the border of light and dark, of life and death. In some more embellished tales, he would ride his flaming chariot across the sky, circling the sphere, sharing light with all ends of the world. But since then, the old mother Sol died, and her only burning son rests above the land of Day. Attrayer could no longer ride his chariot. He grew spiteful of the other angels, and thus he fell into the endless Pit."

"But those stories aren't real, are they?"

"Clearly, Mister Wyer, the Empress believes they are."

"And this is his key?"

Aquinas nodded with certainty.

"Have you been looking for this your whole life?" Jono asked with a sense of dread.

"My dear boy," replied the sympathetic tumnkin, "everyone has."

The center jewel was brilliantly red in the dim tunnel light, begging to be touched.

"From the fields of Ma Haila to the depths of Ka'or Zval, anyone who knew of it and had an inkling of the form it would take, have kept a keen and watchful eye for the wake that the key of Attrayer would once again appear upon the Earth."

"But why?" Jonothon asked.

"The age of balance between the Dark and the Day was always finite. The teachings of the Fellowship say that when Attrayer returns it will signal the final wakes of this era. He will unlock that which binds the burning sun and will issue unto the world a choice: remain in darkness and be consumed by frozen oblivion, or rejoin the Old Mother beyond the veil in the light of paradise."

Jono stared in awe at the key resting in his palms. His eyes met Aquinas's.

"You should take it," said Jonothon. "You'll know what to do with it."

Aquinas shook his head. "I dare not take the key from its finder. For more ages than are on record, the key has been in hiding. The angels chose to offer it to you. There must be a purpose in your finding it, Jonothon."

"What do we do?"

"We leave," answered Aquinas. "I have warned what friends I have to prepare for the worst, but there is someone we must seek out, first most. It is from him that I learned what the key would look like. He may have records that could be critical in unlocking its secrets. After that, my dear boy, we must continue to the safest haven under heaven. This key will be sought after by the entirety of the Empress' vengeful might, and we are going to need more than a hand or two in protecting it. We must go to where the grass grows lush and the sky holds blue and the son of the Old Mother wraps your body and soul in light."

Aquinas waved his staff at the wall, and the dirt crumbled and an opening spread from the center outward. Beyond the tunnel was a dense forest.

Celeste's yellow head poked from behind a tree, and she warked with curiosity.

Aquinas rested his hand on Jono's shoulder.

"We go to the Day."

In the Belly of the Mountain

*W*ith every step the yellow bird took, Jono felt the life he once knew fade into memory. With every step he moved further from what he was supposed to do and deeper into the dangerous unknown.

There was a part of him, behind the walls of fear and doubt, which trembled with excitement. That part of him had been dreaming of adventure his whole life.

The other part felt guilty for leaving his family frozen at the whim of the Empress of the Dark End. Jonothon told himself he had no choice, but in his heart he knew what he chose and he desperately wished he was right. The boy and the tumnkin stalked silently through frosty woods. They hung close to the trees, and occasionally stopped when they spotted dark figures soaring through the air.

Wakes and sleeps came and went.

They sheltered under a heat cloak and prayed it was enough to hide them from the terrible eyes that searched for them. Jono slept strapped to Celeste's back as Aquinas led them on. They ate sour rolls and muscow jerky, unable to risk heating food.

The icicle-crusted forest splintered up the mountain side. Bird, boy, and tumnkin made their way through the narrow crags of the Smaug Mountains.

"We can tread a little easier now," said Aquinas. "Even her spies have yet to see this place. The Eyes of Eies see much of the Dark End, but not all."

The crag was barely wide enough for Celeste to walk through. Gray and jagged rocks ran all along the crevasse's walls which bent high above them so the sky itself was blocked from sight.

It was far colder in the mountains than in any place Jono had ever been. They were well beyond the environment conditioned zone and the greenhouse clouds around Polari. Jono set his coat to maximum heat, and he still had to wrap himself in the heat cloak to keep from freezing. He kept his mask on, despite the crisp clean air, to keep his head warmer. Each breath caked the inside of the plastic eyepiece with frost, cocooning him from the outside world. Plumes of vaporous air puffed out the vent of his mask with each deep and teeth-chattering breath.

When Celeste's bumpy trotting finally stopped, Jono wiped the frost from his eyepiece only to see the end of the crag blocked by an avalanche of rock and ice. He looked to Aquinas, to ask what they should do next, but the Tumnkin was already on the ground beside the cliff wall. Aquinas touched his gemmed staff to the wall, and the stone contorted and morphed into a doorway.

"We will have to travel through the mountain for some time now. The historian lives far into the steeps, near a trader outpost. I wish I could tell you our travels will be short, but Blue Skies are still very far indeed."

Aquinas helped Jonothon climb off Celeste and the three entered the belly of the Smaug Mountains. The stone door shut behind them, trapping them in a cavern. It was warmer than outside, although it was still tremendously cold.

This was no miner's tunnel of dirt, metal, and cement. It was a natural cavern created in the mountain's innards, full of dangling and dripping rocks. Every few yards, a mechanical bat with a plump belly clung to the wall and lit the way. The ro-bats' lights were dull or dead.

As they passed a lifeless one, its body now a dark, skeletal frame sprawled upon the perch like a victim of a crime, Jonothon thought about the sad and lonely life they must have led. He wondered if they could to talk with other bots wirelessly, but then he remembered the cave was a secret; whoever put them there would not want any connection to the outside world.

"We should rest here while we're safe and warm," said Aquinas. "We can eat well and sleep with both eyes shut. The path to the Historian is weathered and rough, but not too far off now."

Jono huddled against a spire of rock beside Celeste. Her feathers were crusted with ice, but he brushed that off and leaned into her warmth. Aquinas removed a small box from the bird's pouch and set it close to them. The box opened like a flower and sparked to life in a whirling blaze. Crackling light from the fire flower lit up the cave in a brilliant orange but emitted no smoke.

"Do you think everyone is still frozen?" Jono stared at stalactites and hoped his family was alright.

Aquinas nodded. "Orpheus drought is healthy to endure for not more than three hours. By now the parade has probably resumed and concluded, with no one the wiser. Who is to say whether the Empress appeared to them or not? I imagine the crowds were probably left disappointed."

"Would they know that I'm gone?" asked Jonothon "Or that anything has changed?"

"I don't think so." Aquinas stirred the flowering embers with a stick. "The army will probably be ordered to act as if all is well. The Empress wouldn't want any whiff of weakness on her part to reach her people. No need to fret. The whispers tell me your family is well, Jono."

"How did you know she would attack?" Jono was warming up and the tunnel made him feel safer from the Empress. "You had that door and the tunnel ready. How did you know?"

"Before I joined the Fellowship and traveled the world caring for old shrines, I lived in the Day. On that End of the world, stories of the Empress' incriminating deeds are not hidden or whispered only in secret. In the Republics of Sola, people know full well the tragedies and deceptions that mark her character. Any of us that dared to enter her lands are all well practiced at the notion of being prepared for the worst possible outcome. There are no second chances once she has decided to come after you."

"And we are going to where you're from?"

Aquinas nodded as he prepared a flank of frozen snakefish on the fire.

"It seems so far to get to," said Jono, "as far as we've gone, and the sky hadn't changed."

"That's true as the word. Dark End patrols the ground and the Terralunan blockade sky and space. Our journey will not be comfortable. But hold to faith, yet, Mister Wyer. We are not alone in this venture, and the angels will speed our steps."

Jono pulled the relic from his pocket and looked it over in the fire light.

"The key of destruction . . ." Jonothon mused. "What does it do?"

Aquinas sighed. "The specifics are unclear. That's why we have to speak to the historian. Few in the world know even a sliver of the ancient tales that he keeps. We will get some answers, and some hope, when we meet with him."

Jonothon wrapped himself in the heat cloak and shivered. The clacking of his teeth echoed as he breathed. He tried to look as unfrightened and thoughtful as he could, but the cold was undeniable.

Aquinas looked at him with a hint of remorse in his eyes and tried to get his mind off the cold long enough for the fireflower to warm them.

"It seems Shiva's thread of fate has entwined us together on this path," Aquinas said with a smirk. "Permit me to share a little more about myself. You see, I never dreamt I would be in the Fellowship."

"Then why did you join?"

"Well, I didn't know about them. Not at first. I wanted to be an archeologist. When I was a child I found the skeleton of a whalerusaur. It was underneath our garden, a rib bone in the rutabaga."

"What's a whalerusaur?"

"A huge beasts. Mouth the size of your house. They're all extinct now, but eons ago they roamed the plains of Ankarak, eating bushels of leaves. The mud caked on their backs was the home for birds and lizards and all sorts of smaller creatures. It was fascinating. So I studied the past, but the more I learned about what was lost, the more I wanted to preserve the good that remained in the world. What seemed like a chance meeting with a Fellowship recruiter at the time now feels like the guiding whispers of the angels. Then came my assignment to Polari. It seemed so random at the time."

Jono yawned, but Aquinas responded with a smile.

"The point is, Mister Wyer, that sometimes the Narrow Path takes us to most unexpected places."

Jonothon did not know what to say. His entire life had changed— twice in one wake. He was certain that he made the right decision, but every step he took away from Polari reminded him of how much about the world he did not know. It was all so wonderfully, horribly strange.

"Don't think too much on it," Aquinas reassured him. "It won't help either way. There are still many steps ahead. You should get some sleep."

Jono leaned his head into Celeste's wing. His aches and pains eventually faded as he slipped into the world of dreams.

The final stretch of road through the cavern was steep but mostly free from obstacles. Along the way, Aquinas continued to recall the tales of his past.

"When I began my studies of the ancients it was at the seminary in Emmin Mal. I was top of my class. By special invitation I had the honor of studying under the historian, to study under he that studies under none. While my tenure with him was shorter than others, I soaked in every scrap I could. He had books hidden away that had not been read in ages. It was on one such page that detailed the return of the key, that one image remained burned into my mind. It was the very same as that relic which you now carry."

"If the historian knows so much, won't the Empress know to find us with him?" asked Jonothon. "Will she be expecting it?"

Aquinas shook his head. "I doubt it. The historian keeps in hiding, off the line of the world, he is always watching but is rarely seen. I was told once, that in the wakes before his isolation, he was renowned for his knowledge of the past across all the Rings of the world. He was a welcome guest in the golden halls of Caer Midus and the starless caves of the Crown Castle alike. But as the balance of Dark and Day grew more strained, the sorrowful truths that only he could truly comprehend grew ever more apparent. He withdrew from the bickering nations and the wayward people, and resigned himself to his study of the past. Thusly, his name was lost to the breath of the waking world."

The exit to the caverns came in the form of a particularly large stalagmite.

Aquinas laid the crystal end of his staff against it, and there flashed floating green letters. He typed a word into the air, Litmus, and the mineral pillar melted down and outward to reveal a white field of blistering, snow filled winds.

"Welcome to Bramblebar," grumbled Aquinas.

Chapter Ten

The Man in the Toppled Tower

igh across the snowy peak stood their destination—a speck of grey through the veil of violent white.

It was the home of the historian.

In centuries long lost, it must have been a terrific and imposing tower, but as they trudged through the frozen top layer of snow, all that remained were the three bottom stories surrounded by large broken pieces of stone and metal littering the white hill like scattered raindrops that refused to melt and be forgotten. On the top of the tower was a coned roof made of yellow thatch. Vines of purple wild flowers grew sparingly through thick layers of snow and up the base of the tower.

The three travelers approached covered in crispy layers of snow.

The wind around them slowed to an eerie stop. It was as if they passed an invisible wall that kept the violent winds out. One side was a white flurry of snow, the other calm. Jono tested the strange barrier by poking his head back and forth from snowy side to clear.

Near the tower, a simple wooden fence stuck out of the snow, and behind it, a pair of tuskyaks shoved their muzzles into a trough of slop. As Jonothon neared, the beasts' beady eyes peered up from their food to stare questioningly at the strangers. They didn't charge— content to snort and bare their tusks, informing their new guests they could crush their skulls without the slightest bit of effort.

"Move slowly and don't look directly in their eyes," advised Aquinas, and the brown furred creatures returned to the delights of their stinky meal.

For the first thirty three times Aquinas knocked on the small wood door at the foot of the tower, they waited patiently. When no sign of an answer came after the thirty fourth attempt, Aquinas hopped off the stairs and walked around the side of the tower.

"Stay there and keep knocking," he instructed Jonothon.

"Where are you going?"

"Around."

"What are you going to do?"

"I'm going to have to find another way."

Jono stood on the stairs, knocked intermittently, and wondered what Aquinas had planned, until he heard it.

It was the sound of a snowball colliding and self-destructing on a thick pane of glass. It was followed by another snowball that thudded against the window.

When the tumnkin came back around the other side, after numerous more snowball attempts, he was visibly annoyed.

"There's no use to it," said Aquinas, stamping his feet. "The old man must have gone deaf."

"Wouldn't some students hear us though?"

"No. That was a long time ago. I suspect there haven't been any more students after the last of us left."

"Maybe he's dead."

Aquinas looked nauseated. "You'll have to wait here. I'll leave the heat cloak and some jerky. There's a trader's post at the far end of the valley, along the backside of the mountain. If the historian is no longer here, we're going to need more help sooner than I had hoped."

"Can't I come with you?"

"Even out here, the Empress may have eyes on that town. It's best if you stay here where it's safer." Aquinas climbed onto Celeste. "I hope to be back before two hours pass. Don't let anyone see you and stay as warm as you can."

Jono watched as his only guide disappeared into the flurry of white upon his yellow steed. The distant lights that must have been the Bramblebar town were far off, and Jono worried about what might find him before Aquinas returned.

He curled up in the arch of the doorway, his back to the door, and pulled the heat cloak tight around him.

Jonothon sat alone for what seemed an eternity. He had almost slipped into sleep when the door slid open and he fell backward into the tower.

"Huh?" said an old man with long white hair and beard. He poked his head out of the door and looked to both sides. "I thought he had gone."

"Aquinas went into the town." Jonothon stumbled on the floor. "He'll be back though."

The old man grunted his disapproval and then squinted at Jonothon as if he had carrots growing out of his ears. The old man looked over Jonothon's shoulder, out into the snowy fields. Finding nothing near an explanation outside, he returned his gaze to the boy in front of him. The old man straightened himself and cleared his throat.

"And who are you?" he said, seeming to have just noticed Jono wore an air mask and carried a heart reg with him.

"Jonothon Wyer," Jono responded as he picked himself up. "Sir."

The old man squinted then shuffled back into the tower. He didn't slam the door in Jono's face, which Jonothon took as an invitation, and closed the door behind him as he stepped inside.

The round tower was stuffed with paper books and electronic scrolls; shelves overflowed with them. There were desks stacked upon desks and covered in books. It wasn't only books and scrolls, but parchments, boxes, flat computers, mechanix parts, and relics of all kinds strewn over the whole of the tower.

Wood and metal support beams lined the walls and circled in the middle. A staircase ran along the wall and up to the second and third floors. Bookcases divided the first floor like walls. Beyond two shelves that felt like a hallway was a kitchen with a simple but comfortable-looking tattered pink chair. Jono crept inside and then stepped into the kitchen. The man rummaged through a reizofridge.

"Why are you here? Do you know me?" said the old man.

"I heard you study the history of the worlds," Jono said meekly.

"That so? Defined by my habits am I? Well, that's probably a good enough introduction, then. And who, may I ask, are you?"

Jono supposed he was old enough to forget things frequently, but the sparse few minutes that elapsed was a bit surprising.

"Jonothon Wyer, sir."

"Oh, right. Just your name, then? It seems you are applying two separate criteria of definition." There was the sound of clinking glass from the other side of the old man. "It will have to do. It is a pleasure to meet you, Mister Wyer." He turned with a hearty, if forced, smile and held up a slab of muscow meat.

"Care for some lunch?"

The two story homes of Bramblebar were colored in earthy browns, sharp reds vibrant yellows, and all trimmed with snow. Balconies on nearly every window and banners, blankets and clothes hung from half of them. Plastic planks made up the covered sidewalks.

Aquinas walked down the street with Celeste behind him, trying to appear as normal as possible. Townsfolk wrapped themselves in thick furs and looked menacing and distrustful at everyone else. Aquinas kept a casual smile plastered on his face and nodded politely when anyone walked by.

In the heart of town, amongst the snow-covered street vendors and fur traders, there was an inconspicuous nook along a red brick wall. A series of red and yellow drapes hung loose, dooring the alcove off from the road.

The short tumnkin sat on a stool in front of a window set against the brick wall. On the other side was not the inside of the building, but an open field of green under a brilliant blue sky. The face of a beautiful brown woman glistening in the sunlight changed from joyous to serious as they spoke. Her skin was dark with tiny sticks and green leaves protruding from it. Her green, leafy hair swayed in the breeze like loose branches.

"Of course, I'll inform him immediately," said the wood dryad. "If she is already on the move, Alexsayter . . ."

"I know. Many thanks, Daphne. I know he is swift."

"You be as well. Her evil seeps unhindered in those lands."

Aquinas nodded and slipped from the stool. "I have to get back to the boy."

"Seraphim be with you," she said as Aquinas moved through the drapes. "May they speed your steps."

The window to the Day vanished and became a blank brink wall.

The historian had his sleeves rolled up as he chopped onions beside a pan of frying muscow meat.

"It's not often I get guests, you know."

Jono bit into his sandwich, not knowing how to respond. He had relayed the story of his archeological find in the woods and his subsequent escape from the Empress.

The historian finished putting together the lean cuts of meat, cheese, and fried onions of his own sandwich and sat down by the table on a stack of books.

"Aquinas said you could tell me about a relic I found," said Jonothon. "He said you were pretty famous, or something."

"I have been many things, a professor among them, for ages now," the historian replied. "I have had the pleasure of meeting people of every species on the planet as well as exploring more than my share of the mysteries and meanings of the life. When I tell you I am the singular most informed historian in the known world, do try to appreciate the weight of it."

The old man took another bite of his sandwich.

"So let's see this relic of yours, then," he said with a cheek bulging full of food.

Jono pulled the relic from his pocket. "I don't know what it does, but if you press the red gem in the middle . . ." Jono's hand moved over the red gem.

"Don't!" said the historian.

Jono stopped and carefully laid his hand on the table.

The historian took the relic and lifted it up to the light, squinting to see it better. He ran his thumb across the central gem, but did not push it in. His eyes transfixed on it as he chewed. He set it down and bowed his head.

"No mistaking it," he said almost to himself. His wrinkled blue eyes met Jonothon's wide ones. "That *is* old."

"Aquinas thinks, well, he said that it looked like a drawing he'd seen here, that this may be Attrayer's key, and that the Empress is after it."

The historian took another bite of his sandwich and added a slice of a crapple into his mouth. He chewed ominously.

"I know," the historian said slowly, "and she would be after it, no question. Tell me, Jonothon, what do you know of history? Of the world as it is now? There are many legends and tales of the nature of the past, some more true than others—the Dark and the Day, the Empress and the sages and the Terralunans above the sky."

"I, well, I don't know much."

"There is a measure of truth in all legends. It just isn't as it is presented to be. Have you ever heard of the tale of the great Manturin?"

"Yeah. That was a turtle so big that people lived on him like an island!"

"Exactly right! Well, that tale is true! Manturin existed—only not as the story says. He didn't sail endlessly around the liquid seas. The poor fellow was caught in a storm current centuries ago and pulled to the eastern ice sheet. The ice just grew right around him and has trapped him ever since. What was once real had, in his absence, become exaggerated. Mythological. The point is, there are legends, and then there is truth—often the two intertwine. It is the duty of the honest researcher to separate them."

The old historian grew somber and leaned against his hands. He stared at the relic on the table, and Jono mimicked the manner of his stare.

"Attrayer's Key, they have called it," spoke the historian. "So long lost that many labeled it myth. Others have hunted for it with a zeal that cannot be understood through mere words. Even as the legend of it permeated the world's mind, its true identity, its purpose, had been lost. Leaders and scholars across the world have coveted it with all their being, but never do they question why. It is a trickful thing, Jonothon, the values and esteem of the living.

"We live upon a world of delicate components. It is a world nearing the edge and now I fear we have reached it. The key we have here with us is capable of changing everything. This is no trick of fancy. It was destined to occur. The hour the key returned marked the beginning to the end of the rule of night and day, and much more. There will be hard times ahead, but I must impress upon you the absolute certainty these wakes are coming. It is only a matter of time and only a question of what those in possession of the key choose to do with it."

"So the Empress is looking for it? She wants it to take control over everything," said Jonothon.

"In more ways and for more reasons than you understand," answered the historian. "That is just the beginning. Keep your mind alive, Jonothon—alive and vibrant. What creeping destiny comes, only truth will see this world through. In these latter wakes of woe, all things of man and nature cling to existence with a tenuous grip. How will the balance tip? Who shall rise and who shall fall? These are the musing of destiny. It will come. It will come with a war at Dawn."

The moment Jono lifted the sandwich once again to his face there came a frantic banging on the door. He squeezed the slices of bread in fright. The muscow meat slipped free and smacked against his nose. The two humans shared a look of concern.

"Front door—open," commanded the historian.

The door obeyed and opened to show a wide-eyed Aquinas.

"Oh. It's you." The historian sat down, disappointed.

"Yes, sir. Jonothon, you are well?" asked Aquinas as he came into the tower, the door shutting behind him. "I didn't see you by the door so I—"

Jono wiped mustard from his nose. "I'm fine."

"Good," continued Aquinas as he stepped forward. "Sir, we come with terrible news. The key of destruction has—"

"Yes, yes. I am well aware." The historian waved a hand like he was batting away a fly. "The child and I have already discussed it, Mister Aquinas."

"You do remember me, then?" asked Aquinas with a hint of suspicion.

"My memory is as impeccable as ever," said the historian matter-of-factly. "Never forget. That's my rule, Mister Wyer, and you would be good to adopt it. The preponderance of problems in life could be easily resolved by the simple, thoughtful recollection of one's own experiences, or lessons of all those that came before."

The old man waved his finger as he said it, as a way of asserting the unquestionable truth of his statement.

"I would like to review some of your records regarding the key, if I may," said Aquinas.

The historian shrugged. "They are sorted the same as always. Help yourself."

Jonothon's first thought was that by the appearance of it, the historian's definition of 'sorted' must have meant flung and stacked randomly about the tables, shelves, chairs, stairway, and floor.

Aquinas initiated his search, scanning book covers and shifting teetering stacks.

"I have a policy," said the historian to Jono, "of never denying anyone aid in the honest search for truth. Uncovering it is difficult as it is without throwing up additional obstacles of pride or greed in the way. You only need ask. That's another rule you should hold to."

The old man's finger waved again as he sloppily bit down on his sandwich.

Chapter Eleven

The Shadows Come A Hunting

*J*onothon left the relic with the historian and curled up on a tattered couch on the toppled tower's second floor, unable to sleep. He was exhausted from the journey, but the torn covering on the couch poked at his skin and stuffing coming out of the cushions made him itch. He hadn't received any straight answers from the historian about just what the Attrayer's key was for, but he'd confirmed Aquinas's impression of how important it was.

The equally exhausted tumnkin scoured the large collection of books. He touched their covers, searching words and phrases throughout the book, desperate for any hint of knowledge about the key.

Jonothon wondered why he didn't simply pester the historian with all of his questions. Surely an item like Attrayer's key would be important enough for him to have known about it thoroughly. There was a clear unease between them. Whatever reason Aquinas had for leaving the toppled tower, it wasn't good.

The hatch to the third floor was open slightly, but it was enough for a chilling draft to creep in. Jonothon wrapped a brown, holey blanket around him and climbed the stairs to shut it, but as he reached for the latch he heard a shuffling noise on the floor above. His body stiffened for fear that the mech-guards had found them. He stayed motionless as he caught his breath and assured himself that if he were to succumb to every tiny fear then there was no sense in dreaming of a life that consisted of anything more than climbing out of bed twice a wake to use the toilet.

To sleep and feed? A beast, no more.

Jono cracked the hatch open further, just enough to see two legs below the historian's thick brown coat. He opened the hatch fully and when the old man didn't move, he continued to come out.

The thatched roof was separated from the stone and metal walls enough to see all around them clearly. Jono approached the wall near the historian politely, not wanting to startle him if he couldn't hear his footsteps. He reached the uneven wall and leaned against it. The top of the stone met his nose, so he was able to see out. They were above the thick white winds, tall enough he could see to the horizon in every direction.

The sky above the snow-filled winds and glistening peaks were a brilliant violet. The distant edge of world beyond the Smaug Mountains to the south hinted a trim of pink clouds.

The historian, however, stared coldly to the northern mountain peaks that were crowned with black and stars.

"What do you know of history, Jonothon?" His words sounded almost sad.

There was a sense of importance to his question, but Jono's reaction was to contemplate what he might really be getting at and to try to give the best answer to that goal that he could.

"I have learned some things," Jono responded, wanting to prove his worth. "We read about the creation of the Imperial Congress this year. Also, there was a lesson about how the original Empress traveled to the Dark End and built warmth out of the cold, and light out of the dark. I bet she just brought that stuff with her originally, though. My teacher said she built cities on other planets and some in moons or just floating around in space. But the Day betrayed her to the Terralunans and then they shut her down and made the blockade. So now we're just here, on Earth."

When the historian did not respond, Jono searched his memory for the furthest history lesson.

"There was a time when all people were unchained to the sphere and could travel the stars, further than you could see," Jonothon said, although he doubted the historian would be impressed.

The man's sunken eyes didn't stray from his gaze into the black sky, as though he hadn't heard Jono speak at all. "We are a bold people. Our stories stretch through millennia and to a depth beyond imagination and yet we find ourselves fighting the same wars and staining the same gifts. We are bold and unrepentant."

Jono peered at the distant stars alongside him and said nothing.

"You do not yet know what sorrowful times you have been born into," said the historian. He turned to Jono and met his eyes with piercing honesty. "But do know that I am sorry for it."

Their gaze held for only a moment before the old man retired to the warmth of the tower and left Jonothon to the cold but windless world.

Jono looked toward the tiny flakes of brightness that seemed unreachable and struggled to grasp the depth of all the changes he had experienced and the uncertain life and deeds that lay before him.

When his toes began to shiver, Jonothon returned to the uncomfortable couch. He found the heat cloak and added that to his cocoon before lying down. He tried shifting sides and then laying his head at the other end, but the poking tears and disgruntled lumps in the couch were too much of an annoyance. However, his exhaustion won out, and he was soon taken by a restless sleep.

Jono fell in and out of chaotic and senseless dreams.

He would wake for a moment only to find a new position to fall asleep in. At one moment, as he turned over, his eye cracked open and glimpsed something outside a dusty window. Jono kneeled over the back of the couch and rubbed the dust off the window with his sleeve.

Through the whirlwind of snow that bordered the tower, the ground appeared darker in one part than everywhere else. It was as though shadows crawled along the ground all by themselves.

And they were coming closer.

He had first noticed the patch of shadows to the right, but now there was another coming up the left. As they passed the invisible barrier into the calmer winds the shadows grew upward like living oil, forming black creatures of wispy flesh. One became large and bulky with a low head and huge arms. The others were far smaller; the middle became wolf–like, and the last took the shape of an imp.

"Fel shades!" exclaimed Aquinas. He'd looked over Jono's shoulder and grabbed him tightly. "They are her spies and hunters. They slaughter without mercy and are nearly invincible to attack!"

Jono jumped from the couch, he knew they had to escape. He looked over the edge of the second floor loft, just as the historian stepped out the front door with a bag of feed over his shoulder.

Jono ran to the stairs. Aquinas grabbed him by his shoulder. The burly fel shade charged forward just as the old man looked up to see it. The black shadow of the beast swallowed his entire body.

"It's too late for him," Aquinas whispered with a fury as he pulled Jono away. "We have to run! Out the window, Jono, quick as you can."

They moved to the back of the tower. Jono slipped on his mask. He found a belt and tied his heart reg to his back.

Aquinas snatched the three books from a table and shoved them into a pouch under his cloak. He pushed open the two old windows by the table and they climbed out onto the stone. The exterior wall of the tower was slanted and the disorder of protruding stone blocks made good handholds for them to climb down.

They struggled down the stones and once they neared the bottom, Jono leapt to the ground. Aquinas grabbed his hand and pulled him around the rear of the tower.

"We are in more danger than you know. They are but the hounds hunting for their master. She must be near! Demon in the guise of woman, the Empress is upon us!"

"What do we do?"

Celeste was tied to a hitch in the rear of the tower. Aquinas cut her reins loose and held her head to his.

"Run swift down the western pass," Aquinas told her. "Stay to the swept roads."

"She's leaving us?" said Jonothon. "How will we escape?"

"She will hopefully divert their attention. Without our weight she will be swift enough to avoid them. Beyond that she can no longer help us. I only pray there is enough time."

They ran along the icy cliff side. To the left of them was a vertical cliff that dropped into jagged rocks until being consumed in a clouded abyss.

To fall would mean certain death.

Jono stumbled in the deep, crusty snow. He pulled his hands into his coat sleeves to avoid touching the ice as he pushed himself up. He glanced back at the tower. The fel shades charged after them. The three dark creatures moved quickly over the snow without leaving any imprint.

"They're coming!" yelled Jonothon.

Aquinas spun around. There was no chance of outrunning them.

"Stay to the edge!"

They reached a peak where the snow wasn't as deep, but they were in arm's length of the cusp of the chasm. Aquinas drew out his staff and held it up to their oncoming foes. The crystal shard burst with a brilliant glow.

"Stand back ye who fell from the light!" commanded Aquinas.

The light flashed through a rainbow of colors as the fel shades came upon them. The creatures screeched and spread out around them. Their shadow bodies grew flat and wide and seemed to blend into each other as though they were forming a dark net to ensnare their prey.

"Stay thy hand and return to the Endless Abyss!"

The wind roared all around them but even with its violent screams, Jono's ears caught an altogether different sound.

There was flapping!

Jono spun as another creature thudded behind them. This was no brother to the fel shades. Glistening ivory feathers covered its body. It had the chest and head of an eagle, but its body was thick and strong—a thin tail with a tuft of fur at the end stretched behind the creature. Golden horns grew from its head and neck and continued down its back. Its wings spread wide and rustled in the terrible wind.

The ivory griffin dove forward and snatched Jono in its claws just as the wolf-shade leapt at him with barred black teeth. The shade crashed into the snow.

"Thomas!" exclaimed Aquinas.

The griffin flew along the edge of the cliff, and Aquinas and Jono climbed on the griffin's back before the other fel shades could claim them. Thomas spun and dove with his two riders down the side of the cliff.

"Not a moment too soon, eh, Alexsayter?" said the griffin, laughing.

They soared down the jagged cliff then swooped upward past the flurry of snowflakes.

Thomas's eagle head arched back to eye their followers.

The shades spread wings from their shadowy forms and leapt off the cliff in pursuit. They swooped behind them. But the strong winds were too much for their thin, almost vaporous bodies, and they lost control.

The griffin and his riders swung against the cliff, and the fel imp smashed head-on into the rocks.

Thomas flew deep into the chasm with Jono and Aquinas holding desperately to his back.

"Hold on!" The griffin commanded.

They gripped tight to Thomas's curled horns as the griffin snatched a boulder from the cliff. He spun on his back and flung the rock behind them.

It soared through the center of the wolf and brute shades, which had to dissipate to keep from being crushed. Their pursuers tried to return to a flying form, but the winds were too harsh and they spun out of control and disappeared down the chasm.

The griffin laughed triumphantly. "Only three fel? The Empress must have thought you'd be an easy catch!" Aquinas adjusted the floppy hat that, by some miracle, managed to stay on his head. "Wiser not to tempt fate."

"No need for worry, Alexsayter." Thomas gave a hearty sigh and winked at Jono. "From now on, we'll have smooth soaring . . ."

They burst through thick clouds. Over a sea of gray clouds and island mountain peaks, in the distant horizon grew a luminous thread of pink.

Jono smiled wide at the light and clenched the curved horns tightly.

". . . and clear skies!"

Chapter Twelve

The Sage of Ages

louds spread across the air like melting ice-cream: marble pink, orange, and red against the violet sky. Ascending over the horizon, Sol lit up half of the world. It looked small and unimposing, like an ornament hanging without a string; but its light changed everything.

They had entered the Day.

It was known as Sola, or the land of Blue Skies.

Jono huddled against the griffin's back, his head buried in its bushy feathers. The wind was cold, and his hands were sore from holding tight to rigid horns for hours.

The clouds soon thinned, and the rainbow colors of Dawn faded until they were only spots of white puffs against an opaque blue atmosphere. The sunlight was warm despite the wind's chill, but it fogged up Jonothon's mask.

Below them stretched an endless green forest spotted with shimmering lakes. Blue streams snaked through the land, and waterfalls tore down mountainsides.

"Look to the east, Jono," said Aquinas over the whipping winds.

Jonothon's eyes ached from the light, but even through his squinting and the foggy mask he saw brown, arched roofs and cobblestone roads.

"That's nothing. Just wait until we arrive," said Thomas with a happy grin to his beak.

The
forested mountains gave way to rolling hills and valleys filled
with farms. Thatched roofs and stone castles littered the world below
them.

As amazing as the sight was, Jonothon was exhausted and hot. His
thick coat made him sweaty and stuffy.

At first the castles below them were small and simple, but as they
flew deeper into Blue Skies, larger and more ornate castles covered the
land.

The sun was a quarter arch above the horizon as towering spires
jutted into the air. The griffin weaved around the towers. The sight of
the republic of Day made Aquinas laugh with joy.

Banners and flags hung and fluttered in the wind, blue with gold
trim, symbolizing the sky and the sun. Upon them was the crest that
united the republics of Sola: the seraph Shiva in the form of a white
dove crowned with light and spreading her six wings.

On the wave of hills that rolled before the towering Epoch
mountains rested a glistening castle that spread into a village below.
Open green fields mixed with stone buildings and courtyards of the
great golden castle.

"You have arrived to the last true haven upon this troubled world,"
said Thomas as they descended amongst the gold spires. "Home to
the Sage of Ages and the center of the Republics. Welcome to Caer
Midus!"

Thomas sailed down to the central courtyard. His two passengers
toppled to the grass and cool cobblestone floor. Jono tore off his

mask and covered his eyes. A soft breeze met them, carrying warm, clean air.

"Hold thyself still!" said a gruff voice from beside them.

The blade of an ornate polearm pointed directly at Jonothon's face. On the other end was a knight with a cat-like body—a feli'yin. His muscular, furry form was tall and lean, and he wore emerald armor. He had powerful looking legs and a long, swishing tail. A mane of hair grew from below his helmet and down to his chest.

"All visitors must arrive and register through the main gate," yelled the feli'yon. He looked at the heart reg that Jono held close to his chest and snarled. "No exceptions, Thomas, and especially not for a Dark Ender!"

"There is no time, Aramis," said the dryad, Sir Daphne Briar, as she pushed past him. "They've barely escaped the Empress with their lives."

Daphne knelt and hugged Aquinas. "It's good to see you safe again." She smiled at Jonothon and took up his mask and coat. "You will need armoroil before you burn. So pale. Never touched the sunlight, have you? Follow me. You'll need goggles, a cloak, and ointment. The Sage would speak with you immediately, Alexsayter. I will join you when the child is ready to endure the light of Day."

"Right, right," replied Aquinas. "Nary time and the Empress is already on the march." He turned to Thomas. "You've carried us so far. Could I trouble you to take me a little further?"

"It's never trouble for a friend," Thomas said.

"I will see you shortly, Jonothon," said Aquinas as he waved. Jono waved back while Thomas, with Aquinas on his back, stretched his wings and leapt into the air.

"This way. Every moment counts," said Daphne.

Jono had never seen either of Daphne's or Aramis's species of peoples before. Her dark wooded body was draped in a gown of leaves that brushed ground as she walked. A branch from the end of her gown caught on a crevice in the stone floor and tugged her back. She turned to Jono with a faint blush and pulled the gown free.

"I should get that trimmed."

Jono smiled back awkwardly.

Daphne led him through golden hallways that absorbed the sunlight to glow a luminescent yellow. Beautiful marble statues decorated the halls of Caer Midus. Statues of men, woman, and children—mostly humans but some of other species—lined the halls and stood guard at the corners of archways. Their stone faces were always pleasant, softly happy as they stood frozen in dance, reading a book or stretched to hold up the ceiling.

The dryad brought Jono to a room and presented him with a blue crystal jar, a dark blue cloak, and round goggles with nearly black lenses.

"You will need to cover your skin in this, all over, even under clothes. They may seem solid, but there are no crannies that the Light can't creep." Daphne smiled sympathetically. "The transition can be extremely difficult for such a pale night child as you. I'll leave you to it in private, but don't take long. The Sage is eager to hear from you."

When Jono had finished smearing the clear, sticky substance over himself, he donned his coat and goggles but left his stuffy mask off. He slipped the strap of his mask over his shoulder and wheeled his heart reg into the hallway.

"It can be uncomfortable, but at least you won't spontaneously combust. This way," said Daphne.

Beyond a white arch, they entered a garden, glistening in sunlight. Vines climbed up castle walls, wound up pearl columns, and clothed marble statues in their brilliant yellow and pink flowers. Bushes were groomed into the shapes of animals and carriages, all bursting with colorful flowers in full bloom. Streams of clear water poured from statues and cut lazily through soft grass.

Jono squinted through the brilliant light. The lush plants loomed terrible and magnificent above him. Faint clouds of pink pollen floated in the air, their particles shimmering in the sunlight. He clenched his heart reg as frighteningly gentle vines reached out to carressed him as he passed under a flowery arch.

At the center of the garden sat a circular pavilion with seven pillars. Vines that wound up each pillar grew inward, offering inconsistent shade.

A crowd had gathered at the stone steps, including Aquinas and Thomas the griffin. Inside the pavilion, a willowy tree had wrapped itself around a marble chair. The tree had striking violet eyes . . .

The Sage of Ages.

His chocolate, bark-like skin was covered by a leafy beard that flowed down his chest. Branches and leaves draped his shoulders and wrapped around him. His rough lips curled into a sad smile. The patriarch of the duchies of Blue Skies raised his hand and summoned Jonothon to approach.

The murmuring crowd fell silent as Jonothon walked to the pavilion. Jono felt the shock and disgust in their gaze. Every step he made felt like he was violating something sacred to them. No one moved, but if they attacked, there would be nothing he could do.

Aquinas stood beside the Sage with the books he had taken from the historian in his hand. One of the books was opened to a page with the drawing of Attrayer's key. Aquinas and Jono exchanged a worried glance.

"You have nothing to fear here," spoke the Sage. "You are most welcome in my home. To risk all that you have, there is no question you are a true friend of the Old Mother, and of the Day. Come, night child, and learn the truth the Empress seeks to hide."

Chapter Thirteen

Of Legends and Prophecies

"Alexsayter told me of your journey," said the Sage. "The angels keep special watch upon you. I wish I could welcome you under a more cheerful sky, but fate, I'm afraid, has brought you here for somber business indeed."

The crowd began to whisper, but the Sage did not react to their worried words.

"By the lines in your face, child, your involvement has brought you to the limits of what passes for education in the Dark End. It is time you know the truth, the secret that has been veiled in the darkness of her lands. It is the truth of our world of dark and light, and of the Key and the Keeper."

The Sage raised a wooden staff laden with uncut gems. The sky above the pavilion darkened with a solid blanket of clouds. Motes of light flickered and zipped around like fairies before they merged into the image of a human man and a woman. The woman cradled a child against her chest.

"At the birth of this world, when old gods were young and involved with the matters of the Earth, all was made to exist in perfect balance. The sun and the stars took turns with the world. All obeyed the commandments of nature."

The fairy light flickered apart and transformed into image of the planet Earth.

"But those that favored the Dark grew ambitious and hungry for power. They turned away from their creators and lusted after the secrets of the abyss. In their zeal, the armies of corruption committed the gravest sin for which all their descendents bear burden: they blacked out the light of their Mother. Their ambitions had turned to madness. Were it not for the Mother's loving grace, all life would have been extinguished. It was at the world's greatest moment of sin that She bestowed upon us Her greatest gift. The world was abandoned by the Father and the Mother, but She left us Her only son, who shines upon the faithful, and She left us the seven seraphim, the earth-bound angels that look over us and guide us in this dangerous era along the narrow path toward heaven.

"And so was born Dark and Day—the fleeting gift of a second chance at redemption. But second chances are fragile things. This tenuous balance has not the strength of nature. It cannot last. The whispers of the remaining seraphim have foretold the wake when Attrayer, herald of destruction, wayward angel, will return from the endless Pit. He will claim his key and unearth the sins of old. Judgment will shake the Earth. The narrow path will take the faithful through fire and light. Only then will the sins of the past be faced and forgiven. Only after we meet the whole of our mistakes and overcome them will the veil be lifted and the Earth cleansed to join the kingdom of heaven."

The Sage waved his arm through the fairy image; the crowd looked on in silent awe.

"At the Gates of Dawn rests the guardian of the fragile balance. The angels entrusted the Keeper to await the return of the Key. But prophecy is only as certain as our will to meet it. It is the key of destruction, but will it destroy evil? Or will it destroy those that seek heaven? It is within us to decide."

The Sage returned to his seat, and the fairies dispersed into a ring of light around the forum.

"These are troubling times. It is a pity such dire news weighs on one so young," said the Sage. His remorseful eyes searched Jonothon's. "Child, show me the relic you uncovered in the twilight forest. Show me Attrayer's key."

Jono was bursting with pride.

He had found the key the world had been waiting for. The planet would be safe from a freezing Day or burning Dark and it was all because of him! He would be a hero, even greater than Illius. The Day could probably fix his heart and lungs with magic, and he was sure that even the Dark End would see reason and be proud of his choice.

He had done it. He had saved the world.

Jono reached into his pocket, but it was empty. He felt the pocket on the other side, the back, and every tiny pocket he could find. He checked them all twice, three times, but the icy fear filling his veins was only confirmed.

"Burning stars!" Jono swore.

"No . . ." slipped quietly off Aquinas's tongue.

The Sage grasped their meaning. He grabbed Jonothon by the shoulders.

"Where is it, child? What has happened to the key?"

Jono froze with shame and fear.

After everything he had learned, after the chance to save the world from destruction had landed so carelessly into his hands, he had lost it.

"I left it on the table," Jono said in shock, "in the kitchen at the tower."

The crowd gasped.

Aquinas sat on the marble steps. He looked like had been sick for a week. "Where the minions of the Empress overtook us and slayed the historian."

The crowd's murmurs grew loud and fearful.

"Let none deny it. The last wakes are upon us," said the Sage of Ages. The Sage turned to the feli'yin guard that stood from the crowd. "Aramis, send word to all families under the Blue Skies that we must gather swiftly but in silence. The Dark Machine will set her eyes on us to see what we know. Alexsayter, the Assembly of Lords will need to hear from you to know what has transpired. Make ready, all of you. The sphere will feel the tremors of the Pit if the Empress' plot is allowed to unfold."

The crowd dispersed quickly and Jono turned to follow them.

"Jonothon," the Sage called, pulling him back. "I will need you at the assembly to confirm the relic you found was the key. The lords will be wary and for good reason. I'm afraid it's not safe for you to return to your home in the twilight. To return to the Dark in these coming wakes would bring you only a swift and certain doom."

"I'm sorry," Jonothon squeaked, overcome by the gravity of his mistake, and on the edge of tears.

The Sage laid a hand gently on his shoulder. His eyes reflected Jonothon's sorrow. "I know."

Chapter Fourteen

The Assembly of Lords

The waiting made Jonothon's stomach feel like it was on a centrifuge. He sat alone on a terrace above the main gate, overlooking the hill leading to the village. Over the following hours, a few delegates arrived through the tunnel of gates at the front of the castle. Most, Aquinas had informed him, would appear directly in the Round Hall when the assembly began.

Lord Peregrine, the Duke of Diremarc, marched through the golden entrance with his banners waving and an entourage of green-skinned gromlin servants. His thick, red beard and chiseled jaw were intimidating, even from a distance.

The Sheik of Systine came not long afterward in a carriage led by four white stags. The sheik's golden haired daughter, whom Jono surmised to be around his age, wore an elegant pearl gown and glistening veil.

As all the arrivals settled in the courtyard, Jonothon watched her in particular. He went into the courtyard and struggled to gain the courage to say hello, but when the white-gowned father and daughter walked by, nothing came out. The corner of her eye followed his as she passed. For the rest of the wake, Jono was plagued with second guessing over whether he had smiled back or gawked at her.

Horns trumpeted from the walls of Caer Midus.

At the center of the castle, high in the main tower was the Round Hall. The marble room was lined with large stained glass windows whose colorful light danced against a domed ceiling. At the side opposite the door stood a towering statue of the seraphim, Shiva. Her pearl wings spread before a frosted white window that opened on the unmoving sun, just above the mountain top. The angel had six wings, and her gown melded into a throne for the wise and weary Sage of Ages. In his brown, knotted hands he held the three old books that recently belonged to the historian.

The delegates and lords of the far reaches of Blue Skies entered in front of Jonothon or flickered into existence already seated upon marble benches that encircled the room. The lords represented every species and region of people in the Day.

The seven highest ranked lords sat at a round table in the center of the room. Jonothon noticed a knight with long, blond hair and brown eyes glaring at him. The man's eyes were cold and angry. Jono felt the anger and blame that must have been shared by the whole of the Day. He had failed and they must have thought he did it on purpose.

The instant the door shut there was a torrent of questions from the delegates.

"Is it true the key has returned?" shouted a centaur dressed in yellow robes.

"Is she coming?" asked an elvayn woman in a green robe.

"Alistair, what news of the Keeper? We cannot let her pass, key or not!" said the muscular Lord Peregrine.

"Our intelligence has seen no movement toward the Keeper," replied Alistair Vahlor, the Sheik of Systine. "The Empress dares not step toward the Dawn quite yet."

The Sage raised the book from the historian's tower and the crowd fell silent.

"Noble Lords of the Day!" The Sage's voice commanded attention. "We have two among us that bear witness to this truth! The Empress of Eies and her minions have slain the historian and taken the relic in question. From the records we have recovered, Attrayer's key is manifest."

The Sage waved one page of the book above his staff. The image of the page appeared above the round table. It was gigantic in size and rotated for all to see. A collective gasp came from the crowd. Some of the lords fell into chairs and laid their head in their hands, while others stared, frozen, at the image hovering above them.

"Here on these ancient pages is described the return of Attrayer's Key. Upon it is drawn a distinct image. We have the one who found the relic, and he can attest to its image. Come forward, Jonothon."

Jono stood from his seat and approached the table with every pair of silent eyes in the hall fixed on him.

"Is this the relic you discovered in the Twilight Ring? Is this that same relic you held in your hands, which the Empress now holds in hers?"

The crowd held their breaths for the answer. Jono looked up at the giant page upon which was drawn in ancient ink a round key with a red jeweled button in the middle.

"It is."

The crowd gasped again.

"Then there is no room for denial," spoke the Sage with unquestioned authority. "The key of Attrayer is in the hands of the Empress of Darkness. For all our steadfast efforts, all our valiant diligence, our greatest fear has been born. The age of ascension is undeniably upon us."

"I'm sorry!" Jono burst into tears of shame and terror. He couldn't hold it in anymore. The guilt had swelled in his heart to where he felt he would die if he didn't reveal it. "I wish I could get it back! I wish I hadn't—"

The Sage stepped from his throne and knelt beside Jono, silencing him with the action. "Jonothon, these are the deeds of a heartless tyrant. She is to blame. Your hands are clean of this."

"But they aren't!" Jono knew his actions had born the fruit of disaster. "I'm the one that left the key. I was scared and the shadows were coming and I couldn't fight them. I couldn't do anything, and now she has it because of me!"

The Sage laid his moss covered hand on the trembling boy's back for comfort. Jonothon choked on his words until his sobs ran freely, honest and open.

Rage boiled inside of him, eclipsed only by despair. He hated to be weak, to be incapable of what his heart begged of him to do. Even now his painful confessional was tempered with a deeper mind that held him back; it watched the beats of his inconsistent heart, always cautious, always distant, separated from everyone else and never fully alive.

"The light is not yet set, Jonothon. There is still hope." The Sage turned to the assembly of Lords. "We must rise to protect the Keeper from her grasp. We must seize the time that remains and make our final stand at the border of Day and Dark. The Empress marches to murder the sun and destroy us all, but we shall stand and meet her with our courage full."

The Sage clenched the page into his fist and slammed it into the stone table.

"We will cut the Empress down before she strangles the light of life!" said Aramis.

"Her monsters have always been covetous of our lands and our purity," said the Duke of Diremarc. "She would freeze our End out of spite alone and slay our children as they slept."

"She wouldn't do all that! She couldn't!" Jonothon cried in the desperation of his own guilt and stinging betrayal to learn the truth of his own homeland. "I've lived in the Dark my whole life and I've never heard of her doing anything that bad. Maybe she is as afraid of you as you are of her?"

He pulled back. The glare of the assembly made his face flush with embarrassment as though he had committed a heinous breach of trust.

Jono looked to Aquinas, whose wide eyes and stark face moved side-to-side in obvious warning. The lords' initial look of shock turned to disgust, but the Sage spoke before any of them could.

"She would," spoke the Sage of Ages in a grave and definitive tone. "She has slaughtered and pillaged her own people for less. Never forget Eve's Dale! Never forget the Wandering Star! Never forget the shattered halls of Lailet Dem! Rally all your noble knights! Call for aid from all the children of the Day. Our final chance lies at the Keeper of the Dawn! I cannot tell you what awaits us on the road the angels wish us to walk, but through meadows or through fire we will stay to the path of the seraphim! We will bring glory to the Day!"

The crowd of Lords cheered and applauded while Jono sunk back. He dared not respond. He only stood still and afraid until the Sage's deep stare finally left him and returned to his council of Lords.

Aquinas slipped toward Jonothon and led him out of the great doors and into the glowing golden hallway.

"Despite being born of her lands, you are completely unaware of her treacheries. I know she keeps the truth hidden from you and all of her subjects. You enter this difficult work at the middle, Jonothon."

"Can't we get the key back somehow?" asked Jono, ideas racing through his mind. "Or maybe explain it to her, make her see reason? Or trick her into giving it up?"

"You can't ever trust the Empress," whispered Aquinas. "And I would caution you from even thinking about it. Once you open the door to her falsehoods, they will find a way to corrupt your judgment. She has long since chosen her path, and power is the only altar she worships. Our last hope is the defense of the Keeper."

"But what if we could steal it back?"

"No one here would dare to breach the Dark End, certainly not so far as Eies, into the cursed halls of the Crown Castle itself!"

"I could get in," said Jono. "Before we left Polari, I was going to go to school there, remember? If they let me in then I could find out where they key is!"

"That's absurd!" said Aquinas. "She would find out. Her eyes crawl over all earth and sky beneath the stars. Treachery lurks in the heart of every creature that calls itself friend."

"She wouldn't find me." Jono felt a rush of power within himself, a desperate need for hope. "I'll be really careful. People always underestimate me because I look sick."

"You are sick! That is precisely why you can't go. The cold would kill you before you ever reached the city. You can barely survive as it is, let alone make it through the barrens of the Dark End."

"But they won't suspect me."

"No, Mister Wyer. Within the Dark End there are dangers you cannot imagine. The Empress knows the end is certain, and it is her fear, her desperation that makes her fight against it. Do not give in to fear, Jonothon. The light does not bend to shadows. We cannot choose the Empress' path for her, but we can stand and fight. We will win this battle."

"But what if you don't?"

"Do not let doubts cloud your mind. She is a machine of doubts and calculations. Turn to your heart and know that life is good. The seraphim will not let it be extinguished in the void. Not here, nor after. You should rest. You must be exhausted."

Jonothon walked away, feeling more helpless than ever. Voices of the lords of Sola crept through the stone walls, stalking him like ghosts.

"Do the Terralunans know of all that has transgressed? Is it not our duty to inform them?" asked a lord.

"They must know already. It's the Dark Enders we need to keep an eye on. And to think that mechanical Empress was only just here speaking of peace and cooperation! And now she stabs us in the back!"

"Never trust the Dark!"

The rallying cried was repeated by the many lords of Blue Skies. "Never trust the Dark!"

Chapter Fifteen

Princess Suriana

Everyone at Caer Midus castle was busy except for Jono. Over the following wake, Jonothon slept as much as he could in a room Daphne had assigned him. She had blacked out the windows for him, but the unaccustomed warmth made it hard for him to sleep.

Jono felt useless while everyone else prepared for war. Even though he'd helped them, their stares and sideways glances told him he was not trusted.

In the fields, knights saddled bulky mulamals with weapons and draped them in tattered brown sheets to look like pilgrims. Someone spotted Jonothon, and when the army glared, he turned away but still caught their whispers.

"Watch yourself, here it comes."

"Probably lost it on purpose."

". . . spying on us."

Jono wasn't spying, of course, at least not for anyone but himself. He had nothing else to do and there was certainly nothing more interesting to watch than the forces of a strange realm preparing for battle: the feli'yin, centaurs, and elemental dryads practice military drills.

It was mid-wake when Jonothon spotted something out of place.

Four human men slunk down the shimmering yellow hall. The odd thing was they all looked like a variation of Jonothon. Their skin was made to look pale, and they all wore coats similar his. They were in disguise!

Had no one ever seen a person from the Dark End before? Jonothon thought.

Jono followed them closely, careful to lift his heart reg up to not be exposed by its squeaky wheels.

The entourage of false Dark Enders snuck down winding stairs to where the sun was no longer the only light. At the end of the stairs, Jono heard a door opening. He poked his head around the corner just as the last of them had entered a room. He scurried as fast and as quietly as he could and stopped the door from shutting behind the last imposter.

From the crack of the door, Jonothon peered into a circular room with a ceiling so tall that it opened up to the sunlight. The men walked to a tall stained glass window floating in the middle of the room. The colors of the glass lit brilliantly, although the light didn't come from behind it but from above. On the windows, stained-glass figures of an elvayn, human, rock golem, and wood dryad awoke and moved to the center as their guest approached.

"You'll have to know the answer," spoke one of the stained-glass people in the window.

"Did you bring it this time?" snapped one of the disguised men.

"It wasn't my job to bring it last time," replied the other man, "but yeah I got it."

"Then speak, friend, and enter," said a green stained-glass dryad in the window.

"Or spout out the wrong one and you can all end up on the ice plains," said the rock goddess in the window.

Jono held his breath as the man stepped forward.

"The answer is the autumn wind."

The mirror began to glow brighter, and the shards of colored glass shifted in quick succession, making the room light up in a flickering rainbow.

"Oi!"

Jono felt a tug on his clothes and was lifted into the air, picked up by a powerful hand from behind. The hand spun him around to face the fierce and furry head of a grimacing centaur.

"I . . . I was lost," Jonothon lied. "The Sage sent for me so I could tell him what I know about the Dark End, but I've never been in a place this big before."

"The Sage's forum ain't downstairs," snorted the centaur. "It's by the front courtyard, you rotter! I should gut your pale hide right now. No one here trusts you didn't give the key to the Dark Machine on purpose!"

"I didn't! I'm here to help!"

The centaur glared and snorted in his face.

"I . . . I really have to see the Sage . . ."

"We're watching you, Dark Ender." The centaur set him down.

"Alright, thank you."

"Well then, get!" The centaur kicked at him, but Jono had moved away just in time to avoid the blow.

Jono looked back, and the centaur snarled at him, but his gaze was fixed on the crack of the door and the now empty room.

"How long have you been in here?"

Jonothon lifted his head from a pillow as Aquinas entered his room.

Jonothon shrugged. "It's hard to tell the time here."

"I know this must be hard on you. Exposed to the light for the first time, and so much has changed." Aquinas sat on the bed next to him. "I thought you may want this."

In his hand was a scroll.

"It's from the library. There're thousands of books on it."

"Thanks." Jonothon accepted the scroll.

"You know, you don't have to stay locked up in your room. There are plenty of kids your age in the village. Why don't you make some friends? I heard that the sheik's daughter was asking about you."

"Really?"

"Here." Aquinas reached into his pocket then handed Jonothon a single silver coin with a fat gnome engraved on it. "Take some money and go explore the village. You're finally under Blue Skies! Go see the sights. Have an adventure! Trust me, you're going to love it here once you give everyone a chance to know you better."

Aquinas put his thumb on the coin image's face. "Transfer ownership."

Jono placed his own thumb on the fat gnome's face. "Accepted."

Jonothon had no idea where he would find her, and even less of an idea of what he would do once he did.

Jono made his way to the tunnel of gates at the front of Caer Midus. The road wound down the hill and into the village. Jonothon hesitated. The green field felt like an ocean parting him and the pointed-roofed buildings below. Jono wondered what chemicals his brain released to make him feel so insecure and timid, a trigger to the fight or flight instinct. Jono took a breath of the crisp, warm air. If he could analyze it, he could overcome it. One step forward and he was off!

The village was a collection of cobblestone roads, brown ginger breaded houses, and pots of flowers in every window. Every corner was fresh and clean.

Even at the market square, Jono could tell that the people were preparing for war. Below the surface of their smiling pleasantness, they were afraid.

Shoppers and diners in cafés tried not to stare at him. A group of children entered the Melting Heart café, and Jonothon followed them in.

"What'll you have lad?" asked a kindly barista when Jono approached the counter.

"I'm not sure," Jono replied as he slid the coin onto the counter. "What will this get me?"

She touched the coin. "Oh, this is more than you'll need. Do you like franks and fizz?"

"I've never had them."

The lady smiled. "Trust me, then. You'll love it."

She pressed her own thumb against the coin and the spot on the counter lit up for a second. She gave him the coin back.

"You can just ask the gnome how much is left on him." She handed him a piece of meat wrapped in a bun and a small can with a straw.

"Thank you."

The frank was spicy, but the sauce on it was sweet. He'd never eaten anything like it in Polari.

He sat in one of the many wicker chairs at a table in the middle of the market square.

He couldn't help but smile.

The Day was bright and warm. Birds sung from every direction. Mighty trees loomed over the peaked roofs and their leaves glistened in the light. Jono's eyes had grown more accustomed to the darker tint of his goggles, but when he looked at the wide-open skies spotted with billowing clouds, he did long to see them in their natural color.

He was looking up at the clouds, amazed they were naturally white, when a chubby orange and red bird flapped down to his table.

"Mind if I have a snip?" it squawked.

Jono recalled seeing a talking animal like it in a book he had read—a paratiel, if his memory served him.

He tore off a piece of the bun. "Sure. There you go."

The bird stuck out its head, snatched the bun from his fingers, and then fluttered away.

"You really shouldn't feed the paratiels. You'll only encourage them." A girlish laugh from behind Jono followed the words.

The daughter of the sheik strolled up to him. An entourage of girls wearing similar white and gold saris accompanied her. The other girls stood back from his table and sneered.

The blond girl seemed to not notice her friends' behavior and sat in the chair beside him.

"Do you have those in the Dark?" she asked, pointing to his food.

Jono shook his head.

"How do you like it?"

"It's very good."

There was a moment of silence and Jono slurped on his fizzing drink.

"There's a great sweets shop at the other end of the square, Beetleguise. You should try the fruit comets."

"Oh, yeah?" He smiled at her nervously as he failed to think of anything to continue the conversation.

"Forgive me," she said, tilting her head down, "but is everyone on the Dark End as pale as you are?"

"No. I'm just, well, there are all types of people," Jonothon stammered. "Humans, yeton, mustecrates, grudgon . . ."

The girl leaned toward him and stared at his face calmly.

"Remarkable," she said. "I would think that only a certain type of person could even endure such a place. The terrible cold and all that . . . machinery."

"It's really not all that bad," Jono said because that was the only thing that came to his mind. "Of course I've never been past twilight before, but the night still has trees and glowing mushrups. In the steam season, there are huge clouds of pixieflies that swarm from the forest into town. It's really . . ." He swallowed. "Pretty."

The girl looked neither convinced nor impressed. "Simply remarkable," she said, mostly to herself. "And to have you here, under the light of the sun? This must be a very profound experience for you."

"Yeah." Jono smiled, thinking she might be alluding to something other than the obvious but not sure what that was. "Yeah, I guess it is."

"I wonder if all night children can come through the Dawn, or maybe if there is something about you—something different?"

She looked over his face like she was inspecting an alien specimen. He was sure the blue veins on his face made him look like a monster.

He tried to change the subject. "I'm Jonothon. From Polari."

"Yes." She smiled politely. "I know you are."

"Oh." Jono hadn't made the connection that his presence there would have been something of an item of interest for the locals.

"Although you're supposed to be a secret," the girl said. "The presence of a Dark Ender inside of Caer Midus? Well, that's more than loose lips can hold, isn't it!"

They both smiled awkwardly, and Jono noticed that the girl had a few dots of brown in her emerald eyes.

"Yeah, I guess," said Jono. "Have you ever crossed the Dawn into the Dark End?"

"Ha! I should think not!" She covered a snorting laugh with her hand.

"You should sometime. You could visit Polari or the Jupiter Gorge. That's pretty famous."

"No," she replied in curt politeness. "I don't think that would be wise. Besides, when the Day finally returns to the Dark End, it will all have to change. There will be a great flood, so the Old Mother can wash her wayward children clean. There's plenty of grime built up there. Waste and refuse produced by the machines. It's unhealthy for the planet, but I'm sure you know."

She glanced at his heart regulator. She didn't say it, but Jono got the notion she assumed all people on the Dark End were as sickly as he was.

"Machines are poisons on the earth." The girl sighed. "They say the bodies of the dead are destroyed to feed the living."

Jono made a face and said, "That's gross."

She nodded.

They both noticed a young knight pass on the other end of the square, holding the hand of a pretty woman. They smiling at each other as the knight placed a flower behind her ear.

"The knights are preparing for it." The girl leaned in to whisper. "Most don't know what it all means, but we do. It's probably best for them not know how bad it is. The Dark Empress may be watching, and the knights need secrecy."

"Your father's a knight, isn't he? Will he go with them?" asked Jonothon.

Her face lost its air of mature control and, in that instant, betrayed the truth that she was a worried young girl. She looked away, unable to answer.

Jono felt a surge of guilt rise in him. He hadn't meant to be mean or make her upset. He got the sense that her father was deeply important to her and maybe they'd been separated before.

"I don't . . ." she started weakly.

"Come on, Suri," nagged one of the other girls as she grabbed her by the arm. "We're late."

"Oh, right!" She stood and stuck out her hand. "I am Shay Suriana Vahlor. Pleasure to make your acquaintance." She waved as her friends pulled her away. "Bye, Jono."

He shoved the last of his frank into his mouth and smiled back with puffy cheeks.

As they walked away, the girls mocked whispers to each other.

"You shouldn't talk to him," said one girl.

"Why?" said Suriana.

"He's probably a spy," said another. The group all glanced at him suspiciously, and Jono quickly looked down at his empty plate.

"He's . . . interesting," insisted Suri.

"He's one of them."

Jono slurped from the straw of his fizz and looked at them from the corner of his eye.

"He's probably thinking about how he's going to kill you."

"You can't trust him. The Dark Enders can learn your secrets by eating your brain."

"Yeah, I've heard that too," said another girl. The others nodded, which democratically confirmed it as fact.

The Shrunken Door

onothon had a sun ache.

By the time he returned to his room, his head was swimming and his body shivered even though he was hot.

He slept through the sleep hours and had breakfast delivered to his room.

He used the scroll Aquinas gave him to find one of the first stories he'd ever read, The Voyage of Illius. He pulled the bed covers around him and read those familiar first words.

The breeze skimmed the salty water and gathered up a boutique of dust in its ethereal grasp before greeting the young prince on the castle terrace.

It was almost like being home.

Even thousands of miles from his family, in a realm that would burn him alive, he felt normal. He was Illius saving the princess from a Cyclops. He was a man of daring and courage that never wavered in the face of overwhelming foes. Illius was hope—a blue print of what a great person could be. And he was fictional.

What mattered was Jonothon believed in him, in what he stood for.

Jono stopped the scroll and looked around. Even when the world was nearing its end, here he was, hiding, curled under the covers. He wasn't Illius at all.

Jono threw the scroll against the wall. He leaned over, and the copper memory watch slid from his shirt pocket and dangled on its chain. He picked it up, wary of the device as if it were a pot of boiling water. He summoned his courage and flicked the lid open. His thumb ran across the dial and stopped on a random recording.

His dad's face popped up on its holographic screen. The image tilted sideways and fixed on Dahlia and his mom. They were all there, laughing.

Jono remembered this.

A roaming fair had been set up at a muscow farm outside Polari. They must have recorded it when he was in the tent with the fortune teller. While the old woman told Jonothon he would have a dangerous encounter with a tortoise, his family gave him their own fortunes in exaggerated, mock-fortune teller style.

Charles held his hand against his forehead, eyes shut tight. "You're going to do great at the academy, and be the youngest person ever to become Commander!"

"Ok, it's my turn!" said Dahlia, lifting a hand to her forehead, mimicking the fortune teller. "I can see it all now!" Their mother laughed at them both. "No, no, listen. You will be the most popular kid at the academy! All the girls there will giggle at the sight of you and even the professors will consult with your great wisdom."

His mom took the recorder. "I can see it in the future, just as I saw it in your eyes. You're going to be happy, just as you've been meant to be. All you needed was the chance. You are here to do great things in this world. All you have to do is do them."

Jono shut the watch.

He didn't bother wiping the tears from his cheeks.

It was time to get out of bed.

Jono marched across the second tier hall over the courtyard. He'd packed his few belongings and tucked the scroll into his coat pocket.

The stained glass room must have taken the imposters to the Dark End. All he had to do was get there, explain he was late for the academy, and find a transport to the city.

He was almost out of the courtyard when he saw her again.

"Suriana?"

The girl turned with a perturbed look on her face. When she saw that it was Jonothon calling her, she smiled.

"Oh, hi!" she said. "My friends just call me Suri."

A shock ran through Jono. Did that mean she considered him her friend? He shook himself of the feeling and asked, "Are you alright talking to me?"

She smiled at the absurdity of his question. "Of course."

They sat on a bench overlooking the courtyard.

"I promise I won't eat your brain," Jono said.

She smiled. "I know."

"I've never even heard of anyone doing that on the Dark End, really."

Suriana looked at clouds drifting high into the flat, blue sky. There were buds and blossoms on all of the trees in the courtyard.

"The world is warm here, you know," Suriana said and then turned her gaze to Jono's coat. "You don't have to wear that heavy coat all the time."

"It's alright. It's stuffy but it keeps the sun off my skin."

"So the sun is harmful to you, then?"

Jono shrugged.

"Hmm. That's amazing." She seemed to find all the differences about him fascinating. She stared more intently at him, intrigued by his eyes and his pale, blue-veined skin. "Just as the world is divided, so too are all of its people. Earth and the angels push us to either end by burning skin or chilling the bone."

"It seems natural enough to go where things are more suited for you." Jonothon reasoned this was exactly why he should return to the

Dark End.

"Maybe." Suri shrugged. "Crossing the Dawn is like being on another planet." She touched one of the buttons on his old coat. "You Dark Enders do wear the strangest things."

"What do you mean?"

"You burn over here, but do you still freeze in the Dark?"

"Well yeah, I do, but not all people are as thin-skinned. I'm kind of . . ." Jono pulled his heart reg closer to him. ". . . different."

"Still . . . take these odd bobbles for one," Suriana said, reaching for the buttons on Jonothon's coat. "These little carved pictures, are they retellings of the legends of your people? Do you know what this weird, gnawed edge symbolizes?"

A rush of embarrassment flushed Jonothon's face. His clothes were a patchwork of hand-me-downs re-stitched by his mother. He'd never had a shirt or jeans or coat that wasn't once part of a bigger garment that came from charity.

Suriana squinted, transfixed by the mystery of the simple, forgettable button. "It's such a different world there . . ."

"I'd like to see more of the Day," said Jonothon.

"You should." She smiled, staring directly at his eyes. "Once the trouble with the Empress is set right, I'll show you the best places myself!"

"Are you so confident everything will be alright?" Jono said it to himself, but the words slipped out for her to hear them.

Suri nodded. "It's just the truth."

There was a crash at the front gate, and both of them jerked their heads upward at that same second they heard a snap, and Suri held a button in her hand, its torn string dangling from it.

"I'm sorry," She said. Her face was flushed with red. She was upset at her carelessness. "It wasn't my fault . . . it was that sound! I couldn't help it."

"The Fell!" shouted guards on the third tier just as a group of fel shades melted out of the shadows.

The shadow demons spread apart, taking all kinds of terrifying forms. An ogre fel shade solidified his fist and smashed against a pillar that held up the terrace.

"Run!" yelled Jono.

They ran along the second floor toward the open hallway on the other side. If the fel was attacking the Day, then it may already be too late. Jono feared that the Empress was about to use the key, but he still didn't understand what would happen. He glanced up at the sun, but it made no sign that it was about to explode or disappear.

Lord Peregrine was in the courtyard when the fel shades laid siege to the castle. He drew his sword in a glistening arch of light. He swung at a wolf shade, but the creature leaped through the blade like it was air and charged at another man.

"They are shadow born!" Peregrine exclaimed.

The bells of all the towers rang, announcing the attack.

A fel shade leapt onto a feli'yin soldier, knocking him to the ground. The shadow's body, at first in the shape of a werewolf, spread around him, cutting him by the mere touch.

"Flames of Calla!" yelled the Peregrine as he clasped the hilt of his sword. The blade ignited with orange, electric flames. "Send these demons to the Pit!"

Peregrine swung through the shadowy figure, and this time the flames tore a clear gash. The flames spread across the fel shade like burning tendrils that wrapped and swallowed the black figure whole. Its limbs crumbled, and in moments its only remains were sparking dust in the grass.

An instant of enjoying his conquest was all the opportunity the ogre shade needed to send Peregrine flying with a single punch. The knight smashed into the second floor wall and thudded helplessly onto the terrace. His burning blade clanked onto the stone floor and went dull.

Jono and Suriana were next to the doorway, but Jono couldn't leave the knight to die. He had to do something! Jono spun back to help the fallen knight. Jono knelt by Peregrine and shook his head. "Wake up! They're coming!"

Peregrine moaned. Jono grabbed his shoulder, but he was too heavy to move.

Jono didn't have any time to think, only time to do. He snatched up the sword and repeated that incantation of ignition.

"Flames of Calla!" Jono yelled, gripping the hilt, and the blade burst alive.

"Jono don't!" called Suri.

Jono turned to see Suri at the edge of the door. Her eyes begged him to run with her, but he stood his ground.

"Run, Suri! Now!"

"Look out!" she screamed.

A winged fel-panther lunged through the air. Jonothon swung the sword and dove away from the fel-panther at the same time. The sword missed the fel-panther entirely, slipped from Jonothon's fingers, and spun recklessly through the air.

Jono was sprawled on the floor, frozen in shock.

The spinning sword fell to the courtyard just as the fel-ogre raised its fist above a knight, the flaming sword cut straight through its back. The ogre roared as it flared and turned to ash.

On the second terrace, Jono scrambled without a weapon. The fel-panther growled, toying with its prey. Its claws cut at the ground. The beast bared its teeth and charged. Its snarling mouth was inches from Jono's face when the panther froze. Blue sparks shot into the air and a blue cut of fire tore through the panther's skull.

The dark shadow matter dissipated to reveal the blond knight wearing a glowing blue gauntlet.

"I am Eljin of the White Guard."

He stood triumphant in silver and white armor with tunic matching many other knights. His long hair unfurled in the gentle breeze as he reached out his hand.

"You can trust me."

Jonothon took his hand and stood up. Behind Eljin, a group of fel charged at them.

"There are more coming!" Jono yelled.

Fel-imps leapt from the third tier and darted at them.

"Into the hall!" Eljin commanded.

"We can't leave him," Jono said, pointing at the fallen knight.

Eljin looked, growled and then slung the unconscious Peregrin over his shoulder. "Move!"

Jono grabbed his heart reg, and Suri pulled him into the hall.

Eljin turned to protect them, but the fel-imps burst into a hundred tiny imps.

The imps ran into the walls, exploding like villainous firecrackers. Dust and rubble flooded the hallway, shutting them off from the courtyard.

"We need to go! Quickly!" Eljin coughed as he led Jono and Suri through Caer Midus.

They ran down stairways and further from the battle above. When they finally stopped, Eljin motioned for them to be silent. Eljin slipped the limp Peregrine off of his shoulders and set him slumped against the wall.

Jono tried to catch his breath, but even he could hear it—footsteps charging toward them. Eljin ignited his gauntlet and spun around the corner.

The gauntlet's bladed fingers stopped a centimeter in front of Aquinas's throat, its flames singeing the hair on his chin.

"What in the seraphs' names are you—" Aquinas shouted, but then interrupted himself. "Jonothon!"

Eljin lowered his arm.

Aquinas went to Jono, but he turned back to the knight.

"You?" gasped Aquinas.

"Hello, Alexsayter." said Eljin.

Jonothon and Suri looked at each other, each looking for explanation for the spark of recognition between the knight and Aquinas.

"Burning stars!" said Aquinas. "Eljin! The last I had heard, you left the Fellowship. That was years ago. And here you are, a knight of Caer Midus."

"It has been a long evolution, my friend."

"Of course, many spoke ill against you for leaving, I regret to say," Aquinas replied. "And yet we meet at this fortuitous crossroad. I suspect the seraphs guide you still."

"As they to you." Eljin smiled. "But time ain't our ally."

"Indeed. Jonothon, I've been looking for you," said Aquinas. "We need to get you somewhere safe."

"We're deep in the castle now," said Eljin.

"Is it safe here?" asked Suri.

"It depends on their forces," Eljin answered. "No telling how many fel are attacking."

The knight looked up and listened as the clash of battle crept through the walls and snuck between Jonothon's bones.

"Will they be alright?" asked Suri.

Eljin nodded. "Caer Midus is tougher than a few shadows, no question. The shades can't be trying to win. They must have something else in mind."

Eljin continued down the hall. Jono followed on his heels, mulling over what he meant. He glanced back at Suri, who was clearly worried about the knights fighting on the levels above them.

"They're still fighting up there. We need to help!" said Jono.

"There is a way you can help, but not here," said Eljin. "I heard you from the great hall. No one under the Blue could get the key from the Empress, but you, Dark Ender, you have a chance. They all may doubt you, boyo, but I saw you fight the fel. You be the one to turn this war around."

"Eljin!" Aquinas yelled. "I hope you are not suggesting we send him into the clutches of the Empress."

"You want to go back?" asked Suriana, her voice almost cracking. Her hands were clasped tightly together, holding something.

"The Sage's plan needed to be a surprise," said Eljin. "Fel shades are at the gate. Our only chance to try something the Empress won't expect. You, Jono, are exactly that."

"They'll know what happened to you!" said Aquinas. "That Jono was the one who discovered the key."

"But the Empress has the key," said Eljin. "They'll probably greet the boy as a hero. It's you, Alexsayter that should be afraid of returning to the Dark."

"Jonothon, don't go," pleaded Aquinas. "It isn't safe. You need to trust the Sage."

"There's nothing certain these wakes," said Eljin. "Sometimes the greatest events hinge on the smallest choices. You may yet be the one that saves us all. The angels don't set up coincidences. They started you on this path. I believe you can do this. You were meant to do this."

Jono looked back at Suriana. Her wide, frightened eyes spoke the words her voice couldn't muster.

If there was any way he could help these people, Jono was determined to do it.

"You can accept your destiny," said Eljin, "or you can hide from it."

Jono nodded. "I'm done hiding. There's a glass window that takes people away. They were going to the Dark, I'm sure of it."

"The shrunken door?" said Aquinas. "How did you know about that? It can't take you to Eies. There is no gate under the Blue that sends that far."

"Don't let that stop you," insisted Eljin. "Every town in the Dark is tied to the city somehow. Find that connection and you'll have your way to Eies."

"I can do it," said Jonothon.

"Follow me, then," said Eljin. "The shrunken door isn't for anyone to use. The Sage may not like it, so we better be quick."

"The Sage isn't the only one against it. The rainbow ladies that guard the door are not so permitting," said Aquinas. "If you don't know the answer to their question, well, they don't take kindly to trespassers."

In the depths of Caer Midus, the four descended until they came to the room with the stained glass window.

A pillar of light illuminated the rainbow glass. They stopped at the door, and Eljin urged Jonothon to go on.

Jono set his heart reg down and wheeled it through the shrunken door. He looked at the glistening colors of the glass window. On it were the images of four women; a wood dryad, a human, an elvayn, and a rock goddess.

"Who goes there?" asked the dryad.

"Trespassers beware," said the elvayn.

"Only the permitted shall pass," said the human.

"What they said," added the rock goddess.

"I'm Jonothon Wyer. I need to get through. It's a top secret mission for the Sage of Ages."

"Oh, ho! Says the Sage sent you, does he?"

"Even still, he must know the answer."

"Alright then, child," said the dryad. "Who cringes from the Day's light? Who hides behind those that stand in the sun? Who rules throughout the Night, but flees from the glory of the Day?"

Jono thought about their question.

It sounded like a riddle, but it could just as easily have been a password or something to trick anyone who didn't already know the right answer.

The faces of the women grew ever more intimidating.

"He doesn't know it," grunted the rock goddess.

"He still has time," said the dryad.

"I say we fry him where he stands," said the elvayn.

Their four pairs of eyes grew red with power. Jono was beginning to sweat. He was smart, his test scores proved it. He could figure this out. The Day was always looking down at the Dark, so it could be an insult somehow. If it was a riddle, it could be something obvious. Something natural that they Day would know about that the Dark wouldn't think of. Time was against him. . .

"No more time, boy, what's your answer?"

"It's, um . . ."

"We should leave, now!" Aquinas called to Jonothon.

"You fool!" said the four women in unison. "Do not attempt to cheat the gatekeepers of Caer Midus! Now you will serve as an example to all those . . ."

"Don't hurt him!" yelled Suriana.

"A shadow!" yelled Jono. It was the only idea in his mind, but it fit the clues and the Day seemed to be afraid of spaces without light. "The answer's a shadow!"

The shimmering shards of rainbow glass parted. Light bore down upon Jono with every color imaginable. The finality of his choice seized him and in that last instant he turned to look back at the tumnkin who had led him thus far and the young girl of the Day, but the white that had encompassed him became a deep and endless black.

He felt nothing.

Chapter Seventeen

Stranger in a Strange End

*J*onothon blinked.

He was wrapped in endless oblivion.

After an instant he could feel his body tingle to life. He blinked again. His re-existing fingers rubbed his eyes and, slowly, hints of light brought the world into view.

The white glow of Terralunis cut to the earth with jagged reflections off a net of branches that surrounded him.

Jonothon stood in the ruins of a stone cabin that had long been overtaken by these gnarled woods. A deep humming below him slowed until a heavy click silenced it for good.

By the look of things, there was no way to return to Caer Midus. Jonothon suspected the shrunken door required much more energy and size to send someone than the exit needed to receive them.

A bitter wind cut through leafless branches. It pricked goose bumps on Jonothon's skin despite his thick coat. Wherever he was, it was cold and dark. The sting of air only hinted at the greater chill that surely lay deeper into the night.

Above him, a crisp black sky sparkled with stars.

Through the gnarled woods, Jono spotted a cluster of orange lights and billowing purple plumes above them. Even far into the woods as he was, he could still hear a soft clanking of whatever large machines brought the town to life—and probably made up some of its inhabitants.

Jono pulled his mask off his shoulder and slipped it over his face. The lights and steam from the town crept menacingly through the trees.

It was time to get moving.

Jono trudged through moist soil, and when he finally arrived, his pants were covered in thorny seeds and needles. He settled behind a tree and inspected the strange town from a distance.

Crooked roofs separated a dark sky from the glowing orange-lit cobble stone streets.

There was a sign, not far from the nearest building, standing on a road that ended abruptly at the edge of the forest. Written in cracked maroon paint were the words "Welcome to Dollup, Where the Tough get Going!" The sign was old and conquered by generations of vines. Jonothon wondered if the sign was referring to the same town as the one in front of him.

Jonothon's first thought was to dart into the street and pretend like he been there all along, to blend in. He stopped when he realized the house closest to him had eyes, ears, a nose, and a wild beard.

It wasn't a house at all.

Taller than the trees and leaning casually against a crooked two-level house was giant mechanical man. Half of his body was made up of gears and mechanix. He had four wide legs that supported his enormous weight. One metal arm scratched the wires at his backside, while the other held up a skinnier man whose mechanical parts seemed to stretch to allow his neck to be held at such a height.

"Bet my ticker on it, I do," said the skinny man. He pounded his chest as he dangled from the other man's hand.

"I'd eat a char ox whole before I believe that tripe!" grunted the large one as he dropped the other man on the ground.

"I saw it with my one good eye, true as gravity," replied the skinny man, who had now shrunk his body parts into what seemed a more comfortable, although odd, triangle shape. He appeared unconcerned about his recent manhandling as he brushed off his loose military uniform. He was a soldier of the Dark army. Jono gasped at the sight and wondered if he would be made into such a mechanical oddity. "She was there in person, cold as the winds and honest as the sky."

"Didn't you rent those eyeglasses from that thief in West Rouge, Wedge?'

"Right you are, Biggs." said Wedge, the skinny one. "That does not impede on the integrity of the product, as he was very reliable . . . up until the stinging betrayal, of course."

Biggs stomped his massive foot, crushing a butterfly that happened to flutter by.

"That's just the way of the worlds." Biggs shrugged his massive shoulders. "Crush or be crushed."

The two monstrosities stood between Jono and the road into Dollup.

Jono thought it best to avoid them and snuck quietly around, holding his loud breathing for as long as he could. Jono slunk into an alley a block away. Black bags smelling of rotting food piled up against the wall. A mirecat poked its head up from its sticky dinner, but since Jono didn't snatch away the two-wake-old fish guts, the animal happily went back to eating. Warm air crept out of window wells and floated into the chilly alley.

Dollup's cobblestone streets were orange in the light of rows of lamps. The first few steps made Jono's heart reg bounce, sending a shock to his chest. Exhausted and with muscles aching.

From the look of the street, Dollup was nearly abandoned. It then occurred to Jono that he had lost all track of sleep and wake hours while under the sun.

Further down the street Jono turned a corner and was accosted by colorful lights and music illuminating a bustling promenade.

The street was filled with shops, taverns, and people of the oddest of species chatting casually to each other. They were all well dressed and cheerful as they meandered and socialized among barking shopkeepers.

Many of the patrons, but humans especially, had bionetic implants installed on their bodies. A group of grudgon strolled the street with guttural laughs as they waved their glasses in the air, repeatedly spilling the green, frothy liquid within. They were all short and round with scales that looked like brown, muddy rocks lumped together.

Mustecrats and yetons popped in and out of shops with hover carts floating dutifully beside them.

Jono pulled his mask close and hoped it and his heart reg would help him to blend in.

Jono passed a tall and elegant ayleen woman with gray skin and long, slicked-back hair tendrils. She leaned against a wall wearing a feminine peach-colored suit. She looked at her watch with a hint of annoyance on her face.

The building beside her was Lungdon's Robot Non-stop Fix 'em Up Shop. Its garage was open, and the greasy mustecrat inside shoved a wrench up the chest cavity of an unsuspecting robot. A tube burst, and black liquid dumped all over the mustecrat's furry face.

Jono nearly collided with a red-skinned gromlin coming out of Zizzly Physics Shop with a stack of boxes in his arms.

"Watch it," snarled the gromlin.

"S-sorry," Jonothon stuttered, but the gromlin shot him a nasty look and continued on his way.

Halfway down the promenade was a circular plaza with a stage at its center. Chairs circled around tables and nearly all of them were full. The surrounding restaurants spread into the plaza and their seating intermingled with one another. It reminded Jono of the market square in the village of the Day.

On a balcony above the crowd, an onyx skinned ayleen in a white dress lounged on a chair while playing on a golden harp. Her haunting song mingled with the gentle rhythm of the vibrating cords. Her eyes were shut, and she seemed to ignore the world below her.

Below the performer, in the open air tavern called "The Rusty Joint", Jono spotted a group of people in black uniforms with silver trim and skull-like masks. On the shoulders of their jackets was the red semi-circle peaked with a star on top of the crown.

They were soldiers of Eies.

The soldiers crowded around a table too small for the six of them, which was over loaded with bottles, mugs, and half-eaten burgers. Their laughs were loud and uninhibited and fit perfectly with the rest of the tavern.

"I don't suppose you'd reconsider?" blurted a burly soldier with a metal arm.

"With you, Horus? No. I think I'd rather lose another leg now and save myself the travel," said a woman with strange metal wings folded on her back.

Beside them, a man with a hawkish nose, caramel skin, and a black goatee tapped on a panel in his hands and small holographic images appeared. It changed with every tap. He sipped his lambic ale quietly.

"Mel-o-dy!" cooed Horus. "Come on, Sweets. It's only a little sneak and boom job. I could use someone with your talents, that's all."

"You mean my ability to get the stars out of danger when you inevitably blow our cover?"

"Exactly!"

The hawk-nosed man looked up, and his red eyes met Jono's. In that instant the smile beneath his mustache changed ever so slightly.

Jono ducked around a spiraled bush. He began to second guess his entire plan.

What if they asked him why he was here instead of in Polari? Hadn't he escaped from the Empress as well as her soldiers? What if they knew he went with the people of Sola? Did they know he was in Caer Midus when they sent the fel shades to attack? What would they think if they found him here, hundreds, if not thousands, of miles away from his home?

It was too dangerous, too far from the city. Jono had to find another way to get to the city, but how?

Jono snuck away from the promenade, back to Dollup's quieter streets.

He needed to find out what the town's people worked. In Polari, the main industry was the black rock mine, and there was a train that would carry the mineral to the city. All he had to do was discover what they made in Dollup and how they sent in to Eies.

He needed a better view of Dollup.

Jonothon found a park at the top of a hill. He climbed as high as he could up a bent tree. The view from the park wasn't obscured by houses, so he could see far into the distance.

In the north edge of town was a set of wide buildings lit up in a pale green light. It was just what he was hoping to find—a factory!

A wide road led out of town and to the gates of the factory. Jono rolled his heart reg down the road, sticking close to the shadows.

Jono was tired and hungry.

His only money was the gnome coin, which would buy him nothing in the Dark End and draw lots of quick, and well-armed, attention.

The factory gates were locked, and cameras lined the fence guarding it. Whatever they made in there must have been shipped to Eies. If he could sneak in with the cargo, Jono could rest the whole trip, maybe even find some food. There was no telling how often things are sent to the city, so the sooner he got on, the better.

The fence was old and most of the cameras seemed to have broken and not been replaced. Jonothon hoped somewhere was a crack large enough for him to squeeze through.

Jono crept through the bushes and gnarled trees that surrounded the factory, taking his time in moving around the perimeter.

On the back side of the compound was a promising break in the wall. Jono crept closer, but realized a sturdy metal patch blocked his way through.

Twigs snapped behind him.

Jono ducked for cover behind a hollow log. His heart pounded and he pulled his regulator close and checked the connections.

He waited as still as the stars, but no one came for him.

Jonothon poked his head out from the log and saw two glowing green circles flash away from him. They were green eyes attached to an oblong metal head and small humanoid body. The strange creature hid in the shadows between the lamps that hung along the fence.

Jonothon watched cautiously as the figure brushed its hand against the patch in the wall. Instantly, the wire mesh separated. The humanoid darted through the wall and disappeared into the factory compound.

Jono grabbed his heart reg. This was his only chance, and he knew he had to take it.

The patched wall began to reform as soon as the creature snuck through. Jono ran as fast as he could but slammed against the wall just as the last link went back into place. The mesh rattled and clanked but wouldn't give in.

Jono laid his head against the metal links, defeated. He pushed again and this time the wall opened. He toppled to the other side.

There was no sign of the green-eyed creature.

The compound was quiet.

Jono made his way around, hiding behind crates. He didn't see any workers, but he could hear the rumbling of machines at work.

At the compound's central building, two huge doors were cracked open. Jono slipped inside.

His jaw dropped at the sight of the four gigantic metal legs of an even more humongous machine. It looked like a bulky, mechanical centaur. Its head and arms were not fully assembled, but huge drills and guns covered its body. The walls were cluttered with robotic arms, as the building itself put the metal beast together. Jono thought back to what Aquinas had said of the Dark End's machines and industry of death.

Jono shivered.

"Do you like it?" said a gleeful voice behind him.

Chapter Eighteen

Kirin's Kontraptions

ono spun around, tripping over his heart reg and tumbling to the floor. A pair of glowing green eyes leaned over him. A pair of hands reached out to help him up.

"The design was originally my idea." The voice was not nearly as menacing as its silver head suggested.

The metal only covered from the tip of the nose and up. An honest smile assured Jono that he was, in fact, not going to be eaten alive.

"The Argonaut," the green eyed mech-person stated proudly.

"It's amazing," Jono said. "Kind of scary, though."

"That's the whole point," the metal head replied, excited by Jono mentioning the machine's ferocious appearance. "That's why they liked my design. It would put fear into the hearts of our enemies. Make those Solans go running for the hills when this baddie charges across the Dawn!"

A fleshy smile below its metal head was wide and proud as its green eyes turned to the product its imagination brought to life.

"When will they do it?" Jono asked.

"Do what?"

"Attack," Jono said. "When is the Dark going to use this to attack that Day? Do you know?"

"What are you talking about?" the metal head replied. "I was just joking. I mean, it is a military tank mech, but it's just to scare them into not starting anything stupid. It's a deterrence to keep the peace."

The person said the last part as though it had heard it repeated a thousand times.

"Oh." Jono recoiled.

They looked at each other in silence, which was broken by a nearby gurgling. The green-eyed person held its stomach and smirked.

"Sorry," the person said, blushing. "I haven't eaten in while. Let's go make something."

Jono knew how that felt. He hadn't eaten all wake.

The metal-headed person led Jono up clanking stairs and across a rickety catwalk to a door with a port hole in its center. Above the door hung a poorly painted sign that read "Kirin's Kontraptions."

"Who's Kirin?" Jonothon asked.

"That's me. Keiko Kirin. My uncle is the chief engineer here. He let me set up my own shop. I get to use whatever spare parts I want."

The room was a graveyard for robots. Old machine parts were piled upon the countless shelves and stacked in tiny mountains that nearly reached the ceiling.

Keiko nonchalantly slid off the metal part of her head to reveal that of a perfectly normal human girl: eyes, nose, ears, and all.

"You're a girl!" It slipped out on Jono's mouth before he even knew he had said it. She couldn't have been far from Jonothon's age. Her black hair was tied behind her head in pink tethered pig tails.

"Uhh, yeah." Keiko Kirin raised an eyebrow at him then turned away.

"I mean," Jono stammered, "a human. I just, well, I thought . . ." He looked around, looking for something to prompt a change in subject. "What's that?" He pointed to an odd mechanical bobble that glowed a light purple.

"Huh? Oh, that's just a lamp." Keiko smiled and opened a reizofridge next to them. "I hope you like beetle worms."

"What?"

Keiko turned around holding a plastic bowl full of slimy, chubby worms with pincer legs all over their bodies and five or six snapping mouths.

"Do you want mustard with yours?"

Jono mumbled an answer that made no translatable sense, however, Keiko took that as a yes. She laid the beetle-worms flat between two pieces of bread and squirted mustard on them.

"Are you sure that's okay to eat?" asked Jono.

"Sure I'm sure. They're a little gooey after you get through the crunch but packed with nutrition!"

"They look like they'd bite my tongue off."

"Not if you bite them first." Keiko smiled.

Keiko squished the bread down, and the creatures squirmed to poke their snapping mouth-heads between the slices. She set the sandwich on a plate then handed it to Jono, who took it.

Jono slid his mask off and looked at the sandwich closer. Every centimeter he brought it closer, his face twisted in a new unfathomable discomfort. He gulped. His mouth was dry.

Kirin looked at him, eyes wide, and her stern lips quivered. Jono opened his mouth and inhaled a deep breath before his mouth surrounded an out-stretched worm . . .

"No, no, no! Don't do it!" Kirin squealed before falling into a fit of giggles. "I'm sorry, I couldn't help it."

She plucked the beetle-worm sandwich from his hands and dumped its contents back into their container. "We really don't eat those. Seriously, I didn't think you'd take it that far, I promise!"

Kirin still giggled uncontrollably.

"Oh." Jono set the plate down, relieved but annoyed.

"They eat up rust and ice off the machines and leave a grease that protects the metal from the cold. Don't you, little guys." She petted their squirmy backs.

"That's pretty disgusting."

"It was really funny though."

Jono let out an airy laugh which, more than anything, revealed that he had no idea what he had gotten himself into.

On the other end of Kirin's shop was an open balcony that overlooked the frosty marshes behind the factory. They sat together, their legs swinging over the edge, and sucked down bottles of protein juice.

"That mech, the Argonaut, does the Empress have a lot of those in her army?" Jono tried to hide his concern for the knights of Sola. He hadn't seen any earthshaking monsters while he was under Blue Skies. He imagined the Argonaut could crush twenty knights with one step.

"Nope," said Kirin, "the Argos models are brand new, so there's only a few. There's other mechs, sure, but none like my Argo. We made a lot of surveillance bots and hover carriers in the run before this." Keiko tried to slurp from her straw and talk at the same time. "We ship a ton of spare parts to the city, too. We have to keep them well stocked because it's a long trip on account of those *Terraloonies* blocking the high skies."

Jono recalled what the Sage of Ages said about the Dark Ends ingrained spite against the Tills. Polari just tried to keep to itself, but here, far from the Twilight Ring, the animosity was clear. Jonothon looked at Keiko's brown eyes as they scanned the open sky. He wondered if, just maybe, the truth was different from what he had been told. "How far are we from Eies?" asked Jono.

"Far. A few hours flight, depending on what you take."

"Why not have a factory closer to the city?"

"There are plenty, but they don't have the ore like we do. This stuff's precious, and Eies doesn't want one gram of it going to the Day." She pointed to a spot where the trees disappeared and it looked like the earth sunk in on itself. "This planet's old. The world has been stripped thorough of its ores, so if you find a good spot, you don't let it go."

"I once read that Pseudo," said Jono, "where the ayleens are from, it is one of the youngest planets to form sentience. There's got to be plenty to mine there."

"I heard something like that about Grutnee. I don't see why the grudgon, or anyone else for that matter, would leave a thriving planet for this poured-over heap with a dead star. And with the Terralunans blockading us from space like they own it, I bet they've regretted settling here for generations."

Jono slurped on his juice and wondered what other worlds must be like.

"Why doesn't Eies just fight the Tills?" he asked.

Keiko shrugged. "That's what I think, but we don't. I don't know why. Maybe the Loonies have some weapon that the Empress doesn't want to go up against."

"Worse than all your death machines?"

Keiko squinted at him. Jono stopped, feeling like he had said something wrong.

"It's really not like that. I know the Argonaut is big and scary and all, but most of what we make isn't even able to break low space. It's all transport, mining, and construction mechs, really. Well, like ninety percent of it is.

"Stronger power keeps the peace. If Sola or the Tills thought for one second that the Dark was weak they wouldn't hesitate to break all pacts and invade us. You would think the Day would back us against the Till, force them for our freedom, but those burnt brains don't even want to be free! They're happy to be lorded over like children before Giftmas. Head down and do what they're told. Straight and narrow and blinders a' plenty, right?"

Kirin put her hand up to the sides of her eyes like blinders and made a disgusted face. Jono hadn't gotten that impression at all from his wakes under Blue Skies. Of course he was only there for a short time, but the open air and the gentle hospitality had made him fond of Caer Midus and its inhabitants. It was only their blanket distaste for the Dark that smudged their quality in his mind.

"I don't think it's as bad as all that," Jono said.

Keiko spat out a laugh. "It's worse than that for sure. Have you ever been to Blue Skies?"

Jonothon shoved the straw in his mouth and shook his head.

"My uncle has. Back when we were trying to help them out. The Empress had the notion that all ores should be accounted for and measured, under blue skies or starry. So my uncle went there with a bunch of miners and smelters to see how we could help them. You know what he found?"

Jono shook his head again.

"They were still doing it the same way it'd been done two hundred years ago! No digger bots, no particle spreaders. He said they would lose over thirty percent of the ore on account of all that waste. And the energy waste of their smelts was even worse! He was amazed they could heat those stone castles of theirs. Only thing is the sun watts keep coming, so they don't have the need to be efficient. And worst still, when he was going to send them a bunch of our diggers and spreaders, they turned him down flat! Those burnt brains thought we'd spy on them with the bots. Spy on what? Their old dirt sorters and Stone Age houses? They'd squander whatever they get just because that's the way they do it over there. They're so terrified of change and they don't grasp that change is the only thing that keeps you afloat."

"That is really strange." Jono was confused. He tried to reconcile this new information with what he'd experienced.

"It's dangerous, when you think it to the end," said Keiko. "They'd rather ignore the facts and put their fate in the hands of the tyrants of

Terralunis than face reality and be responsible for themselves. They can't stand how we work to live, you know? They'd leave us power-out in the cold if they could."

She shivered and frowned. She appeared upset at the very idea of the people across the Dawn.

"The Day pretends while the Dark ascends," said Jono.

"Huh?"

"It was something a soldier of Eies said to me in Polari."

"You're friends with a soldier?"

"I met some when they were supposed to take me to Windom."

"Wait. Hold on. Windom?"

"Yeah, it's an academy. They have this test to allow kids from all around to enroll at no cost."

"I know what it is. You're going to Windom? To the academy at Eies?"

"Yeah, that's what they said. I was supposed to leave for Eies over a week ago, but . . ."

"What are you doing here? The term's already started!"

"I was, well, I on my way and—"

"I'd give my biological body to go to that school!"

"Actually, that's what I came here for," replied Jono. "I missed the convoy so I thought that a place like this would have to ship things into the city. I needed to sneak on. I didn't have any other way. I have to get there!"

"By the burning stars, you do!"

"Can you help me? I don't have any time to wait. I have to get to Eies."

"Do you even know what a great opportunity it is?" Keiko's eyes looked remorseful. "This is your chance to do anything in the world. To learn from the best and have no limits on what you can do. And here you're just skipping it?"

"I didn't mean to . . ."

They both fell silent. The crickets in the frost marshes chirped at the unforgiving cold.

"There's a ship alright. It flies out on the wake," Keiko said.

"Really? That's fantastic!"

"It's not an easy trip. Not like a train, or straight flight path." Keiko explained. "It's Bad Lands between here and the city. No straight roads so the shipment won't get sacked by night pirates. They go through rough places, mountains and crags, across deep ice. We have to avoid anyone who'd want to steal our parts, you know?"

"Can I do it?"

Keiko nodded. "It's all automated by the hollow pilot."

"Perfect!" Jono beamed and then became serious when he noticed how sad she looked. "Why are you still here? As smart as you are, I bet they'd take you if you wanted."

"They didn't," Kirin replied. "I applied already. I got the highest score in my whole school, too. I guess they just don't want me."

Jono turned to Keiko with a gleam in his eye. "We can make them."

Jono let his mission to get Attrayer's key slip to the back of his mind. "If you help me get there, I'll help you get in. You can come with me. I know you're smart enough. I could never build anything like what you've done. We'll just explain everything to the school when we get there."

"Yeah, right." Keiko laughed. "They'll just kick us both out."

"They won't." Jono felt excited at the idea of helping someone else. "When the recruiter talked to me he said the Empress herself was proud to have me join. I'll make them choose. They take us both or I won't join."

"Both or nothing, huh?" Kirin said cautiously.

"Both or nothing."

A small grin cracked into her frown, and then spread her lips into a full smile. "You are serious, aren't you?"

"Of course!" insisted Jonothon.

Keiko's face brightened. "It's gizmos, but alright. Let's go talk to Cid!"

Chapter Nineteen

Of Pixels and Installs

Nestled in a hammock in a corner of the tallest tower in the factory slept a snoring man. His face was scruffy, and his oily black hair shimmered in the dim light. Half his body was made out of machines.

"Uncle Cid!" Keiko squealed.

The man startled, and the hammock flipped, spitting him onto the floor.

"Cid, I have the best news! You know how Roger Hyland was the only kid the Academies took from Dollup this year? This kid passed the test. They sent soldiers out to take him to the academy and—"

Cid cracked his neck and glared up at them with a red, squinting mechanical eye. "What? Slow down. Who's this?" he said with a wave of a metal finger at Jono.

"This is . . ." Keiko looked back at Jono. "What's your name, again?"

"Jonothon Wyer."

Cid shook himself awake and blinked at Jono.

"He's enrolled to go to Windom," said Keiko.

Cid frowned. "I only had the Hyland kid on the list. You know how strict they are against false cadets. Dollup had one recruit and that's it."

"He's not from Dollup," Keiko said. "Jono tested in Polari."

"Polari!" Cid pulled back and raised an eyebrow. "How the still burning stars did you get clear out here from Polari?"

Jonothon froze; he didn't know what to say that would excuse his unusual travel.

Thankfully Keiko broke the silence.

"We have to get on the parts shipment to Eies," Keiko insisted. "The term's already started!"

"And you say he's a recruit?" Cid said, squinting his one biological eye. "Did you miss your transport, boy?"

"Uhh, yes."

Cid winked his mechanical eye and a list of words appeared in the air. Cid waved his hand to scroll down until it stopped at a word written in capital letters – POLARI. Below the town was a single name – Jonothon Wyer.

"You see," Keiko said, smiling. "He's there. Jonothon says he can pull some strings to get me in too, we just have to get there soon."

Jono hadn't quite said that, but he figured she needed to sell her uncle on the idea.

Cid frowned again. Jono didn't know if it was because he'd been rudely woken or because he didn't like the idea of his niece and some strange boy making the trip to the city in the depths of the Dark End. The image flashed with *Priority Zero*.

Cid sighed. "By your test scores . . . You've been designated for the covert operations program."

"The Cloaks?" asked Keiko excitedly. "You're going to be in Cloaks, Jono!"

"That's right," said Cid. "There's going to be installs. I have kits for all the entry grades, but it says here that you are promoted to tier three. Strange."

"You're going to get third year installs?" Keiko cheered. "Welded! Most recruits only get linkers and brain storage. Poor clunkers without any of the real soldier powers. I think the Cloaks track gets you spy wires and later you get cloaking skin, stealth darts. You're a lucky one, kid."

Cid frowned at the hovering report. "I've never seen this priority tag on a cadet's account before. You must be something special. I'll see what I have."

"These installs?" Jonothon's interest perked. "Are you going to fix me?"

"Fix you?" Cid looked at him, confused. Cid glanced at Keiko, who shrugged innocently. "You mean, on account of that mask and beat up regulator you're dragging along?"

Jono nodded. "They said that they would fix up my heart and lungs once I joined."

"You don't say?" Cid knelt and looked over the heart reg for a label. He grunted. "What I meant by installs were the ones all recruits get for their first year. Eies ships them to us regional hubs. I don't normally carry any other bionetic parts. We deal in straight mech-tech here."

Jonothon kept his face still to hide his dismay.

"I may have some old bits that would be better than the junk you're using, though. It could tide you over until you get a proper install."

Cid went to a stack of bins by his hammock then dug through a plastic box, tossing unwanted parts into a new pile behind him before he held a small, circular item up to the light.

"Ah ha! I do have this one. This piece used to be the standard for monitoring suits under pressure. A bit outdated and a little dented, but it sure beats that junkware you're plugged into."

Cid kneeled in front of Jono. He lifted up the boy's shirt and unplugged the heart reg from his chest.

Jonothon froze and focused on each cautious beat of his heart.

Cid ignored him and fastened the small harness over both shoulders and around his waist then plugged in the new round heart regulator at the center of his chest.

"That'll have to do for now," said Cid. "Lungs are a different story though. Changing those out will be a big project and I ain't got nothing to replace them with. I can give you some air filters. Every now and again you'll have to cough it up and replace it. Here's some spares."

Jono swallowed at the thought of something sticking down his throat.

In Cid's hand was a plush cream-colored beetle the size of his thumbnail.

"Just put it in your mouth when you're ready," he said. "It'll know where to go. Now hold still."

Before Jono knew what was happening, he felt a sharp prick on the back of his neck. He yelped.

"It's alright, boy. It's just pixels. They're microscopic robots. They'll flow through your blood and grow you the bionetics you need for the academy. Be sure to eat plenty over the next few wakes so they get all the parts they need."

Jono rubbed his neck. "They make parts out of food?"

Cid pricked him again.

"And that one's for your Cloak installs."

Jono rubbed his neck and took a step or three away from Cid.

"Do I have to be in Cloaks?" Jono asked. "They've already chosen what I'm going to be, and I haven't even started."

Cid shrugged. "Like I said, they pegged you for the Cloaks from the tests you took. They're pretty spot on with these things. If not, you better learn to love it."

"What about you?" Jono turned to Keiko.

"She's already got her installs," answered Cid. "We kind of jumped the gun, back when we thought, well . . ."

"It's alright. Thanks to Jono, I'll get to use them after all." Keiko's smile was wide and honest.

It made Jono hope to the stars that she was right.

Among the towering transport ships that filled the dock was a cargo ship only slightly bigger than the Wyer's old truck. It had rotating engines on every side and a patchwork of shields covering its hull.

Cid opened a hatch on the back and put a cooler into the ship. It was stuffed with food, drinks, and candy for them to smuggle into their dorms.

Keiko was wrapped in a thick pink coat. She had hastily packed a yellow suitcase that walked to the ship on its own robotic legs.

Jonothon was glad he'd remembered his blue coat and the library reader he kept from Caer Midus. He'd left his heart reg and breather mask in Cid's office, and even though he didn't need them for now, he felt naked without them.

Cid hugged his niece and lifted her into that back of the cargo ship.

"Now if things don't work out for the school, and I'm not jinxing it here, just keeping you prepared—for whatever reason, you just have Alvin bring you home. Okay?"

Keiko nodded dutifully and pulled a seat down from the cargo ship's wall.

"It was good to meet you, Jono," Cid said as he shook his hand. "There's a com near the front. Just say the name of whoever you're looking for once you get to Eies, and Alvin will get a hold of them."

Jonothon nodded. "Thank you."

"Bye, Cid!" Keiko wave as her uncle shut the doors.

The cargo ship shook as it lifted off the ground, and with a whirling hum it soared out of the docking bay and into the starry night.

Jono curled against the wall. He was grateful for Keiko's help in his otherwise desperate situation, and although he had no idea if he could convince the school to accept her, he hoped with all his heart it would work out.

It was awfully nice to not be alone.

"Alvin?" said Keiko.

"Who's Alvin?" asked Jono.

A gnomish man popped into existence in the air above their strapped cargo. He had a pointed hat, pointed ears, and wore a purple robe over his portly body.

"Alvin's a hollow," Keiko explained. "Just the ship's A.I. pilot. Not a real person."

"I take objection to that," said the holographic gnome.

"Not biological is what I meant." Keiko responded before leaning close to Jono and whispering, "He's a little sensitive. Have you ever met a hollow before?"

"No." Jono shook his head.

"I don't get passengers often," said Alvin with a lisp. "It's great to have you."

"Thanks for taking us," said Keiko. "Could you set the ship to clear walls? We'd like to see where we're going."

"Most certainly!"

Without a moment's notice, the walls, ceiling, and floor disappeared. Jono shrieked and jumped on his seat.

Keiko and Alvin glared at him, and he put his feet back down on the now invisible floor.

Dark treetops rushed by below them. Pockets of underground steam spewed a cloud that clung to the vegetation.

"Have you ever been to the city?" asked Keiko.

"No," said Jono.

"It's amazing. I haven't been there before in real life, but I did a hollow tour once at our library in Dollup. The real thing is much bigger. I hope we can tour the Crown. It's amazing what the Empress has made of it all. The Dark End was nothing before her, just a waste of ice and rock. That's her philosophy—spreading life to places without it."

"I wonder if she wants to spread off planet," said Jono.

"You have to keep pushing the boundaries, don't you?" said Keiko. "You need to test your limits to see what you're capable of."

"Would she use the army to do that?"

"I guess. You would have to make sure it's safe before you build anywhere."

"That makes sense." Jono tried to look as though he meant it. "Do you know if they're going anywhere now?"

"We did ship some construction mechs to Aires awhile back. That's closer to Dawn. But Aires isn't new. They're just building it taller and better."

"Is Aires close to the Keeper?"

"The who?"

"It's a . . ." Jono hesitated. "I don't know exactly what it is, some old monument near Dawn, I think."

Keiko shook her head. "Never heard of it."

After cramped hours, the forest below transformed into rocky hills, frosted with layers of ice.

There were pillows and blankets stored in the walls, but the floor was ribbed to carry the pallets of cargo and hard to sleep on. After tossing and turning, Jono's body finally gave in to exhaustion.

Chapter Twenty

The Guardian's Grasp

ono dreamed he was sailing with Illius over a frozen ocean. The wind was so strong that it pushed the full sails across the icy wasteland.

He woke up hours later feeling refreshed but hungry.

Keiko offered instant dinners in a can. Jono popped off the lid, twisted the knob, and then the food heated up.

He carefully ate the searing steamed-bean sprouts and cambotai stew while Keiko curled against the wall with the scroll Jonothon had taken from the library at Caer Midus.

"That's funny. This has almost nothing about Eies or Windom." She looked at him, confused. "Not a map or shops or anything. Windom isn't even listed at all."

"Yeah . . ." Jono struggled to come up with a lie. "It's really old, and I got it for books mostly, for my birthwake and it was in storage for years, so there's probably a lot of data rot on it."

Keiko accepted his explanation without question and searched for something else to read or watch.

If they could have flown in the high skies, the trip to Eies could have been made in a matter of hours instead of wakes. That option was far too dangerous for more reasons than bandits or pirates, although no one really spoke of what the danger was exactly. Everyone knew it had to do with the Terralunans, who blockaded the high skies from outer space.

The mountain peaks below them became small islands as the ice from the Ullr Ocean spilled into their valleys. The frozen plateau was crowned in icy claws that shimmered like soft blue fairies, calling travelers to embrace their beauty and freeze their skin off with a single touch.

Above the ice, the full moon glowed stark white. The Terralunan home hung so close Jono felt as though he could reach out and snatch it from the sky.

Keiko wrapped her fingers on the table and stared pessimistically at the five cards in her hand.

"Are you going to keep beating us all hours?" she said.

Jono blushed.

Keiko had brought a deck of Kings and Creatures cards. Jonothon had won four games in a row, and was on the brink of winning a fifth.

Keiko placed down a watery stallion, named Oxygen. Alvin held his chin and stared intently at his cards as they hovered in front of him.

"Two to make it," said Alvin.

"A single arrow," Jono said as he laid down the cards with a smile, "and Hydrogen, King of Fire, Carbon, the Black Wolf."

"Humph," replied Alvin with exaggerated gloom.

The cards laid out made a design of three fire cards, two water cards, one earth golem, and one black wolf connected to each other with five single arrows and one dual ax. The cards lit up in a chain reaction. It was the chemical nitro methane.

Jono had won again!

Keiko threw down her cards and shook her head, all the while retaining a smile. "I don't suppose you want to trade hands? All I had was a dual mace and the Iron Banshee Queen."

Jono shook his head. "We used to play this all the time at home."

The image of his family sitting around the fireplace on a chilly wake entered his mind. It was a simple life, but they were happy together. He imagined his mom at a town council meeting, his dad fixing steam pumps and Dahlia chasing her friends around the streets in Polari. He doubted that they had any clue that a war could start at any moment. He wondered if they would be proud of him for trying to stop it.

"I bet you were the grand champion," said Alvin, pulling Jono out of his thoughts. "It takes a lot to beat my quadrex processing brain power."

Jono blushed. "I was pretty good. Most times it's just luck of the draw."

"You're going to do great at the academy," said Keiko cheerfully. "I can tell."

Jono smiled but didn't believe her. "The recruiter that came to my school said that my mathometry scores were really good. I thought I'd go into that, not Cloaks."

Jono shuffled the deck of cards clumsily as he thought he had to be the least qualified person at the academy to go into the spy trade. Maybe they were planning on giving him bionetic legs so he could run super-fast or cloaking skin so he could be completely invisible.

The deck of cards slipped for a third time, but this time he had an excuse other than his uncoordinated fingers. A shadow had swept under the white ice beneath them.

"Did you see that?" Jono's face was wide with amazement.

"Do you think it was . . .?"

"An ice dragon," said Alvin. "The ice is always thin around this sector during Augustine. They come to feed off the claw whales that try to lay their eggs."

Jono and Keiko pressed themselves against the clear walls, searching for another sign of shadow under the ice.

"The whales come to these frozen shores against the Alps to lay the eggs," said Alvin, continuing his lesson. "It's quite odd, you may think, given the intense cold the surface. The eggs are very large and filled with blubber to warm and feed the calf while the ice covers it up again during the winter season. It stays trapped for a year until the calf has reached the full size of the egg and the ice thins once again. There are, of course, occasions where the timing doesn't match up and, well, as I'm sure you can imagine. The calf starves and remains frozen in the ice. There are quite a few skeletons that remain, even after being picked clean by snargs or bandits, but given the complexity of the process it's amazing the success rate is as high as it is. Despite the danger of the cold, it is within the liquid waters beneath the ice that the greater predators reside. There is an enormous ecology below, from the moss that grows on the bottom of the ice to—"

"There it is!" Jono shouted.

A shadow beneath the cracked ice appeared for only a moment before it fading away.

"Have you seen any come to the surface, Alvin?" asked Jono.

"The whales do breach the surface quite often around this—"

"No, the dragon," they both replied in chorus.

"You're submersible, right?" said Keiko. "There's got to be an opening somewhere so we can see below."

"Oh, no no no," said Alvin. "The land may be barren up here, but as water keeps a more even degree of temperature, it is full of all manner of life. There are enough dangers that live under the ice to make us beg for pirates or bandits. Didn't you just hear what I said about the eggs?"

"Fine." said Keiko. "We'll watch from—"

"It's back!" exclaimed Jono.

The shadow of the ice dragon returned to the cracked surface. The three travelers looked over plains of ice before seeing the reason why the dragon had returned. A white horned seal was resting near the edge of a large crack in the ice.

The water was a brilliant blue.

"The color comes from the soft fluorescence of the algae in the water." said Alvin.

"It's hunting," said Jonothon.

"Run seal," Keiko said. "We should warn it."

"All things have to eat," replied Alvin.

The shadow began to move. Its snakelike figure curved against the rugged white ground. A clawed hand reached from below and dug into the bottom of the ice.

"It's coming!" Alvin froze. His voice cracked in genuine terror.

The ice dragon snaked under the surface toward the unsuspecting seal.

"We're leaving. Now," said Alvin.

Keiko flipped open a hatch on the invisible wall and pressed a now visible red button. "We're alright, Alvin. It can't see us. We're cloaked and high up in the air."

The seal slid unknowingly toward the water, and the shadow under the ice became still.

"That's not it at all! You must release that override!" Alvin was shaking and floated in front of Keiko's face. She kept trying to look around him.

"Maybe we should—" Jono began to say.

"Look!" said Keiko.

The seal turned away from the crack in the ice just as the ice dragon burst from the water and lunged forward.

"Keiko Kirin, for your life, please release that lock!"

The ground shook violently with a thunder that cracked open the ice into giant shards that splashed in an uproar of violent blue and white. The ice dragon's head burst into the air just before it dove again, its glistening white body arching into the water until it disappeared.

The humans ducked against the wall, eyes wide.

"Bandits?" squealed Keiko.

"Was it the dragon?" asked Jono.

"Worse," said Alvin.

They all turned around to see it.

The sky behind them, once filled with clear stars, was as black as death. Like a monster from a nightmare, the enormous beast had landed on the sharp mountain peaks that pierced the cracking ice around it. Its black mane spread around its lion head and rippled in the wind like flames. Tattered bat wings spread to cover the sky. Jagged horns lined its head, shoulders, and back. Six black snakes splintered out of its tail and slithered along the shattered ice. Black fur cracked and teemed with white fire.

Jono couldn't tell if it was organic, machine, or both.

The three travelers were frozen with terror.

"The Chimera," Alvin whispered.

A giant black foot stepped onto the thicker ice. Flames flared from its paw and steam burst out from the melting ice.

"Oh burning stars," said Keiko. "It's a Guardian!"

The obsidian Chimera stared directly at the cloaked ship.

"Can we outrun it?" asked Jono.

"We can't outrun it," the others said in unison.

"What does it want?" Jono asked.

"It is a guardian of the skies," said Alvin. "They are the enforcers from Terralunis imprisoning us on Earth. They are the destroyers and seeders of fear."

The chimera snorted in the icy air and breathed out vengeful steam. From its glowing mouth it bellowed an announcement. "Slaves of the Night, do not dare run, nor hide. The eyes of my masters see further than those of your Empress and we have known the omegan mechanic has moved into the Dark End."

"What is he talking about?" asked Keiko.

"Quick, put your gloves on," said Alvin, instructing them in a panic. "No, not just your coat. Put on these seal fur ones."

A door swung open on a closet of adult sized thermal clothes. Jono grabbed them and handed one set to Keiko. His mind was racing. *They know*, he thought. The Tills had found out about the key and now they were searching the Dark for it.

The Chimera stepped onto the ice, its black wings opening wide against the sky.

"Submit now, Dark Enders," it roared. "You have violated the pact. You now belong to the Lords of Terralunis."

"If it catches you, it will never let you live," said Alvin. "Grab hold of that lever, there on the floor, both of you!"

They did as they were told. Jono looked at Keiko for any sign of hope, but she just shook her head. She was as lost as he was.

"Land and submit!" the monster roared.

"I'll lead him away as best I can," said Alvin.

"How?" Jono began to ask, but a metal sphere wrapped around them. The cargo ship flicked into visible light and the beast of white fire leaped at its prey. Alvin dove forward and shot an escape hatch out along the ice floor before bursting his engines from under the leaping chimera. Jonothon and Keiko zoomed across the plain, tumbling toward jagged mountain peaks.

Alvin spun around the Chimera's leg and charged to the sky, but the monster's snake tail sprung at him. Fanged mouths sunk into his left engine and tore it completely off. Alvin spun out of control. He flared his engines again, trying to stay just ahead of the beast. He spun in circles, back and forth; each time the Chimera's strike narrowly missed him.

The escape pod bounced against the rocks and finally crashed into a mound of snow against an icicle-crowned cove. Jono's head smacked against Keiko's as they slide to a stop. The cloaked ball left an indent in the snow before opening like a cocoon, and then dumped them onto the freezing snow. The sphere spread into a wall that reached the stone of their alcove. They peered around its edge at the black creature as it swatted and leaped at the impetuous ship.

Ice cracked and steamed beneath it. The Chimera leaped into the air, its wings flapping twice before it dove onto the helpless ship. The weight of the beast smashed through the ice just as its claws wrapped around Alvin's metal frame. Its fiery claw crushed the hull of the ship; the metal melted, hot and orange in its grip.

Alvin release one last burst of his right engine and blasted the Chimera's hand, breaking his body free but losing his last bit of power. The flare of engine was the last thing Jonothon saw before the ship disappeared into the translucent blue water.

The Chimera roared. Its wings flapped as it hovered in the air. Its face was alight with fiery rage. The monster landed again, scanning the area. It must have seen the escape pod release. Jono was sure it could see into a spectrum where the cloak couldn't hide them. They would have to run. Maybe if they could get on the other side of the rocks, they would be better hidden.

"What should we do?" asked Keiko, but before Jono could think of an answer, the Chimera's search had stopped with its gaze fixed in their direction.

The Chimera charged at them, each fiery, crushing step bursting with sublimated ice vapor. It leaped into the air to pounce, and all they could do was hold each other and cringe against the stinging snow as impending death fell upon them.

The instant before they were crushed, a high pitched zip rang along the mountain peaks and the side of the monster's head exploded in orange and black. It lost control and crashed head-first into the snowy embankment. The collision flung Jono and Keiko into the air. They slammed and slid against the ice ocean plain.

Jono scrabbled to his feet and grabbed Keiko's hand. The ice was rugged despite looking smooth from above. They ran as fast as they could, careful not to fall or touch the ice with their skin.

A roar of pain and fury swept across the ocean. The Chimera had risen again, and Jono glanced back long enough to see the scarred and broken chips of its black skin thrashing with white flames.

Above them came a deep mechanical growl just before a black, silver, and blue object slammed into the Chimera and set it tumbling onto the ice. Jono couldn't believe it! It was the mechanical soldier he had seen back in Dollup. Biggs!

"Get them, Ramsus!" shouted Biggs, whose arms split into wings, his legs giant engines. Biggs flew to their direction. His engine-feet cut out, shifted downward, and then skidded along the ice.

The children were frozen and held their arms up against the flurry of ice shavings that flew at them. Biggs's midsection opened up like a mouth and, just before it swallowed them up, Jono saw another familiar face.

"Wedge! We need that tyrant chained!" said the bearded, red-eyed soldier from the café. Ramsus grabbed Jono and Keiko and pulled them safely into the large cavity of Biggs's chest.

"Biggs, give us a flyby, and then gun it!" Ramsus shouted over the roar of the engine and the wind.

Jono looked at Wedge, who was fidgeting with knobs around his neck.

"This is always such an imposition." Wedge told Jonothon with a shrug. "Can you hold this for me?" Wedge removed his own head and placed it into Jonothon's hands. Jono was so shocked he almost dropped it.

They zoomed over the Chimera and pummeled it with the gigantic

mortar from Biggs' arm cannon.

Wedge's headless body saluted and then jumped out of the doors. It fell through the sky as his arms and legs splintered and spread out like wire claws that carved into the ice around the obsidian Chimera. His body had transformed into a net, pinning the monster to the icy surface. The monster slashed at the metal cables that were once Wedge's arms, but the cables separated before they could be cut, and shot off countless smaller cables to bind the savage beast.

"How dare you defy the pact!" roared the venomous Chimera. "Usurpers! Your treachery will not go unpunished! You cannot defy!"

Biggs blasted the ice with rockets. The air exploded in orange and white fire.

"Oh? But I love defying!" chuckled Biggs.

"Now's our chance!" yelled Ramsus. "Full burn!"

The engines exploded with a burst of power, and the bearded aircraft, along with his two new and terrified passengers, soared out of the reach of the writhing Chimera, over the sunken mountains, and toward the very heart of night.

City 'Neath the Stars

"Are we safe?" asked Keiko.

Ramsus nodded.

"Are you sure?" asked Jono.

"Certain as the stars," replied a smiling Ramsus. "Wedge's body was designed to shut down tanks. It's not quite the same against a Guardian, but it will buy us enough time get to the city."

"That was amazing!" Keiko flopped onto a chair with a shocked smile on her face.

"That's what I get for being so ridiculously useful," said Wedge's severed head.

"Poor Alvin . . ." said Jono.

A hand came down on Jonothon's shoulder and gripped him firmly. Jono and Wedge's head looked up to find the peculiar sight of Ramsus's rugged military face bursting with a smile.

"You're him, aren't you?" said Ramsus.

Jonothon froze. "Him?"

"How the stars did you ever escape?" Ramsus continued.

"Escape?" muttered Jono.

"From those sun-burnt Solans!" said Ramsus ecstatically. "You are him? The boy that was kidnapped from Polari? The one scheduled to be a recruit for Windom? Those soldiers were pretty upset when you disappeared from the pickup. Polari ain't a convenient drive, as you know. Not to mention your parents. I hardly recognized your face from the alert that was sent out, on account of that mask you were wearing before."

"Right . . ." Jono played along. If a kidnapping was what the Dark believed happened then he would be wise to let them keep believing it.

Keiko looked at both of them, confused. "You were kidnapped?"

"Yeah, that's why I was in Dollup," Jono lied. "I stole a ship from the Solans, but it crashed in the woods."

The red-eyed soldier grabbed Jono's hand and shook it. "That's one burn'em story! I'm Ramsus. Ramaadi is my sur. It's a pleasure to rescue you."

Despite Ramsus's gruff exterior, he was thin and muscular, his pointed features, hawkish nose, and bushy black eyebrows expressed a deep friendliness.

"The Solans are burn'em slave traders," explained Ramsus. "That's why the Terraloonies like them so much. They will steal innocent kids and sell them to the Tills for slave labor. Not much grows on the moon, so they need all the resources they can get from a living planet: soil, food, animals, and slaves. They probably use them as food too, when they can't work anymore."

Jono cringed at the thought.

"I don't believe I've seen you before, Miss." Ramsus smiled at Keiko.

"This is Keiko Kirin. She wasn't kidnapped," said Jono, "but she's coming to the academy with me. There was a mistake. She's supposed to be going to Windom too."

"That's why you were on that transport, then?' said Ramsus. "Good thing we spotted you leaving Dollup. Not to worry. The generous Mister Wedge here will send a call up ahead. It'll get back to your parents and the academy and let them know you're alright and on your way. You're late for your first year at the academy and those hard noses aren't going to like that." Ramsus gave him a sympathetic smile. "You are in luck, though. I'm headed in that direction myself, so in addition to the flight in ol' Biggs, you two get the pleasure of my incomparable company. Toll free!"

The compartment inside Biggs was cramped but large enough for Jono to stand upright. There were two port holes that were hard to see through, but Jono could tell they were flying close to the ground again, dashing left and right through mountain canyons. The sky below them was now thick in greenhouse clouds that clung to mountain peaks.

Kirin peered out a port hole. "Why did that Guardian attack us? We didn't go anywhere near the high skies."

"This ain't the first time those devils have broken their own pact and come to the ground," said Ramsus. "I don't recall it being as bad as it's been this past week, though. We've received reports of attacks all across the Dark End. Almost every transport is getting stopped and searched. The Loonies are back to their old nature—being bullies."

Jono knew it wasn't just brutality that made the Guardians stop all the transports. They must have known Eies had Attrayer's key.

"Did you go to the academy?" Keiko asked Ramsus.

"Sure. Anyone who enlists has to go to one of the three."

"How was it?" asked Jono.

"Did you have to study all the time?" asked Keiko.

"Oh yeah, there's lots to study," Ramsus replied, "and it was as good a time as it could have been. We didn't spend the whole years indoors and underground, though. We had our share of travel, as young as we were."

"Really?" Keiko's face brightened.

Ramsus nodded. "Trust me, Polari-min. I've been across more'n half the sphere. There's nothing so educating as adventure."

Outside the window a jagged, snow covered horizon glistened in the moonlight.

"It's so dark here. Are we close?" Jono whispered.

"I should say so. Eies is a spare few hundred kilems away and the Windom academy is just at the edge of it."

"I mean are we close to the end? To the middle of the night?"

"Oh burn'em no!" laughed Ramsus. "We're deep in the Dark alright, but we're plenty far from the middle of it."

Jono blushed. He felt like he should have known that, but didn't.

"It gets far too cold out there at the true end," Ramsus explained, "and too . . . unstable. Nobody really lives at either ends of the world. The things that do live there, those things that survive when all reason says they shouldn't, well, you don't want to come within half a kay kilem of something like that."

Jono glanced at the soldier, only to see a harsh and resolute stare. He wondered what could possibly be worse than the Guardian they had just escaped.

"Just got a call with the Shield," boomed Biggs' voice. "We're clear to enter."

"Look, we're at the sentries now," said Ramsus. "Welcome to Eies!"

The children peered out of the port holes as Biggs flew over the crest of the mountains. Illuminated white clouds filled the enormous ring of mountain peaks. The entire city was built within a wide basin in the middle of the mountains. Greenhouse clouds covered the surface like a lake, brilliantly lit up by the city beneath. It was a pearl of light in an abyss of darkness. Peaks of towers stuck up through the clouds like metallic islands.

Along the far mountain range was the home of the Empress, herself: a castle that spanned half the ringed mountains. Sharp black spires jutted into the starry sky like an obsidian crown adorned on the city of Eies.

Biggs flew down along the city before diving into the blinding clouds. After a few moments of rushing white, they emerged into the city exploding in light and activity. Keiko squealed and grabbed Jono's arm tight. "We made it!"

Biggs soared over roads of flashing lights and ducked under sky bridges. The city was a maze of towers and roads interlinked in all directions beneath thick clouds. White lights mixed with spots of red, blue, green, and yellow, igniting the clouds in a rainbow glow.

Hordes of people of all species speckled the web of roads. Many were unlike anyone Jonothon had seen before. Creatures with thick fur and monstrous appendages wore top hats and coats. Androids and grudgons scurried in and out of shops while humans and ayleens strolled along streets. No one took notice of yet another mechanical man flying through their crowded sky.

Lights flashed by the port holes, and a creeping fear snuck into Jonothon's mind like a trespassing spider. Somewhere the Empress was waiting, holding on to the key to the balance of the world and plotting its destruction.

The center of the massive city soon fell behind them as they approached the northern cliffs. Towering supports lined the mountainside and disappeared into the thick lake of clouds. The rock wall got closer and closer . . .

"Look out!" yelled Keiko.

Jono clenched his eyes.

And then he opened them. Nothing had happened.

White clouds whipped around them, and Keiko shared his look of confused relief. They both looked out the window just as Biggs burst through the clouds that seeped out of a crack in the mountain like a lazy waterfall. The darkness of the night once again surrounded them. From their height they could see far into the horizon: a dark world of jagged mountains all the way to the dark end of the earth. The white light of Terralunis only served to sink the sense of dread into Jonothon's bones.

Biggs shifted his engines into feet, his wings tilted their angle, and they descended along the cloud-fall as sharp teeth of rock rose to block the moon's light and gobble them up.

There was a bellowing thud as metal feet landed on the stone ground. The cabin shook and tilted, but Biggs landed far more gently than would be expected by one with his burly appearance. An eerie orange light crept into the cabin like a probing fog; before them stood the towering gates of the Windom Academy.

"We're here," said Ramsus as he led the way down the ramp coming out of Biggs' waist.

Fierce orange flames lit up the obsidian basin and danced off the sharp black edges. Jono felt as though there was some creature looking back at him from the dark, prowling but unseen.

Across the whole of the mountainside were windows and balconies jutting from the rock. It was like a stone city peeking out of the veil of the mountain.

Beside the Windom gate were immense stone statues of kneeling knights, their large swords held beside them. Round, spiked armor covered their bodies.

Gray gargoyles lined the pillars and edifices of the gate. Above the closed stone doors were carved strange marks that could have been words if only Jonothon had known how to read them.

"You can leave me here," Wedge said to Jono, as he had almost walked off with his severed head still clutched in his hands. "This old brute owes me a new body."

Keiko turned to Biggs. "Thank you so much."

"Yeah, thanks," Jono added as he handed Wedge's head to Biggs.

"All in a wake's work," grunted Biggs. "We'll see you back at the station, Ramaadi?"

"Right. Be sure to fix up Wedge before then," said Ramsus.

"Oh? Can't I kick him around for a bit first?" laughed Biggs.

"Only if he consents," laughed Ramsus, "but don't break him anymore than he is!"

"Yes, sir!" the burly mech-man said with a laugh as he lifted into the air.

Jono watched Biggs soar away before scurrying after Ramsus and Keiko. He slipped off the thick fur coat then realized it was still too warm with his blue coat on. Even though it was deeper into the Dark End, Eies was far warmer than Polari.

Keiko nudged Jonothon's arm and pointed at the hunched stone knights.

"They're watching us." She grinned.

The heads of the statues moved ever so slightly, keeping an eye on them. The stone goliaths gripped their enormous swords, motionless but prepared to strike.

Ramsus reached the gate first and just before he collided into it, the solid stone peeled away like a cloth curtain. Keiko and Jono both stopped and looked at each other. Ramsus poked his head back out. "Don't stop now."

Inside the mountain, the academy was vast and dark. The central hall was wide and lined with the black pillars wrapped in spiraled stairs that reached the distant arched ceiling. White torches hung on the walls. All around them, gargoyles clung to the rock. Their stone bodies were motionless, but Jono could feel them watching.

The three walked down the hall and turned through empty corridor after empty corridor. They wound through halls lined with windows that displayed different locations around the world, as if they were really there. One hall was like walking under water, while another seemed to be a desert under a dawn sky.

"It's been ages . . ." said Ramsus, more to himself than to the children. "I hardly remember where we are at all."

"How do you know where to go?" asked Keiko.

"Them," said Ramsus as he pointed toward the gargoyles.

Jono was ashamed he hadn't noticed it before. All the gargoyles around them were pointing, fingers, tails or heads, in the same direction. They were guiding them down a path through the massive cave. To where, he had no clue.

They came to an open room with an arched doorway. Upon its shut doors was a carving of a tree. Beside the door was a crescent shaped desk, behind which sat a stern and skinny elderly woman. On either side of the desk were growling spike hounds with chains around their necks. Their glowing red eyes seemed to lust for blood.

Keiko slipped her hand into Jono's, and he glanced at her. He was surprised but tried to hide it. She had a smile on her face, but it was in the wavering corners of the smile that betrayed how nervous she was. A powerful sense of responsibility boiled up in him. He could tell she was depending on him to see her through. He wasn't going to betray his new friend no matter what; he would find another way to the key if he had to.

"State you identity and purpose," came the lady's harsh voice.

"Captain Ramsus Ramaadi. I'm here escorting a student."

Ramsus nudged Jono to speak.

"Um, Jonothon Wyer. Student."

"A student, are you?" said the snooty woman. Her desk held a plaque that read *Cadet Warden—Elberta Drudge.*

"I'm deeply sorry," she said, although she clearly was not, "but late admissions are strictly forbidden." She waved her hand at them. "Good bye."

Chapter Twenty-Two

The Windom Academy

"We can't leave!" Jono blurted out in shock. "We've come so far. I know I was approved!"

"Do you realize it has been a full two weeks of lessons? This is highly inexcusable!"

Jono was certain it hadn't been a full two weeks yet, but he didn't argue. "I was, um, kidnapped . . ."

"By Solans, ma'am." added Ramsus.

At that word, the laying spike hounds snarled and charged as far as their chains would allow and bared their vicious, saliva covered teeth.

"Brutus! Cassius! Do be silent! You shan't be eating any entrails unless I expressly command it!" Drudge wiggled her nose and straightened her glasses. "Come forward, boy. I can't test you from a distance."

Jono looked warily at Ramsus, who nodded approval. Keiko clenched his hand, and then released it, giving him courage. When Jono reached the desk, the woman extended her open hand. She obviously expected Jonothon to put something in it, but he had no clue as to what.

"Your hand . . ." she said without looking at him.

He placed his hand in hers, and she held it firmly. In a flash she had retrieved a metal butterfly and pricked the skin on the back of his hand. She lifted the metal butterfly and set it on her black marble table. Static blue holographic faces flashed in rapid succession above the desk until stopping on his.

"Very well. Your identity has been verified. You are indeed enrolled, Mister Wyer, although I have never heard of anyone with such disrespectful tardiness meeting any level of success at the Windom Academy. The dregs at D'Arrow may tolerate that lack of manners, but we, sir, have standards. Go on then and get settled," she said with a harrumph. Her eyes then stopped on the little girl that stood resolutely beside Ramsus. "And who is this?"

"She's Keiko Kirin." Jono cut in. "She came to join, too!"

"To join?" Ms. Drudge spat like the words were molasses in her mouth. She checked her holographic list and raised her eyebrows sharply before looking back at her work. "I have no such name in my registry. There are no allowances for admittance without an invitation. I'm quite sorry," she said, although she clearly wasn't, and flicked her wrist at them. "Goodbye."

Keiko didn't say a word. Her forced smile disappeared, and she stood there, staring blankly like she had been shot.

"No!" Jono said. A fire flared up from inside him. "No, she has to attend! She deserves it."

"That is simply impossible."

"It isn't! She took the test and there must have been a mistake. Keiko is already stars smarter than anyone I know. She's built mechs! And bots and she can . . ."

"I hardly see how that is relevant."

"I'm not lying!"

"I don't care if you are!" the snarly woman spat. "That child has no invitation to enlist and therefore . . ."

"Jono . . ." Keiko said, her voice betraying her defeat.

"No, you don't understand," he said, his voice pleading. "I promised and if you only knew her you really would want her to join."

Ms. Drudge' voice was full of venom. "She cannot be allowed to attend under the enlistment program or any other and must leave immediately!"

"You have to let her in, or I'll leave with her!"

"Highly unusual!" she scoffed. "You are in no position, you presumptuous whelp, to make any shape of de—"

A red light flicked on the hologram.

". . . demands . . ." Drudge finished weakly. She hid the message she just received. She read it over thrice before glaring back at the two children. Her face contorted with controlled spite. She clasped her hands together and glared at Jonothon, who tried his hardest to not show how terrified he was.

"Upon extreme circumstance, I will allow her case to be reviewed," she growled. "The commander will be finishing his class shortly. It may take some time to review her case, or, in the Commander's wisdom he will see that you are both an infusion of hopeless trouble and send you back to whatever frost covered hut you crawled out of."

"You, child." Drudge pointed to Keiko. "Wait in there until your fate is decided." Her finger flicked in the direction of the solid black doors that looked like they never opened.

The spike hounds' chains fell, letting them free. They encircled Keiko and led her away through the door. She looked back over their spiked fur at Jonothon.

He couldn't see much of her face and he didn't know if they were really going to let her in, or if they were simply trying to trick him. The doors cracked open automatically and boomed as they shut.

"As for you, Mister Wyer, take yourself to your dorm immediately. Capricorn corridor, room twenty nine." Drudge looked at Ramsus. "You're excused, sir."

Ramsus clicked his heels together, saluted Mrs. Drudge, and then returned the way they had come.

"Have a great time Jono!" Ramsus waved as he disappeared down the hall.

"Um, ma'am?" squeaked Jono.

"You're still here? I was quite sure I—"

"But I don't know where Capricorn corridor is."

The women sighed and pointed to a dark-gray gargoyle now facing him. It pointed to the right.

"Just follow them."

Jonothon started to leave then turned back.

"Also, I was told I'd be fixed here. I was supposed to get a surgery for my heart and lungs."

Drudge glared. "All pre-enrollment installs are to be completed on or before the first wake of school, which, as I have stated was—"

"Two weeks ago."

"Don't be snide. I will look into the doctor's schedule, but due to your tardiness I would not expect anything sooner than the third week of Decsomber."

"What? But I won't be able to keep up in drills or—"

"Do not whine. It is unbefitting a Windom cadet, and I haven't the patience for it."

Jono looked at her with as much purposeful sadness as he could muster. The woman only rolled her eyes.

"Go see the resident bio-mechanic once you've settled. He may be able to help you with something in the meantime."

"How do I . . ."

The woman clenched her jaw and by the acid in her eyes, he could tell she was an inch away from violence.

"Oh, right. Ask the gargoyles. Ok. Thanks."

Jono slunk away before she could insult him again.

Jonothon followed the gargoyles' directions to a statue of a creature whose head and chest resembled a goat with a dragon's tail instead of hind legs. At the end of the hall was room number twenty nine. Jono turned the handle on the door and pushed, but it wouldn't budge. He tried by pulling, but also to no avail. He looked around, confused.

On the front of his door was a silvery blue goat head with a knocker in its mouth.

"Do you mind?" said the knocker.

"Oh," said Jonothon, startled it could talk. "Sorry. I was just trying to get into my room."

"I don't have you registered. This room is off limits to non-academy personal and unregistered students."

"But the lady at the desk told me this is my room. I'm late."

"Alright, then," sighed the capricorn. "Look at me and state your name."

Jono stared at its beady eyes and said his name. The Capricorn looked down, blinked twice, and then sniffed.

"Ah, it is you," bleated the capricorn as the door then swung open. "Welcome to your new home, lad."

The room behind the door was circular with bunk beds and dressers alternating along the wall. A balcony on the far end looked out to the northern night sky.

Jono walked to the balcony. There was no wind and when Jono reached out his hand, he discovered a clear, curved surface. He couldn't tell if it was just glass, or if the image of the outside world was an illusion.

While most of the bunk beds were covered with bags and books and clothes, Jonothon noticed one untouched bed had an old but familiar suitcase underneath it. Jono pulled it out and confirmed it was indeed his—stacks of paper books, hand-me-down clothes and all. The soldiers must have brought it to school even though he had gone missing.

There was something comforting about having his things, his clothes and books. He almost forgot his mission to find the key and just let himself enjoy the small sense of success at finally, actually, arriving at the academy.

Jono unbuttoned his shirt and sat on his bunk. He could see the lump under his white undershirt of the smaller heart reg he got from Cid.

He was exhausted but couldn't avoid his worrying about Keiko and Attrayer's key. He lay on the bed and tried to listen to the sounds of the cave-like academy.

The room was quiet.

Jonothon wondered why he hadn't seen anyone else yet. The school should have been roaring with students. If they had found out about his plan to get the key back, they could have moved all the students somewhere safe and have a troop of soldiers ready to lock him up at any moment.

He tried to fight the feeling that he'd led Keiko to her doom. He was terrified she wouldn't be allowed into the school and would probably be sold into slavery herself, or sent to be food for the Terralunans. Horrible ideas swam in his head. He tried to fight his doubts and fears, but he was too tired to stop them.

His eye lids sunk like lead in a liquid sea, and sleep dragged his waking mind into unconsciousness.

Green and Lumpy Aliens

"Don't wake him. He looks sick."

Jonothon was still fully clothed and as exhausted as he was when he first collapsed into bed. Footsteps clacked against the stone floor. His body was heavy and sore. He cracked open his eyes, but everything was dark and blurry.

Something green and round came close to him then moved away.

"Hey you!"

Jono felt something blunt poke him in the ribs.

"Don't do that!" whispered another voice with an odd accent.

Jono blinked and forced his weary hands to rub his eyes, and then the room became clearer. He jumped back once he saw the two heads that leaned over his bunk, inches from his face. One head belonged to a green-skinned ayleen, topped with orange and red spines that flopped backward like thick strands of hair. The other was covered in brown, scaly lumps and had a sharp-toothed smile that could only belong to a grudgon.

"Oi!" said the ayleen. "No one's been in that bunk since the term started. Are you new here?"

Jonothon nodded.

"Don't you know you're late?" grunted the grudgon with a guttural laugh.

Jono nodded again.

"So I guess we're bunk mates then," said the ayleen. "We were just about to get dinner, if you wanted to come."

Jonothon stared at the two strange species. "Actually, I'm starving."

"Good. You can sit with us," said the skinny ayleen. "I'm Isaac Ohm and this is Oscar Bohrs."

Oscar waved. "Pleasure." His lumpy brown face spread in a wide, spiky-toothed smile.

Jono suddenly remembered. "Keiko! I need to find Keiko to see if she got in."

The ayleen and grudgon shrugged at each other.

"It's dinner," said Oscar. "Everyone will be there."

Isaac smiled. "And it's nice to meet you, Cadet . . .?"

"Oh, sorry. I'm Jono, er . . . Jonothon Wyer."

"Well then," said Isaac with a smile. "Welcome to Windom, Wyer!"

"Thanks." Jono forced a polite grin at the reception.

"Come on!" insisted Oscar. "I haven't eaten since lunch!"

The three boys marched out of Capricorn Corridor and through flame-lit hallways, the distant roar of children reverberating through the stone walls. A tall teacher in black robes glared at them as they scurried past him.

"On your way," said the teacher.

They soon arrived at a pair of massive stone doors that opened onto a cavernous room. The dining hall rose high up the mountain. Balconies jutted from the walls—the higher the seats seemed to indicate the older class of students. The youngest students crowded tables on the ground.

Most of the students wore black uniforms with red sashes and ornate silver designs on the shoulders and sleeves. Isaac slipped his jacket on when they entered while Oscar wore only the pants and white undershirt.

The enormous hall was overwhelmed with students climbing the walls and leaping between balconies like a chaotic circus. Cadets swooped above them from balcony to balcony. A girl with puffy black hair climbed with a half-eaten burger in her mouth.

Nearly every person older than Jonothon had some form of strange power. A feli'yin boy hung upside down on the underside of the third tier with curled, dark wings wrapped around him. A professor rolled by on wheeled legs. Another teacher read from book held up by a third mechanical arm. On the fourth tier of the room, an older female cadet slouched in her chair while three odd rodents—which Isaac informed him were called edelmice—passed a spoon of mashed mushrups from the plate on the table and into the human girl's expecting mouth.

On the second tier balcony, a boy with black hair ate a crustacean sandwich while his identical twin walked clean through a row of students to the next table.

On the third tier a boy squatted on the top of a table. He transformed into long-haired gorangatang. The crowd around him exploded in laughter as he waved a tray of food over his head and pointed his finger with mock indignity at those around him.

Jono, Isaac, and Oscar pushed through the crowd on the ground, looking for an empty place to sit. They neared a blond boy who leaned toward a girl with her back pinned against the wall. The boy's lips curled into a proud smile. On his bare arms were shiny metal circles.

"Trust me. I can hold it for as long as I need to," he boasted.

The girl had a smile on her face, but her eyes wandered uncomfortably away from the boy's intent gaze. The circle on the boy's shoulder grew orange and hot. The boy glanced at his arm.

"These things are dangerous, deadly to the untrained squab. But in the right hands, it's one of the strongest powers here."

Jono stopped to watch.

An orange sphere popped out from the blond boy's mechanical shoulder. The orb hovered in the air as flames swam around the ball like a current of rushing water.

The boy caught Jono staring at him, and that moment of distraction was all it took. The boy's face was full of fear, but it was too late.

The ball burst with a gooey fire, and a harsh bang echoed through the dining hall that sent Jono tumbling backward onto the ground.

The girl blurted a loud laugh before she could stop herself. The instant of embarrassment that washed over the blond boy's face quickly transformed into a fiery anger.

"Don't they check for brains before enrolling you recruits?" The boy stomped forward and grabbed Jono by the collar. "Are you looking for an excuse to bail out already? You see fire, dumb-drop, you don't stick your face in it!"

Jono lay on the ground, frozen. The circles on the boy's arm glowed hot again, and Jono couldn't tell if this raving boy would shove another fire bomb in his face. He looked around for help, but the girl against the wall had taken the opportunity to slip away. Isaac and Oscar looked back at him. Their worried expressions and equally frozen bodies weren't going to help.

"You're like a burn'em sun-burnt Sola!" The boy laughed loudly, trying to take the attention away from himself. "Stars! Can't you grasp that fire bombs ain't the type a thing stick up your nose? Why don't you go live under the sun and get fried!"

"Hey, Nick!" shouted a boy from the third tier. "Nice flare!"

"Yeah. It is. Want a closer look like the twig here?" Nick yelled back. "I'll singe those four whiskers off your chin until you can grow somethin' proper."

"Are you coming or are you just going to cook the kid all hours?" shouted a dark-haired girl on the same tier.

Nick growled and pushed Jono back down before he leaped onto a table and climbed to the higher decks to meet his friends.

Isaac and Oscar scurried over to help Jonothon up.

"You got to watch out," said Isaac. "This isn't like any wherever you're from. Things are serious here. The power we get comes with responsibility."

"Yeah," said Oscar, "like, don't burn your face off. That's Nicklus Knox. I'd suggest not being enemies with him."

The three bunkmates found a space big enough for them sit beside a row of burly yetons that looked too old to be on the ground floor.

Jono kept his head down and rubbed his seared face. It hurt, but not as bad as his pride. Part of him always dreamed life in the academy would be a second chance to do everything right; he could be popular and successful, instead of who he was in Polari.

At the center of their table was a statue of a gnome sitting cross-legged. Isaac touched its round belly of the gnome and leaned in to speak.

"I'd like some halibut and crisps. Oh, and some gazberry milk. What do you guys want?"

"Mugaluk, please," said a smiling Oscar. "I like it hot an' spicy."

Jonothon was bewildered. "Can I get anything?"

"Of course," said Isaac. "They conjure up whatever you want."

"Alright." Jono leaned toward the gnome so it could hear him better. "Just some thaipan, please."

After a few moments, a plate of thick brown noodles slid through a hole in the table. Jono grabbed a fork and slurped up the noodles. He tried to not think about Keiko, but the longer he went without seeing her, the more he started to believe the worst had happened. The pit of his stomach sunk.

Isaac munched on a breaded fish stick and flipped through a floating magazine screen that the gnome was kind enough to project. Oscar slurped down what looked to be a soup made of mud and insects. Jono was mesmerized by how he ate it up, despite the uneasy sounds of crunching and buzzing.

"Have you heard about this?" said Isaac, pointing to the image on the floating screen. It was a huge green light coming from a metal box.

"What is it?"

"It's the inertia reactor on Ares, the red planet," answered Isaac with honest excitement in his purple eyes. "It's a new test engine for hyper space travel."

"I wish we could go there," grunted Oscar.

Jono looked at him, surprised. "You can see news from the red planet?"

"Oh, yeah," said Isaac. "Just because the Terraloonies don't let us off the planet doesn't mean we can't get signals from the others."

"The Empress should blow up that old moon, and then we could go to any planet we want," said Oscar.

"Yeah, burn'em Loonies, and the Solans," agreed Isaac.

As Jono looked at the crowd of bionetic-powered cadets he noticed he was scratching the back of his hand. His first thought was of the prick he got from Ms. Drudge, but that had been on his other hand. Come to think of it, the itching wasn't just his hand. His shoulders, neck, and other spots across his body itched. Maybe there's something in the air, he thought. It didn't hurt, but the more he paid attention to it, the more he wanted to scratch.

"So, are you both from the city, then?" asked Jono, trying to distract himself.

"Oh no, I'm from Eckleclypse," said Isaac. "But I've been to Eies plenty of times before now. My dad works for the Crown, so we get to see a lot of places."

"I'm from here." said Oscar, smiling. "Born and raised under Eies, down in the East Trench."

Isaac finished his fish and shut the magazine.

"It's getting late," said Isaac. "I'm going to find David before it hits sleep hour. We were going to play some Monster Slayer in the den."

"Oh, I'll come!" said Oscar. "Did you ever beat that zombie warlock?"

"No," Isaac replied, "we didn't have the right amulet to slay zombies, so we had to go around him. But David got a new sword, so we're going to try it again. Do you want to come along, Jono?"

Jono did have a growing interest in the game they were talking about, but somewhere inside him was a nervous and growing need to keep moving. He couldn't let himself just have fun when there was so much yet to do.

"I was supposed to meet with a bio-mechanic actually."

"Really? You have more installs you need to get?" asked Isaac.

Jono hesitated about talking about his weak heart and lungs.

"I met him before, that clunker ol' Edgar No Eyes," said Oscar as he chomped on a mugaluk covered centipede. "That guy's more mech than biological. I think his brain spark's wired wrong, but they still let him walk around the school freely. Bloke's far too creepy for me."

"Too right," said Isaac "I wouldn't want to head his way alone."

They shook their heads agreement. "Anyway, see you later Jono."

His two bunkmates pushed their way through the crowd until they disappeared. He stood to leave but was overcome by a lump in his throat. It started to itch terribly, but not like what he felt on the back of his hands. He tried to swallow, but the lump only got thicker. It was blocking his throat. Jono coughed violently, trying to hide it as he stumbled out of the dining hall.

Some of the other students stopped and stared at him. People turned at the sound of his coughs. He made it to the dining hall door and fell to his hands and knees, coughing uncontrollably. What if his mission to find Attrayer's Key had been found out? What if they had poisoned his food? What if the Empress had let him come this far only to kill him?

In one final, heaving cough, Jono spat out a black oily ball and realized what had happened.

"That was horrible," Jono gasped out loud.

The once white filter beetle was now fat and bloated; its body was completely soaked in a gooey black substance made of a mixture of the filter oil, saliva, and all the dust and grimy particles he had breathed in from the air. There was no way he was going to put another one of those things down his throat if he could help it.

Jono picked himself up.

He hoped that whoever Edgar No Eyes was, he could fix him right away. He walked down the corridors, breathing slow through his nose as gargoyles pointed the way.

Crazy Edgar No Eyes

The dark hallways of the underground academy twisted and wound in and out of each other like the tunnels of an ant colony. They eventually gave way to cold, carved rock supported by metal lattices. The last gargoyle pointed Jonothon down a tunnel scarcely lit by a dim, flickering track along the top of the wall.

Jono crept down the jagged tunnel until it abruptly ended. An enormous chasm cut through the mountain, the distant bottom lost in a menacing fog. A rickety metal bridge continued across the chasm to meet a door on the other side.

Jonothon stuck his head out cautiously as a howling draft chilled him through his coat to the bone. He should have brought his overcoat.

On the other side of the bridge, the mountain continued. A rust covered door was bolted into the rock and seemed to have been forgotten for ages.

Jono took a careful breath, stared straight forward, and charged across the bridge. His feet clanked, and the railing rattled with no guarantee it wouldn't collapse. Jono leapt the final step onto the stone ground. He grasped the rust-flaking door handle and pulled with all his scrawny weight until he heard the spiteful click of its latch. He had to push his foot against the wall to open it, but once in, he shut the door easily and shivered with relief.

It took more than a moment for his eyes to adjust to the darkness.

The moist, mildew cave around him seemed more like a junkyard than a mechanix shop. Even Keiko's shop had some form of order. This place was filled with everything from books and mech parts to rotting sandwiches and mushrups growing in the dirt. Vines wrapped around stalagmites of garbage. An entire ecology had been created out of the muddy waste that permeated the cave.

"Who be you then?" snarled a voice from the shadows.

Jono held close to the door. "I'm, well, I am a student here. I came to get installs to fix my . . ."

"A student, are you?" Out from the blackness walked a haggard man onto the hill of decomposing dirt and garbage. His weathered face was far beyond his years and made him resemble a moving corpse. Edgar No Eyes spread his arms wide and his near toothless smile seemed to spread wider. "I see. I see. Come to my kingdom, have you? Come to learn the secrets of the world? The secrets of power and destinies, eh?"

The man's back was hunched, and long, white hair crawled over his back like translucent worms. A thin beard hung wild from his wrinkled face to the gears in his knees. He was draped in a rotting coat covered in holes. His body was assorted in a jigsaw puzzle of flesh and metal.

The fleshy hand attached to a mechanical arm snatched up a book from beneath a lump of garbage and waved it in a scolding manner at Jonothon. The man's eyes were wild even as their sockets were empty. Edgar dug through piles of trash, held a tea pot up to his blind, empty eyes, and then tossed it aside.

"I, well," Jonothon squeaked, "I thought you installed parts that would fix my heart and lungs."

"Fix? Oh yes, I can fix . . ." Edgar No Eyes snatched up a metal contraption that looked like the joint to a mechanical arm. Edgar's wrinkled fingers pried open Jonothon's mouth as he held the joint up to his empty socket for the inspection. "I can fix the things what need fixing. You got to keep things running. Got to keep my empire strong, eh!"

"Right," mumbled Jono with the metal tube in his mouth.

"No problem with the heart, as far as I can see," said Edgar as he flung the joint into a pile of old shoes.

Jono wasn't sure if he should argue with his obvious misdiagnosis, or seize the chance to escape.

"Of course we could make it better," continued Edgar. "There's always room for improvement! Better sun, better skies, better truth, better lies."

Edgar shoved a new metal part against Jono's chest. This one looked like a circular saw with spider legs. He began measuring Jono's chest with a protractor.

"It's a descent fit for your size," Edgar acknowledged humbly and picked up a spiky, rust-covered clamp he began to open and shut. "I'll just crack you open a bit, only in the middle, and make it all as right as raindrops. With a few of these old boys gearing you up, I'll have you back to the barbeque by Greenwake."

Jonothon was convinced he had made a mistake. "That doesn't look right."

"It's not about the right part, but that which is made to be right in the end, eh?" Edgar's toothless smile stretched with certainty.

"No, but thanks for your help," said Jono as he stepped back to avoid the blind man's approach. "I actually should be getting back. There're people waiting . . . expecting me. They're probably coming here as we speak and I've got classes in the wake so, really . . ."

Edgar dashed at him and grasped tight to his shoulders. He squinted through his hollow eyes and surveyed Jono's face. "Beware what the others say. You can't trust them like you can me. They want it, you know, but I alone . . . I'm comfortable with my empire of dirt. Don't let it fall. It's crumbling. I can hear it, all the cracks is crinkling." Edgar trembled and hung his head in dismay. "Go on then. Go read the book and look upward."

Edgar released Jono from his grasp and pushed him away.

"Go on and get to it. Study for good marks. Don't forget salt. In grains or otherwise." The dirty mad man turned and slunk back into the shadowy stench.

Jono slipped out the door and, as he crossed over the rickety metal bridge, he remarked to himself how happy he was to have his own faulty organs, just so long as they hadn't been ripped out and replaced by the crazy man's junk.

The second time over, the chasm didn't seem nearly as terrifying.

The following wake, Jono rose early, not so much because he intended it but more due to his nervous mind that wouldn't let him sleep. He had a fresh filter beetle down his throat, and buttoned up his new school uniform that had be delivered to his room while he was at Edgar's.

He stared out the fake window, across the cold sea of starry black and shimmering mountain peaks. It was hard to stay calm about starting his new school when the agents of the Empress could discover what he had really come to do at any second.

Jono pondered what to do next.

He knew that he needed to find out more information about the castle. He needed to find where they were hiding the key and where they were keeping Keiko.

He was surprised that no one at the academy seemed in the least bit aware of the danger that was pushing the world to the brink. They didn't know the Empress' greed was about to bring destruction raining down upon them. It was a burden that Jonothon carried alone, the knowledge and the fear, and most of all the responsibility.

Lost in his thoughts, Jono barely heard Oscar stumble out of bed and mumble about breakfast.

"Are you all ready for your new life?" asked Isaac as he leaned off the top bunk with a smile.

Jonothon smiled back and shrugged. "I don't think I've been ready for anything. I just keep going."

"I know what you mean," said Isaac. "This is so different from school back in Eckleclypse. Two weeks on, I'm starting to get used to it. What classes do you have coming?"

Jono held a scroll that had been left with the uniform. "It's Redwake, so chemix is first."

"Are you alright? It's Bluewake," Isaac corrected him. "That's a good one, though. You'll like Dr. Stone." Isaac snatched the scroll from Jono's hand and looked it over. "Let's see here. Oh, we'll have Mechanix and the Mind together. That's great! Have your installs grown in yet?" The ayleen leaned back to get a view of the back of Jonothon's neck and nodded. "Yeah. It looks pretty close."

Jono felt the back of his neck and sure enough, there was something small and metallic growing out of his skin. The pixels that Cid shot him with were changing inside him. It made a chill run down his spine.

"Is this normal?" asked Jono squeamishly.

"Normal? It's optimal! We all need them. We've been working on using the computers installed in our brains mostly, but tomorrow Professor Wishe will take us into the library."

"The library? What's that have to do mechanix and the mind?"

Isaac smiled. "You don't know? Well, I'll leave it as a surprise then. I'm going to grab some breakfast. Are you coming?"

Jono nodded.

"Stars!" exclaimed Isaac. "There's no time! We're late!"

Jono looked at the clock on the wall. The start of the school hours had snuck up on them.

"Mathometry's your first class this wake, right?" said Isaac. "I'll show you the way."

"Thanks," said Jono.

Jono was good at mathometry and glad that his first class was something he thought he would be comfortable with.

They charged out of Capricorn corridor and down winding halls packed with students. The air smelled of bacon and syrup and made Jonothon's belly grumble. He wished he hadn't lost track of the time. The crowds thinned as students shuffled into their rooms.

"It's just down there," said Isaac, pointing to a winding staircase. "You take the third left, I think, and then it will be on your right."

"Thanks. I'll ask the 'goyles if need to."

"Ok. I'll meet you for lunch?"

Jono nodded. "Yeah. See you."

Isaac waved and ran down the hall.

The path through the halls to his first class was easy enough to follow. He was even beginning to gain a sense of direction around the tunnels of the academy, but with each step, nervousness built up inside of him.

He was finally more of a normal boy than he had ever been. No more mask or clunky heart regulator trailing him wherever he went. No more standing out as the weird kid with problems. He could start over without anyone knowing he was different.

The halls were empty by the time he reached his classroom. The door to Mathometry was in a hall lined with statues all the same shape, except for one. It wasn't a statue at all, but a muscular man with mechanical arms.

The man stood in the shadows of the hall lamps at the far end of the corridor. His metal arms were made of dark materials that glistened against the light. Pumps and pistons had replaced his muscles.

Jono paused to stare at the strange man then slowly turned back to the classroom door.

The mathometry class room was narrow, and its seats were already full of students. Geometric math problems hovered above each desk in glowing blue script. At the front of the room stood a squat man in black and purple robes beside a wall screen.

"I was informed there would be a late attendee to my class," said the toadish Professor Lumph as he stopped his lesson and glared at Jonothon.

The rest of the class stared as well.

Jono tried to creep to the nearest open seat without making eye contact.

"I did assume, however, that Ms. Drudge was referring to your untimely arrival this semester, and not your tardiness this wake."

There was a muffled eruption of giggling across the room.

"I'm sorry, sir," said Jonothon meekly.

"You have two weeks of catching up to do, young man, and I will not tolerate negligence and apathy in my classroom. If you can't keep the pace, cadet, then you will be trampled in the path of our education. Are we clear?" Lumph snorted at the last part.

"Yes, sir."

"Very good. Now, Mister Eddenwood, could you please continue to inform the rest of us on how you came to the answer of forty three point six two eight, when, as you can all see on the screen before you, that the answer is clearly fifty seven point nine three?"

Jono kept his head down but let his eyes survey this hostile territory as the unlucky student in the crowd in front of him tried to stutter out an explanation of where he must have got it wrong in the equation. A feli'yin boy caught Jono's eye and gave him a disparaging look.

Throughout the course of the lesson, Jono caught mention of the brain computers and Professor Wishe - all of which left him clueless.

The math problems were easy enough to him. On more than one occasion, Jono almost blurted out the answer before Professor Lumph had finished explaining the process for it. The answer seemed almost natural.

By the time they had gone through a previous assignment, a bell chimed across the academy. Jono left the room with a scroll full of downloaded assignments and the sinking feeling that any time to look for the key would be whittled away by class work.

The Decision of Dvaniur Grail

Geo Studies turned out to be no less demanding.

Professor Teresa Talmage was a middle-aged human woman with light skin and faded red hair tied in a bun. She wore a serious look as she pointed to various places on a floating globe. A holographic moon circled Sol 3, with a web of lights that made up the Terralunan cities.

The Professor began lesson six with a description of the Urenial prefecture of the eastern Dark End and its relationship to the economies, cultures, and survival statistics of the neighboring Morrasse and Vingalba regions.

There was a test next Redwake.

Jono scribbled down the notes over downloaded maps on his scroll computer as Talmage continued a diatribe about the significance of imported muscow dung played in the various businesses of the Urenials.

Jono's mind wandered. He scribbled senseless designs that evolved into a rendition of Attrayer's key as well as an elaborately decorated name: Keiko. When he looked up from his scroll, there was an image of an old grudgon with what amounted to a beard of crusty scales floating beside Professor Talmage.

"This was thanks to the mayor, Thadisius Scrapgrut, whom originally established the dung trade infrastructure across the entire east quadrant of the Dusk Ring. As we noted before, it was this that allowed the entrepreneurs in Vingalba to take full advantage of their nitronated soil and produce all those chilled beets we know and love."

In Jonothon's short travels, he had already visited far more interesting places than dung fields. He had no interest in beets, chilled or otherwise.

As was becoming a dangerous habit, Jono found himself caught deep in his own thoughts when the scraping of chairs awoke him to the end of the class. He downloaded the new books he was assigned to read. All the while keeping his gaze down in fear that Professor Talmage had seen he wasn't listening and would call him on it.

By lunch time, Jono had gone without any other student acknowledging him in any way. He disappeared into the crowd of healthy, normal children. It was both a relief and a disturbing experience. He followed traffic through the corridors, feeling as though there were eyes lingering on him, but no one gave any notice.

His skin itched again.

Jono noticed the pink spots on his arms had begun to peel away the skin to find tiny metal circles. The crowd pushed passed him and clogged the wide dining hall doorway.

The small black dots itched violently across Jonothon's arm. There was a second of pressure, and Jono moved his head away just in time to avoid the metal cable that shot out of his arm. The cable snaked through the crowd and bit down on the stone arch of the door. Jono's arm was yanked across his face and he stared in horror at the metal wire that cut through the line of students.

Jono could feel the tension in the wire like it was a part of him. Somewhere in his mind he could control it. He made it wiggle, but he couldn't make it release it grip on the stone.

The other students gave him annoyed glares, but he pretended to ignore them. He focused on the snake-like wire. His mind commanded it to move. Just then three other wires darted out of his back, legs and shoulder. They flung wildly in all directions and even more started to fling out from his arms. One stray wire wrapped around a tall human girl. Two cables from his legs latched onto the upper arch of the door and pulled Jonothon, dangling in the air, between the outstretched cables.

The students around him ducked and dove out of the way. The rest of his wires whipped around before flicking back to wrap around his body like a cocoon.

Jono dangled helplessly in the air above the crowd like a spider caught in his own web. He felt a tap on the cables that wrapped around his face. Hands tilted his hovering body until he saw the grimacing face of Nicklus Knox.

"Good job there, Twig," Nick snarled. "You could 'a tore someone's eye balls out with all these snapping snakes flying everywhere. This girl here . . ." he pointed to the red headed girl wrapped in the dark cable but did not move to help her. ". . . she could be suffocating even as we speak. Look at her face! You could squeeze the life right out of her with your stupidity. You can't even control your own wires."

"Stab your eyes, Twig, that's fear in 'em. You can't get all feared out now. Is that how you're gonna act when we have to fight the Solans? Or the Terraloonies? Are you gonna freak out and cut your own squad up with your wires flapping everywhere? You'll have yourself all wrapped up, nice as a Giftmas present for the Loonies to carry you away to be a slave on their rock." Nick grunted. "If I ever get put in your squad, stars, I'd shoot myself and have it done with."

Nick ducked under the mess of wires. He held onto Jono and only released him when he disappeared into the dining hall. Jono swung back and spun in his tangle of metal webbing.

It was half way through the lunch period before Isaac found him and called for help. Ms. Drudge arrived first but only supplied a barrage of insults comparable to Nick's. She eventually summoned for Edgar No Eyes, who cackled and laughed about an imaginary conversation he was having with an asparagus.

Edgar adjusted the dots on Jono's body without acknowledging that he was even doing it, and the cables slurped back into Jono's skin. He thudded hard onto the cold ground. The last cable finally freed the red-haired girl it had wrapped around, and despite losing most of her lunch time, Kirstin Orbit assured the embarrassed cadet that, although he had a serious amount of practicing to do, he would eventually get the hang of controlling his spy wires.

Jono refused to go into the dining hall and face a thousand staring eyes. Instead he made his way to his next class.

The rest of the wake continued on its steep turn downward. His mechanix teacher didn't show because she accidentally exploded her own house, with herself inside it, and needed to replace her bionetic legs, arm, and get her neurals checked. Instead, the class was forced to suffer Ms. Drudge's glaring eyes as they did worksheets that described the diagram and functions of a basic robotic digestive system.

Drills class wasn't any better.

The class took place outside the academy in a forested crag in a valley. The students were ordered to run around a booby-trapped obstacle course by their hairy, smelly, and altogether unpleasant instructor—a fuglian named Boargrin Krust.

"Give me three laps, you clunkers," snarled Krust. "Now! Timer's ticking!"

Jono lagged behind the rest of the class as he ran along the trail. He caught red and blue flashes of light cutting through the woods, accompanied by the screams and cheers of his classmates. He charge forward but a burst of blue light exploded in front of him and pushed him backward. Jono scrambled behind a boulder and tried to catch his breath.

He peeked around the rock and there in the woods was the most absurd wizard he could have imagined. A lanky robot had dressed in a blue gown and pointed hat with bright gold stars on it. The robot waved around a mechanical version of a wand. It was as unrealistic as the Day Enders thinking everyone from the Dark looked like him.

The wizard bot sent out another beam of green light through the woods.

"Look out!" Jono yelled, but the imitation magic caught another cadet and lifted him into the air.

Jono started to get up to help, but he was slammed in the back as another student tripped over him and landed face down in the dirt.

"What are you doing, hiding?" the student growled. "They're not real spells, burnt brain!"

The wizard bot leapt from the woods and shot spells out in all directions. More students charged past them, dodging the spells and firing back at the bot with arm cannons. A red spell knocked a student down. Another cadet held up her arms and created a blue shield to block a spell. The spell reflected off the shield and back at the caster, blasting the bot's head off of its shoulders.

"Get up, recruit!" someone yelled. "If you can't get through a wizard bot, you don't stand a chance against the real thing!"

By the time Jono had made it around the course once, most of the wizard bots had assumed the lesson was over and had left the course. The rest of the class had been finished for ten minutes.

Instructor Krust leaned over Jono as he lay on the ground, gasping for air. "You are the worst soldier I have ever seen."

Jono dragged himself through the halls of the academy, stopping by the dining hall long enough to grab a plate of tenderloins and mashed corn, and then headed back to his dorm room.

Near the center of the boy's dorm hallway was a room called the Den. It was musty and cluttered with tables and lots of old, comfortable chairs. Jono sat down and ate his dinner alone.

It wasn't long before the first few cadets started to filter into the Den. Some brought in their dinner trays and ate while other did their classwork or watched movies on floating screens. A feli'yin and mustecrat sat in a corner, playing a holographic fighting game. They teamed-up to punch and kick a variety of ninjas and demonic spirits as they ran through an ancient wooden dojo.

The room came to life with loud, rowdy boys watching videos and playing games.

Jono tried to catch up on class work, but after losing his place in a paragraph five times, he decided to check out what the others were doing.

Oscar slouched on a tattered leather couch watching the news. One the screen, a pretty dalphemyr woman described the opening of a new Environment Conditioning plant somewhere in the mountains of the Dark End.

". . . bringing a much needed update to the prior system. The new comfort radius will cover the full Gordric valley and allow for hundreds of new homes and new jobs to come to this pristine area. Back to you, Tom."

The screen switched to a human man, clearly a former soldier by the look of his bionetics, who sat with the view of Eies just below the cloud line.

"Thank you, Cheryl. It's great to see all these great new opportunities that come with progress. In national and local headlines, the chancellor of space development planning, Helmut Hoggs, has resigned due to health reasons with his deputy taking the reins of the beleaguered department. Collin Greaves has the report."

"That's it then?" said Jono, worried about the coming war at Dawn. "Nothing's happened, yet."

"No, no. You missed it!" said Oscar.

"What? What happened?"

"They showed this porcupie eating contest they had on at carnival in D'Arrow." Oscar snorted with laughter. "I wish I was there. It was amazing. Those guys can really chomp it down! The smaller ones were passing out from the spices."

Jono forced a smile and returned to his seat in the back.

Whatever the Empress was plotting, it hadn't happened yet. He still had time, but it was slipping like water through his fingers. Somewhere in the darkness of the obsidian crown, she was preparing for something horrible.

At the front of the den, Isaac and his friend David had taken over the game system. They laughed as they cut through zombies with holographic swords. Isaac cast a fire ball from his hollow staff in the swampy ruins of an old castle.

The sight of all the fun was like a canyon between Jono and his classmates. He couldn't help but be taken aback by the realization of it.

They don't know.

The Empress must keep them insulated from whatever is going on in the Day, he thought. She'll keep them secure and happy and by the time they finally see the truth of the rest of the world, or learn of the history of her evil deeds, it will be too late. She would tell them about glory and righteousness as they flock to their deaths.

"You don't suppose they know that you're watching them, do you?" came a deep voice from behind him.

Jono spun around. Drenched in the shadows at the corner of the room was the same muscular man with piercing silver eyes and shiny, metallic arms that had stalked him in the halls. He leaned against the wall with his arms folded and a stern look on his scarred face. His smile was as honest as it was intimidating.

"They're like this every year." The man waved a metal finger at a boy hanging upside down on the ceiling. "They're showing off their new installs to each other. It's a healthy part of the adjustment process, so I'm told."

"I saw you earlier," said Jonothon.

"You don't know who I am, do you?"

"No, sir."

"I am the commander of this school. My name is Dvaniur Grail, but do not presume to address me in the familiar." His silver eyes looked over Jono, sizing him up.

"Yes, Commander."

"By what name do they call you, recruit?"

"Jono," he said. "Jonothon Wyer, sir."

"Jono . . ." replied the commander. Grail seemed to be trying the name out to see if he liked it. His lack of further response indicated the negative.

Together, they looked at the students in the den playing and laughing and being kids.

"The imperial forces are not an easy lot to live with. Are you sure you are prepared for this commitment, Cadet Wyer?"

"I think so," Jonothon stuttered.

"Thinking is good, critical, but make sure that what you think is correct," said Grail. "There are many possible roads one can take in life. Some are led by dreams of what may be, some by good intentions, and others by the inertia of the life around them. All of that, you scan me clear, all of that is worthless if it doesn't square against reality. That's where people actually live. Whatever dreams you hold, whatever hopes you have for this venture into the empire's army, don't lie to yourself. Forget about what you want, or how you want things to be. If dreams aren't tempered by reality then reality will crush them without hesitation. Above all things in life, Wyer, be right."

Jono nodded, not wanting to disagree with him.

"This is a difficult life and success is not something easily achieved alone. Build strong friendships early; ones you can trust. They will be invaluable wherever life takes you. Your friend, Ms. Kirin, is a good one to start with. She is just as smart as you told Ms. Drudge and fiercely loyal. It is not our custom to bend any of our policies and late admissions are strictly prohibited but to tell you the truth, and this is just between you and me now, I enjoy breaking all rules I can when I know I'm in the right. We have approved the admission of your friend. Be certain to demonstrate that our trust is well vested in the both of you."

Jonothon's face lit up. "You knew . . . and Keiko, she's in?"

"She is." Grail stood and touched his hand to the wall. The stone seemed to contort itself away from him and opened into a dark passage. "She's being prepped for our mechanix program and she'll be starting classes on the wake."

Jono was wide-eyed and triumphant. Commander Grail looked back at him with a grim smile. He nodded and then, with a swift step backward, he disappeared through the wall.

"Best to get some rest, Wyer," said Grail from the other side of the wall. "It's all up hill from here."

Chapter Twenty-Six

The Metal Professor

The Capricorn doorknocker had barely bleated out the time before Jono was up with his black Windom jacket pulled over his shoulders. He tried to rouse his bunkmates, but both Isaac and Oscar responded with delirious grumbles from beneath their covers.

"We still have plenty of time," said Isaac.

"No! The green crystal melts the burn'em zombies!" snarled Oscar deliriously.

The dining hall was already saturated with delicious breakfast smells when Jono arrived, but the benches and terraces were all but empty. Jono devoured the steamy egg and potato hash he'd ordered from the table gnome. He tried to keep from burping as it made the fresh beetle filter twist around his throat like a hairball settling in.

Students filled the room, drowsily eating breakfast and finishing school work. All the while Jono's eyes were on the lookout for a particular black-haired girl. He waited and wondered if she would even know to come there. He certainly wouldn't have known if Isaac hadn't shown him where it was, although there were always the gargoyles he could have asked.

Oscar walked over with a plate covered in sticky red goo that stank worse than mugaluk. Soon the room was too crowded for Jono to even tell who was who.

After breakfast, in what Jonothon considered a particularly clever idea, he followed the gargoyles to the entrance to the girl's dorm wing. Surely, he would be able to find Keiko there.

The girl's dorm hall didn't look much different from the boy's, though it did have a statue of twin mermaids near the entrance. Jono waited impatiently, but when no one left the rooms for a while he was convinced it was no use. He must have missed her.

Jono wanted to avoided being late to class two wakes in a row, so he gave himself plenty of time and left the girl's dorm.

The chemix room was down a large corridor. Its doors were tall and wide. The moment Jonothon cracked open the door light spilled out like a rolling fog. The room was unlike any of the other cramped, dark classrooms he'd been in. It was brightened by a series of arched window screens that covered the walls. Actually, they were shaped to look like windows but instead of showing carved stone wall that surrounded them, it looked as though the room hung over the edge of a cliff overlooking a sea of green trees and rivers under clear blue skies. Jono peered into the distant fields. He was unnerved by how real it felt. A flock of pink and orange birds burst from their perches near a distant waterfall and clouded a portion of the sky as they flew over the room.

The gray stone walls that stretched to the tall vaulted ceiling reminded Jonothon of the inside of the old church near his school in Polari. The walls were lined with lab equipment full of bubbling liquids, glass tubes, and shelves of bottles filled with a rainbow of powdered minerals.

Jono walked to the front of the room and set his bag on the closest table to the black screen. Alone in the room, his curiosity enticed him to inspect further. Around the teacher's desk he discovered a pile of mechanical rubble. His first thought was that they must have been parts to be used in a class exercise, but on closer inspection it looked more like parts for a mechanix class, not chemix. There were gears and pistons and circuitry but no sign of anything biological.

Jono peered into the pile of dark materials. Beneath the clutter copper gears clicked away. A piston moved and shot steam at him, causing Jono to stumble away.

Out of the gray metal, two amber-colored circles appeared. They glowed against the metal, unmoving; and then they blinked. The metal beneath the circles formed to resemble a mouth.

"So are you early, or are they all late?" asked the metal pile.

"I'm, well . . ." said Jonothon. "I think I'm early."

"Alright then." The metal face smiled. "It hasn't been spoiled."

"What hasn't?"

"The surprise, of course!"

Jono began to worry. "Are you supposed to be here?"

"I don't see why I would be anywhere else."

"Who are you?" asked Jono as he prepared to make a run for it.

A full metal head popped out from the rest of the rubble and extended its neck closer to Jono. It had a benign expression on its mechanical face.

"I, my curious cadet, am Doctor Zacharias Stone. None other than your chemix teacher."

The teacher's metal eyebrows were raised and a decidedly goofy grin spread across his face. A huge metal hand almost bigger than Jono's whole body zoomed out and offered to shake.

"How do you do?" said Dr. Stone.

"Good. Thanks," replied Jonothon, unnerved.

The head and hand quickly returned to the pile.

"Are you a Hollow?" Jono asked. "Under the metal, I mean."

The metal man stopped. "Oh my bits and pieces, no," laughed Stone. "I'm not just a program. I'm human—or I was once, and still consider myself so. I moved over to this fantastic physique when my old body became . . . unfixable, shall we say. Aside from the occasional groan inducing joke that slips out, my brain's still healthy and whole as ever." He tapped his head and winked.

"Really? How old are you?" asked Jono, amazed by the strange robotic man.

"That depends on when you start counting."

"How did you lose your body?"

"Are you always this forward?" asked Dr. Stone.

"Oh, no. I just wondered." Jono blushed.

"It was a long time ago. Another life, some might say."

"Were you always a chemix teacher?"

"I was, well . . ." He looked at the door with a worried expression on his metal face. "Actually, I'm in the middle of something. The other students have only seen me in my larger form. I want to keep things interesting, remind them the world is full of things you don't know. So naturally, I'm going to pop up and surprise the rest of my students. Catch them off guard and give them a bit of a shock, so if you don't mind?"

"Oh." Jono smiled. "Okay then. Sorry."

"Grand. You sit there and look normal," said Stone, and then changed his mind. "Or bored, rather. Yes. Look bored."

The head disappeared again within the pile, and Jonothon sat down at the front desk.

"Don't give me away," Stone insisted.

"I won't."

It was a few minutes before the door creaked open and let the first unsuspecting student in. A girl with long brown hair sat in the back row. When nearly all the seats were filled, Jono could sense that the other cadets became restless. They looked around expectantly.

"Where is he?" said a dark brown boy.

There was a murmur of agreement amongst the students.

An amber eye winked at Jono, who tried to disguise his smile.

"Chemix is here!" boomed a deep voice that made all the students look around for its origin in awe.

"Where is he?" asked a grudgon boy.

"Maybe it's a recording," replied another cadet.

"Chemix is all around and within us!" Stone's voice boomed even louder. "It runs through our veins and wires our scrolls. It is the clothes on our backs and the stone at our feet."

The lights of the windows dimmed, and white dots spotted the air like stars.

"It powers everything from your homes to the distant stars."

Flames erupted from torch holders on the walls.

"It is the chemical makeup of everything from the tiniest bug."

A clanking roar came from behind the desk, accompanied by a massive shadow that kept stretching higher and wider until the lights burst on to reveal a gigantic clockwork golem.

"To the mightiest of creations!"

There was an eruption of fireworks in the tall ceiling. The students gasped and cheered. The doctor's golden gears clicked inside his gray frame. He was a behemoth machine, smiling with benevolence.

"We are chemix! Alive and breathing and participating in countless chemical interactions throughout our bodies."

There was a wave of contagious snickering from the students when Stone tapped his own metal chest at the last part.

"Oh, yes," Stone said. "There is chemix at work in mine, too."

Stone pulled apart the metal plate of his chest and looked down at the mesh of gears, hydraulics, and flickering lights on his hardware.

"Though it's not exactly the same, is it?" Stone added with a smile. "We have talked about the basics elements of chemix, but now I will take you from the lessons and into the reality of chemix in the world all around you. It is a world of functional magic where the fundamental elements of chemix will guide your understanding of how the world works, and how we are able to create things anew.

"Chemix is the study of how the smallest things in existence create everything around us. It is an indicator of a universal truth: everything is more complicated than it seems." Dr. Stone kneeled and pulled a yellow, bushy plant from beneath his desk.

"I will assume that by now most of you have seen these or other plants grow in the wilds of the Dark End."

He held the plant up for the students to see.

"All life must consume energy to survive, and plants are no different. Most don't eat cheese burgers, like you and me, so where, do tell, do these rooted, fragile things get their energy from?"

There were few moments of silence, wondering if it was a trick question, before a blonde girl raised her hand. "The leaves eat light, and water from their roots."

Dr. Stone nodded. "That is partially true. The plants that have evolved across the border under Blue Skies use the chlorophyll in them to photosynthesize energy from light into sugars that it can use, but consequently, I was strolling out in the gardens of Eies the other wake and I noticed a critical dilemma."

"We have no sun," blurted a boy in the back.

"Exactly! The plants on our side need another source of energy."

Stone set the plant on the top of his desk and suddenly there was a huge leaf floating above each of the students' tables.

"Look closely at the veins of the leaf as I apply a drop of rain water from the valley."

The image of a floating leaf was blurred with the clear liquid. The imaged zoomed in closer, and they were looking at tiny squares floating quickly along a vein. These squares glowed red and yellow and, as they touched, the tiny vessels faded back to green.

"Hydrosynthisis. Not only is the water used to nourish, but a chemical reaction that occurs creates energy for the plant that is spread throughout its limbs and stored in the stem. Not only that, but do you see these bristles?" The image zoomed closer. "These bristles and vents pull in the air and collect dust and microorganisms full of proteins and sugars."

Stone lifted the yellow plant off the table again, the images of the leaf disappeared.

"While that is all well and good for the plant, the next question is, what can we make of it?"

The students were silent.

"Thankfully, answers have already been found for us. This, my intrepid learners, is the napalm plant. It can be found naturally across the night and twilight rings, and is of particular use to us. Note the bulbous tube along the stalk."

He tore a small bulb off and held it up to the light.

"Now, the plant milk is usually benign, harmless that is, in fact you'll find palm milk in anything from facial wash to food supplements. This natural stalk, however, creates a unique concentration that when, exposed to sulfron . . ."

Stone broke open the bulb. Milky goo trickled out. The instant he dropped a tiny yellow pebble onto the open bulb there was a booming explosion that pushed the air against everyone's faces and echoed in the stone room.

Dr. Stone chuckled as his metal smile appeared through the dissipating smoke. His face was covered in soot from the blast.

"Don't ever try that unless your entire body is made of reinforced metal—and you have excellence insurance."

By the end of class Jono's cheeks were sore from smiling.

"On your way out, Jono, be sure to download the three books on the shelf by the door. Look over the first three chapters and don't be afraid to read ahead about anything that seems interesting. More knowledge is always better than less!" Stone said. "The rest of you, continue reading chapters four and five in the *Chemix and Me* and then we'll get onto the special topics next week. Be sure to read the chapter

The Problems with Cloning."

Jono held his scroll up to the bookshelf. The yellow book was titled *What you need to know before processing Uranium in your Grandmother's Basement: and other essential Chemix lessons.*

Jono was so caught up in the class that he almost ran into someone as he was leaving. Jono nearly dropped his scroll.

Directly in front of him, in full black, red, and silver uniform and unmistakable pink-ribboned pig-tails stood Keiko Kirin. A mischievous grin spread across her face.

Jono froze, not knowing what to do. She stepped forward and looked him over like she was inspecting a faulty machine. She poked the blue veins on his cheek and smiled. Jono started to speak, but before he could get a word out she had wrapped her arms around him and was giggling ecstatically.

"You did it, Jono! They let me in!" Keiko squealed.

"I heard. That's fantastic!"

"I knew you'd figure out a way." Keiko's brown eyes were full of joy.

"Yeah, I . . ." Jono didn't want to let her know he really didn't do anything. "So, you were in this class?"

Keiko nodded. "I got in late 'cause I was looking for you and then I saw that you were already at the front. Figured I would hang back and spy on you."

"I didn't see you," said Jono. "You should have told me you were there."

"Then it wouldn't have been a surprise, would it?"

"I guess not, but—"

"Come on! We don't have a lot of time before the next class." She grabbed his arm and pulled him, running, out into the hall.

"Where are we going?" asked Jonothon.

"This way."

They turned the corner and came to an intersection of halls. Keiko stared down both halls with a quick and ponderous look about her before darting to the left.

"Do you even know where you're going?"

"We're exploring, Jono. I already found a gear shop and the thermal viewing room this morning. There was lava everywhere. That must be how they power some of this place. It was pretty far down."

"If you want to go somewhere, you can just ask the gargoyles to point you there."

"What?" She stopped in her tracks.

"They'll tell you how to get anywhere."

"That's amazing!" Keiko sighed. "I love this place. I hope the rest of our classes are as interesting as that one. What else do you have this wake?"

Jono pulled out his scroll and tapped on the 'schedule' icon. "I'm going to meet Isaac in the library for Mechanix and the Mind."

"Really? I'm in that too!" Keiko beamed. Every little thing was like opening a new Giftmas present.

"That's great! Maybe we should explore our way towards class?"

Keiko gave him a mock frown, but as soon as it was there, it disappeared and was replaced by a smile. "Alright."

They started to walk off, but then she turned around.

"Jono," Keiko looked at him seriously. "Thanks for getting me in."

She didn't hold back on her smile, and he couldn't help but give in to her excitement.

Jono smiled back and shrugged as if he did that sort of heroic thing every wake.

"No problem."

The Code World

*T*he gargoyles clung to the darkly lit halls with fingers and tails pointing to the library.

Jonothon and Keiko came to a room larger than anywhere else in the academy. Pillars were shelved with books and winding stairs. Walkways and study areas connect pillars like the threads of a spider's web.

The distant ceiling was a domed window that opened to the dark abyss of space and stars.

A student on the seventh floor carried a stack of book toward her desk. No one would have noticed except that she stumbled and the top two books slipped over the rail and flailed helplessly toward to the floor. Before the books had fallen to the thirteenth floor, a gargoyle swooped off its perch and snatch them mid-air.

"Those are the librarians," said Isaac as he stepped from behind them. "They only do the material books in here, though. They're good at being nosy, I've learned that already." Isaac looked at Keiko. "Is this her?"

Jono turned his head, trying not to blush. "Yeah."

Keiko smiled. "Keiko Kirin."

"This is my bunkmate, Isaac Ohm."

"Pleasure." Isaac bowed. "So, you're in this class too?"

"Yeah, both of us."

"Where do we sit?" asked Jono as he looked around.

Isaac chuckled. "This is just the material library. Come on. Our classroom is down here." Isaac pointed to stairs that descended in the middle of the library.

A pair of wooden doors slid open, ushering them into a dark, circular room. There were a few students already seated. Isaac, Keiko, and Jonothon found a place to sit on plush leather seats. Jono bounced a little on his cushion.

A flash of white light burst from the darkness in the center of the room. Keiko gasped at the white, glowing woman that appeared in front of them. She sat cross-legged in midair. Long strands of white hair flowed from her head like waves of water. Her skin was a dull white with elaborate designs curving and crisscrossing all over her body and the flowing robe she wore. She floated, slightly transparent, like a ghost, in the middle of the room.

The woman smiled pleasantly and raised her hand. "Welcome. Welcome. I know you all have been eager for this wake's lesson. Please have a seat. I see our two new cadets have joined us. My name . . ." The woman waved her hand and instantly the letters appeared right in front of them. ". . . is Persephone Wishe. As the rest of you know, it is my duty as teacher of Mechanix and the Mind to facilitate your studies of two of the more remarkable creations to be born of the thinking mind."

The woman floated to the center of the stadium-seated room. "We have worked on the introductory elements to your first year installs, and this wake we shall put our Linker lessons into practice."

Jono leaned over to Isaac. "What's the linker?"

Before Isaac could answer, Professor Wishe floated over to them.

"I confirmed with the Ms. Drudge, and she says the tests show both of your installs are fully functional. Since that is the case, let's continue with the lesson and try to keep up as best you can."

Professor Wishe floated right through the rows of students. Jono spotted a butterfly-shaped projector in the middle of her transparent chest. It was the hollow-heart that projected the professor's image.

"We are going to start slowly for those of you who have not taken any linking prep classes. This is probably most of you." Wishe focused on a nervous looking mustecrat boy who was scratching his furry cheek. The attention seemed to calm his nerves, and the kind expression from Wishe's green hollow-eyes inclined him to think it was going to be alright.

"For those of you that have . . ."

Jono saw Isaac nod knowingly.

". . . then these will be helpful refreshers. Practice is an ever fruitful tree.

"For this wake's lesson we will go over an introductory linker exercise and take a peek into the library." She took in a deep, thoughtful breath, which was unnecessary for the hollow. "The connection of the mind and the electronic is a tenuous one. It is the imagination that creates the best connection of the biological mind to the hard wired one. It solidifies the graphical interpretations of the information presented to you. Embrace the illusion and use it for your benefit. Now, if everyone will lean back in your chairs—relax and place your left hand on the arm beside you."

Jono looked around at Keiko and the rows of other students, all leaning back as they were told, before he followed suit.

"Close your eyes," said Wishe in her soothing voice, "and imagine yourself standing alone in a black room."

Jono shut his eyes and stared into the black. He imagined himself standing in a cave far too dark to see anything. He couldn't tell where he was but he could feel it was somewhere dark and empty. After a few moments it began to feel as though he was indeed looking, not at the dark under his eyes, but in an unlit stone room.

"Feel the coolness in the air around you. Breath it in," encouraged Wishe's voice.

Jonothon breathed deep from his nostrils.

"Imagine that on either side of you stand the stone walls of a hallway."

Jono cracked his eyes open—not in reality, but to the hallway in his mind. He could feel the cool air that permeated the black abyss.

"There is a cool, gentle draft coming from in front of you," Wishe said. "Let yourself feel it brush against your face."

The teacher's voice was quieter now, as though Jono moved further away from her. The soft air gave him goose bumps.

"Now, look into the distance ahead. Out of the darkness, you can see something. Right at the center . . ."

The distant voice trailed off into the black Jono was walking away from. He saw the thing in front of him: a soft light that slowly grew in intensity. As he stepped toward it, the light grew brighter and began to reflect off the stone walls and wood buttresses around him. The closer he got to the center of the room, the wider the room became. He passed books that floated in the air as he came to the source of the light.

A clear crystal ball floated above an ornate stone pedestal. A live, constant flame burned on the sphere from the outside in. He soon noticed more of the strange, round candles hovering around the circle room. The floating books hung in thick groups to create walls around the inner circle. Banners of different colors hung from wooden arches.

"So you're the first, are you?"

Jono spun around despite the calm demeanor of the voice behind him.

Persephone Wishe stood beside him, not as the holograph in the real world, glowing and transparent, but with the look and quality of a real flesh and blood human. She raised her hand at the wall as a tan girl with jewelry above her eyes appeared as though she was a reflection of the flame, blending into life out of nothing. Jono stepped back and soon another student flickered into life.

The room then filled with students.

Keiko stepped from behind a red banner with a delighted smile on her face as she flickered into the room.

"Awesome," she said, beaming at Jono.

"Gather 'round the center, everyone," Wishe said as she waved them to come closer. The students kneeled around her in a circle and whispered to each other about the oddity of the code world around them.

"Can we do anything here?" asked a girl.

"Can we fly?" asked a mustecrat.

"Or ride on a tiger?" asked an ayleen.

"This room," Wishe explained calmly, "is a learning utility. While it is primarily a library, it can serve to teach you about anything from aerodynamics to zoology. It is not only a world unto itself, written in code and networking with your brain, but it is a connection to the physical world at large. If one were so informed, this room could be used to connect to nearly every city in the world as if you were there yourself. We can visit the Endless Coast or the yellow desert of Sa Rah without so much as breaking a sweat."

Jono thought of the Round Hall at Caer Midus and how many of the lords had only appeared there as if by magic. "So you mean we could talk to anyone in the world from here?"

"That is not all," replied Wishe. "You can actually see the world as though you were really there. The people talk and see you as well. I would love, if some wake, we may even visit the Blue Skies. However, their bureaucratic quagmire and inability to see the reason for such an exchange has left such propositions inaccessible for the foreseeable future."

"I don't want to go to the Day even if it's in hollow form," snorted a turtlup boy, his scaly neck shrinking into his thick shell. "Just sitting under that star would probably burn away an IQ point per second."

"That explains a lot," said an ayleen girl. "They got brain burn."

"Since that idea does not seem to appeal to you," interjected

Professor Wishe, "I am hopeful to arrange such a visit with the Empress herself, later in the term."

A rush of terror came over Jonothon. The students began to murmur excitedly, but Wishe merely continued with the lesson.

"The first thing you will need to understand is how to navigate within the system of the library." Wishe took a leather-bound book floating beside her and opened it. The wall to her right pushed away and revealed a new hallway lined with books.

"This world is a computer system, and as such it has structure and purpose. This book is not just a book. These walls are not just walls. They have ulterior meaning here. They represent a functional element to the system, the organizational structure by which information is stored. In the library, books are both sources of information as well as keys to subcategories of information."

Wishe pointed to the hanging tapestries, the green one.

"That is the biological."

She pointed to the red one.

"Historical."

Her explanation continued with blue being "Fiction", purple referring to the "Mechanical", "and so on. You must remember that everything here has an order. Categories will lead down into far more specific areas and details. Everything is connected to other categories. This world of knowledge is yours for the taking. It will be as focused . . ." She pulled her arms in and made the room shrink around them. They lost sight of the walls and the light of the candle spheres flickered against their faces.

". . . or as wide . . ." Wishe spread her arms and every stone surface around them instantly spread far away.

The students gasped as the floor itself disappeared down an endless and dark tunnel of rooms and hallways and books. The ceiling expanded up a hundred stories before bursting with bright sunlight as it opened to the illusionary surface. The children cheered at the amazing sight. Most had probably never been further than the Twilight ring, Jonothon thought, so the sight of a blue sky with a fully beaming sun was absolutely remarkable.

". . . as you can imagine!" Wishe finished with a sense of satisfaction.

Jono couldn't help but stare, transfixed by the white clouds glistening above them.

Keiko grabbed his shoulder to get his attention. White birds with long tails flew upward from the abyss, toward the Day's light above them. Isaac had grabbed one by the tail and it pulled him up without any strain at all.

"Let's go see the blue!" Keiko cheered to Jono as they both grabbed a tiny bird.

A warm wind howled past them as the birds floated up and breached the surface. It was breathtaking; perfect green grass covered rolling hills that strolled lazily into the distance. Moss-covered stones thrust out of the ground around them. Jono spun around with a smile. They weren't just stones, but the ruins of gigantic statues. A huge gray hand protruded from the grass, and gripped around a broken stone staff. The first year cadets scattered themselves to explore the new world.

Jono walked to the base of two giant stone feet cut off unevenly just below the knee. He ran his hand against it and smiled at the cool feeling of rock.

"I wonder if this is real," he said to Keiko and Isaac. "Somewhere, I mean. Under Blue Skies." He touched the stone. It felt cold to his mental hand. "The ruins of an ancient civilization."

The three of them strolled through thick grass and moss-covered ruins.

"Who do you think these are supposed to be?" Jono added with a gesture to the broken stone humans.

Isaac shrugged. "They could be old kings or something."

"I bet they got a bunch of slave bots to build these for them," answered Keiko.

"You're very nearly right, on that," said a squeaky voice.

They turned to each other, as that was where the voice had come from. Between them fluttered an azure-winged pixiefly; its tiny white body resembled something like a big-eared elvayn.

"Excavation of the ruins of Port Pius indicates an ancient nation known to us as the—"

The pixiefly was cut off by the roar of a tiger and the shrill laugh of a group of students. Keiko nudged Jonothon and they ran over to see the tiger walk toward Isaac. The entire left side of it was skinless, and every time Professor Wishe pointed at it, another layer was lost. Muscles stretched as it moved and then disappeared to the bones surrounding pumping organs.

"The heart itself is a fascinating organ. Look how it pumps blood, pushing it all over the body," said Professor Wishe.

The students scattered and after a good deal of time exploring the sunny surface of the library, a crucial thought came to Jono's mind.

"How do we get out?" he asked the professor.

A group of young heads turned to look at him as though he alone was spoiling their fun and would end their time in the library.

Wishe smiled. "That is a very astute consideration." She came closer and leaned down to Jono. "Is there any reason in particular? Do you want to leave?"

"No. I just . . ." Jono felt uncomfortable defending himself when his question seemed so obvious and appropriate. "I just wanted know."

"It is time, isn't it?" said Wishe. "You've all done very well, but we must be moving on. We will depart the library the same way we came in. Remember, this world is a trick of the perceptions. It is a tactile interface for the electronic files and data. In truth, you are all sitting comfortably in the lecture hall. Now shut your eyes to this world. Shut away its impulses from your mind. Let the light fade from you."

Wishe stood in the center of the students pushing the world away from them.

"Step back into the dark . . ."

A black cloud grew from around her and spread over the children. The grassy ruins faded into oblivion.

". . . and awake. Focus not on your sight, but on your body. Breathe in deep and exhale slowly. Feel yourself breathe. Feel the muscles tense and slowly release. Come back to the physical by being aware of it again."

Jono focused on the feeling of his clenched eyes, and then cracked them open.

"When you are ready, open your eyes."

The round hall was still dark, but Jono could see it so much clearer now that his physical eyes were more accustomed to the dark.

The professor was once again a floating hologram.

"Please stand and stretch a little. I know that the first time in the code world can be a little unnerving. Some people will clench muscles without knowing it and come back feeling sore. Do be careful as you stand."

The doors from the round hall burst open with a roar of cadets recounting their experience to each other. Everyone was invigorated by their illusionary world, but Jono proceeded with trepidation, trying to grasp the depths and connections of a world with such amazing things in it, a world he had barely begun to know.

A molten ball collided in the air with an altogether innocent pie. The force from the glowing orange ball of fire thrust the helpless dessert in the opposite trajectory and, in an explosion of burning purple berries and brown sweetened crust, directly upon the face of a snarly gargoyle. The direct hit was met with an uproar of cheers from the dining hall terrace, but the gargoyle simply licked the pie from his face then flew away to wash it off.

Nicklus Knox pranced around on the edge of the third year terrace, emboldened by his stunning victory over the dastardly pie.

A barrage of berry bits sprinkled down on the table below, and neither Jono nor his friends were spared at least a dab of the pie shrapnel in their hair. Isaac stopped a teacher—the lanky, black cloaked Professor Mortis—as he passed by and pointed out the indiscretion.

"Shouldn't you make him come down, or stop?" said Isaac. "That's dangerous. And annoying."

Mortis only lent a half interested glance up at the pompous boy, and then shrugged. "Actually, I think this is quite an appropriate opportunity for Mister Knox. If he indeed falls and breaks his neck, well then, that lesson will be far more learned than if I were to explain it to him. Or if, perchance, he succeeds in impressing the girl he keeps smiling at, well, then that lesson would be learned as well. The pie, of course, is a great pity though." He whipped a clump of purple goo from Isaac's shoulder. "Why did it have to be schnazberry?" He shook his head and walked somberly away, leaving a gaping Isaac annoyed at the celebrating boy's second victory.

Keiko came over to them from a nearby table of giggling girls. She had already made friends with all the girls in her dorm hall and was saying hello to more people than Jono had ever talked to at his old school in Polari.

"Marin said they had a huge welcoming ceremony this year in a stadium in the city," she told Jonothon.

"Oh yeah, you really missed out by being late," said Isaac. "They had cool fireworks and the charger from the Eies Explorers made a speech. There were new students there that were going to the other academies, too. A lot were just in hollow form. I'm glad I'm not going to D'Arrow. Those kids look crazy."

Keiko smiled at Jono. She was elated to be at any academy at all.

Oscar and David agreed that Windom was the undisputed best academy. Jono ordered a plate of gruel cakes. The food was good, but soggy.

"That's just the beginning," said David. "Last year some of the fifth year students snuck an intoxicated dirt troll into the girl's dorm on Giftmas Eve. It smashed up their presents then sniffed its way to the kitchen and ate half the school's stock of mince meat pies. It took a gaggle of gargoyles stinging it with venom to bring it down." David laughed.

For the entire span of lunch, Jonothon had forgotten about his search for the key, about the impending doom between the Dark and Day. For the first time in his life, he sat with friends, laughing, eating, and not once did he worry about being made fun of.

For the first time he felt like a real, normal boy.

Chapter Twenty-Eight

Cloaks

"*I* bet they smell."

"All of them?"

"It's a proven fact their bodies emit sweat pheromones to attract a mate."

"Right."

"Also, all that heat there makes them emit even more sweat, and that makes them smell."

"You would think all the light would at least make their eyes really good."

"Nope. It's too much for them to handle, so their eyes limit themselves on what they take in. They actually have duller sight then we do."

"I bet it's just all that sun burning their brains like boiled eggs."

"That is not precisely accurate, my dear partners-in-learning," pointed out Professor Ronver Viscus as he took control of the open class discussion. "The biologically-founded intellectual inferiority of the Sola population comes from an extensive and clearly understood science."

The curved front walls of the classroom of *Modern Histories of Sol 3* had transformed from their apparent cold gray stone into the image of a bright open field of crisp green grass, blue skies, and spotted wooden houses surrounded by trees. Along the right wall strolled a couple of Solans with pleasant demeanors.

With a wave of his wand, Professor Viscus froze the image of the walking human and dragged him from the wall and into the center of the room. Half of the human lost its outer layers to show his bone structure and major organs.

"The evolutionary process over millennia shows us how the environment of the Day has naturally selected certain characteristics as to thrive, such as exaggerated self-image, relaxed work ethics, and superstition. This is similar to how the Dark End has conditioned ingenuity, integrity, and vitality to propagate within its own population. There are certainly cultural catalysts that exacerbate these trends, but it is all grounded in the effects environmental conditioning have upon biology and culture.

"I believe Mister Espinosa brought up pheromones and mating. That is a critical factor in what I will now describe." Professor Viscus waved his wand again, and the walls displayed a row of half see-through humans all with blue circles around a part of their exposed brains.

"We all know the increased source of light makes agricultural production far more prevalent under the Day than on our end of the world. That aspect of an ease of survival, including the docile nature of the preponderance of beasts in their farm regions, created a natural lack of incentives for efficiency and technological advancement along with instilling an intense value in favor of personal activity. It is simply an easier life under the Blue."

While the right wall retained the circled brains, the front and left wall projected video of Sola societies enacting the precise behaviors the professor described. Smiling Solans played and lounged in an outside bistro beneath the shade of thick trees. Jonothon thought the buildings looked similar to those he saw in the village below Caer Midus, but there was a distinct lack of decorative plants and the smiles on everyone's faces looked forced and artificial.

"When that pleasure oriented focus turned their societies away from production and toward cultural status, the mating habits turned with it. No longer were mates looking for the better farmer or the better miner. Instead, they sought out those that exhibited culture quality values, such as fixations on unproductive activities, games, art, or consumption. And it stands that those individuals biologically predisposed to succeed at such activities also emitted a particular class of pheromones. Those people mated at high percentages and created more offspring. The production-minded segments of their population were far less reproductive. When you extrapolate that trend over ultra-millennia, you can see how that pervasive condition created the modern flaws in the bipolar and shortsighted culture that exist currently.

"Even more confounding than the ingrained laziness of natural Solans," added Viscus, "is the fact that this has spilled over to affect our own society. Their isolated perception has led to their tragic support of the Terralunan blockade on our planet, as did their disdain for advancement and change and their altogether celebration of mediocrity. What else do we know about the common characteristics of the cultures of the Day?"

A feli'yin boy raised his hand. "They have a fragmented government which makes sure nothing gets done quickly, or at all."

"They worship the son of the dead star," said a girl whose hair was tied back in black fuzzy balls. "Like its magic or something."

"After they harvest they'll have huge parties where they waste almost a third of what they've produced."

"In the Day," said Clarissa Bauer, as she played with her red braided hair, "they still have temples to worship the Seven Seraphs. They still think they're real."

"So?" asked Jono, feeling lost by the surrounding conversation.

The classroom ignited in uproarious laughter, even Oscar, sitting next to him couldn't contain his toothy grin and guttural chuckle.

Jono looked around, embarrassed. "Or, I mean, weren't they real at some time or based off of actual people or . . . something?"

"Actually, this relates to my point earlier, doesn't it?" Viscus smiled.

"You see, this is another example of the cultural activities that rule the Solan lifestyle. The prevalence of mythologies throughout Sola illustrates their fixation on fantasy and ideals opposed to the functional reality appreciated in our own lands, correct?"

But Jonothon had met Solans, and they weren't all that bad. There must be more to it, Jonothon thought. "I guess, but, well, it seems not everything over there would be just because it's easy or comfortable. Maybe they just like to do different things." Jono paused before adding, "This all just doesn't seem . . . correct."

Professor Viscus stepped in front of his desk but tried to not appear too aggressive. "Do you think, then, that the methods to describe their limited intelligence are not properly scientific?"

"Well, no, I guess it's not that . . ."

"Do you propose an alternate theory to the cause of their mental limitations?"

"No, it's . . . I'm just not so sure all that is true."

Clarissa audibly choked down a laugh.

There was a wave of loosely concealed snickers across the other desks, but all eyes were on the professor who wore an artificial smile plastered on his face.

"My boy, the wide world is far more different than what you may have encountered in some beast herding, mineral town secluded on the distant ends of the Dark. There is real method to the beliefs and a web of truths below the surface of illusion. If you keep your mind open to the idea that some of us may have something to teach, you just may find a little room to learn."

Jono slouched in the chair and wished he could shrink down so small he could hide behind an atom. He didn't say another word for the rest of the class.

Jonothon's first Cloak Operations Training course was held in an incredibly dark room in the bowels of the academy. Only the dim flicker of sparse torches differentiated the room from the endless shadows. But he could tell he was not alone in the black. He heard the soft scuffling of their feet but couldn't see them.

"I don't think he's old enough," said a voice through the wall of shadow.

"Are you sure that this is right, professor? He doesn't look like he could do first year drills, let alone keep up with us."

"Sounds clunky to put a first year in a third year class."

"Too right. He'll probably just get himself killed. Remember that booby trap run we did at the end of last year, Elise? Even Hector busted his arm. This twig will probably break something permanent."

"That's true, as I can see," answered a girl's voice. "It must be an error."

"No," growled a snide, deep voice from behind the shadows. "There is no mistake that Mister Wyer is designated for this class." A lanky form materialized out of the darkness, as if its molecules were being assembled from nothing. Professor Thelix Goest stood tall with gray skin and pointed features. His ears pointed back and small gray bones jutted out from his skin. His black hair hung thick around his head. Jono had never seen a dalphemyr this close before.

Behind the professor materialized the forms of a boy and a girl; they were the twins Jono had seen with Nick during his first trip into the dining hall.

"Do you even have your cables?" asked the boy.

"Doesn't look like from here, Kain," said Elise.

Jono assumed they were referring to the snake-like wires that had come out of his arms, and he nodded an affirmative.

The girl snatched his hand and held it close to her eye. She grunted at the metal dot on his arm and then tilted it back and forth to test how the light reflected off his skin.

"No cloaking skin," she concluded.

"Look!" said Kain, pointing at Jonothon's face. "He still has his original eyes." The exasperated tone in his voice made it clear he didn't approve. "Oh, come on! This has to be a joke."

A few more students joined them in the sparse light.

"Regardless of the peculiar circumstances of our meeting," Professor Goest informed the rest of the students, "we will fulfill our task with absolute attention. Regardless of the reason, it falls to us to get this child prepared for what awaits."

Goest grabbed Jonothon by the shoulder and made him stand in the center of the darkness. The room lit up to reveal the balcony of a brilliant castle where a clouded sky glowed in peach and pink. The walls were laced with gold trim and decorated in ornate lettering.

Jono reached out to touch the wall, but his hand went right through it. It was a simulated world much like the game in the den, but far more elaborate.

"It is my belief that the greatest teacher is experience," said Goest. "You will try, you will fail, you will learn, and then you will try again. The area before you is a simulation of the castle of Systine, a stronghold of the Solan military located in the Mor'Ning ring. Your mission is to infiltrate the communications network and disrupt their ability to transmit data to the thirteenth division of the Sola ground fleet. Make it look like a physical system failure. A basic illusion virus will be sufficient. Are we clear on your instructions?"

Jono struggled to find which of the near infinite questions he should ask first, but Goest didn't wait for him to straighten out his thoughts. He could only gape at them.

"Why am I not surprised?" Goest shook his head and disappeared behind a marble wall.

The balcony reminded Jonothon of what he imagined Illius would have stood on. Jono snuck through flapping violet drapes and into the first room of the castle. The rugs were plush, and the carved wood furniture seemed like delicate relics of a time when such things were made by hand and blade. The room was clearly not designed for communication hardware; it was more of an extravagant office.

The arched double doors at the front were only a hologram, but when his hand reached its place in the air the image reacted as if it were real, and the door opened. He poked his head out and spied a hallway beside a wide stairwell. He couldn't see anyone, but he could hear footsteps to his left so he seized the opportunity and ran as fast as he could to the right. He charged through the white and gold hall and cut around a sharp corner just as the knight spotted him.

The knight lifted his gun blade without hesitation and fired. The loud blast shattered through the hall and Jono stumbled backward, tripped over his left foot, and hit the floor.

The simulation froze. His chest actually stung from the blast. He touched his hand to the metal regulator over his heart, surprised the room could actually make him feel pain.

"Try again," said the unpleasant Goest from behind the illusionary walls.

The false world reset to the balcony, and this time Jono tried to find any way to use his cables to link into the communications system. He searched for and found a plug near the center of the opulent office. He was able to break into the security cameras, but a guard walked into the room. Jono hid behind a desk but was spotted, and shot, again.

They tried the exercise again and again for what seemed like hours. Every time Jono found a solution to one problem, a whole new one was there waiting to defeat him.

"Why do you think you were wrong?" asked Goest after Jono was caught exiting a vent to the communications room and subjected to a full body barrage of stun blasts.

"I . . . I don't know." Jono trembled on the ground, feeling sore and abused.

"What did you learn about this test?"

"It's, well, it's difficult. I don't have enough information about where things are."

Professor Goest slammed down an invisible button on the wall. The room returned to black shadows and cold stone.

"Of course you don't have enough information. You have to be smarter than that! You will never have all the information you want. That does not change the fact that you must find a way to succeed. Do you think the Solans are going to give you any second chances? Do you expect the Terralunans to invite you into their prison stations for tea and then let you leave? If you, all of you, are not performing at peak standards, then you might as well pack your bags for the slave pits or the torture chambers of the Terralunan tunnels. It is not good enough to simply succeed, such success is more coincidence than not. You must be so far superior to them, so thoroughly prepared and flawlessly executed that you can actually be expected to return to service alive." Goest turned to Jono with a chilling stare. "I do not know for what purpose you were sent here, boy, but I will not release you to any venture without the proper training. You cannot go into the pit of the enemy unarmed for the dangers that await you."

Jono held his breath, terrified and unable to reply. There was a vicious look of curiosity in the professor's eyes he couldn't shake. All of their eyes searched him, questioning why he was there, questioning every aspect of his existence. They were trying to understand, and Jono knew then what a danger their intense scrutiny was to his mission to recover the key.

One thought repeated in his mind, over and again, as he sullenly traversed the halls after class: his cover would not hold long under their scrutiny.

They are going to find out.

A Boy in Wolf's Clothing

ono didn't meet with his friends for dinner. He grabbed a bowl of dejaaj stew and retreated to the back of the boy's den.

His time was running out.

He poured over news clips, looking for any sign of the coming disaster. He scoured the table's computer screen for any information he could find out about the Crown castle. There were simple schematics and maps of the Crown and the academy. The structure of the castle itself was not only the exterior crown that ran along the mountain ridge; it extended through the vast tunnels throughout the entire mountain itself. Looking closer, there were numerous places where the academy and Crown connected, but what Jono really needed was some way to search the rooms of the castle. He needed to know which rooms or areas to look for the key.

He needed to spy on them.

"What are you doing?"

Jono jumped so suddenly that he almost fell. Keiko was standing in front of him. "I thought only boys could come down to these dorms?" Jono stuttered.

"Yeah," Keiko laughed. "The gargoyles stopped me the first couple times, but I fooled them." Keiko pointed to her clever disguise: a big, ugly hat and a baggy overcoat. She leaned over the table and looked at the schematic. "What's that?"

Jono shut the screen off. "It's nothing." Jono tried to smile casually. "I was just studying."

"If you say so." Keiko stepped back with a mischievous smirk and a shrug. She winked at him and strolled to the tattered couch.

Jono wondered if she knew something was up. He was sure she wouldn't turn him in, but he didn't know what to make of her learning the truth.

The boy's den looked like a dungeon lorded over by teenage boys who never had any mothers. Despite the clutter of bubble cans, hollow game controllers, stacks of water worn books, and enough mechanical parts strewn about to make one think that an army of robots exploded, it had a certain charm to it. A few tapestries and posters colored the gray walls. Foam chairs that littered the ground were comfortable, conforming to offer support in any odd position, and the maze of shelves and secluded crevices made it feel like a home Jono never knew. The rest of the boys arrived and filled the room with noise.

A hovering screen displayed the news where a smiley mustecrat and a well-groomed ayleen woman described the important events of the wake, critical to the lives of all Eies citizens. The broadcast was universally ignored until there was mention of a Sola shipment of supplies that had been sent passed the atmosphere to the Terralunans.

"Those sun-burnts are unbelievable!" said Nick to a murmur of approval around him.

"Too right," said Isaac.

"Why don't they just let us alone and hide under their blue?" grumbled Oscar.

"You can't reason with those that think reason is the path to the Pit," said Nick, slouching on a foam chair. "The Empress won't take much more of it, neither. We need to firebomb a few of their capitals to get them off our backs and us back to the stars. Just wait. It's coming."

Isaac and David returned to a corner of the room wearing black gloves that projected the image of a sword in David's hand and a gem encrusted ax in Isaac's. The hollow-realm of a haunted forest flicked into existence around them and the two friends proceeded to hack their way through giant spiders and evil gnomes, all the while collecting gold and items dropped from the satchels of holographic creatures.

Nick slouched in a chair in the far corner as he chatted over a screen with someone. It sounded like he was bragging.

Keiko fussed with her disguise and cheered on Isaac and David as they smashed through a barrage of gromlin warriors. On occasion she would turn her head and flash a smile at Jonothon.

Jono returned the smile, more authentically each time. He reached into his pocket and pulled out the memory watch Dahlia had given him. He ran his thumb over the phoenix and the capricorn looking at the star. A part of him yearned to be home in the old wood house where the sky was always twilight, but his fearful heart reminded him that it was also the place where he was weak and alone and nothing would ever change.

He looked at the others in the room just as Isaac swung his fiery ax through the head of a skeleton. Isaac caught his eye and held up his ax with pride. They all looked so happy. The world was only beginning to them, and they had a lifetime left to explore it.

It was only Jonothon who knew they didn't. The end was coming and neither the Empress nor the Sage could or wanted to stop it. He breathed in a slow, cautious breath and let himself enjoy a simple smile at all of his new friends. The beetle filter tickled his throat, but he suppressed the urge to throw it up. For a moment he wondered if they would hate him if they knew his true purpose, but then he quickly disregarded the possibility. They were good. They were just living a different life. Jono sat there in the musty room, and tried to soak in the shouts and laughter through his skin, knowing it was temporary and precious. Whether he succeed or failed, he would be an outcast in both sides of the world. So instead of searching for the key, or doing his class work, Jonothon sat quietly in the midst of the rambunctiousness and held onto the joy with the entirety of his mind.

The thunderous collision of solid book against stone desk sent a collective gasp among the classroom. Jonothon's eyes flicked open in shock and saw the sweaty face of Professor Lumph staring back at him.

"I am hoping you had only been removing dust from your eyes for the past five minutes while we reviewed yesterwake's assignment," said Lumph.

"I was paying attention," Jono insisted.

"Then you wouldn't mind sharing your answer for problem seventeen."

Jono cleared his throat. His mind raced, and the computer embedded in his brain seemed to click away as it helped him process the answer.

"It's forty two point nine six degrees."

Lumph snarled at the correct answer and turned back to the rest of the class.

Jono sighed and sunk back into his chair. He had downloaded the schematics of the Crown to the computer that the pixels had built in his brain and every moment he could spare he spent with his eyes shut, scouring the mental map for signs of where the Empress might be keeping Attrayer's key.

He had found a wing of the castle that he was certain was an armory, and another that was a gigantic information processing bank. He imagined that it had something to do with the infamous spy camera network the Empress used to oversee the whole of the Dark End—the "Eyes of Eies" they called it.

Jono had wanted to do nothing but search for the key; however his early wake was unfortunately filled with the usual series of inconvenient distractions one could expect from a military academy.

In Geo Studies he was berated by Professor Talmage for trying to sleep, but it was only in the darkness of his shut eyes that he could see all the detail of the schematic that projected from his brain.

"Find your own pieces, you dust mites!"

Jono stopped at the corner by his mechanix class to catch Edgar No Eyes beside a disassembled suit of armor. Edgar swatted at the air with a disembodied metal arm. A line of cadets held tight the opposite wall as they snuck by the crazed man, unnoticed.

"Hey, stranger!" Keiko popped up from behind Jono.

"Hey, you're in mechanix this hour?" Jono was surprised to see Keiko had yet another class with him. He imagined Commander Grail might have done it intentionally, thinking back to his advice about building strong friendships.

"Yeah." Keiko's smile was weaker than normal. "I thought they let me skip ahead from first year, but I guess they bent the rules enough already." She shrugged. "I'll just have to show off a little until they have to move me up." Her infectious smile was back.

So was their regular teacher.

Professor Raina Helios was a dark skinned woman with a wide smile and bubbling energy. The class broke up into teams of two and was assigned a box of mechanix parts and a tattered schematic of the robot they were supposed to build.

Jono was convinced Keiko could have pieced the robot together blindfolded, but instead she insisted Jono learn how to do it.

He held up a bent piece of metal he couldn't find on the instructions. After he thought about it for a little too long, Keiko explained what it was.

"Knee joint cap," Keiko said with a glance. "See the little lip on the inside there? That means it goes on the right side."

They sat apart from the class near a clear wall that protected them from the lava on the other side.

"Isn't Windom fantastic?" said Keiko with starry eyes. "And this is just the beginning—you're missing a pressure hinge—and from here on out, we're going to be able to do so much more. We'll get more installs and go on field trips all over the Dark!"

Jono was still surprised at her enthusiasm. "Yeah, but you lived at that factory. You got to help build the biggest mechs on the planet."

"I didn't actually work on things much myself," Keiko admitted without hesitation. "That black piece needs oil and connects those pistons—but it's more than that. We'll get to see places all over the whole Dark End, and maybe even breach atmo. I think it's coming. The end of the blockade. The world is going to open up and we're going see it all. We'll be a part of making that happen all because you happened to stumble into my shop in Dollup."

Jono tried to attach a piston to what could have been the arm of the robot, but when he spied Keiko's disapproving look from the corner of his eye he moved it to the leg.

"I had a cousin that was in the academy," she said. "Not Windom, though. He graduated from Crossridge."

"Really? The sheriff at my home town went there too."

Keiko nodded. "He did really great, too. They made him second captain by the time he graduated."

"Is he abroad, or in the city?" said Jono, trying to be engaged. "We should try to meet up with him."

"No. He died a long time ago, in Eve's Dale. I only know him from recordings. It's not easy to make the world better, but I think the gears are moving and we're going to help, Jono. That's what being here means."

Long before the end of class they had succeeded in assembling the simple robot. It walked between the two of them, poking at their shoes and staring up at them with a ponderous look on its simple metal face. On the back of its robotic skull were connectors similar to the one Jono had used in his Cloaks class.

"Can you link into it?" Keiko pointed to the tiny plug on the back of the robot's head.

"I don't know. I can try." A wire snaked out from his forearm, and Jono plugged it in. In front of his eyes his eyes flashed lines of odd, untranslated code. The strain made his head ache, but he managed to get the robot to dance. Its tiny metal feet skittered across the floor as it flailed rhythmically.

Chapter Thirty

Great Expectations

rills class was worse than before.

Commander Grail had joined the class to oversee the progress of the first year cadets, and instructor Krust was even more snarling as he belted out impossible orders. The cadets ran along the obstacle course, and Jono tried his best to keep up with everyone else. He'd changed out his beetle filter, but even then his lungs and heart weren't used to pumping blood and air through him so quickly.

On his first lap, he had managed to dodge a levitation spell and fire breath but stepped on imitation vine mines, twice. His ankles and hands were gnarled as he broke free from the briars.

Jono stumbled to a stop and leaned on his knees to catch his breath. He had two more laps to go.

"Wyer! Are you waiting for mage knights to run you over?" Krust spat from across the track. "Keep running!"

Jono glanced at Commander Grail's stern face. It was hard to say if he was disappointed, but he was clearly not impressed.

A crowd of students charged past them, completing their second lap. Jono bowed his head, took a deep breath, and then ran on down the course.

Jono sat quietly at dinner. He nodded politely as Isaac and Oscar debated whose favorite band was better, *Inconsolable Crush* or *The Valence*. After a while, Jono said he was going to bed early because he was sore from drills. This was absolutely true, but more importantly he needed the time alone to search for any sign of the location of the key.

Jono lay in his bed with an image of the castle hovering in his closed eyes. He'd stared at it for hours. Jono rubbed his eyes. How was he ever going to make it in?

"Aha!"

Jono leaned over the bed and was surprise to see Keiko's head poking out of the stone wall.

"Jono!" she giggled with joy then disappeared again into the wall.

Jono slid out of bed and walked cautiously to the wall.

"Hello?"

As he was about to touch what looked like hard stone, Keiko's head popped out again just in front on his face.

"There are tunnels everywhere! Come on!" she said.

"How did you find them?"

"I tried to get over to the boy's dorms again, but the 'goyles kept stopping me, so instead I went exploring and I found a tunnel behind the old knight statue over by the Chemix room. I've just been wandering around and here I am!"

Jono squinted. "Those are probably only for the teachers to use."

"Then it probably goes somewhere interesting," Keiko replied.

"What if they kick you out for it?"

Keiko shrugged. "What if I live my life worrying more about consequences instead of seizing opportunities? It's the same thing with me coming with you across hundreds of kilems of barrens on the slim chance that I could get into a school that already rejected me, and that turned out okay."

Keiko's head disappeared into the wall, and this time, after a moment of doubt, Jonothon followed her.

The tunnels wound through the stone halls; tiny cracks let them spy into empty classrooms and a tattered mech shop and a teacher's office. They came to a wall where a stone column twinkled differently than the ones beside it.

"It's a false wall," Keiko said.

"Where does it go?" asked Jono as he searched the wall for any crack to show to the other side.

Keiko shook her head then pushed against the stone. It bent but wouldn't open.

"I guess it's locked," said Keiko.

The tunnels ascended the cavernous school inside the mountain. Keiko and Jono climbed steps and came to an arched door. The door itself seemed to fade as eerie orange dust hovered in the air, shimmering like drowsy fairies. The glistening cloud was cut as a large figure stomped through the hall. The two explorers ducked back and, as the figure walked away, they could see the light reflect off the man's metal arms.

"Let's follow him," said Jono, and Keiko nodded excitedly.

Commander Grail's footsteps were loud enough that they could hear them clearly from the other side of the stone wall. The hidden path followed alongside his path through the hallway and up a series of stairs until the commander stopped at a particularly nasty looking gargoyle sitting in an alcove. The commander whispered to the stone beast for a moment before it stepped aside and Grail walked straight through the wall.

Jono and Keiko froze. Was the commander in the tunnels with them? They scrambled for a place to hide. They ducked into an alcove where the shadows hid them from view. When the deathly silence finally assured them no one was coming, Keiko built up the courage to nudge Jonothon forward to find out where Commander Grail had gone. A new shard of light cut through the shadows in the tunnel ahead of them. Jono crept up nervously, until the light met his eyes.

On the other side of the wall, Commander Grail sat in a leather chair. Grail was surrounded by floating screens that showed rooms all over the academy. The image on one screen was moving. It turned to its side and showed a gargoyle looking back at it. The image on the screen then leapt outward and dove from its perch and soared around a spire of the castle. The wastelands of night were on one side, the brilliant clouds of the city on the other. Not only were they looking through the eyes of the gargoyles, but they were spread over the Crown castle!

A trembling excitement grew out from Jonothon's heart and all over his body. These were the castle's security screens! Wherever the Empress had the key, she would certainly have her security network looking over it.

On the screen directly in front Grail there appeared a metal door with an intricate lock system. Jono's eyes widened with recognition. Whatever they were protecting behind that door was clearly valuable.

"That's it," Jono said, the words slipping from his mouth.

"That's exactly it, Mister Ohm," said Persephone Wishe as Isaac spread his fingers across the page in the history book inside the Code World of the library. "And how, then, do you select the more specific event you want to review out of the historical period?"

Isaac's proud smile was glued to his face as he demonstrated the clockwise motion of his finger around the title picture above the chapter in the book. The grassy hill beneath the blue sky morphed into an open throne room with a black clothed human holding a chalice in front of a cowering king.

"Well done." Wishe smiled and initiated a round of applause. "I would like you all to experiment with this process. Mimic how to do it correctly at first and then try new things to see what else you can come up with."

The teacher strolled around practicing students, nodding and acknowledging their own use of the technique. The class was a flurry of murmuring that filled the grassy plain with competing historical images. Jonothon took the opportunity to slink to the back, trying to go unnoticed. He cracked open a book and started searching.

"Eve's Dale?" spoke a voice behind him.

Jono looked up to see his holographic teacher peering down with a gentle but concerned countenance.

"Where did you learn about that?" asked Wishe.

Jonothon didn't know what to say. He muttered a few unintelligible noises before stating, "I heard someone mention it once." He shrugged. "I didn't know what it was."

Wishe knelt beside him. The tiny pictures on the book were filled with blue light creeping through a thicket of trees. "Some things are best avoided, Mister Wyer, until one has a more appropriate perspective to learn the truth of them."

"I don't understand," said Jono.

"That will take time." Professor Wishe smiled gently. "For now, I think it would be advantageous to explore topics of slightly less sensitive nature. Do you have a favorite sport? Or favorite animal?" She said it in such a kind and tactful tone that Jonothon couldn't help but oblige her. She smiled with a nod, and turned her attention to the class at large.

"Your assignment for this wake is to pick a subject that interests you, be it space travel or bug guts, and create a chart of the path you used to find it. Then find a partner and run a comparison on your two topics. The purpose of this exercise is not only to find the thing you are looking for, but to find the connections between your topic and any other. I want you to visualize just how much there is to learn, to grasp the scope and interconnectedness of reality. I want you to see how all the elements of our world are connected."

After a while, the field of the code world was a mess of hovering images. Jono waited for Wishe to become preoccupied with the larger group before he backed further away from the class. He deliberately caught Wishe's eye before going far; she smiled pleasantly at him but made no move to follow.

Jono snuck further and further away until the other students looked like heads poking up from the tall blades of grass.

He found a large flat rock.

Jono knelt on the soft soil and touched it gently. Cracks formed across its surface. They splintered and came together to create a word: "Communication".

Jono poked his head above the grass. All the other students had spread apart to research their own topics. Jono picked up the rock, which was large but light, and strolled to a short tree groomed in the shape of a mushrup. Tall, wild grass grew up so high around the tree that it touched the low-hanging branches.

Jonothon ducked under thick leaves and sat on dirt and spiraled tree roots. He opened up the side of the rock as if it were a book. Tan pages flipped open. He looked around once more before he wrote the words Caer Midus with his finger on the blank page. The book produced a drawing of the massive golden castle. He ran his finger along it, turning the image around, searching for one room in particular.

When he found the small arched window, he zoomed in to look through the mirror at a cramped and cluttered bedroom.

Alexsayter Aquinas looked far more tired than when Jono had last left him. His face fur was untrimmed and gnarled; his eyes exposed a lack of sleep and a restless spirit. The tumnkin sat in a wooden chair in the corner of the room, surrounded by old, dusty books. He pulled a quill from on top of the stack of books beside him and placed it on the scroll in his hand.

"Aquinas," Jono whispered as loud as he could.

The man looked up at the vanity that now showed Jono in its mirror and tumbled off his chair.

"Jonothon!" Aquinas gasped as he struggled to the mirror.

The shout came through loud. Jono covered the rock book with his hand to muffle the volume.

"Where are you, lad? Are you safe?"

"I'm alright. I'm in Eies, at Windom."

"My soulless stars." Aquinas wiped his brow with his hat before replacing it on his head. "I had feared for your journey. Those plains of icy death that fill the realm of Night are as unforgiving as the Empress who rules it, but thank the seraphim, you've made through! And you're well? They haven't discovered you?"

"Yes and no. I've been enrolled in the school. They've even selected me for Cloaks training."

Aquinas laughed with relief. "Angels be praised. The Sage was right not to fear for you when I told him what happened. The seraphs do indeed watch over you like no other, child, but you must of course be cautious."

"We don't have a lot of time."

"I know that," replied Aquinas. "The Sage and his mage knights have gone in disguise as pilgrims and have secured the Keeper. There is no sign yet that the Empress has moved toward him, but I fear the hour is drawing very late!"

"We can stop this, Aquinas, but I need your help. I found out where they are keeping the key in the castle! I am going to try to get it, but I don't have a way to get it back to you."

"Jonothon, this is far too dangerous." Terror lined Aquinas's face. "You are talking of invading the Obsidian Crown! The heart of the

Empress' reign is surely guarded by such beasts of evil that it is death just to imagine them." His fur shivered with fear and disgust.

"We don't have any other choice. You have to trust me."

Aquinas looked down at the scroll of revelations in his hands and swallowed his fear. "You are right. There is no more time. We must continue on the path laid before us and trust in the seraphim to guide us, as they have already guided you. This is our only hope. The Light has the Keeper and now it is up to us to fulfill our end. If the Empress charges with the key in her possession, there will be . . . devastation. Countless lives will be laid to rest, even if the Light does end in victory. You can save them, Jonothon, angels willing. If we have the key, then the Empress would not dare attack!"

"I'll get it, Mister Aquinas. I will find a way, I promise!"

"I trust you. Jonothon, if you can brave the wastelands of darkness and steal away to the pit of the Night Machine herself, then I can manage to rescue you from it." Aquinas grabbed a satchel and began throwing supplies into it. "I still have a friend or two under the stars. I will secure an escape for you. It will not be easy, but I will return you to the side of Day. The Sage and knights of Blue Skies will stand with salvation in our grasp and danger at our heels. I will be ready. Call me at this gem to speak in private."

Aquinas held up a round green gem that hung from a chain around his neck and touched it to the mirror. The image of the gem popped up on the page in Jono's book.

Jonothon nodded. "Okay. Thank you, Aquinas."

"I'll send word to this location once I've reached the city. Be swift as the seraphs, my boy. May their wings keep you safe."

Jono tore out the page from the stone book, folded it, and stored it in the privacy of his code world's jacket pocket. He shut the rock and closed his eyes.

How would he break into the castle? He would have to scout out the maps further. If he could only find the window to the room that held the key, perhaps he could find a way to fly up to it.

"Was that the Day?" squealed a voice above him.

Jono leapt backward and fell onto his back. Above him, Keiko Kirin sat in the branches of the mushrup-shaped tree, her face bright with amazement. "Was that someone from Sola? In the real world?"

"It, well, yes, but . . ."

"That's amazing!" Keiko's face lit up. "Are you already on assignment for the Cloaks? Do they already have you spying on the Day?"

"Keiko," said Jono as she hopped down through the branches, "there's something I have to tell you. You have to promise not to tell anyone. We're all in grave danger. This isn't an assignment from the Empress."

"What isn't?" said Isaac, his head poking through the grass.

Jono stared back at his new guest.

"Jono's spying on the Day!" said Keiko.

Chapter Thirty-One

The Study Group

"Really?" exclaimed Isaac. "That's fantastic! You must be excelling in Cloaks!"

Jono sat frozen. He was caught. He thought about letting them continue to believe themselves, but it would probably get back to someone that a first year cadet had "excelled" in Cloaks so much to be put on assignment only a few wakes into his studies.

"So who's the Keeper?" asked Keiko.

She had heard, Jonothon thought, *probably all of it.* It would be no good excluding them. He would need all the help he could get to sneak into the castle and get the key back. Jono looked at her. She trusted him. She befriended him. He couldn't succeed alone. It was time for him to let go of his fear, and that meant he needed to trust his friends.

"Come in, and come down," said Jono, waving his friends closer. "This can't be shared with anyone else, okay? I mean it. No teachers, no friends."

The seriousness of Jono's words only seemed to pull Isaac and Keiko in further and to make them more excited.

"You weren't kidnapped, were you?" said Keiko. "It's alright, I suspected as much. Just wish you would have told me."

"I'm sorry. You're right, I wasn't kidnapped. Not exactly," said Jono.

"So what's going on?" asked Isaac "Are you a spy for them? You don't look like you're from the Day."

"Jono wouldn't do that," insisted Keiko.

"I'm just asking," rebuffed Isaac. "No sense in avoiding the obvious question."

"I'm not a spy for the Day," said Jono, although he kind of was. "The truth is, I was supposed to come here, just like everybody else, but then I found something, back in Polari. It was an ancient key that people from both Ends have been looking for, for centuries, maybe longer. They called it Attrayer's Key! Whoever has it has the power to control the light of the world!"

Isaac and Keiko stared at him, transfixed.

"The Empress stole it from me and now she's going to use it. The world was once in balance and it was only a matter of time before it had to return to that balance, but she doesn't want that to happen. She would lose all her power if the light came to the Dark End, so instead she is going to use the key to black out the light for good. The rest of the world will be Dark."

Isaac shrugged. "What's so bad about that? I like the Dark just fine."

"The Solans are not like us. They can't live without the light. They'd freeze and die, all of them. I need to get the key back. I need to stop her or anyone else from using it."

"That's gizmos," said Keiko, though by her unsure tone Jono knew she still believed him.

"It is true. You have to trust me," said Jono. "Please."

"Jono, you seem welded," said Isaac, "but Kirin is right, that story is gizmos. Why would the Empress want to destroy half of the world? We want to leave this rock and get back to the stars."

"Only she knows how to really live in the Dark," said Jono. "If she had the only means of survival, then she would rule the sphere with no one to stop her. The Terralunans on the moon need food shipments from the Day. If the Empress could stop those, the Tills couldn't keep the blockade going."

Isaac thought about it. "That's actually quite a clever plan. It may even work."

Jono grabbed him by the shoulder. "Millions of innocent people will die!"

"No, no it's evil, sure," Isaac agreed, "but clever."

"So what do you do once you actually get this key thing?" asked Keiko.

Jono swallowed. "I don't know. All I've thought about was that I need to get it back."

"That tumnkin you were talking to," said Isaac. "Is he coming to take it?"

"His name's Aquinas. He's good. I trust him. There's no bone in him that likes the Empress, but he lives under Twilight. He wouldn't let anyone in the Dark be harmed either."

"This thing can't go to the Solans," insisted Isaac. "If this Aquinas will help, that's one thing, but you can't trust the Sage or any of the knights. They may talk nice when they think the Dark is powerful, but once they got their hands on it they'd start doing all the things they said the Empress would do. They'll burn the Dark End in light and call it goodness." Isaac was resolute, and Keiko nodded in agreement. "If she'd do it, then they'd do worse."

Jonothon sat against the tree with the weight of his plight bared down on him. "It's my fault she has it, and that the Day thinks all is lost already. I just have to get it back. I need to set everything right. We can't leave it to chance that everything will work out. We have to stop *both* of them from using it. We have to destroy it."

Keiko and Isaac agreed.

"You'll help me?"

Keiko laughed. "I hopped on a flight to a city I've never been to so I could enroll in a school that rejected me already, all trusting a kid I just met! Do you really think I'd turn my back on adventure? Besides, you're good luck, Jono."

They looked at Isaac.

Isaac shrugged. "I'm already four weeks ahead in all my classwork, and however this filters out, it promises to not be boring."

"How do we get it?" asked Keiko.

"Firstly, where is it, first of all?" asked Isaac.

"If this key is so important, the Empress would have it in the castle with her," said Keiko.

"There was that room we found," Jono said, "the one where Grail was looking at all the screens from all over the castle. I think that connects to the same security network that watches everything in Eies. There was one room with guards around it and the whole door was this big lock. We need to find out more about that room. I think it's a treasure room."

"If we could find a hard line to that security room, you could cut into it and see it all with your spy wires," said Keiko. "We just need to follow the cable to find a better place for you to link into it."

"But we'll still have to get into the Crown in order to get this thing once we know its there," said Isaac. "That will be hard. There're guards everywhere and 'goyles, and the Eyes of Eies will be watching."

"If they catch us, there is no telling what they'll do," said Jono.

"We're kids," said Keiko, with a grin. "What's the worst that could happen?"

"A rocket weighing seven hundred and twenty two pounds is flying through the air at a steady speed of two hundred and ninety seven kilems per hour with an altitude of two thousand feet. At what degree must it descend on a ground level target three hundred and ten kilems away?"

David Kepler looked up from a mathometry book at his three companions sitting at their round table. He'd found Jono, Keiko, and

Isaac in the back of the den studying and had offered to help out since he was a second year cadet and had done reasonably well in mathometry. Despite saying they were determined to stay and figure out the next few chapters, the three first year cadets didn't seem to be studying all that much. Isaac glared down at his own book and scribbled notes onto a scroll while Keiko scratched her head beneath her floppy hat and tried to make it look as though she was not completely exhausted.

Jono had closed his eyes. He envisioned the scenario of the rocket cutting through the clouds with the ground far below it. He tried to match the numbers of the weight and speed of the rocket and what angle the fins would have to be for the missile to hit the target dead on.

The boy's den had been loud and active for most of the later evening, but as the late hours grew nearer, the crowds faded to only a few stranglers and Jonothon's weary study group.

"Why not just use an adjusting navigation system and forget the whole thing?" said Keiko with a whack of her pen against the table.

"Because that's not the problem," answered Isaac.

David rubbed his eyes and shut the book. "Alright, that's it for me. If you need any more help let me know, but I got drills tomorrow. Good sleeps all."

The three half-heartedly waved goodbye, but the instant Kepler left their energy perked up.

"I still think we should tell him," whispered Isaac, leaning in.

Keiko shook her head. "We have to keep it simple. No complicating things while we gather intel. Right?"

Jono looked at the rest of the cluttered room. Another older boy was leaving with a half-built robot in his arms. The room was empty, save for themselves and Nick Knox, who was spread awkwardly on an old orange chair, snoring.

"Yeah," said Jono. "I think it's clear."

They'd picked this room, and that particular table for a specific reason. After following all the hard lines into and out of the security room they'd found Commander Grail in, they discovered one such line was just outside the boy's den in the secret tunnel Grail himself had used. It was a security line that connected the schools network to the castle. One of Jono's spy cables, the one that came out of his left leg, was designed to be able to cut into the line and attach a dual port so the information would still transfer like normal, but he would be able to search it as well.

For the past four evenings they'd pretended to be a study group so Jono could access the security cameras and continue their search for a way into the Crown. They'd already confirmed the guarded room on Grail's screen was truly unique to the entire castle. There were no cameras beyond the door, and the locks were unlike anything any of them had seen.

"It must be where they are keeping it," Isaac had concluded.

The others agreed. The predicament they found themselves in was an apparently impossible task of maneuvering the entangled tunnels and exposed bridges to get to the locked room and then escape without being detected.

The spy cable snaked out of Jono's pant leg and curved under the table. He made the cable slither in the shadows created by a ceiling lamp as it wound along the cold stone ground toward the crack in the wall. The first time they attempted to sneak into the security network he had spent nearly the entire evening just getting the port connected. Every time after that, Jonothon was able to simply plug in and start searching.

Images flashed in front of his eyes, and he shut them to see more clearly. Putting himself into the computer was almost like being in the code world of the library, only it wasn't designed with the same elaborate and realistic interface. The world of the security network was a harsh file system of folders and data. The information was more of a maze of glowing green columns. Whenever he pulled one of the visual files out, it took over his whole field of vision. It was like he was actually sitting in the corridors of the castle, looking through the eyes of the gargoyles, goliaths, shadowcats, or mothdragons that all connected to the ever watchful eyes of the Empress. He removed an image like taking off a mask in his mind, and then tried another file.

Jono peered over the edge of the ornate rim of the doorway that led into the soldier's dining hall of the Crown. He'd seen that room twice before, only from a different angle. On each occasion he'd spied a fascinating display of the powers the full-fledged soldiers of Eies possessed. This time he saw Ramsus Ramaadi sitting alone reading from a hovering scroll and eating a breaded chicken leg. He wasn't showing off anything particularly unique, which left Jono wondering what his powers must be.

Jono removed the dining hall file from his face and pulled another one out of the directory. This time it was from a balcony that looked out onto the city. A sea of clouds sparkled with all the city's lights beneath it. The eyes of the mothdragon was a roller coaster view as the small creature fluttered down a tower and turned into an open window. Jonothon tracked its position against a map of the castle that hovered at the side of his vision. They were in the second column of the western ridge of the Crown. He continued to scan each room, looking for connections that could lead them from the academy through the innards of the mountain and to the castle top.

He cracked open an eye to check up on the physical world. The information network wasn't as consuming to the mind as the library was; to leave the library required a concerted effort to refocus the mind. Leaving the file system was much easier. He could actually be in both at the same time, but it was like seeing two worlds merge in and out of each other; an activity which concocted an exponentially powerful headache.

Keiko and Isaac maintained the façade of tired students with striking authenticity.

"What about jetting on the outside of the castle and then slipping in through a vent or window?" asked Keiko when she noticed Jono's open eye. "Any luck with that?"

Jono shook his head. "Still nothing. There are eyes all over the outside and no cover as far as I've seen."

Keiko's head sunk in disappointment. She'd offered to build them a small sky jet they could fly up to the Crown, though their escape would still depend on Jono's Tumnkin friend. She was eager to show off what she could do with mechanix, but as of yet, her services had gone unneeded.

"I could probably crack that lock, once we get there," she added, half-heartedly. "Uncle Cid always said I had a knack for locks."

Jono shut his eyes again: more hallways, more storage rooms.

Across the room Nick snored loudly. He reached up to scratch his face and tumbled spastically off the chair. The three students looked over at him and stayed still. Jono tried to lean over his cable to keep it hidden. Nick grunted, and then yanked the blanket off of the chair and pulled it over his head.

They looked at each other, worried. Jono shut his eyes again and resumed scanning.

"Oh stars!" whispered Isaac.

Jono opened his eyes.

"It's late. We better hold off until tomorrow."

The hour had grown late, and they packed up and left, dismayed and exhausted.

Sleep came quickly when Jono and Isaac finally returned to their dorm. Oscar was already sprawled about his sheets with his mouth open wide and his guttural breathing filling the air. Jono kicked off his shoes and crawled into bed. Despite the anxiety that rushed through his blood, his body was weary from the recently shortened sleep hours and ever increasing class work.

The Spy's Spy

After what seemed like both an instant and an eternity, his eyes cracked open again.

The world was blurry and strange.

Jono rubbed his eyes and shut them again. A dull light flashed in front of him. He blinked. There was a pale yellow light in front of his face. Did one of the lights turn on by mistake? Was it already wake? Jono blinked again to try and clear his sight.

In front of him was something like an imp.

"Wake up!" whispered the tiny man.

Jono squinted. The man was stalky, only about three inches tall. He had long, blond hair and a gruff expression on his face. He stared directly at Jonothon, but when Oscar rolled over and his bed made a creaking noise, the tiny man ducked behind the pillow.

"What are you?" said Jono.

"What do you mean . . . what?" replied the tiny man.

Jono rubbed his eyes again, but the little man was still a bit of a blur.

"Are you an imp?"

"I . . . what? No. Listen to me. We've got to get you out of here. Something is going to happen soon."

"What's going to happen?"

"Something big. I know what you've been up to!"

"Who . . . How do you . . ."

"Burn'em!" the tiny man cursed. The room's lights flicked on, and the gentle wake music began. The tiny man dove behind the pillow.

Jono lifted the pillow only to see the man climb off the bed and dart along the ground. Jono leapt up to chase him, but the imp man disappeared. He rubbed his eyes again. His body ached from head to toe.

"Already up, are we?" said Oscar, smiling and licking his lips.

Jono forced a smile and nodded even though he felt like he hadn't slept at all.

Dr. Stone downloaded the graded reports on examples of environmental adaptation directly to their scrolls. Jono had almost forgotten the upload deadline was the previous night, but thanks to Isaac's reminder, he sent it in before they left the den. He wasn't exactly proud of his work; most of his free time had been consumed with practicing with his cables and searching for the key.

Jonothon was able to throw together a couple paragraphs about the woolly frogs native to his own Twilight Ring, but his lack of effort gave him a uncomfortable feeling as he looked at the closed scroll. He didn't want to see his score or read whatever advice or corrections Stone had written.

The rest of the wake dragged on.

He felt increasingly oppressed by the teachers' pressure over his inability to keep up with the class work. He couldn't afford to spend extra time on it. Finding the key was what truly mattered.

After a dreary succession of classes, Jono, Keiko, and Isaac made their way back to the den, which felt chillier than it had ever been before.

They sat on soft puff chairs without saying a word. Their plans to find a route had all been dead ends, and time was certainly running out. There was little left to say.

The room around them had never seemed quite as oppressive before, but now Jono felt claustrophobic in the midst of the dusty shelves and tattered furniture.

Isaac tapped his thumb against the end table. He squinted his purple eyes as though he was mulling over ideas, but whenever his mouth opened to say something, it only hung open for a few moments and then shut again. They all desperately wanted to come up with a way to solve their dilemma, to rescue the key, but nothing came to them.

"At least we know she hasn't done anything with the, err, thing yet," said Keiko, trying to be cryptic. "The world hasn't ended. We'd of known if that happened."

Jono and Isaac looked at her.

It was a simple observation but clearly correct. In all the time since the raid on the historian's tower, the Empress had yet to make a move to use the key. What could she possibly be waiting for? Jonothon thought. What was he missing? For a moment he felt impatient and annoyed at her, but then he stopped himself. It wasn't as if he wanted her to use it and destroy the balance of Dark and Day. He certainly didn't want the sky over Caer Midus to go black, all the plants dying in moments and the poor people of the sun being caught unprepared for the terrible cold of darkness. What really upset him was that he didn't understand what was really going on. If he didn't know what was going on, how could he stop it?

"She must be waiting for something," Jono finally said.

"But what?" asked Isaac.

"Maybe it can only work at a certain time," said Jono. "That's what I've read in a lot of stories, like during an eclipse or when the planets all align or something."

"Is there anything like that coming up?" asked Keiko.

Isaac shook his head. "I don't think so. There was the closest point of Shatner's Comet just before school started."

"I don't see why any of that would really matter, though." Keiko shrugged. "I mean, planets lining up? To do what? They're still so far apart anyway. It kind of sounds a little silly that you'd have to wait for that to happen to unlock the orbit of the sun. No offense."

She was right. It didn't make a lot of sense, but then again, neither did destroying the world.

Isaac slipped out of his chair.

"Sorry, Jono, I have to finish some work for tomorrow."

"Yeah, we should all get to bed, I guess. We'll think better after a full sleep anyway," added Keiko. "Good sleeps, Jono."

Jonothon didn't move from his chair but managed a weak wave of his hand.

The room had emptied except for him, so he took no efforts to disguise his spy wire connecting to the castle network again. There was a spot, hidden among the files that monitored the supply and restocking of D salts for the many plants, where there was a different type of file. It was right where he planned. The page of the communication book he used in the library was reset to save anything there instead of the library's own memory. Jono downloaded the communication file onto his brain computer and erased it from the castle's data bank. He then shut his eyes and played it.

On the black side of his eyelids an orange light flickered and then came into full glowing focus. There was a blurry brown creature that stood in the shadow of the light from a street lamp coming through a window.

"I've made it to Eies," said Aquinas excitedly. "This place is even creepier than I remember. I hope you receive this in time. I have secured a means of transport. All they are waiting for is the signal from you. Deep down I knew it would come to this, that you would recover us from doom. I do have faith in you, my boy. Your family would be proud. Our kinsmen await us at the gates of Dawn. All you need to do is call me once you're ready to take the key and I will not fail to be there." Aquinas was smiling wide, joy and pride filling his eyes. "The seraphim will unite us soon and sweep us to victory. Trust in that, child. Farewell."

The message cut to black, and when Jono opened his eyes he realized they were wet. He wanted to hide somehow, to run away from the responsibility that was forced on him. It was too much. His gut wrenched. It can't be done. For all his travels, all his success, he had come to this point and realized he couldn't go any further. Maybe he should ignore the whole mess about the key. Nothing bad had happened so far—it was possible that nothing would. Or maybe it would have to be another thousand years before it could be used. He could just enjoy his life at the academy with his new friends and let whoever wants to deal with that mess of prophecy and world destruction deal with it themselves.

Of course, he could never again return to the side of Day. They would know of his failure and the shame, at the very least, would be unbearable. They might even come after him for letting the Empress have it. Maybe he should just go home to Polari and live the rest of his wakes out on the house on the hill reading books, eternally separated from the world by a thick red comforter.

Jono looked at the clock. It was later than he realized. By the time he finally left the den and walked through the halls toward his room, the halls were empty and deathly quiet.

"Hey!" spoke a quiet voice.

Jono looked back and then forward down the hall but saw no one.

"I've been looking for you all wake!" The voice was whispered and electronic, but somehow familiar. "Down here!"

It was the tiny man from that morning! He poked his head out of a crack in the wall, and waved Jonothon over to him.

"Who are you?" Jono asked.

"Shhhh!" demanded the tiny man. "They can hear you. Only my

sight and voice are coded against the Eyes of Eies. I'm safe. You just stay quiet and listen to me."

Jono leaned in. The little man looked around nervously, like his safety was not as certain as he said it was.

"It's you!" exclaimed Jono in a whisper. "The knight from Caer Midus? Eljin, how did you get here?"

"Be silent! We are on the edge of death as it is!" said Eljin as quietly as he could. "Would you push us over into her grasp?"

Jono froze and shook his head.

"Good. Now stop looking at me. Sit against the wall and start adjusting your shoe." Jono did what he was told. "Good."

"What are you doing here?" Jono whispered, trying to not move his lips.

"I am here for the same reason, I presume, you are," answered Eljin. "We are both here because of him, and it is his guidance that has led us to the cusp of victory."

The Sage! thought Jonothon, and his heart leapt. The Empress may have spies and eyes littering the planet, but the Sage of Ages must not be without his own.

"His sight goes further and in more disguises than the Empress herself," Eljin continued. "We have known for a long time that she was desperate and now we have our chance to do what need to be done. We're going to have to be clever and careful, boyo. There's danger all around us."

"But we've tried. There is no way into the Crown."

"There is!" said Eljin. "Or at least there will be."

"Does Aquinas know?"

"We have your furry friend in place. It's the key that's the deeper matter. You must be prepared for it. At the crack of the wake I have arranged for a way for you to get to the Crown. There's going to be a distraction that will take their eyes off us, but there's not a lot of time. You're going to have to take full advantage of every second to make your escape. Can you download schematics into your brain's computer?"

"Yes."

"Good." Eljin's image began to flicker and fade. In his tiny center was a small, floating worm - his hollow heart. A tiny wire stretched out from the heart on connected to the plug in Jono's arm.

"Take the plans and the timelines. Do not stray an inch or I assure you, all will fail."

"I won't," said Jono, and with that Eljin disappeared. The tiny worm floated back into the crack in the wall.

Jonothon finished tying his shoe and hurried down the hall. He didn't wake Isaac when he returned to their room. He climbed into bed and pretended to sleep.

He poured over the schematics again and again, where they would enter the castle, exactly at what time. He decided to tell Isaac and Keiko everything before breakfast. They would be ready when the chance came. The morning was going to get very busy and he didn't want to have the crucial piece out of place when things started. He was brimming with excitement and relief that there was still hope.

It was hours before the blue lines of the schematic finally faded and Jono succumbed to sleep. Tomorrow he would risk everything for this one, last chance.

Chapter Thirty-Three

A Simple Distraction

even on the nose," bleated the capricorn door knocker. Jono's eyes burst open.

Isaac was already up and buttoning his uniform. He looked back at Jono with a forced smile, but Jono darted out of bed and grabbed him by the arm.

"We have to get to breakfast and find Keiko!" Jono whispered.

"What? Why?"

"I'll tell you both all the details. I found a way! But we don't have a lot of time. It's going to happen soon."

They ran out the door and through the halls. The dining hall was already packed with students and the smell of bacon.

"Keiko!" Jono called at her away from the group of girls from her dorm. "We should get some food. We don't want to be hungry."

"What are you talking about?" Keiko asked.

"Jono's found a way," said Isaac, "but it has to be this morning."

"Right," said Jono. "It will happen before classes, when everyone is separated."

Jono ordered an extra helping of stork eggs and toast. They found a secluded table in the corner.

"Ok, now tell me everything," said Keiko.

Jono told them about the plan to sneak into the crown while Eljin had arranged a distraction.

"He said Aquinas knows too, so he'll be ready for us on the castle terrace when we leave."

"We should get started. Where are we meeting him?" said Keiko.

It started to really sink in that this was happening. There was no time left for doubt, no telling where their journey would take them before the key was destroyed and the two ends of the sphere were made to see reason.

The hall by the front gate was drowning in a sea of students that moved in all directions.

It was ten minutes before the first class began.

Jono closed his eyes and could clearly see a map of the school. An arrow pointed down a hallway.

"We're supposed to go to the north wing. Then head down in the mountain," instructed Jono.

"How do we get up to the castle by going down further?" asked Isaac.

"Eljin will know," Jono replied. "He'll meet us there and then he'll show us the rest of the way."

"Can we really trust this guy?" asked Isaac.

Jono didn't answer at first. His friends were risking losing everything they had ever known.

"I don't know of any other way. Every wake we wait and do nothing may make us too late."

Pebbles on the floor began to rattle like popcorn kernels before a rumbling bellowed through the halls and shook the walls around them. Windom became a maze of frozen students while the noise grew louder and closer. Even the gargoyles looked around with worry.

"Earthquake? Isaac said.

"This must be the distraction," whispered Keiko.

Jonothon, Keiko, and Isaac pushed through the crowds. The rumbling grew louder as they entered the north wing until the shattering thud of footsteps echoing through the halls.

"Something's wrong," said Isaac.

"What's happening, Jono?" asked Keiko.

"I don't know," Jono said.

A tremendous thud kicked up dust that rushed through the hall. Keiko squinted one eye at the sound of clanking metal and stone.

"That sounds like—" Keiko voice was cut off by a thud that reverberated up through their knees.

Out from a giant archway stepped the black metal figure of the Argonaut. The four legged mech was even more terrifying in motion than when Jono first saw it at Keiko's shop. Its jagged mouth stretched open and unleashed a terrible roar that shook the room around them and blew the tapestries lining the walls. A flurry of gargoyles soared like a glimmering silver cloud toward the mech, but the Argonaut lifted his arm and a sparkling turquoise shield lit up around it. The metal arm swung through the air, smashed gargoyles aside, and crushed the third level terrace. The black and copper stone shattered into chunks and rained down around them.

"Run!" Jono shouted.

They charged across the open room toward the interior hallways, but the Argo was not alone. Three mantis mechs ran out of the hallway, their mouths and bladed hands snapping menacingly at the air. Jono pushed Keiko and Isaac against the wall just as the crazed robots leapt passed them. The mechs continued leaping and snapping around aimlessly, as though they had gone insane.

Keiko grabbed Jono's hand and they turned to go down the dark corridor, but froze again as the hall ignited with fire. A mechanical embermander strutted forward, unflinching through the wall of flames.

"Go back!" Keiko yelled.

They ran back into the large hall of screaming students as the crazed mechs smashed into pillars and shot lasers into the ceiling. The entire academy trembled under the footsteps of the legion of war mechs gone mad.

All the exits were blocked.

The Argonaut's claws cut through stone. Its mouth swung down with bared teeth ready to snatch them up and slice them to bits. The three cadets dove backward. Out of the corner of his eye, Jono saw a silver glint sailing through the air.

Commander Grail landed at the base of the Argo's neck and spared no second breaking through a joint in its metal armor. With his mechanical fist, Grail crushed the monster's spine and tore its metal tendons apart with terrifying strength. Grail ripped the mammoth head of the Argonaut free and hurled it into the mantis mechs, smashing them against a wall. The Argonaut's legs slipped from beneath it, and its humongous body crashed onto the floor.

Grail clung on to the collar beam when the monster fell, and then ran to the students.

"Sabotage! This is the Day's doing!" said Grail with greasy fluid covering his hands like black blood. "Run to the nearest classroom and order the room computer into lockdown. The code is 'Armadillo'. Go now!"

Across the corridor another series of clanking steps in the distance assured them the chaos was not over. Grail gave them one last commanding stare, shouted, "Move!" and then ran headlong into the direction of danger.

The three ran through the hall, Jono guiding them with the map that floated in front of him. They descended stairs; the noise of rampaging mechs grew distant, until they finally came to an empty classroom.

"This is as far as I have," said Jono. He blinked, and the floating map that only he could see disappeared.

"Is he coming here?" Keiko asked.

They looked around at each other, confused. There was a crash against the hallway just outside of the room—a thud followed by a screeching of metal against stone. Jono poked his head out of the doorway just as a metal dragon shoved its head through into view and stretched its neck as its flame-lit tongue flicked wildly.

Isaac poked his head out to see as well, and then quickly yanked Jono back inside the room.

"Get to the back of the wall!" yelled Isaac.

The dragon's head was stuck at their open doorway, but its burning tongue snaked in. It set the wood door on fire and seared the chairs and tapestries. They screamed as the fire tongue swished closer and closer.

"There you are!" said a tiny voice beside them. The imp-sized Eljin was sitting on a shelf on the wall beside them, looking impatient. "Who're are these lot?"

Jono looked at Keiko and Isaac. "They are helping. We can trust them."

The tiny Eljin sniffed. "More the merry, I suppose. What's all that. . ."

The burning metal tounge slammed against their door. "Mechdragon tongue! Come on!"

Eljin hopped to the floor and ran straight through a nearby wall. The others were quick to follow him through the false wall and into the tunnel.

They ran behind Eljin through secret passages, occasionally coming out through a regular hall or room as the chaos and destruction around them grew. Sirens blared instructions for everyone to remain calm and stay in a safe room and all would be resolved shortly.

The stone halls around them eventually became rock and metal. The only light came from the glow of Eljin's tiny body.

They clamored through the cold rock tunnel until coming to a complete stop. The path ended as the mountain gave way to the misty chasm. Jono recognized it as the same crag near Edgar No Eyes' home.

The light of Eljin's hollow heart flicked off, and they were left alone in the darkness.

A trickle of Terralunis moonlight crept through the chasm and silhouetted a shadowy figure that sat stood near the edge. The figure stepped forward and raised his hand, illuminating a floating sphere. The true, full sized, but still short, Eljin smiled at them triumphantly.

"You did all this? You made the mechs go crazy?" asked Jono. He was surprised at the extent of damage the crazed mechs were doing.

"Impressed, are you, boyo?" Eljin winked proudly. "But a good trick like this only works once, so we have to make the most of it."

"But those mechs were blowing up the academy!" said Jonothon. "People may be hurt!"

"That should keep their eyes all the more occupied," said Eljin. "We have to go. Time is slipping."

Eljin turned to the open, freezing air of the chasm. He took one step into the empty abyss, and they gasped. Eljin looked back at them, standing solidly in the empty air: invisible stairs.

"No time to be surprised," laughed Eljin. "The key won't steal itself!"

The Treasure of the Crown

long the rocky chasm that hugged the side of the mountain, four figures crawled carefully up the invisible stairs. The highest spire of the Crown castle melted into black sky, distinguished only by the lack of stars and the subtle reflection of the city's light below it.

Eljin, Keiko, Isaac, and Jonothon climbed to the crest of the chasm where the black mountains were capped in white ice.

The sky above was clearer than Jono had ever seen. The stars glowed brilliantly, the blue of the Milky Way creeping through black space. Space was so clear that Jonothon felt he could fall into it simply by staring too deep. The twinkling sirens beckoned him into their black oblivion.

Jono spotted a burning flare in the sky, bright and pulsing, but not a star. It was small at first, but as he squinted he could tell it was coming closer. The moment Jono recognized it, he stepped back in fright. He lost his footing and would have tumbled over Keiko and Isaac and been lost into the chasm below, but his back collided with something hard near the stairs. His eyes were wide, and he didn't dare move. But why didn't he feel the cold, the chill of the mountain air? He then realized they were in an invisible tunnel. That was what kept the deathly cold out. Keiko and Isaac looked at him, confused.

Eljin turned around and glared. "You alright, boyo?"

"We can't go up further! Look!" Jono pointed to the flying object in the distant. "The Chimera is there! It's going to spot us!"

Eljin tapped the nothing in front of him, and it made a deep metallic sound. "We are as invisible to them as this tunnel is to us. We're completely safe."

"I see it," said Keiko. "It's the Chimera. That thing nearly killed us!"

"If it's coming to Eies with the Terralunans, then the Empress must be getting ready to attack. We don't have much time!" said Jono.

"Why would the Tills come to Eies?" asked Isaac.

"She must be plotting with the Loonies?" Keiko said, disgusted. "I never thought I would see that."

"No time to waste gawking, then. Quickly now!" said Eljin.

The invisible tunnel crawled along the mountainside and continued up the castle wall.

The monstrous guardian of black flesh and white fire soared over them without any hint of seeing them. The Chimera landed against a balcony; its back paws dangled and clawed for stability as its forepaws held tightly to the dwarfed stone balcony. Cloaked figures emerged from the creature's chest and disappeared into the castle.

Along the Crown's central spire, Jono and the others came to a narrow entrance in the rock. They had to squeeze and crawl through the opening like worms digging through a stone earth. If Eljin were any larger of a man, he would not have made it. They squirmed upward as hot air rushed around them.

A clutter of voices crept through the cracks of stone in a manner that, at first, resembling a pack of rabid wolves fighting over a carcass, but as the group crawled nearer they could distinguish actual words.

"You cannot deny what we have witnessed," spat a venomous voice.

"I only contend with the assumptions that you've brought here," replied a steady voice.

Through a crack in the stone, Jono could see an ornate and simultaneously drab room with a long wooden table and plenty of chairs, although no one was sitting in them. He stopped to slip a wire from his shoulder through the crack and closed his eyes to peer into the room beyond.

There were three people standing opposite of a half dozen Eiesans. Terralunans! They wore dark purple gowns and their skin was pale, almost gray, covered in wrinkles.

"Eies has breached the Pact of Revelations!" one of the Terralunans hissed.

Commander Grail stood opposite them with his metal fist planted on the table. His face was flushed and his teeth were clenched.

"Do not dare lie to me!" said Commander Grail. "We have guarded our End. This is your betrayal. You made a prison of this sphere while at every turn we have been trustworthy stewards. Even this wake you sick your dogs under blue skies to sabotage my academy!"

"Connivings and contradictions!" spat another dark coated Terralunan. "We are well aware of the intense search perpetrated by the Dark End for centuries. You have looked beyond your boundaries for fear of others and have since instilled that fear in them yourselves."

"We demand the Empress explain her actions immediately," coughed the third member of the Tills.

"You will make no such demands while you stand on our soil," answered Grail. "The Empress will speak to whom she chooses, when she chooses."

Jono felt a leather boot kick his head. He opened his eyes to Eljin's stern look. Eljin shook his head. He was right. Every second counted.

They moved onward until they were on the inner side of two stone walls. It was narrow path, but there was room enough to stand. They found a wall that faded a little when they touched it. Eljin motioned Jono over, and he sent another wire out of the false wall to search for trouble.

"There's no one around," Jonothon whispered. He sent his spy wires further. It looked around like a curious snake. "No guards."

"They must still be cleaning up the mess in the academy," said Keiko.

"Or meeting with more Loonies," added Isaac.

"Come on then," said Eljin, leading the way through the wall.

The knight turned to the right and started to run as quietly as he could.

"No," said Jono, the hollow map hovering in front of his face. "The treasure room is down this way. We're close."

"Don't worry. Just follow me," said Eljin with gritted teeth.

"We have to get it," Jonothon insisted.

"Trust me, Jono," Eljin whispered. "We have to—"

"Look!" Keiko pointed at figures of shadow that were now moving with a life of their own.

"The fel!" gasped Jono.

The shadowy monsters swarmed toward them. It was impossible to tell what was real shadow and what was a monster of surging death. Jono looked to Eljin, but the man had no flame blade this time.

The monsters cut through the air. Their shadow forms spread together across the whole of the corridor, turning the hall as black as the pit.

"Jono!" Eljin called out, but the fel shades had already overcome him. Their ghostly form passed right through him, swallowing Eljin into the utter darkness.

Isaac grabbed Jono's shoulder and pulled him away. The three bolted down the hallway, not daring to slow down. Every hallway was empty. They dashed from the fel, turning corners and running with all their strength.

They spun around a corner and there, at the end of the hall, they saw the door they had been searching for. It was large and covered in locks of every kind.

"There it is!" said Keiko.

Jono looked back but the Fel Shades were not there. He turned to

Keiko, who was looking over the locks intently.

"Do you think you can undo it?" Jono asked.

Keiko fiddled with a couple knobs and gears. "I'll try. I don't quite know which to start with . . ."

The metal clanked, and the gears began to move. Jono and Isaac looked at her, but Keiko gave a shrug like she wasn't sure what she'd done. The gears unlocked on their own, and the door opened automatically.

Jono, Keiko, and Isaac stepped cautiously through the doorway. The room was dark, but they could see glistening lights like jewels scattered in every direction. The doors slowly shut behind them with a groan, and the locks clicked. In the front of the room, a dim light grew brighter until it illuminated the stone floor and a red and silver carpet the cut through the middle of the room. The twinkling lights were computers stations, not jewels.

At the far end of the room, with the black threads of her hair pulled back to connect with the computer all around her, was the Empress.

"Welcome." She spoke softly. Her crimson gown was bold against the black, throbbing metal of her throne. "I've been expecting you."

Jono shared frightened and confused glances with Keiko and Isaac.

"Please. Come closer," the Empress requested in a soft tone.

Jono's blood seemed frozen and every impulse in his body screamed for him to turn and run, but instead he stepped forward.

"I know about Attrayer's Key," Jonothon said. "I was the one that found it and I can't let you use it."

"Is that so?" The Empress smiled softly, in a way that reminded Jono of his mother. "And just what is it that you know? What have they told you I would do?"

Jonothon swallowed a breath. "They're afraid you will stop the light. Without it the Day would freeze, and the Terralunans couldn't survive without support from the Day. They said you would destroy half the world to break the Terralunan's hold over Earth."

The pale, young Empress looked back at him, contemplating his answer. "And do you believe them?"

"I don't know," Jonothon stuttered. "I just don't want anyone to die."

"It is wise to reserve judgment." The Empress was not as terrifying or threatening as Jonothon had imagined. She seemed reserved with sadness behind her black, shimmering veil.

"There are no monsters here. Do not put faith in the words of the old tree and his congregation of the blind. Pride without function inflates their ego. They are lost to fear and loathing. Destruction disguised as virtue. Think for a moment of what the Day would do if they had the key. Their zeal would unleash it without question of consequence. The Dark End would be set ablaze and the ineptitude of the Day would bring their fragile realm crumbling around them. Do not place faith in that, it is folly."

Jono stepped in front of his friends, courage taking the reins of his body. "Why should I trust you? You hunted for it once I found it in Polari. You froze the entire town to get it! I know you want more power and you have always wanted the key."

The Empress bowed her head. "I can't risk losing it to fools. I can only imagine the tales of me they must have conjured for you. I will not say there is no seed of truth in them. Governance and progress can be messy things. Only know that none could live up to the completeness of that caricature, and no one is pure good or pure evil. We are all of us, shades of gray. I have sent our people to war only when necessity demanded, and for that they call me warmonger. When faced with disaster, I have created opportunity. For that, they call me greedy. I have built a home out of the dark corners of nature that spurn life. All this to be called a monster."

The Empress' youthful appearance could not hide an ancient wisdom.

"There was a time when we were all united. We built great cities and explored across the black. But time is a trickful thing, and the spirit of progress faded from their hearts. I was like you, once, although you would not know it. There were great deeds we had done, plucked from our imagination and birthed into reality by our own hands. I didn't want that to end. There is so much more to explore, to create. They grew comfortable in our successes. Yet I was not content. The stars were always there to wish upon, always showing the depth of the glories yet to be known. I humbly ask you to trust that, Mister Wyer. Trust that I believe in the greatness of our potential. We can explore the universe if we only release our own fearful grip on comfortable ground and free ourselves to be the people we dream of being. That is the true world in front of us. What would you do with such opportunity? Would you turn your back on the stars?"

The Empress slid from her throne and stepped gracefully along the path of soft red carpet that cut through the sea of cold, gray stone. She stood in front of Jonothon, cupped his head in her gentle hands, and looked him over, searching, as though she could see through to his soul.

"What would you do?" she asked.

"I wouldn't hurt them," said Jono, thinking of Isaac and Keiko, and everyone in the Day.

"You are very thoughtful, and yet have much to learn." The Empress sighed, both honest and sad. "Tell me, did you ever consider the coincidence that you arrived on a mission to spy and steal for the Day and you were so conveniently given the teaching and tools to do so? You needed to spy on me, and thus you became a spy?"

Jono didn't know how to answer.

"Did it not occur to you that your miraculous return would be suspicious? Fortunately for me, Mister Wyer, you are not a very good spy, not intentionally, anyway. Once you were spotted on the Dark End, I chose for you to be selected for the Cloaks training. I watched as you searched for the key and heard every word you spoke with your

Sola agent. I have learned the secret the fool of Ages has struggled to keep hidden. The Day is coming. The army of Sola has already moved on the gates of Dawn."

"The Day?" Isaac looked at Jono then to the Empress. "Are they going attack us?"

"No. We will end this," the Empress said resolutely. "They do not have the key and they dare not threaten us."

"You don't have to fight. There must be another way," said Keiko.

"I did not want this," said the Empress. "But we cannot bend to every bully. We cannot let ourselves be forced into a tighter prison. The stars are all of ours to explore. It is a crime against our nature to bottle that up, to abandon who we are. We cannot bend to this mad injustice any further. We will let the Day and their belligerent benefactors know we will not stand idly by as they tear down our progress and condemn us to their own decay. Who is it that wages war now? Who attacks through fear and instigation? Who has seized the ruins of the Keeper and dares me not to meet them?"

"You don't have to do this!" said Jono.

"The Day has itched for war at every chance," replied the Empress. "Even now at the Keeper of Dawn their zeal boils for war. I am afraid that the time to end their madness has come."

The doors flung open on both sides of the throne room and burly metal guards marched in.

"Keep these three safe," the Empress commanded. "Children, we will talk again when stability has been restored."

The Escape Seals It

*J*onothon, Keiko, and Isaac were brought to a room in the castle that looked over the city. The clouds were thick and illuminated, but outside the circle of Eies, the world was dark and cold.

Even looking directly south, there was not a hint of Day's light.

Jono imagined the Empress would be joining the council of Terralunans to assuage them of their fears, all the while her forces would prepare for battle. There was no way he could stop it now. They were left to wait it out.

"Do you think she'll use the key?" Keiko looked at both of her fellow prisoners.

Isaac had no answer and only stared out across the skyline.

Jono shook his head. "I don't know. She'll fight them and if Day's knights are strong enough, it may come to that. I don't even know how it works . . ."

There was a bang on the door and a guard burst in. Despite the surprise, Jono noted the guard's uniform was particularly worn-out.

"There you are!"

"What?" said Jono.

"Who are you?" asked Keiko.

The guard tore off his helmet.

"Eljin!" exclaimed Jono.

"How did you escape the fel shades?" asked Isaac.

"No time. We are leaving, now!" The knight in soldier's armor grabbed Jono by the shoulder and pulled him into the hall.

"We can't leave without the key!" exclaimed Jonothon.

"She'll black out the Day!" said Keiko.

"Not without this." Eljin reached into his pocket and retrieved the metal ring with the ruby gem in the center: the key of Attrayer!

"How did you get it?" gasped Jono.

Isaac reached out to touch it, but Eljin pulled it away.

"You have to come with me," demanded Eljin. "There will be plenty of time for explanations once we're in the clear. Come on!"

They ran through the halls as fast as they could. A map hovered just in front of Jono's face and pointed him in the direction of their rendezvous with Aquinas. It was all left to hope that the tumnkin was prepared as he had promised.

Imperial guards lay unconscious along the hallway. Eljin shoved a balcony door open with his shoulder. They were faced with the glistening light of Eies and the glowing clouds below them.

On the edge of the balcony hovered a thin silver jet.

A chill ran through Jono's body. He spun around.

Three fel shades—the wolf, the brute, and the imp—surrounded them. He turned back to the jet, looking at it as a means of escape from the fel shades.

A hatch on the jet opened to reveal a face Jono never expected to see again—the Historian! The man's weathered face and hair seemed to have aged twenty years since they last met.

Jonothon stopped as he felt his gut drop, like a stone sinking to the bottom of a chasm.

"Come on," said Eljin, shoving them all forward, "there's no time to dawdle."

"You're here?" Jono said. "You're alive . . ."

"The ruse is complete," Eljin told the Historian as he approached the jet.

"Get them all on," commanded the Historian. "Our exit window is short. He will be more than enough to seal her decision."

Jono turned to where the Historian looked and saw a figure cloaked in red with a large hat lying unconscious in the corner.

Jono's eyes widened. "Aquinas!" He tried to run to him, but the brute shade picked him up. "Is he alright?" Jono demanded. "What are you doing?"

Neither Eljin nor the Historian gave him any notice. Jono stared at them; he hadn't noticed it before because of all the hurried commotion, but there, on Eljin's arm just below his sleeve, was the lowest edge of the tattoo of the dead sun. The same tattoo Jono had seen on the wake he left Polari.

"Sergeant Tombs? You're Eljin Tombs?"

Everything seemed to click together at once. Eljin was in Polari. He was in Caer Midus when the Fel Shades attacked. The Historian was the one who controlled the fel shades, not the Empress. They'd used him from the beginning!

"She never had the key," Jonothon said. "You . . . these fel shades were yours? At the tower in Bramblebar and at Caer Midus?"

"Are you certain their armies are committed?" the Historian asked Eljin.

"Completely," replied Eljin. "The Dark army prepares as we speak. With the full weight of the Day's army at the Keeper, the Empress and the Terralunans are convinced that Attrayer's key is in play. There is no going back."

Jono looked at the two men, back and forth. Eljin handed the key to the Historian. Inside the jet was a book with the same symbol Eljin Tombs had tattooed on his arm, the mark of death: the Dead Sol.

"We have to be swift to cover our tracks," said the Historian. "Put them all in."

The wolf fel shade grabbed Isaac by the back and the imp snatched Keiko.

Above the balcony came a terrifying howl. A huge blade covered in turquoise lightning cut through the sky and sliced through the fel-imp with Keiko in its arms. Keiko fell to the ground in a dust of electrified ash and looked back at the assailant.

Gripping the end of the blade which sprung from a gauntlet was a raving Edgar No Eyes.

"Usurper!" yelled Edgar. "Where do you think you are? I will not let you betray the true Empire of the Earth! This is where your treachery ends!" He swung at the fel wolf, but with every move the shade rippled and contorted its body to avoid destruction.

"You have long given up the rank of honor!" replied the Historian. "I will not heed the ravings of madness!"

Eljin charged at Edgar, but the mad man's mechanical arm, although rusting and bent, was still in good use. Edgar deflected the attack and flung Eljin into the fel-wolf who dropped Isaac as it dispersed around Eljin. The fel-wolf formed again on the other side just as Edgar swung his shock blade through its head.

The fel-brute was already beside the jet and flung Jono inside.

Keiko started to help Isaac climb to his feet when she saw Eljin scramble to the jet. He fumbled for a weapon inside the jet, yanking some strange gun free and aiming it at Edgar. They both ran after him, but a glowing blade cut into the stone in front of them, stopping them cold.

"Stay far from this viper!" Edgar ordered the children. "I'll see to the other—"

Edgar's voice was cut off by a deep bellow, and his head jerked to the side violently. His whole head was covered in a gelatinous sphere, almost as clear as water. He grabbed at his face and tried to remove the bubble, but it was stuck to his head, suffocating him.

Eljin pulled the trigger on his weapon a second time. The bubble gun bellowed deeply and another bubble collided with Edgar's chest. It flung him off the balcony. His metal body flailed as it disappeared through the clouds.

Eljin wore an arrogant grin for a moment before he saw more figures descending from above. He turned the bubble gun upwards and shot, but missed all three new attackers. Eljin turned to see the door on the silver jet shut, with Jono inside.

Eljin darted for the jet, but the engines flared and the ship rocketed away. He looked behind him with just enough time to duck out of the way of a metal hand sweeping toward him.

A line of black shadow stretched onto the balcony, and Ramsus slid down it. His eyes were black with glowing red pupils. The shadow gauntlet in his left hand swept over the children, protecting them in a black dome.

"Get back!" yelled Ramsus. "Wedge! Are you waiting for an invitation?"

Wedge flung himself at Eljin, who covered him with bubbles. It made no difference; Wedge didn't have to breathe.

Eljin shifted the settings on the gun then fired again. A green, sticky substance shot out and stuck Wedge's appendages to the ground. Eljin then turned, running to the edge of the balcony as if he were going to jump off, but Ramsus' right blaze gauntlet blasted a pulse of red spheres that hit Eljin's arm with such force that he spun around.

Eljin's arm went limp, but his reflexes were still sharp. He snatched the falling gun with his other hand and pointed it at Ramsus. He couldn't pull the trigger before the shadow gauntlet swung forward. It morphed into a hand that seized Eljin's whole body and swung him backward. His face smashed against the door, shutting it with a thud.

Ramsus ran over to Keiko and Isaac.

"Are you alright?" asked Ramsus.

"Save Jono!" yelled Keiko.

Ramsus turned to see the jet heading upward, away from the city and toward the black night.

"All defenses engage now!" Ramsus yelled to Biggs who transferred the command to the defense ring around the mountains.

Isaac nudged Keiko and pointed up. Above them a dome of lights now shone over the entire city. Sentry guns sprang up in a line all along the mountain ridge.

The silver jet spun away from the weapons, and darted downward, toward the city.

Wedge had freed himself from the bubbles and with one stretched hand, he lifted himself and Ramsus onboard as Biggs swooped past them.

The historian's jet swerved through clouds and spun around buildings trying to lose them. Ramsus crawled into a gunner's hole inside Biggs' chest. He could see at all angles and shot out a gray spider-web-like adhesive just as the jet darted downward.

"You've got to get me a clear shot, Biggs!" said Ramsus.

"Yeah, you tell that to them!" answered Biggs.

The silver jet dove through the city and swerved over a crowd of people at an open market. The rush of wind sent a volley of hats flying off peoples' heads.

Biggs grabbed the bridge above him and swung his massive body around to follow the quickly changing course of his prey. The jet spun around rows of pillars, trying to confuse and lose them. Biggs locked onto its position but instead of heading straight toward them, burst upward, through the clouded sky. He flew over the array of pillars while Ramsus shot a wide, sticky net over the whole area.

They dove again and spotted the jet just as the outer layer of its hull burst apart, like a snake removing its skin. The jet was free from all the sticky lines holding it in place.

Biggs darted forward with Ramsus blasting webs into the city. The webs caught random people in their grasp, but the jet was too fast.

The jet ignited a full engine burst then shot in a straight line through the city. It skimmed the cloudy surface and cut through the crack in the mountain before its afterburners burned out the cloud fall on the other side.

The sleek jet was designed for speed, ideal for a getaway, and there was no way Biggs could keep up on a straight shot. The jet released a hard burn of fuel with a brilliant flame behind them. Jono's body pushed into his seat. His cheeks pulled away from his mouth.

Sentry guns blasted volleys of bullets after it, but the jet released decoys and shifted to stealth mode. A burst of cold air hid the jet from heat seekers and thermal detectors.

Mortars exploded randomly in the chilling air, but Jono, the Historian, and the silver jet were lost in the darkness of night.

The Key to Destruction

"*I*t had to be the Day," said Isaac to a glaring Commander Grail when he met them on the balcony.

"They must have tricked Jono into it," insisted Keiko. "He wouldn't help them on his own!"

"I trust you on that point," Commander Grail replied. "The wretches under the Blue are not above exploiting the innocent."

Grail looked over the city's skyline. Far to the south, the Day was ready for war. He would not be the one to let them invade the Dark if there was anything he could do about it.

"The ship did head toward the south," added Ramsus. "They must be headed to the gathering army. Our engineers will start cracking the mind of the one we caught, but odds are his knowledge is limited. He keeps saying, 'We are the tomb of the world. We are the Tombs.'"

"Tombs?" Grail pondered the word and what it must mean to the man in their prison.

"This Eljin may not be of great use to us in the time that remains," said Ramsus.

"Do they really have it?" asked Commander Grail as his eyes met Isaac and Keiko. "Do the Solans have the key of Attrayer?"

The terrified look on the eyes of the two children confirmed the Commander's worst fears. He couldn't tell what tricks the Day was up to, but his students were honest pawns in this disaster.

"I saw it," said Isaac. "The old man took it with them. He had that same tomb symbol on a book."

"They would burn us all alive!" exclaimed Biggs.

"They'd turn their sun against us." Wedge said, nodding. "They'd steam the ice and make our skin boil." He looked at Biggs' metal body. "Well, those of us that have skin."

"The Empress must already know of it," said Grail. "We sought to calm a rebellion at the Keeper, but now it seems the worst has come to us."

The commander turned to the arched doorway. He knew what was coming. He could feel the war stirring in his bones. Time was more precious now than before and the consequences were about to lead them to the edge of oblivion. That wasn't his call to make. Only She could see them through this.

"Follow me. The Empress will have orders."

A crystal-black night watched from above, emotionless and indifferent as a speck of silver sped across snow-spotted plains dangerously near the surface of their humble planet in the middle of nowhere.

As they traveled across the globe, the stars above them, once brilliant and undeniable, receded into memory as the great abysmal expanse struggled against the illusion of sky, and with those twinkling spots faded Jonothon's hope.

Darkness clung to the sky as best it could, but there slipped a cloak of colored light across the sky. The belligerent hem flailed above that desperate empire of dirt. Piercing clouds morphed in the wind, content with their perpetual madness.

In that broken land on a distant edge of the globe lost between the worlds of Dark and Day, ran a fissure in the earth that cut through its mother, stabbing against the heavens. It cast a vengeful shadow over all lands to its north, denying them the warmth and light that waited beyond its southern ridge. Trees were scarce and none but the most despicable of creatures chose this land as their home. The ground itself melted in unnatural contortions, sharp and merciless.

It was a valley of death.

Crouched in the swaddling shadowed arms of that fissure, blue and gray skyscrapers clawed up from the soil like broken fingers yearning for freedom. The fault line spread a shroud over what was once, in eons past, a great and thriving city. Surrounding the city were vast fields of gray squares rising from the ground, cracked and broken and filling the land far into the horizon.

A bitter wind butted against the silver jet, shaking the vehicle. Jono gripped the side of his seat as he looked out the window. He felt as though they were flying through time as the vessel grew nearer and nearer to the ancient ruins.

Two skeletal skyscrapers tilted high together like a crumbling gate. Rebar stuck out from cement walls like bones of a corpse. It was one of a thousand tombstones in this graveyard of a forgotten world.

Jono stared over the horizon of decayed buildings, feeling full of regret. It was as though he had discovered the death of someone he never knew existed, someone whose life had been remarkable but only ruins remained.

"Where are we?" asked Jonothon.

"Home," said the Historian, and nothing more.

They continued above desolate streets and swerved between rectangular tombs. Somewhere in the jagged ground an unseen monster howled. The terrifying sound reverberated through canyons of buildings and shivered up Jonothon's spine.

The jet flew through a hole in the heart of one of the larger buildings. Its countless floors shared the same cavernous gap that tore down the center of the building like a vicious scar. The craft floated halfway up the building before it came to a rest on the cold ground.

The doors swung open, and the old Historian shuffled out. The interior of the building reeked of ancient decay. Only the floor that they arrived on had been renovated with thick rugs and tattered couches in the attempt to make the building livable. Its scattered decor looked out of place against the gray rubble. The floor was cracked and crackled beneath Jono's feet. The cluttered room resembled the Historian's tower, but in even more disarray.

Hovering along the walls in every direction were video screens that displayed news and images from across the whole world. Jono held his breath once he recognized what it was. One screen depicted a festival full of brightly colored tents that illuminated a strange swampland. Another screen revealed the construction of a twisted white tower in a blindingly bright desert. The screens peered over valleys and forests, cities and towns, inside homes and shops of every kind. A knight marched down golden halls; a young girl played with building blocks in a wooded home. It was like seeing the full existence of the world in all its synchronous, chaotic glory.

Earth, Jonothon saw, was much larger than he had really understood or appreciated. It was alive and wondrous and completely unaware of its impending doom.

"This changes everything."

The Empress looked out across frozen wastelands from the balcony behind her throne room. Four soldiers and two children stood behind her.

"We've sent a full squad after them," said Ramsus. "There has been no sight."

"Send more," she said, gripping tight the balcony's railing. Her body was tense, and her face filled with a nervousness that unsettled all of those around her. Her whispered words slipped from her lips and despite being no louder than a breath, they were all heard. "I can't see them . . ."

Keiko and Isaac looked at each other in nervous silence. The children shivered in the freezing air, but the Empress, despite the bareness of the skin beneath her robe, took no notice.

"Our forces, both here and abroad, are ready to deploy as we speak," said Grail.

The Empress nodded. "If the Day indeed has the key, then there is no other path left for us. We have been stripped of our options."

Keiko and Isaac couldn't muster any words at the plans unfolding before them and merely huddled together as the Empress' veiled face turned to them.

"Children, you must go now with your commander. If there is any help you can offer, it will be there at the field of battle." She turned to Commander Grail. "Prepare all of the troops. Prepare the city in case we fail. Let no resource go unfurnished."

Grail nodded, turned abruptly, and gestured to Keiko and Isaac to follow him. Grail led them through the throne room, and then turned to Ramsus.

"Send everyone the instant they are armed and spare no second before attacking. We are in a battle of time and strength. The Terralunans will surely aid the Day in destroying us."

Grail spoke to Ramsus, but his eyes were fixed on Keiko and Isaac.

"We must break free of this guillotine. We go to stare down our fate and defy it. We go to save the world. Make all forces ready! We leave now for the war to end all wars."

Across the tattered stone halls of the Windom Academy, students stood motionless in their dorm rooms and in the cavernous halls. Everyone was looking up. Hovering in the air was the image of their fearless leader.

Grail now commanded his troops.

"You have seen the destruction they brought to our school this very wake. Know now that a greater threat has been unleashed by the Day and if we do not confront it, all of the Dark will burn. Go to the ships at once. We are sending all of our troops as quickly as we can. You are all a part of the army of Eies and there is no time and fewer options. Grab your gear and get to the nearest launch deck. There is not a moment to spare. Move out!"

The image disappeared.

Many were dumbfounded by what their commander was asking them to do. Others moved swiftly to opened walls that hid munitions. Stone walls were alight with colored arrows that pointed to the nearest launch deck.

In the dining hall, older students seemed overjoyed at their chance for real combat.

"We'll show those rotten Solans," said a determined yeton boy.

"So they've finally had enough?" added a feli'yin girl. "It's about time!"

The younger students at the tables on the floor didn't share the same enthusiasm.

"You heard him!" Nick shouted at them. "Get to the ships and be ready to fight!"

"But I don't want fight," muttered Oscar, with a full mouth of mugaluk.

Nick leaped down and smashed the ceramic bowl with his boot. Mugaluk splattered across the table, but the boy took no notice.

"That ain't our choice, now is it?" Nick said as he leaned over Oscar. "You just do what needs doing and don't ever look back!"

"Why do we have to go, though? I thought that—"

"Did you hear what he said, scaly? They're gonna burn us alive if they get their way. Not sometime, not maybe. Now. As in, right now!"

Nick followed a flock of students to a teacher that handed out ammunition beside an open wall. He shoved a pulse gun into the hands of a small grudgon before adding a few more charged magazines to his own pockets and locked into his gun.

"I don't want to die," squeaked Oscar as he stared at his feet.

Nick shrugged and slid the gun strap over his shoulder and snatched a few grenades from a box.

"Nobody does. That doesn't change anything."

The caramel colored stones that were once laid as roads around the ruins of the Keeper were now separated by tall patches of green grass. The entire hillside was littered with broken pillars and stone carvings. Above the disguised army of knights and a thick tree line, the sky was torn in orange, pink, and purple.

A stiff breeze rustled through branches that hung over the Sage's makeshift headquarters. He looked out at the wide valley beyond the woods and the distant mountains that crowned the dark horizon bejeweled with stars.

A cloaked figure bounded up wide steps and passed the guards that protected the Sage of Ages. Aramis's pilgrim cloak sparsely hid his jade armor.

"It is certain news," said Aramis. "The forces of Darkness come now in full. It seems the Empress has chosen her path."

"Exactly as we feared," said the Sage. "Inform the war council to prepare for the worst. The lords of Terralunis surely see the danger as well as we do. Prepare, for she is coming. The full force of the valiant children of Blue Skies will not bend to Darkness without a fight!"

Jonothon felt a chill run down his spine.

More and more of the hovering screens displayed the preparations being made for war on both sides. Knights tested the electric fire of their blades. Soldiers scanned their bionetic bodies and checked their weapons. The gears of war clicked to life across the globe.

Jono shook his head in amazement. "You've been watching everything, everywhere."

The Historian almost snorted to contain a laugh. "It is extensive, certainly, but 'everything' would be presumptuous. I merely see the things I am looking for."

"Are these the eyes the Empress? Are you seeing what she sees?"

The Historian smiled. "You're partially right. We have procured some of the Empress' viewing network for our own purposes. In many cases we have found the need to populate our own means of sight and sound."

"But then, she could see you too."

"The Empress cannot see where she does not look."

The Historian swaggered to a deteriorated kitchen and filled a kettle full of water before placing it on a stove.

"What are you doing?" asked Jono.

The old man looked over his shoulder before returning his attention to the dusty stove. He pulled a tin of tea from a shelf.

"Isn't it obvious?"

"You started all of this." Jono's voice cracked with anger. "We could have made them see reason and not use the key. Or we could have destroyed it ourselves or . . ."

"Attrayer's key?" A sad smile spread across the Historian's wrinkled face. He took out the red and gray relic from his pocket and held it up to the artificial light. "The key to destruction they say . . . how absurdly poetic."

Without a thought or a care, the old man tossed the key aside. It wobbled through the air toward the hole in the center of the building like a leaf carelessly falling to the ground to be forgotten.

Jonothon snapped out of his shock. He leapt forward and barely caught it. He was stunned the one thing that had started all the fear between the armies of the Dark and the Day could be tossed aside so apathetically.

Jono held the circular key gently in his hands, but upon looking at it again, it now seemed simple, ordinary.

"They're in the air right now," Jono said, almost in a whisper, as he ran his fingers across the cold metal rim. "The Dark and the Day are going to war, all because of this?"

"No," the Historian replied as though making a simple correction. "The key was never more than what they made of it."

Jonothon stared back at him, confused. "Then Attrayer's key is just a myth?"

"As with all histories, there is some truth mixed with the fiction."

Jono held the key close to his heart. "But they believe in it! There may still be time. If I take the key to them, if I show them, then I might stop it."

The Historian sighed. "That trinket is not Attrayer's key."

The Gears of Noble War

"*W*hat?"

Jono's first reaction was to object. Of course it was Attrayer's key! He wanted to say that the Lords of the Day saw the exact image and they all agreed, but then he realized the flaws in his own mind.

Had the Historian ever truly said the red gemmed relic was actually Attrayer's key? Did the Lords of the Day have any better idea what it would look like? It was Aquinas that had seen the old drawing and believed it was the key in the first place.

"What is it, then?" asked Jono.

"That bauble in your hands is, by itself, nothing of consequence," said the Historian as he poured a steaming amber liquid into a small cup. "It's just relic. An old beacon. It was a standard peripheral for many ships of its eon. From the thirty seventh age of humanity. Not everything old is of value, Jonothon. At best it might be pawned to a witless collector, but it is certainly no ender of worlds. No, that special claim is reserved for the key that rests in the hearts and minds of those cursed souls that scream across the skies now, hungry for the battlefield."

The wretched facts sunk into Jono like an arrow to the heart.

It had all been a lie.

"You knew they thought it was true. You let them think it."

Jono clenched the relic tight and looked at the book with the cover of the symbol of the dead sun, the symbols of the tombs of the dead. The Historian had set it on a table before taking to his task of making tea. Jono picked it up and flipped through its musty pages.

"What is all this?" Jono held the book up. "Eljin has this tattoo on his arm. What does it mean?"

The Historian sat in a red leather chair angled toward an array of screens. He took a sip of his tea before answering.

"It is a reminder to those that remember the truth. We are the Tombs, a community of honest folk who gaze upon the world around us and know it for the trick that it is. Those of us that wear it or keep it ever close to our thoughts simply know the truth and are not afraid of it. We have embraced the reality that the balance will end. It was only a question of time. There was never a doubt, and now that time is here. I let you become entwined with the two wayward nations as they wrapped themselves in legend and fear. It will be their own hands that will tear down the world they built. That is the duty of the champions of old dead Sol. To help others see the truth. What they do with it is their own fault."

"You wanted them to do this? Why? It doesn't have to be this way."

"But it does. Not every detail is set, but the descent into oblivion is not a path that can be reversed. It is unavoidable. To be a part of the end of all that is . . . that is the last task left to us, the last honor."

"No, it isn't! This isn't the end. All you did was lie and trick them into this!"

"Do not be wrong, Mister Wyer, it is the primary failing of weak people." The Historian glared at him with stern eyes. "I did no such thing. I would not lie to you. Any question you will ask I will answer in truth, to the best of my knowledge. I would like you to understand there is no malice in our mission. Please appreciate that, at the very least. It is merely the fulfillment of a destiny that cannot be avoided. We are all servants of the stars. Despite all that we have created, all of our inventions, we are small, finite. That is the truth, and I embrace this now."

"Did Aquinas know?" asked Jonothon. "Was he a part of this?"

"Alexsayter Aquinas is not one of us. He is just a paranoid idiot, by no means a rarity. The world is bloated with them. It just so happens, this particular paranoia was cast out of my recruiting school and it seems he took it as an insult to his character. His desire for redemption became the instrument of his damnation. It is ironic that my most failed pupil would be the one to deliver the greatest gift. Inadvertent, of course, but pivotal nonetheless."

The old man and the young boy both looked to the monitors of the news as the army of the Day circled the temple of the Keeper.

Each of them felt sharply different emotions.

"Our time has finally come," said the Historian.

On a floating monitor a fierce young woman with fiery red hair appeared. She looked directly at it and smiled.

"Words of war have spread like wildfire across the Diremarc," she said. "I've even heard that a large group of farmers are traveling to join the war at Dawn. There are also whispers throughout our legion about the sacrifice of one of our own. Is it true?"

She clasped a necklace that held the symbol of the Tombs. "If it is, then he is but the first of us all. Praise and peace be upon him."

A new image surfaced, a stone-faced man with red dust behind him.

"I had meant to merely update the network, but the news has made all of us take a moment to grasp the clarity of our purpose. The first of the last wakes is upon us. Let us reign down truth of these final times upon those that hide from fate!"

"There are more of you?" asked Jonothon. "All over the world, making people hate each other. You're tricking them into wanting to fight."

The Historian shut off the monitor to his villainous partners. He didn't turn around to face Jono.

"That is far easier than you would think."

Above a brick mantle floated a screen showing a field at twilight. Tall reeds swayed and it looked warm despite the darkness in the sky. Jonothon wondered how many of these Tombs he might have seen in Polari. He wondered if the call to war had reached the children. He wondered if his parents and sister were still alright. Another screen showed a rally under Blue Skies with people chanting slogans against the Empress and the Dark End.

"Everyone is so fixed in their blame on the other that they didn't see you and what you've done," said Jono.

The historian sighed. "I do regret your unfortunate part in all of this, but innocence is always the victim in revolution."

"This never had to happen!"

"It always had to happen. There is no changing destiny. All life is a wheel. From death, new life is born. To live we must kill. We consume life to perpetuate ourselves and to the abyss of elements we must return. As we destroy to survive, we are destroyed so that others may live. So too are all the stars and all civilizations of the universe. That wheel has turned on the peoples of Earth. It all had to end sometime. This isn't a question of choice."

Jono was tired, lost, and his eyes and heart burned with despair. "This isn't destiny. You made this happen! You tricked the Empire! You made the Day believe this key would destroy them!"

"They had tricked themselves!" the Historian spat, his anger and torment released. "The key to destruction was always within their own minds. It was their fear, their pride that brought us here. When you make saints of yourselves and demons of your enemies, there are no limits to the destruction you can commit!"

Jono looked at the glimmering silver relic with its red sphere. "I can stop this. If only—"

"There is no 'if'. There is what is and there is what isn't! You cannot undo this. You cannot stem the tide of a thousand millennia. One way or another, the end is coming. It has been known long before all this was born into the world. These wakes are the beginning of the long awaited end."

Across the wide screens more images flashed of the world preparing for war. One image caught Jono's eye and made his mouth drop open.

It was Keiko!

She stood in a crowd of children, other students from the academy. They all wore armor too big for them and held guns that would surely knock them over. Light and clouds whipped past small windows that lined the room they were in.

They were flying. Flying to war. Flying to their deaths. The look in all of their eyes was the same sad fear and confused determination.

Commander Grail's voice bellowed through speakers . . .

". . . You are the valiant few that can stop the destruction of our home. You can snatch the lives of your families from the clutches of these Day monsters. Together we will conquer our enemies, who lust for death, and we will spread true progress across the sphere and into the stars! We fight for peace! We fight for hope and life!"

Keiko pulled her gun close to her chest and leaned her head against its barrel.

"We fight for freedom!"

The image shifted and Keiko was gone.

On another screen Jono could see the castle of Caer Midus. The screen was low, and he reached to touch it just as the image changed to another view of the castle. He tapped again and again, searching the castle until he found a balcony with pearl shades blowing in the breeze.

A blonde girl had wrapped herself in her arms. She looked cold despite the warmth of the sun. Her eyes were swollen but stern. Suriana looked hopelessly toward the northern horizon.

Jono's heart beat faster and his blood rushed through his veins. He had to do something! He couldn't let his chance to help slip away. He couldn't hide in his bed or ignore the world beyond his covers.

Jonothon pushed himself up, darted to the silver jet, and then leapt inside. He grabbed the steering column and slammed on the ignition, but the Historian was swift despite his old age.

The old man grabbed his arm.

"Don't go there. You cannot stop this."

"Let go!" Jono kicked at him, but the man grabbed his collar and nearly pulled him out of the vehicle. The jet spun in the air as Jono held tight.

The Historian was yanked off the ground as the jet spun over the chasm in the building. The old man gripped the side of the door with his free hand and tried to get his foot inside. He grabbed hold of a lever, but that only made the car spin vertically out of control.

The tail of the jet smashed against the ceiling and launched through the gaping hole in the building. The jet collided with an exposed support beam and then whipped around violently as it fell to the main room, falling through many of the floating screens. It crashed against the floor and flung the Historian loose. It slid along the ground before its nose punctured a wall and dangled over the many stories below them.

Jono lifted his head slowly.

Every muscle in his body was sore. He was surrounded by blue, protective foam that had already begun to fizzle. Under the jet's contorted metal frame, a fire spread, but a puff of white smoke shot out from below it and quenched the flames.

The jet was dented badly. The screen in the middle of the console was black with a crack running down the middle of it. Jono tapped the screen, but it made no sign of activity.

The Historian was not far from him, his body sprawled limp against the rubble of the old room. A bone stuck out of his leg, and his arm bent in a way it shouldn't.

Jono walked to him, steadfast, *like Illius confronting the heartless king*, and he demanded information.

"Tell me where the Keeper is."

The old man's smile was full of bloody teeth. "Such fire in you! You'll need it. The final times will be a turbulent descent."

Jono grabbed him by the collar and yelled desperately in his face. "Where is the Keeper?"

"My boy, I would not have you dream of things beyond your ability. There is no changing what must come," said the Historian with a deep sympathy in the blood-filled wrinkles on his face.

"WHERE—" Jono's small fist collided against the white-bearded cheek with every ounce of force his could muster.

"IS THE—"

He hit him again and again. His fist throbbed and ached and drew blood from both of them.

"KEEPER!"

The broken old man laughed. He finally succumbed to the question out of pity rather than pain.

"To the west."

Jonothon's red eyes burned with distrust.

"It is the truth. Just follow the Dawn. When you see their armies and fields of the dead, then you'll know you have arrived."

Jono released his grip of the man's collar and ran back to the crashed craft. He hit the red ignition switch, and the jet growled painfully and then died. He tried it again, and the jet craft shook and rattled then thudded again into silence.

A sick weight sank to the bottom of his stomach. He tried to start it again and again and every time was to the same effect. His heart ached and his blood froze. He'd chosen to charge against the war, he had stood against evil and was going to save the world, and only the simple failure of the jet was stopping him.

"I can do this." *Just think it through.* He looked at twisting wires and boxes and blinking lights. He thought of how Illius tricked the goliath. He thought of all the stories and heroes that had snatched victory out of certain defeat. They had found a way. They had helped the ones they cared for. He could do this. He had to do this.

From behind him cackled a laugh of sick despair. It started out guttural and quiet and grew unhinged into the maniacal madness of the dying old man.

"You can't fix it." Tears and blood stung the old man's eyes. "That such pivotal events could be swayed by the simplest of things. This is the sick twist of destiny, boy. The spit and wisdom of your seraphim."

The Historian rested his head against the rubble. He made no attempt to stand. A stream of blood crept down the back of his neck.

"Think before you act. What will you do once you get there? A small boy with a round metal piece of garbage? Will you wave it around in the middle of a battle and hope they notice you and stop? You will never get the leaders of either End to reason after they are determined not to. They will both shoot you down upon approach."

Jono could feel his heart pound inside his chest and his fingers began to shiver. He tried to ignore the old man. *The jet wasn't working. Why wasn't it working?* Jono laid his head against the console as the world closed in around him. He felt alone and weak and utterly helpless; he didn't even think to fight the tears that swelled in his eyes. Above him, he heard a quiet sound that emanated from the remaining screens. The sound slowly became louder, amplified by the synchronous voices of the many screens displaying the same two scenes.

"I come to you on this sorrowful occasion, not as your Empress, but as an emissary of hope. You all know of the dangers that have befallen us. We have been brought to this terrible circumstance through treacherous madness of the Day."

The Empress' voice was gentle but strong as she spoke to the legions of soldiers and all the towns and cities across the Dark End.

"It is the blind ambition of the Machine of Darkness," said the Sage of Ages across all the screens in every building under Blue Skies, "that has reached a peak of unforgivable infamy that now demands the vigilance of all those that love life and peace. We walk upon a dangerous precipice. On either side there is death and darkness, but we shall not stray from our narrow path! We are united for light and for hope!"

"The knights of Day have gone mad with their zeal and would destroy the balance of all our lives for their blind pride," the Empress told all the people under the stars. "There can be no peace if our security depends on the will and whims of thoughtless and aggressive dictators. We march now to end the violence they have wished for, to end the imprisonment of our people and the psychological enslavement of their own. The lords of Day may yearn for war, but our honor will inform them of their terrible error. No fear shall deter our freedom! No evil will turn our hand from justice!"

"We will free our lost brothers from the veil of darkness that has blinded them to virtue!" the Sage bellowed. "It was a prison cast upon them by their own wicked master! We shall defend the light of life against those who would drag us into the Pit!"

"Peace will be the banner of our victory!"

"A world united in freedom from tyranny, oppression and greed!"

"Let all the world know that we have stood against enemies of freedom and never faltered!"

"We stand now for justice!"

"For peace!"

"For the light!"

"For freedom!"

It seemed as though the world itself shook with a swell of cheers, roars of hope and shouts of faith eager to be tested.

Into the Fray

ono smashed his fist against the plastic steering wheel. He imagined Keiko and Isaac screaming for help as destruction reigned down around them.

"You have seen them from both Ends of the sphere," the Historian's voice cracked from across the room. "Do you think that tiny, obvious truth would dissuade them once their hearts are fixed on war?"

The Historian's voice was weak, and he struggled to speak over the pain in his broken body. He winced and propped himself up on his arm. "No. This is the nature of their world. This is . . ."

Jono ignored him and tried the engine again and again and every time it failed. His body shook with fury and fear and . . . his hand moved to his chest. He felt the heart regulator just as he noticed the shattered pieces of electronics that didn't belong to the jet. With the slightest touch, more pieces fell from the broken machine and tumble down the inside of his shirt.

An icy terror seized his body.

Jonothon folded his arms and tried to calm himself. He tried to steady his heart and breathing, but a wave of tremors flooded his body and agitated his throat. He realized something was different the instant before he began coughing violently.

His body revolted against him, and he fell sideways out of the jet, and coughing and clenching at the bare wire ports at his chest. He rolled onto his stomach and gasped for air, spitting out black, oily goo onto the ground. He fought for every half-breath as he peered at the image of a fleet of black ships soaring through a sky riddled with red and violet.

Jono clutched his chest. Another fit of coughs took over every muscle. He curled and hunched over the cement, hacking painfully. Jono heaved and spat in vain until a thick, dark mucus dripped from his trembling lips as the beetle filter, squirming fat and happy, scrambled onto the cold cement.

There was nothing he could do.

The Historian was quiet, and the screens displayed their truth solemnly and without remark.

There was nothing to be done but accept the things that could not be changed.

The room was silent.

The world seemed soaked in a gross and inevitable atrophy. The dead city mocked him; it cursed the world to its own fate.

Jono jerked his head up. He reached forward and slid himself along the floor. He breathed in deep, calculated breathes as he crawled to the screen above the mantel.

There was no way he could bring the key to them, to make them understand. They might not have even believed it was the great key of Attrayer if they had seen it in person, but there was still the Keeper. That was real, and all their eyes would be fixed on it. They would be watching, waiting for either side to unleash its power. Only, that would never come. They would fight to the death thinking the other side had the key and was only moments away from destroying all they loved, unless . . .

Jono grabbed the screen with his wires and pulled it to him. He ran his hand along the side and found what he was looking for. He had to try a couple times before he found the right port. A shimmering black wire slid out of his sleeve and plugged into the network.

He glanced at the Historian, who seemed far older than before. The man's eyes were shut and his body lay completely still.

Jonothon connected his wire to the screen and closed his eyes.

Of Metal & Flesh

*I*n the middle of a brilliant pink sky, Jonothon saw a spot of black. It hovered in the air like an ebony butterfly carelessly surveying the world. Clouds breezed by, above and below, but the serene creature seemed oblivious. The white stars of the violet sky flared in distant twinkling. The black speck flared with white as well, and in that instant, Jonothon knew the Terralunan's Chimera had laid its eyes upon the growing chaos around him.

Jono's view rotated.

He couldn't ·control the motion of his new eye piece. The view turned toward stone pillars and leafy trees littered with camouflaged armaments and knights and mages shouting orders at each other. A dim blue light spread above the tree line. It connected with other crystal towers that pushed the magical blue shield further still.

The camera continued to move until it fixed itself squarely on the north.

The Dark End's sky fleet cut through orange and pink clouds like a thousand stones raining sideways across the horizon.

On the ground, mages stood in circles casting joined spells that shot blue glowing spheres up to blanket the sky. The first volleys of flame and destruction were upon them.

Light flashed all around Jono's view and exploded against the blue dome of light. Shrapnel sparked and bounced across the blue dome but never fell through the shield.

Jono tore the image from his face. His eyes adjusted on the nightmarish realm of the Tomb's code world. It was nothing like the eyes of the Empress. It was chaotic mess of files, images, and data from all sorts of castles, dungeons, cities, and ethereal places beyond the grasp of the Earth. Stars and stone terraces and shards of the world contorted around him. Every direction was up and down all at once.

Jono rummaged through a pile of clutter before pulling a silver platter from a table that had been cut in half. It looked and felt like raw data, but as Jono ran his mind's hand along its surface, he could tell that it was different. The Tombs disguised how they had broken into the eyes of the Empress.

Jono put the silver platter against his face and the realm of chaotic code disappeared.

Mortars exploded around him just as the metal wheel the mech soldier used as a leg shattered into a thousand pieces. Jono could see the green fields, discolored by the light, which led to hills covered in trees and protected by the blue dome. The soldier wasn't moving anymore. The horizon rotated sideways until the electronic eyes smashed against the side of a rock and cut him off from the battle.

Jono dug through the code world again; he had to find a port that would let him speak or be seen near the Sola base. He put a woolly shoe to his face. Trees grew tall around him. Muffled voices crept through the thicket. Jono turned the camera and saw the Sage of Ages speaking to the hovering image of a knight.

"Stop!" Jono yelled, but there was no microphone connected to his viewer. They couldn't hear him.

"The sentries are nearly ready," said the Sage with fierce authority. "Once the fleet has passed over, remove them from hiding and unleash your weapons freely."

"As you will it," replied the knight. "Our forward crystal mirrors are largely destroyed, but we have confirmed they are dropping ground troops to siege our shields."

"Send out what brave souls you can," said the Sage, "and keep a constant cover fire over them. We must not let one spire of the shield fade. Make them hold, good sir, this is the last great thing we do."

Jono tore through the ports that littered the amalgamated code world but couldn't find one with a speaker. The files that the Tombs used were a mess of disorder, hidden and encoded amongst other files from systems all over the sphere. Jono peeled another image off his mind's eye and rummaged through the network to find another. He had to get to the Keeper; he had to find a way to get everyone's attention, to make them stop.

The Empress leaned forward on her black metal throne. Her hands clenched together and her thick black hair spread backward, connected to the machines on the wall and ceiling.

"Has there been any change from the ruins? Any alterations of radiation or internal activity?" Her voice was almost a whisper.

"None," answered Commander Grail's hovering visage. "Even compensating for the disruption of their shields, the readings we have show that the interior of the Keeper has not been breached. It may be that their disdain for technology has stunted their ability to use the key against us. There may yet be hope."

The Empress nodded. "Do not cease, commander. Our fate will be decided on a single breath."

"We siege them by air and ground now. They are well fortified but they cannot last against . . ." The image flickered. Grail's voice crackled until it was lost and the hovering light mutated into a cloud of disorder.

The Empress stared at the aberration until the nebula of static was replaced by a short, skinny boy.

"You!"

Jono squinted as though he couldn't quite see what he was looking at.

"Jonothon! How is this possible?" said the Empress.

"You can see me?" Jono beamed with relief.

"Yes. Where are you? Answer me," she said with deep concern.

"I have the key!" Jono blurted. "It's not what it seems. You have to trust me and..." Static cut into his transmission, "...the attack before...It can't do any..."

"Are you near the ruins?" The Empress stood. "Can you tell me if they know how to use the key?"

"I don't..." The image disappeared and Grail once again hovered in front of her.

"I'm sorry, my Empress, our transmitter seems to have been—"

"I saw the child." said the Empress.

"Wyer?" Grail asked. "My stars . . . Are they holding him at the Keeper?"

"I could not detect from where the image had been transmitted," she replied. "It had been blocked from my sight . . . they knew how to block me."

"Who could do such a thing?"

Her lip trembled. There was a hint of true terror in her voice.

"I fear the Keeper has been lost."

Jono blinked before he saw the Historian's bloody hand clenching the wire coming out of his arm.

"So, you tried talking to them?" said the Historian as he leaned against the tattered gray wall, barely able stand. "How did that work out? I'm sure they are reconciling their differences now."

Jono recoiled and yanked the wire out of the old man's hands. "I will stop it."

"I cannot let you try." The Historian hobbled toward Jono. He whinced with every step as he dragged his broken leg. His wrinkled hand shook but was fast enough to snatch the hovering screen and thrust it through the air. Jono ducked out of the way, but the screen soared passed and smashed into the array. Monitors cracked and went black.

"No!" yelled Jonothon as he tried to keep his heart from beating out of control.

"I am sorry, but I can't let them find us."

The Historian moved toward the screens that hovered over the stove. "The others should be here soon. I'll have to destroy all of these in case I die before they arrive."

The old man grabbed another screen and lifted it to smash it on the ground. Jono lifted his arm and three wires shot out to wrap around the man's ankle. Jono pulled them back, and the old man crashed to the floor.

Jonothon's wires stretched to the other side of the room and pulled back another screen. It was different from the first one. Just as he found the right port to use, a vein-riddled hand grabbed the top of the screen and pulled it away. Jono released a barrage of spy cables that clung to the Historian and lifted him into the air.

"I won't let you do this," said Jono.

The wires thrust the Historian away, flinging him across the gaping hole in the floor to the other side of the crumbling room. His body cracked against the cement floor, his already broken bones splintering. The Historian made a gurgling noise that almost sounded like a laugh.

Jono pulled the screen close and sent all but one of his cables out. Their mechanical mouths snapped down on the floor and ceiling, making a tangled web of metal to protect him. He connected again and with a blink he was back in the code world.

From the ramparts around the Keeper, an army of mages cast a volley of dark objects that shot into the air. One burst into a magical net and latched onto an air ship. The net wrapped around it. Sparks ignited off the metal as the net fried the electronics of its prey. The ship lost control and spun violently through the battle in the sky.

The Day continued to send a storm of spells and clouds of fairy fire from all around the ruins, but the Dark ships destroyed most of them before they could do much damage. The Empress' fleet released a mass of green dots. These gelatinous drops fell on the battlements like rain. When they landed, the soldiers inside them hit a blue panel and the gelatinous sphere around them dispersed. Keiko, Isaac, and other students were among the fray to spread out and fire back on charging knights and casting mages.

A massive flight carrier in the back of the fleet swooped low to the ground to release its cargo. Two Argonaut mechs shook the ground as they landed.

In the base camp at the Keeper, the Sage looked up at the charging army of black metal against the violet sky.

"Protect this land with your lives!" the Sage ordered.

The knights and mages charged forward on armored birds.

"Let loose the sundrakes!" roared the Duke of Diremarc, his sword blazing in the air. "Tear their trinkets from the sky!"

Gold-and-red-feathered dragons burst through the tree line and soared into the sky at his command. Their long, scaly bodies swerved around oncoming fire as they tore into the Dark fleet. Their pointed beaks and titanium talons cut through the metal wings of black ships.

A sundrake landed on the hull of a troop carrier and began splitting the roof apart with its claws. It bore its head down to reach inside but was knocked from the hull into the open air. Its dark assailant had two sets of spined, metal wings and glowed with blue light along the cracks in its black frame—a demon of mechanix and gray flesh.

The demon mech grabbed the drake's arms and cut at its wings as the two creatures fought and fell and flew again, each trying desperately to destroy the other.

"Attack their battlements, but do not harm the Keeper!" Grail bellowed throughout the fleet.

On the ground, giant shelled beasts burst out from the soil surrounding the Argonauts. They clamped onto the metal frames and spread acid-green goo before an Argos snatched one with its giant hand and flung it across the field into the oncoming knights.

A squad of soldiers joined the gigantic mechs against the knights and their beasts. Soldiers shot explosive spheres from their arms and cut at the shells with blades of glowing light from their gauntlets.

Above the chaos, the Chimera, along with its Terralunan masters, surveyed the destruction with cold, calculating eyes.

Jono gazed upon a tattered field and the distant mountains cutting off the northern horizon. He moved his head and he was surprised to see that the view moved with it. He tried to look to the south, but his new head couldn't move much. He looked down and saw the destroyed robotic body connected below him.

Jono was about to leave the port when he saw her. Army gear and bobbing pig tails caught his eyes and almost stopped his heart. Keiko ran across a grassy hill, dodging pixie fire as best she could.

She yelled to someone, but Jono couldn't see who it was. Keiko darted through tall grass and leaped over a robotic corpse. She pulled a metal body on its side to hide behind it. Jono screamed, but the robot's voice box had been destroyed. Keiko looked back and forth. A green head popped out behind a mound of dirt on the side of the hill.

Isaac was close by, calling to her from his chameleon bunker. She dove for the bunker just as pixie fire hit the ground behind her and burst into lashing, flaming vines. The explosion ripped apart the robotic body but luckily sent the head tumbling after her. Isaac aimed his gun out of the hole in the bunker and shot three glowing blue balls that swerved as they flew toward the distant target.

The audio was full of static, but Jono could still hear them.

"Are you alright?" asked Isaac, pulling Keiko close to the inner wall of the bunker.

Keiko nodded. "Have you seen any of the others?"

"Just Knox. He was running toward the fight between the tortogres and the Argonaut. You?"

"Natalie Plank was in a bubble trap over by the center drop zone. I cut her out of it, but we got split up when the knights charged us."

Isaac clenched his teeth as he thought. "D'you think they have Jono trapped on the other side?"

Keiko didn't have an answer. "If he's there, and the Solans have the key, then what are they waiting for?"

They looked at each other, their faces wrought with desperation.

Jono couldn't bear to stay any longer.

The next port he tried seemed at first to be broken and filled with a loud static. Jono's ears buzzed, and then he realized it was the sound of alarms going off. The deck of a ship flashed in red lights, and people yelled at each other without noticing the young boy that appeared out of nowhere.

Jono looked down and saw his arms and his chest clearly in front of him. He tried to touch his face, but he felt nothing. His whole body was there, but it was completely illusionary.

"Can you hear me?" Jonothon asked an ensign sitting next to him.

"Get off the deck and back to the drop hatches, cadet!" the ensign shouted back at him.

"But you can hear me?" Jono asked again, excitedly.

"Of course!" barked the ensign, his face contorted with annoyance. "Now you hear me and get!"

Jono nodded but instead of moving toward the door, he stayed where he was and looked around. On the left side of the deck, where the wall of controls met an array of screens showing the violence outside, there was small vent that shot a steady stream of air into the room. Jono stepped toward it just as the ensign reached out to grab his arm to stop him. The otherwise sturdy ensign fell out of his chair when his fingers slipped through the boy's body.

Jono focused on his dragonfly-shaped hollow-heart, and commanded it to float into the vent. Jono could barely see, but he wound his way through the maze of air vents until he finally popped out the other end and onto the nose of the flying black troop carrier.

Jono was overcome by the sight.

The sky was bloodied with explosions of color and noise from endless swarms of black ships, monstrous flying mechs, and dazzling dragons that darted all around him. Explosions thundered from every direction. A merciless wind roared over the ship and caused Jono's image to flicker. He inched closer to the tip of the massive black carrier until he could see the mesh of forest speckled in orange stone and pillars.

In the center of the ruins lay a carved human face bursting out of the tree line. The face pointed upward, but its gaze veered silently to the south and the distant, burning sun.

In the middle of the shrapnel of exploding ships and screams of sundrakes, Jono stood still and settled his heart. He breathed deep, his image mimicked the motions that his physical body did hundreds of kilems away.

Jonothon charged for the edge and leapt into the sky.

The hollow-heart struggled to descend without becoming lost in the gusts of wind created by the air battle.

The battle exploded across the sky as Jono fell through it.

The image of his feet touched down centimeters above the grass, and he burst into a sprint.

A squad of soldiers charged to one of the shield pillars as knights ignited their fiery blades to defend their post. Jono ran ahead of the crowd, toward the knights. He was close enough that he could see the hesitation in their eyes before they attacked. Jono hopped through the crack between the pillar and the shield and darted through the confused knights.

"A kid?" asked a human knight.

"Is he real?" said a feli'yin knight.

They spun around, unsure if they should follow him or fight off the oncoming soldiers.

"Don't just stand there! Get him!" shouted their captain.

"Where did he go?"

Jono ran through the trees toward the Keeper without stopping. He barreled through the war camp of the Day, occasionally catching someone's eye, but he was gone before they could react.

The Sage studied a living map of the battle inside a tent when Jono passed. The Sage turned and pushed the tent's cloth door aside, but Jono was already hidden behind a tall wall of stone the lined the path to the Keeper.

Chapter Forty

The Thoughts of the Keeper

The bionetic soldiers of Eies tore through the shield pillar and a battalion of knights met them on the other side. Fiery swords clashed with electrified gauntlet blades sparking bullets of light that peppered the air like fireworks.

The Sage of Ages stood at the edge of the clash, his wooden staff held high as the crystal on its crest glowed blue.

"Winds of Odin! Send these invaders back whence they came!"

The group of soldiers were flung back from the blast, and the knights charged at them with binding spells.

A thud echoed through the ruins as Commander Grail landed on the hill. "Sage!" Grail bellowed, the guns on his arms roaring to life. "You must surrender now! End this madness!"

"I will never allow you to black out the light!" the Sage replied with a wave of his staff. A fiery dragon burst from the crystal and circled Grail. It spiraled around him and, just as the fire beast swooped down from above, Grail leaped through the flames and launched a volley of concussion grenades at the Sage.

The Sage waved, forming a fairy shield just as the explosions tore through it and flung him to the ground. Metal chains shot from Grail's arms and snared the Sage's leg and arm.

"Don't let any more of my soldiers or your knights die for this failed cause!" Grail roared over the noise of war.

"Death is all your Empress has in store for the Day. I will not allow the light to end!" The Sage's staff slammed onto the ground, and the earth itself tore upward. Rocks cut through Grails chains, and a burst of stone sent Grail flailing into the air.

Jono ignored the chaos behind him and ran to the center of the ruins, looking for an entrance, but there was none. He found a plaque of information set on the side of the main structure, supposedly for tourists and pilgrims. As he approached, the sign came to life. A hologram of the Keeper appeared, and a pleasant woman's voice began to speak.

"Little is known about who built this ancient structure, or about the true purpose of its being. The mythological belief holds that the Keeper plays an important role in maintaining the balance of the world. When the angels rescued the planet, they established this Keeper to maintain cosmic order while they were away. It is said that when the seven seraphim return from hiding to rule the Earth in its final wakes, the Keeper would give up control to them, and the planet would be prepared to join the absent ancient god in a paradise beyond the veil.

"In recent history, limited excavation projects have confirmed that the seemingly solid structure does hold some open areas beneath it, but no doors have ever been discovered. It is believed this design was intentional to avoid any tampering with the Keeper's mechanix. Due to the sacred and cultural nature of this ruin and the disputed ownership given its geographic location, there have been perpetual limitations placed upon the scientific community that have prevented them from exploring it further."

"There's no way in?" said Jono, dismayed. "That's impossible."

The voice ignored him and continued to prattle on. "While the official pilgrimage occurs only once a solar cycle, there are continuous visitors throughout the year and regular events, both seasonal and historically based, that provide insight and entertainment for travelers from all over the sphere. If you would like more information regarding these events, don't hesitate to ask."

Jono raised his hollow hand against the stone wall. The carved rock was old and porous. Cracks sporadically invaded the rock. There was a particularly large crack near the center. Jono faced it and poked a finger in to measure its width. He tried to see how far it went, but the dim light of Dawn was quickly swallowed up in the shadows.

There was no time and no other way. Jono sent the hollow heart into the darkness. He could almost feel the cool air around him as he sunk through the crack. He swerved and searched, deeper and deeper, into the unknown. The darkness was so thick and he had floated so far that he didn't know which way was up. It wasn't long before he wondered if he could even go back, but after spinning around, he realized he didn't know which way to go.

The noise outside the ruins had become hidden by the solid walls that wrapped up like a cocoon. Jono began to lose track of time. He wondered, if he ever did find a way into the Keeper, would it be too late?

When he first caught a glimpse of light, his immediate fear was that he'd gone in circles and ended up where he began, but he realized that this light was different. It was brighter, more pure. Jono followed the light until it grew and illuminated a cold stone and metal hall around him.

A hint of whispers crept through the hall from somewhere far away, many whispers talking over each other. Jono charged toward the light, turning corners and running down stone corridors.

"Hello?" Jono shouted as he ran. The tiny speaker in the hollow heart shouted as loud as it could.

The whispers grew louder and louder, closer and closer until they stopped altogether. There was utter silence as Jono rounded a final corridor and stopped abruptly at the entrance to the heart and mind of the Keeper. It was an immense chamber whose walls, floor and ceiling were covered like a briar patch with brown stone statues. Their bodies stuck partially out of the walls, floor and ceiling. They all stared intently, and silently, at their young visitor.

On the far wall was the source of the brilliant light.

The hall ended in jagged, rocky teeth and opened to a void of space and clear stars. Just over the lower edge, poking over the horizon, was the burning son of the once burning mother.

Jono wanted to go to it, to walk to the edge, even touch the light of the sun, but the statues thickly covered the floors, and there would be no way to pass without their consent.

"Who are you?" asked Jonothon.

The statues whispered to each other before a woman, sticking waste-up out of the ground, answered in a gentle voice. "We are the thoughts of the Keeper."

"Do you . . . do you know what's going on outside?" said Jono.

"We are aware of all that goes on upon this sphere," responded an authoritative knight whose face poked halfway out of the wall.

"I need to stop what is happening," said Jono. "You have to help me."

"I open for none but the key," replied the knight.

"But I don't have it. I don't even know what it is or if it is even real." said Jonothon.

"Real?" asked another thought. "What does *real* have to do with anything?"

"Any what?" asked a child-like thought. "You mean the key?"

"Yes." said Jono. "What is the key?"

"It is the riddle at the right time," said one of the thoughts.

"Alright then, what's the riddle?" asked Jonothon.

The faces looked at each other, puzzled.

"I'm not sure we would know, would we? Why do you think we are waiting for it?" said a face on the floor.

"Don't be silly," said a feli'yin thought. "The key is a code. Like a potion made from a mixture of plant juices under electrolysis."

"No, no!" said a large-bellied statue sticking out of the lower left side of the chamber. "I'm pretty sure the key is a frame of mind. You know, think the right way or something. That way, only the right type of person could use us."

"No, you're all wrong. It must be some kind of puzzle," said a human-shaped thought. "Quick, say 'key' backwards."

"Umm . . ." Jono cleared his throat and shouted, "Yek?"

They all waited.

Nothing happened.

The human thought looked side to side. "Does anyone feel any different?"

It was greeted with silence before an armored thought said, "I kind of feel like dancing . . . only I have no feet."

The thought looked down, and true enough, his body melted into the wall just below the knees.

The first thought shrugged. "Guess that's not it."

"Wait a second," said a dryad thought. "Didn't we already have the key here?"

"Only when they started us," answered a chubby thought. "But that was many millennia ago."

"Oh, that's right." She sighed with all the importance of a forgotten grocery list item.

"I can't believe it," Jono said to himself. He knelt on the stone floor in despair. *The thing that holds the balance of the world, what everyone is killing over, is completely crazy. It doesn't know what to do either.* He looked at the many thoughts inside the mind of the Keeper.

"Don't you know what's going on outside?"

"Sounds a bit like war to me," said a skinny thought.

"Oh, yes. That again." The dryad thought shrugged. "How boring."

"We've got to stop it!" Jono yelled.

"What's that?" asked a gromlin thought. "We should stop it? Stop the light now, eh?" The gromlin let out a cackling laugh.

"No," said a goat-headed thought. "Stop the fixed position. Spread the light over the world. That's the right thing to do."

"I don't think either of those is quite right," added an old thought. "I was certain we are supposed to shoot the light deep into space."

"No!" yelled Jono. "Don't do any of that!"

"Well, I feel like doing something!" moped a feli'yin thought.

Jono looked back to see the light of the burning sun change. The sun at the end of the room, that orbited the earth, pointed higher and higher until he could see where the light ended. The burning sun didn't shine in all directions, just one, like a flashlight. On the back side of it was a huge, mechanical complex.

On the field of Dawn, the forces of both armies stood still. Not a bullet was fired nor a blade swung. Soldiers and knights stood side-by-side, their eyes transfixed on the sky as the light grew brighter. Dawn gave way to morning, the light blared over them with the heat of Day, and then was followed by twilight, dusk, and the black pitch of night. After a few chilling, frightful moments of Dark, the light came again with the dawn and the Day.

There were moments that each side wondered if they had won. Others wondered if, at any moment, the other side would surrender and victory would be secured. But as the sun kept spinning around and around, a sick realization caught hold of the masses.

Not all was well, or would be well. They weren't witnessing the victory of one side over the other, but the destruction of both.

The warriors of the world dared not move or lose a single moment of lucidity at this, the end of all things.

"What are you doing?" yelled Jono. "Stop it!"

"What?" asked a woman thought.

"Oh, you mean that?" said the chubby thought. "We are just getting things ready, is all."

"Ready for what?" asked Jonothon.

"How should I know? It hasn't been decided."

"You must be the sane one," said a gruff, hairy thought to a pretty dryad girl. "What is it that you think we should do?"

Her answer was simple. "Blow it up, I imagine."

"What?" said Jono.

"Blow it all up," said the dryad. "That sounds about right. Isn't it about time?"

"No!" insisted Jonothon. "Don't ever do that! Don't blow it up! The key will never come so just keep things as they were!"

"Well, for how long?" nagged the dryad.

"Forever!" said Jono. "Never let it end."

The faces all looked around at each other, completely confused.

"Well, that's not computationally possible, now is it?"

"Ha! 'Forever' he says!" scoffed a gromlin thought.

"Alright, do it for as long as you can," Jono insisted.

"Oh. Well, fine. Have it your way, but if you change your mind . . ."

"I won't, and don't ever listen to anyone else who tells you different!" replied Jonothon.

"But what if they have this key thing you came in here talking about?"

"Well, then they're lying and you shouldn't trust them."

"Should we blow ourselves up then?"

"What? No!" said Jono.

"There was plenty of blowing up going on outside . . ."

"I know. How can we stop them?"

"One must appreciate the limits of one's control over others," advised a smug looking thought. "Sometimes, the choices of those who are not you is beyond your ability to change."

"Live and let live, I always say."

"But they're dying!" Jono yelled.

"That's not your place to judge," said a snotty looking thought with a shrug.

"It isn't judgment. It's what they're doing right now."

"Oh, yes. Right."

"I need to stop this, but they have to know," said Jono, his eyes squinted at the beaten relic in his hands. "If they knew there was no key . . ."

"But there isn't any key."

"Yes, but if they thought the key was destroyed or that you wouldn't change the balance, then they wouldn't have a reason to fight."

"Oh, we can grab their attention, but I can't commit to changing their minds about anything," said a thought.

"We could lock the keeper," said the chubby thought. "Fix the system on a perpetual command."

"Yes, but so long as we remain," said the woman thought, "there is a greater chance of a new factor being introduced to us that would change our orders to not change anything. It stands to reason that the only safe way to ensure the near-forever status quo, at least by our part, would be to lock the keeper and destroy ourselves."

The other thoughts nodded approvingly.

"Can't argue with logic."

"It is about time."

"Destroy us, then?" said a contemplative head with his fist underneath his chin.

Jono was dismayed, but it was happening so fast that he couldn't come up with an alternative.

"I knew that was coming!" said a tiny gromlin thought. "Initiate self-destruct!"

"Finally!" said the dryad.

The hillside covered in trees and orange stone began to rumble. Out of the center of the Keeper ruins lifted the giant, stone head with Jono and the room of thoughts inside it. On either side, stone and metal arms raised up and came together over the keepers head.

"Hear me, children of old! There will be no turning of Day and no waning of Night!" bellowed the ancient voice of the Keeper. "The balance will remain. One side Dark, the other Day, no changes can be made. So shall it be done to the end!"

The rotating sun stopped. It was exactly where it had begun and the valley was awash in Dawn. The stone face leaned back until it pushed into the ground once more.

On the battlefield, the knights and soldiers that held their breath now clenched their guns and held flaming blades tense. They stared at their enemies, but no one moved. They waited. They waited for orders. Kill? Or retreat? No one dared make the first move. No one dared to make the decision on their own.

And so, they waited . . .

Inside the head of the Keeper, the statues of thoughts were shaking hands and hugging each other with cheerful goodbyes.

"I'm sorry you have to go," said Jono.

"We understand," said a motherly looking thought.

"It is time, isn't it?" said the inquisitive one, looking at a set of glowing numbers that lit up the floor.

"We'll open the way for you."

"Thank you." Jono ran back down the hall as fast as he could.

"Best be quick!" called the armored thought cheerfully after him. "We've been waiting a long time for this!"

The timer counted down, and the statues in the walls all waved at him. They had opened a path that lead straight to the outside world. The hall shook and began to crumble. A distant door revealed the chaos of oncoming battleships and soldiers from all over the sphere as they charged forward.

Jono ran through the open door, bursting out into the sky as the stone doors slammed behind him.

The sky above was a harsh red and orange as the armies bore down on him.

Jono leapt down the first huge steps of the temple and looked back at the stone giant just in time to see it happen:

An explosion shot up and out like a fan of fire and dust.

Jono collapsed on the stone floor, surrounded by raining rubble, in shock and gripping his heart. Soldiers and knights landed as the last chunks of rubble rained down around him. He could hear pounding footsteps just above the electronic static ringing in his hollow ears.

Shadows covered the sky, guns clicked, and swords ignited—all pointing at him.

Jono looked up as a thick blackness swooped over him and landed with white flames upon the rubble of the ruins. The Obsidian Chimera said nothing, but the two armies stopped and dared not continue against the fiery beast.

Jono curled against the stone. He felt weaker than ever before. The hollow heart must have been damaged in the explosion, and his image had small but growing holes in it. Jono realized how exhausted his real body was.

He could hear voices of the knights calling for the Sage.

Then the Chimera bellowed, "Stand back or you will all burn!"

From the crowded clouds of dust and flying ships, a hatch opened and the fearless figure of Commander Grail leapt through the air, his blond hair whipping in the wind. He landed solidly on the rubble strewn stone. Soldiers of both factions made room for him, and the Chimera only glared, as he pushed through to the cowering boy.

"Wyer? By the stars!"

The war-hardened commander's mammoth metal hands came down to rest on his shoulders, but went right through its hollow form. Sparks danced out of Jono's tiny heart. Half of the dragonfly's wings were broken as it fluttered desperately in a circle. Jonothon's body shivered uncontrollably.

"Wyer," said Grail in his deep voice, both harsh and gentle, "what happened to the Keeper?"

"It wouldn't stop the balance. It destroyed itself to stop the war," said Jonothon with quiet static.

To the commander's left, Thomas the griffin arrived with the Sage of Ages on his back. To his right, a butterfly fluttered by, and a hollow heart flickered to life, projecting an image of the Empress beside them.

"Mercy of the Angels!" said the Sage as he marched toward him. "How have you come here, child? Are you alright?"

Jono looked at them and nodded. "I'm fine. You have to stop fighting. It was all a lie."

The leaders of the world surveyed the destruction in dismay.

"What of the Keeper?" asked the Sage. "Is all lost?" He turned to the Empress. "Your lust for war has condemned us all!"

"It was your zeal that brought us to this precipice," the Empress replied. "You abandoned all reason to get the key!"

"Wyer . . ." Commander Grail spoke softly. "What about Attrayer's key?"

"There was no key. They tricked you!" Jono said. "All of it. It wasn't either End. There are others doing this. They've made you think there was a key so you would destroy each other."

"What monster is behind this?" asked the Empress.

"They wear the symbol of the dead sun," Jonothon replied. "The Historian, Eljin, and there are more! They're all over the sphere, in hiding. I've seen them on both Ends. They wanted this to happen." Jono looked to the Sage. "The Historian said it had to happen, that it was destiny, but that's not true! He wanted the end to come."

Grail ran his fingers through Jono's hollow form. "Where are you?"

"East of here, along the Dawn," Jono whispered, unable to lift his head. "There's a dead city under the shadow of a cliff. There are squares in the ground. It's cold and there are empty buildings . . ."

Jono could hear that they were making sounds, speaking most likely, but it all melted together and became quiet and indistinguishable.

"That's where they brought me," Jonothon whispered as his head grew heavy. "The symbols of tombs are everywhere . . . spying on the world . . . they wanted it . . ."

Jonothon blinked. The ground was no longer orange. It was cold and gray. He was back in the skyscraper. The light from the window seemed brighter and blurrier than before. He curled limp on the ground; it was cool and soothing against his cheek.

He almost didn't mind as the world disappeared.

Chapter Forty-One

The Tomb of the World

A t moments Jonothon heard whispers and caught glimpses of light coming in through open windows and the giant crack in the building. He felt hands on his wires that were still locked in a nest around him. There were explosions and roars of engines, but all the sound was muted and distant.

After a while he gave up on the idea of ever leaving the cold ground.

"Wyer."

He felt an intense aching all over.

"Jonothon Wyer."

He cracked open his eyes, which adjusted to the bright light and slowly fixed on Commander Grail's scarred face.

"You're going to be alright," said Grail. "But very nearly were not."

"Is everything . . ." Jono whispered.

"It's ended," the commander assured him. "The Empress and the Sage will make sure of it. There will be peace, and we will find these traitors. When our ships arrived, there were people here. They had taken most of the equipment, smashed the rest of it. They tried to take you with them, but you held on." Grail smiled proudly at the spy cables clamped tightly into the floor and wall.

"Did they . . ." Jonothon whispered.

"They escaped. I don't know how. They just disappeared. Trust me, Jonothon, we will hunt them down."

Jono looked around, his head heavy with drowsiness. Some of the wires were pulled free from the wall, but most held on.

Flying ships hovered outside the shattered windows, while many more seemed to dart around the dead city, searching for any remaining evidence of the Tombs.

One ship pulled up to the window and, as its door slid down, some familiar faces charged out of it.

"You really did it!" Keiko laughed ecstatically as she and Isaac ran up and hugged him.

"If you didn't come, Jono," said Isaac with a serious but joyful look on his face, "if you didn't make it when you did, we might all be eating dirt. Thanks."

The Empress and the Sage closely followed them.

The Empress' lips curled in uncertainty then broke out in a reserved smile. "You have done exceptionally well, Mister Wyer." She turned to the Sage. "We have both been deceived."

The Sage nodded. "The whispers speak the child's truth. There is toxic evil here that has penetrated both our lands and must be jointly destroyed."

"Agreed," the Empress replied sternly. "It was a trick of fear that was used against us, dividing our ability and diverting our attention."

"A great tragedy has been averted," said the Sage of Ages.

Jono looked at the one remaining screen and saw the hill at the ruins speckled with shattered metal and the plumes of smoke coming from between the trees and across the plain.

Mechanical soldiers carried the wounded on stretchers. Ships had landed, and two separate camps remained to tend to the hurt and the dead. Guns still pointed at each other as they scrambled to help their comrades.

The veil that covered the Empress' eyes could not disguise her remorse. "Even lies can be real to those that believe them."

Jono clenched his fist. "Why did they do it?" asked Jonothon. "Why did they want to create the end of the world?'

The Sage of Ages stepped forward and knelt beside Jonothon. "They had lost sight of the value in the world around them. Weighed against the infinite rewards of an imagined world, the clearest of virtues can be sacrificed. It is those virtues, those simple values that we must never abandon. What is there to gain in heaven if we lose ourselves along the path to it?"

A distant star twinkled on the dark side of Dawn. Jonothon peered up at the leaders of the two Ends of the world. He wanted to believe the clash between Dark and Day had ended, but in his heart he questioned if it were true.

"And what is next for you, Mister Wyer?" said the Empress.

"Yes," added the Sage, "now that the truth is laid before us and peace can be rebuilt, what becomes of the young champion?"

Jono could only stare at the screen overlooking the battlefield. He didn't have an answer.

"I have arranged for the release of your friend, Mister Alexsayter Aquinas," said the Empress "He wishes to return to Caer Midus, but he was eager to hear of you, as I am sure, are others."

"The halls of the academy may have been torn down," said commander Grail, "but they will be rebuilt. If you are inclined to study, Windom would be proud to have you."

Jonothon looked at the Empress, whose covered eyes seemed to glisten back at him. "More than you know." she whispered.

Jonothon looked back at the remaining screen, to the field of battle and the rows of wounded, roaring hover ships, and soaring sundrakes. He looked to the dusty ground.

"Trust your heart, young man," said the Sage. "It has been shown to lead you well."

Chapter Forty-Two

A New Wake

Polari never looked so beautiful.

A gentle breeze swept tall, green-blue grass on a hillside into a rhythmic dance. The valley was filled with a thick, warming fog that made the lights of the town spread into a misty rainbow. Plumes of red and green floated carelessly into the air.

Jonothon watched the town from his distant perch on the grassy hillside with a content smile stretched across his face. He saw his mother peek out the window from time to time. She eventually opened the door and watched him watch the town from the comfort of a porch bench.

He was happy to see his home again. It'd felt as though he'd almost slipped into another world, and it made him feel grounded to see and hear the familiar pieces of his old life. The sight felt comfortable. It was that sense that reaffirmed his decision and made him smile.

The bench creaked as Beky Wyer rocked on it. Jono left the field to join her.

"Dahlia's still unwrapping her presents," his mother said sweetly. "You really didn't have to buy quite that much." She smiled, her eyes bright and proud.

Jono smiled back and forced a false shrug. "It's Giftmas," was the only explanation he offered.

"Are you alright?" his mother asked as casually as she could. "Did they do what they said they would?"

Jono nodded and pulled his shirt down just enough to show off a glowing green circle they'd implanted just left of the center of his chest. It dug through his skin and bone, protecting his heart and regulating his blood flow. If you looked closely into it, you could see his heart beat at regular intervals in pale green light.

The door creaked open and Charles's head poked out. "Are you coming back?" he said with a laugh. "There's still plenty of cake."

The cracked old dining room was covered in loose wrapping paper and open boxes. There were Dahlia-sized clothes piled up on chairs and the table. Cans of food towered beside a sparkling new reizofridge.

Charles held out a plate with a large slice of gooey chocolate cake on it.

"Ooh, I'll have some!" Dahlia said as she snatched it up. She had two spoonfuls in her mouth before she mumbled a hearty, "Oh, thanks, Jono!"

Her brother nodded but didn't move for the cake. His eyes met his father's.

"Are you ready?" asked his father with proud and hopeful eyes.

Jonothon smiled back at him, uninhibited, and nodded.

They all stopped and gathered around him as closely as they could.

"We love you," said Beky.

"I know," Jonothon replied. "I love you too."

She leaned in to kiss his cheek, but her lips only connected with the air.

Jonothon lifted his hand just as the world around him clicked to black. He blinked his eyes a few times before they adjusted to the dim light of the Library.

"Finally!" cheered Keiko as she and Isaac ran over to him.

"We've been waiting forever," said Isaac, only half serious.

Keiko was dressed in a blue gown that ruffled along its edges. Isaac wore a tailored black tuxedo with a red handkerchief with the Windom Academy crest on it. He held out another tux to Jono.

"I brought you my old one," said the ayleen. "Get dressed. It's already started."

"We'll wait outside," said Keiko as she stood. "David and Oscar are already there so hurry up!"

"I will." Jono smiled.

The door shut and Jono threw on the fancy clothes as quick as he could.

The first half of the school year had come to a relatively uneventful close.

Despite being late from the beginning of the term and dealing with the minor distraction of stopping the end of the world, Jonothon studied hard and finished all his classes with a solid 'G' average.

Returning to the rhythm of class work had been made easier by the fact that almost no one knew he had anything to do with the battle at Dawn. The academy and the world of both ends were informed of the disastrous trickery of the secret organization known as the Tombs, and what they had done to bring the world to war. They also knew of a courageous young boy that was caught in the middle of the nightmare, who had exposed the truth and ended the conflict.

His name was Jason Wheat.

As far as the world knew, that imaginary hero was being kept hidden somewhere off the planet. They'd all seen the image of a brown-haired, skinny boy say some nervous remarks about the world needing peace and unity, now more than ever, as he stood on the deck of a floating spaceship with the earth hovering behind him like a round Giftmas ornament.

After the wounded were healed and the dead were laid to rest, all of the blame for the tragedy was jointly directed at the newly infamous Tombs. The Empress and the Sage agreed the Tombs were to be hunted as vigorously as they possibly could. They'd even received a half-hearted endorsement from the Terralunans to search the Sol system for traces of them on the possibility they'd slipped through the blockade. They all agreed the young boy at the center of the plot was to be kept under protection. The child hero was safe on one of the many space stations, and the entire world knew it.

Gossip continued to fill the halls about what had gone on behind the scenes, but slowly the chatter returned to a more personal nature of who liked who and what instructor ought to be fired for making their end of term test too hard.

Jono didn't mind that he wasn't praised or even recognized by strangers in the hallways because his friends recognized him just fine.

The bow tie wrapped itself automatically around Jonothon's neck as he pushed open the doors to the library, slipped through the opening, and darted down a nearly deserted hall. Keiko and Isaac turned with surprise, jumped to their feet, and chased after him.

The halls were abandoned, except the three pairs of stomping feet and the ever watchful gargoyles sulking in the shadows. Jono arrived at the large silver door first and touched the embossed sword that pointed upward. The doors slid open, and Isaac and Keiko got in before he could shut them.

"You're getting faster!" Keiko said as she caught her breath. "I would've still beaten you in a fair race, though."

"If you say so," said Jono.

"She is wearing a dress," Isaac conceded just as the doors shut.

The anyvator darted upward, rocketing through the hundreds of floors of the mountain. A soft medley of music and laughter grew louder and louder until the roar of a party was all around them.

The doors slid open, and a blast of red, green, and white light illuminated their faces. At the end of the hall was a huge room decorated in ribbons, ornaments, icicles, and flying sparklers. Elegantly dressed people and trays of food filled the room in every direction. Pine trees lined the room on either side with stacks of presents that almost touched the towering, arched ceiling.

A crowd of young cadets danced awkwardly in the center of the room, while teachers and their older guests mingled around the edges. Giftmas wasn't officially until the next wake, but every year Windom held their Snow Fall Ball on Giftmas Eve. The party would continue until end-hour, when the clock would officially chime the beginning of Giftmas morning, and the start of a new year. Sirens and bells would ring across the city and everyone would get to open their present from the Empress.

Jono, Keiko, and Isaac made their way, hopping from every appetizer and dessert tray, through the grand hall toward the grand balcony that looked over the brilliant lights of Eies. They passed Ramsus, who gave Jono a wink as the soldier leaned toward a pretty dalphemyr woman beside the punch bowl. Ramsus wore his dress uniform: a solid black coat with tails, elaborate silver trim, and red crimson inner lining. He had a twinkle in his red eyes as the woman twirled a ringlet of her black hair.

They intentionally avoided a crowd of first year cadets that surrounded Nick Knox as he boasted that he personally knew Jason Wheat.

"He was so daft at first," Nick sorted. "I had to teach him everything he knows. He almost got himself eaten by a paranamole his first year. I pulled him away just before it bit his head off, so I guess you could say I saved the guy that saved the world."

Even Biggs and Wedge had come, although Biggs had to hover outside by the balcony while Wedge brought him a tray of cheese crumpets.

The balcony gave them an amazing view of the city. Crowds of celebrations were being held from the island towers to the trenches that bordered the mountain. The brilliant Giftmas lights of Eies were occasionally overcome by bursts of fireworks. Sparkling flowers, dragons, and gears lit up the clouded city.

Jono looked back into the grand hall and spotted Commander Grail on a higher balcony overlooking the festivities with a stern but pleased smile. The Empress stepped out of the shadows to join the commander on the balcony. She raised her goblet, the room fell silent, and then everyone raised their cups.

"A trying year closes," the Empress said solemnly. "And we are left with harsh lessons, but even greater opportunities. We honor the memory of the Lad of Giftmas by welcoming once enemies into our hearts and welcoming the unknown truths into our minds. Drink, laugh, and enjoy the time with those beside you. To those we lost, and to those we love. To us. May we build an ever better future."

"To the future!" Grail's deep cheer carried and shook across the grand hall.

"To the future!" the crowd roared in response.

Cheers and claps and blaring patriotic music burst to life.

David pulled Isaac away to test some of the fireworks. Keiko met up with her bunkmates to exchange gifts, and Jonothon found himself sitting alone in a corner by the balcony.

He pulled out the copper memory watch from his pocket and flipped open the lid. Jono thumbed through the recordings and clicked on a new message. The smiling face of Alexsayter Aquinas popped to life.

"Hello again, Mister Wyer. It was good to hear about your grades. Well done! Oh, and look!" Aquinas pointed to a big, yellow bird behind him. "I found Celeste. It seems she had gone to her hatchling farm in Eve's Briar while I was away. I'll take her with me when I go back to the Fellowship abbey. I'll have to get her under feathers trimmed because of the warmth, but she'll be alright. They want me to help plan out community reconciliation projects all across the sphere. Both Ends are funding it, and they will have their own people involved of course, but I'll be the Fellowship's representative. I know I keep saying it, but I am awfully sorry for all that I said about the Empress and my part in everything. Well, I suppose we should focus on the future. Oh, and don't worry about the shrine. The fellowship is sending a new caretaker and I, well, I don't think that is quite the work for me at the moment. With all that has happened I think there is more that I can do to help. What worth is there for a shrine of stone, if we haven't maintained the shrine of life, right? And with all the new sense of hope I may even get people to restore them again, to remember them. Anyway, I just wanted to wish you a Merry Giftmas, Jonothon. Do take care, and visit, if you can. There is a certain girl from Systine that has been especially inquisitive about your new situation. I gave her your link, hoping you don't mind." Aquinas winked. "Do take care."

The image disappeared. Jono rested the watch against his lap. He stared serenely at the blank screen. With the raucous room, the bright lights and waves of reverberating laughter swelling around him, the world was overwhelming. In that infinite activity, Jonothon let himself focus on one tiny, but just as complex, piece of the world.

A particular sparkle caught his eye, and when he turned his head away, it seemed to follow his face, targeting his attention. Jono looked up to see the many Giftmas lights sparkle around a glistening blue gown as Keiko Kirin stuck out her hand.

"Want to dance?"

Jono laughed at the ridiculous idea, but her hand didn't move. Clearly, she needed further explanation.

"Really," Jono explained, "I don't know how."

"Neither do I!" Keiko laughed back at him. She grabbed him by the hand and pulled him to his feet. "Might as well give it a try, though, while we have the chance?"

Jono smiled. "Yeah, might as well."

The End.

Take a sneak peek at the second book

in the epic Dark & Day series!

The Withering Mark

Prologue

The War Memorial

A blanket of clouds shaded the town of Thistle from the burning sun as it clung to its usual spot, half way up the southern sky. Clouds meant a reprieve from the heat, and sometimes rain. In the Day, clouds were often celebrated as a good omen, but omens can be deceptive.

Culliver Manish sat on the edge of his daughter's bed. She was deep asleep in the early hours before wake. He brushed her hair and recited a lullaby as softly as he could.

"A gentle sun shines under the Blue Skies,

Magic descends to brighten the Day.

It's warm on your cheeks with light everlasting,

Casting a spell that dries tears away.

You never need leave the land of Blue Skies,

Safe where no metal creatures can be.

The spell of the sun is warm under Blue Skies,

Making mech monsters cower and flee.

So sleep with the sun shining on Blue Skies,

All those you love await you in the Day.

Summon a dream of life in the sunlight,

Casting a spell that dries tears away."

Manish kissed his daughter's forehead.

"I did it for you," Manish whispered. "So you'd be safe."

Manish shut the door quietly as he crept out of his home. The village was silent. He had lived in Thistle for the entirety of his fifty-seven years, but on this early wake he crept warily through its familiar cobblestone streets. He was a portly man, well dressed in a tweed jacket and comely tie. He was wealthy enough to have a casual suit that complemented his figure in the best possible way.

Although Manish had memories of Thistle that could be hung on nearly every street corner and doorway, he caught himself, on more than a few occasions, dabbing his handkerchief against his plump forehead and debating which route would be best, if he were to continue onward at all.

He startled himself at the sight of a grotesque black metal spider. It was on a poster stuck to the side of a blue and gold knight's information box. The ornate inscription read, "Are you INFECTED with a machine? Mechs can be smaller than pixie dust! Get checked regularly!"

The box was staffed by a snoring knight that was no younger than one hundred years old. Manish ignored the knight violating his duty and turned to a golden street post with a crystal chamber on top. He touched the post and a wave of rainbow light shined down on him. There were crystal posts all over town, ready to purify any pixels that could have infected its citizens. Most people got checked five times a wake, but there was not a single recorded case of infection. Manish took pride and credit for that fact.

A statue of a small golden gnome sat of the brim of the post. It waved pleasantly.

"You are clean of mechanical infection," chirped the gnome. "Have a wonderful wake!"

Manish smiled warily at the gnome and continued down the cobblestone street.

Culliver Manish had been elected as the mayor of Thistle for nearly two decades and, despite what a handful of obnoxious objectors may say, he was expected by most Thistlans to easily win re-election the following year. He took what small comfort he could in that knowledge. After all, the people loved him. He had shared in their pain and comforted their grief through drought, joblessness and social controversy. He had led his flock though the tragic war at the Keeper and delivered to them a balm for their despair in the most breathtaking war memorial the world had to offer. Last Septishrei, Modern Events Magazine had rated Thistle's Memorial number one across the sphere, and that was as true as truth got.

Overwhelming Thistle's town square, the recently completed memorial of the war at the Keeper protruded from the once quaint cobblestone square as a bold testament to the town's fidelity to the knights and mages of the Day. Thistle stood behind no one when it came to respecting the dead and honoring their sacrifice.

It was almost two years since the battle between the Dark and Day had brought Thistle's farmers across the globe to face the zeal of the Empress of Eies. The Thistlans, however, were lucky enough to have arrived at the Keeper's decimated ruins on the Dawn border only hours after the dust had literally settled and the two armies were packing up their deadly weapons to go home.

The ever-shrewd Manish had the foresight to immediately join them at the Keeper, and demand that bits of the Keeper's shattered orange stone be taken back to the Day to be incorporated into the artwork of the memorial. The town square would blessedly no longer be a gathering place for protests and rabblerousing. The bloated memorial would perpetually stand as a somber reminder of his leadership.

Where there was once an old leaky fountain with a statue of Thistle's founder, Ebenezer Potsworth in his iconic tattered jacket, pants rolled up to his knees, and a stalk of steel grain sticking out of his mouth, now farmers carved from orange stone held up their picks defiantly towards the north. Stone children stood proudly on the Keeper's fragments and bravely faced their enemies.

The Thistle-folk had celebrated the memorial's unveiling; praising its striking form and emotional resonance. The young artist, whom Manish had personally selected, was heralded as genius, and elevated into instant stardom.

On any other wake, Manish would have taken a moment to revel in his success, but reveling had not even crossed his mind more than a little.

The streets around him were barren. Manish could practically hear the gentle snores of his town; his people snuggled peacefully in their beds. He struggled to smile at the thought of their innocence, but as the thought faded and his smile failed, he dabbed his forehead again. A turquoise dragonfly fluttered past his head, and Manish swatted it away, annoyed.

"Back off, you!"

He crept around the corner into the town square. Upon seeing no one else around, he mustered his courage and reminded himself that he was none other than Mayor Manish. He was a man to be feared, not some intimidated child! He straightened his back, glared down at his prized memorial, and marched toward the gate.

The square was protected by a gate that Manish had the key to. He shut the door quietly behind him and walked past the new stone fountains that drained out of the rocks like tears. Scattered around the square were stone peaks, carved with the names of every person from the county that had marched toward the Keeper. Another vertical stone was engraved with all those that lost their lives across the Day.

Manish's pace slowed, and though his chin was held high, his jaw began to quiver. His eyes darted back and forth, as though the proud stone heroes were glaring at him knowingly out of the corners of their eyes.

At the center of the structure was a door to the mausoleum that was dug below the street. The mayor touched a small panel and the door slid open. Stairs led to a dark room, as though something repelled the light from reaching far.

"Hello?" Manish managed to whisper.

After the shadows refused to reply he put a shaking hand on the rail and descended. The dragonfly hovered by the doorway before following him down.

It took a while for Manish's eyes to adjust. Anyone from the Dark End could have seen crystal clear, but for a Day Ender, such seclusion from the light was a rare and solemn thing. The mausoleum was round on the inside with carvings of the seven angels standing watch from all directions. There was a large prayer pedestal in the center with a cushion for kneeling. Upon the pedestal was a strange metal box.

Manish glanced around the room with only the piercing stares of angels as company.

"I do say, is anyone else here? Show yourselves."

In an instant, three cloaked figures flickered into existence. A grey skinned man with an ornate gold mask stood in the middle behind the pedestal. A woman and man were on either side, with silver masks over their faces. Their shadowy cloaks crept around the room with a life of their own.

"And here I thought you believed in patience, Manish?" scoffed the golden masked man.

"I, well, that is, I do not take kindly to your insistence, sir," Manish replied. "I have done exactly as you demanded, and for my part, I must say the execution has been impeccable."

"We will see about that," said man in the gold mask. "Put all the documents in the chest."

Manish drew a heavy stack of papers from his coat pocket, placed it in the box on the pedestal, and shut the lid. He took two steps back quickly and stood very still.

"Do we have it all?" the gold masked man asked.

Manish was about to answer when the silver masked woman cut him off.

"One hundred percent of the documents are scanned and stored," she said. "No sign of corruption, tickers or spies."

The silver masked man studied a screen in his hand. "My copy is pure as well."

"Is that it, then?" asked Manish, resisting the handkerchief in his pocket. "We're done? This was my last errand, right?"

"That is all, sir. We are done with you," said the man in the gold mask. "But a moment if you please, Mister Mayor. I wanted to thank you appropriately."

"Umm, well, you're quite…" Manish wondered how soon until it would be safe for him to make his exit.

"So many others would stay fixed on pride or virtue to do what you have done. You've made the practical choice and your people, if they only knew…"

"You're not going to tell? That was part of the deal. This must all be done quietly, and you said…"

"I said *if*, didn't I?"

Manish gulped.

"You do see it, don't you?" asked the gold masked man. "You've been looking, looking, looking, but now, do you actually start to see? There's no fighting gravity. There's no undoing what nature has built."

A grey skinned mouth smiled below the gold mask as he peered up the stairs.

Manish looked around confused, as though the masked man was talking to someone else.

"It's cute the way you keep trying to get ahead, you know." The man in the gold mask continued. "Do you really think you would be here if it was not exactly what we wanted? We never wanted to hide anything from you. Hiding is your choice, not ours. Now it is time for you to know. Without a doubt, without a crack in certainty. I remember how desperately you tried to understand why I chose to leave. Don't worry. We will show you all soon. It's coming and you can either embrace it, or you can be destroyed in its path."

The gold masked man laughed to himself. "But we already know what you will choose, don't we? You do so love to be on the losing side. For all your trials, all your might and bravado, to be stuck in that dreadful academy? What a waste! But then again, breathing was made for second chances. Do give it an honest thought, will you?"

"I'm certain I have no idea what…" Manish began.

"He isn't talking to you, idiot." snarled the silver masked man. Manish looked back. But there isn't anyone else here. No one …except that stupid… dragonfly…

"As the wick ends, the flame dies. Things are in motion that cannot be undone. The Lord of the Pit stirs and the Abyss grows hungry! Be sure you are ready for it."

The gold masked man waved up at the dragonfly.

"We'll be watching you, Grail."

With one last smile, the three cloaked figures disappeared as quickly as they arrived. A gear clunked from within the chest on the pedestal.

In that final instant, a thought of clarity crossed over Culliver Manish's soon-to-be-evaporated mind.

There's no way I'm getting re-elected now…

The explosion shattered every window for six blocks surrounding the memorial. An orange plume billowed up from the town square, swirling with black smoke. Bits of Keeper stone cut through the thin wood homes like bullets through paper.

In moments, the town was awake with screams and confusion. A defiant stone farmer's face clacked on the ground as the townsfolk poured into the streets; tying on robes and searching for an explanation.

Already, cover ups were being formulated.

A fractured heating crystal? A thoughtless storage of firepowder? An active grenade mistakenly kept from the Keeper wreckage? The one thing the news would state plainly was that it most certainly was not an attack by the terrorist organization known as the Tombs.

Far across the world, past the Ring of Dawn and deep within the Dark End, a single screen instantly turned to static. The rest of the wall of screens saw Thistle and its inhabitants from every angle. They screamed in silence as they held the wounded close to their chests.

Commander Dvaniur Grail pulled his metal fist from the dent in the consul. A close up loop of the man in the golden mask played on a screen in front of him. It was the last moment from the spying dragonfly. The man's grey skin and distinct yellow pupils were conclusive. He had shown himself to Grail on purpose.

The Tombs had wanted him to know.

Grail gritted his teeth as the world arose to another wake.

"Chaucer is alive."

To be continued in

The Withering Mark

About the Author

Jacob **Israel Grey** was born in the Seattle area and has lived in California, Iceland, and Utah. He completed a degree in Political Science at the University of Utah, focusing on international relations. He returned to Washington State with his wife, son and two Pomeranians, Nikko and Pompeii.

Author blog:
www.IsraelGrey.com

A Word of Thanks

It has been many years since the world of Dark & Day first crept into my mind like a rolling fog to settle into most of my waking dreams. Since that long past wake, it has been with the aid and support of a wide range of talented artists, editors, family and friends that brings this world of mystery and wonder to you.

My sincerest thanks go out to Andrew, Tyler, Nick, Mikel, Garrett, Des, Jade, Kelly, Rob, Arseniquez, Lianna, Jenny, Trevor, Ari, Jenn, Kaine, Karrin, Bobby, mom, Mike, Jenna, a horde of beta readers and, of course, my ever loving Ani.

Your spirit is the grease in Jono's gears.
I hope you stick with him for the rest of his adventures.

It is going to be one burn'em great ride!

Art

Jono, Keiko & Isaac v. the Fel Shades by Andrew Hou

Jono & the Twilight Sky by Israel Grey

Jono Wyer by Andrew Hou

Alexsayter & Celeste by Andrew Hou

The Twilight Woods by Tyler Edlin

Jono Lost in the Woods by Israel Grey

The Empress of Eies by Andrew Hou

The Historian by Andrew Hou

Jono at the Toppled Tower by Israel Grey

The Sage of Ages by Andrew Hou

Caer Midus by Tyler Edlin

Face of the Sage by Israel Grey

Princess Suriana by Andrew Hou

Eljin of the White Guard by Andrew Hou

Keiko Kirin by Andrew Hou

Cid Kirin by Andrew Hou

Kirin's Kontraptions by Israel Grey

The Frozen Ocean by Tyler Edlin

The Obsidian Chimera by Andrew Hou

The Chimera's Lament by Israel Grey

Eies – Capital of the Dark Ends by Tyler Edlin

Isaac Ohm by Andrew Hou

Isaac & Oscar by Israel Grey

Commander Grail by Andrew Hou

Commander Grail by Israel Grey

Keiko & the War Mech by Arseniquez

Grail versus the Sage by Andrew Hou

Jono & Dark & Day by Lianna Tai & Israel Grey

About the Illustrators

Andrew Hou is currently working as a concept lead in a Korean gaming company, Reloaded Studios. He's also one of the founders of Udon entertainment. For more of his art, check out www.andrewhou.com and also his DeviantArt page at http://njoo.deviantart.com

Tyler Edlin is a graduate of the Art Institute of Boston at Lesley University. He specializes in landscape art design for films and video games. His work is influenced by N.C. Wyth, Hayao Miyazaki, and Craig Mullins. Tyler is inspired from his years playing amazing video games such as Chrono Trigger, Panzer Dragoon, and Final Fantasy.
See his work at www.tyleredlinart.com and http://gamefan84.deviantart.com/gallery/

Arseniquez is an illustrator born and living in Thailand. He works as a graphic designer and also set up exhibition spaces. He draws manga styles for freelance job in Deviantart. http://arseniquez.deviantart.com/

Lokman Lam is a character illustrator from Hong Kong. http://lokmanlam.com/ and http://lokmanlam.blogspot.com/

Lianna Tai is environment and character artist inspired by fantasy works of Kekai Kotaki, Miyazaki and James Jean. Find her art at http://rydori.deviantart.com/ and http://mynameislianna.blogspot.com/

Grail versus the Sage

By Andrew Hou

A World of Dark & Day

By Lianna Tai & Israel Grey

You can help us continue the adventure!

Share Dark & Day with your friends!

Rate and Review Dark & Day on Amazon.com!

Join the Facebook group!

Thank you, and happy reading!

⚜ Visit ⚜

www.**DarkandDay**.com

Become a Fan and Like the book on Facebook

http://www.facebook.com/pages/Dark-and-Day-book/102844399757795

See artwork at Deviant Art.com

http://jono-wyer.deviantart.com/favourites/#Dark-and-Day-art

Printed in Great Britain
by Amazon

12898897R00222